THE FAMILY

MARTINA COLE
THE FAMILY

headline

First published in Great Britain in 2010
by HEADLINE PUBLISHING GROUP

1

Cataloguing in Publication Data is available from the British Library

ISBN 978 0 7553 7549 3 (Hardback)
ISBN 978 0 7553 7550 9 (Trade paperback)

Typeset in Galliard by Avon DataSet Ltd,
Bidford-on-Avon, Warwickshire

Printed and bound in Great Britain by
Clays Ltd, St Ives plc

Headline's policy is to use papers that are natural, renewable and
recyclable products and made from wood grown in sustainable forests.
The logging and manufacturing processes are expected to conform
to the environmental regulations of the country of origin.

HEADLINE PUBLISHING GROUP
An Hachette UK Company
338 Euston Road
London NW1 3BH

www.headline.co.uk
www.hachette.co.uk

To my new grandson Christopher Whiteside.

And also for my children, and my grandchildren,
and my wonderful new Polish family.

For Timmy and Avril Petherick.

(Or should that be Anvil?)

With love.

Prologue

'Will you stop looking out the window? You're making me bloody nervous.'

Christine smiled. She knew better than to argue with her sister-in-law. Breda was a law unto herself; she could make the rest of the family look like choirboys when she got a temper on her, and that was no easy feat.

The Murphys were a dangerous crowd, and no one knew that better than Christine Murphy, wife of the sainted Phillip, and the mother of his sons. She was related to the local nutters by marriage and blood, and frightened out of her wits because she was sinking deeper and deeper into their world on a daily basis. Sometimes, like now, when she saw her children smiling and laughing together in her beautiful home, saw the love that they had from their father's family, she envied them. That had been her once, caught up in their love, caught up in their excitement, their lust for life. It had been a heady drug to her then, had held her in its thrall for years. Until that day, that awful, terrifying day, when she had been forced to open her eyes and see them all for what they really were.

From her mother-in-law, with her ready smile and open arms, to her own husband, a handsome, romantic sociopath who saw her and everyone else in his orbit as his personal property. But worse than everything else was that her sons were clones of their father. Both had idolised him since they were small. Why wouldn't they? He gave them everything they wanted whether they needed it or not.

Recently she had inadvertently found out that her son had planned a murder. Planned it as if it was the most normal, most natural thing in the world. But then, in the Murphy family that *was* natural. As were death, threats and violence.

All in a day's work to them.

It had all gone wrong, but he would try again, she knew that for a fact. This was the legacy she had given them, this was the life she had brought them into. From birth they had been indoctrinated by this family's so-called code of honour. It was something she had cherished once, long ago, when she had been young and foolish. When she had still believed nothing could ever harm her or hers.

But she had to be honest with herself, in the early days she had lived with it quite happily because she had closed her eyes to it all. She had enjoyed the lifestyle, had sought it even. Her mother had crushed her from a child, never let her have a second to herself, so she had learned quickly how to be clever. How to get out and about without her mother's constant interference. But she had ended up embroiled in something she had been too immature, and too naïve to really understand. She had fallen for the first boy to give her the time of day, and she had fallen deeply. So deeply he was still the only man she had ever known.

Now it was all finally coming back to bite her, as her father had always said it would. He had warned her, begged her to get away from Phillip Murphy, but she had laughed at him. She had been so determined in those days, had been convinced she knew it all. Was more than capable of looking after herself.

Oh, hindsight was a wonderful thing.

She was chuckling to herself now, and she felt the eyes of Breda on her, even though she had her back to her.

'Are you feeling all the ticket, Christine? You seem nervous.'

Christine turned to face her accuser, for it was an accusation.

Breda was like a bloodhound; she could suss out insincerity faster than she could draw on a cigarette.

'I'm fine, Breda. What's the matter with you? Are you trying to pick a fight with me? Because the mood I'm in, girl, you are liable to get one.' Christine's words caused a hush in the room. She saw her husband and sons stare at her as if they had never seen her before. Breda was so shocked she didn't answer her for a few moments.

'Keep your hair on, Chris, I was only asking.'

Christine walked from the room and made her way through the large entrance hall into the kitchen. The heat of the Aga hit her, and she went to the back door; opening it, she stood in the doorway and savoured the cold night air.

It was early December, and there was already a frost covering the vast expanse of lawn. It was glistening in the moonlight, making the whole place look like a picture from a fairy tale. It seemed incongruous that all this beauty hid the filth and the hate that was a part of the Murphy family's genetic make-up.

Even her sons had not been immune, in fact they seemed to thrive on it all. Especially one of them, but she blamed herself for that. She had ignored the signs, had pretended that they didn't exist. She had believed that her boys would somehow be untouched by it, would not be part of it all because they had been given a private education and everything their little avaricious hearts had desired.

Wrong again, as she had been about so many things.

'Everything OK, Mum?'

Her elder son Phillip Junior made her jump physically. 'You frightened me!'

He grinned, the living image of his father as he had been when she had first met him. All jet-black hair, and steely blue eyes. Despite being big and overpowering, he looked as if he wouldn't hurt a fly. But as she had found out to her cost, looks could be deceiving. He enveloped her in his arms, a gentle bear hug that belied his real physical power. He had broken another boy's nose and ribs when he had been fourteen – he had underestimated his own strength apparently. His grandmother was good at making excuses for her boys. Then again she had had lots of experience.

'Please, Philly, don't do this tonight. I have a bad feeling on me. Think of Finoula, she's the important one, she's your wife.'

He laughed gently, but his voice had a steely ring to it as he said casually, 'You worry too much, Mum.'

She knew it was futile to say any more; like his father before him, once he made up his mind there was no going back.

'You know something, Mum, you need to chill out. Are you still taking the meds from the doctor?'

She nodded.

'Good. What you really need is a holiday. We'll sort something out, bit of the old currant bun and you'll be as right as rain.'

She smiled in agreement, even though she felt as if her heart was breaking. 'Perhaps you're right. I just feel tired, that's all.'

They both turned as Breda came into the kitchen; she had her grandchild in the crook of one arm, and a heavy-duty shotgun in the other.

'Do me a favour, Philly, would you take this for me? I need to get it cleaned up and put away before the Clancys get here.' She was holding it out as if it was the most natural thing in the world to have a child in one arm and a weapon in the other. Christine watched as Philly took the gun without a second's thought. He was used to firearms and it showed. He checked to make sure it was empty of ammunition, and looked down the sight, almost by force of habit.

'I'll sort it, Auntie Breda, you feed the baby. He's got a big appetite, look at the size of him already!'

Christine watched as if she was outside of it all, no more than an onlooker. The medication was responsible for that. It stopped her wanting to take the gun and mow the whole fucking lot of them down once and for all. Finish this family off, take them out of the game, as her husband would say. Turning her back, she looked once more out into the garden. She didn't see the shrug of despair from her son, but she heard the long, drawn-out sigh that told her Breda was losing patience with her.

Well, it would all be over soon; she had to keep it together long enough to make sure it was finally finished. She would try to ensure at least one of her sons would live long enough to understand why she had done what she was about to do. She feared her actions would make everyone hate her until the day she died. But that was a chance she was willing to take if it meant they would one day have a crack at a normal life.

Book One

From the deepest desires often come the deadliest hate

Socrates (469 BC–399 BC)

Seest thou a man wise in his own conceit? There is more hope of a fool than of him

Proverbs, 26:12

Chapter One

'It must be love, look at his hair!'

Phillip Murphy laughed good-naturedly; his father was the proverbial wind-up, but funny with it.

He knew he looked good and was attractive to the opposite sex. Women and girls had been giving him the glad eye since he was fourteen years old. It was his size; he was what his mother termed 'a fine figure of a man'. Broad shouldered, he stood three inches over six feet. His thick black hair coupled with his dark-lashed blue eyes spoke of the Irish in him. His thick-lipped mouth made him look amenable, friendly, hid the steel that lay beneath his easy smiles. He always got what he wanted, it was a mantra with him. He believed his mother's advice: if you want something, you'll get it, you just have to want it badly enough. Well, he wanted better than his parents, he wanted better than everyone around him, and he was determined to get it.

Phillip liked Christine Booth because she was clean; clean and innocent in every way. She looked at him as if he was a god, and actually to her he was the next best thing. The thought made him smile again.

His mother Veronica watched her favourite child as he grinned with happiness. She knew this was serious all right; he had never brought a girl home before, not like this anyway. He had brought them to his bed, late at night, and hustled them

9

out with the dawn, assuming she was too dense to work out what had gone on.

This one was different. All she had heard lately was Christine this, and Christine that. But, as pleased as she was that he was in love, she also knew the girl was only fifteen years old. Phillip was twenty-one, that was a big age difference to most people. But then again, five years from now, the difference between them would be nothing. It was the 'schoolgirl' tag that she was bothered about, and there was no getting away from it. Veronica knew that Christine had to be home by nine every night – not that that meant much in the grand scheme of things, people could have a bit of the other at five o'clock in the day. Early nights didn't guarantee anything, she knew that from experience. Look at her Breda. Veronica loved her daughter but acknowledged that she had a voracious appetite for men. She worried Veronica with her attitude to sex. Breda was what they would have called 'overfriendly' in her day, these days she was just called 'oversexed'.

Veronica had met her husband at the Shandon Bells Irish club in Ilford when she was fourteen years old; he had been eighteen and working on the buildings. Fresh over from Dublin Phillip Murphy had danced with her, seduced her, and married her three years later. Her father had not been thrilled but he had come round eventually, especially once her belly started to grow, and her mother had hastily arranged the wedding to save everyone embarrassment. The priest who had married them had christened their child four months later. Her father grew to love her husband Phillip and she had been blessed with a very happy marriage and a lovely family with her three boys and Breda.

These days it was different: girls were looking older, acting older than their years, but were still treated like children in their homes. In her day, a fifteen year old was out working and looking for the man of her dreams; a father for her children. At fifteen, she was assumed to be on the brink of womanhood.

This Booth girl worried Veronica. She was from a good family, well-to-do in comparison with her lot – Catholic too, so that was a bonus as far as Veronica was concerned. But she also knew that Christine's mother was a hard-faced harridan who thought she was better than everybody else. To be fair, though, the father seemed nice enough. Veronica had been to his shop many times, and he had always been very pleasant to her.

Now her son was talking engagement rings and lifetime commitment. Veronica smiled; the way young people talked about their lives today was laughable. Not like in her day. Then, you married in the eyes of God and you took what came your way: the good, the bad and the indifferent. What else could you do? There was no divorce, not for Catholics anyway, not real ones.

Veronica Murphy surveyed her home; it was gorgeous. They had bought their council house and built an extension, so now the kitchen was huge. All melamine units and shiny work surfaces. The floor was her pride and joy, black and white tiles that looked like marble. She was proud of her home, and rightly so. In comparison to the houses around her, it was like a palace. And she had made a good dinner for them all that night. A big roast, with Irish pork and honeyed parsnips. She'd also made roast tatties like the boys loved, along with colcannon and buttered peas. The aroma coming from the oven was mouth-watering. The gravy was all she had left to do, and she knew just how her tribe liked it – thick and dark. A bit like her youngest son, God love him and keep him.

As Phillip Junior began singing along to the radio, Veronica smiled to herself again. He was smitten all right.

Chapter Two

Christine Booth was sick of her mother's voice, it was like a constant stream of irritating nothingness. The woman talked just for the sheer hell of it. She dreamed of the day she could leave home, the day she could finally shut the front door on her mother's constant nagging. Eileen never stopped, her topics of conversation ranged from what Christine was wearing, to how she sat, to what she ate. Or more to the point what she *didn't* eat. Her schoolwork, her future, her lack of decorum were constant causes of criticism. It was as if Eileen hated her only daughter, was already disappointed in her at just fifteen. Every day of her life, Christine Booth had never felt she was good enough, had always felt she had failed somehow.

Even as a little kid she had been aware of her mother's determination to better herself and, in the process, better the life of her daughter, whether she wanted it or not. Christine had never felt comfortable in her own home, always had to make sure she was what her mother wanted her to be. Needed her to be. Which was polite, intelligent, hard-working and, above all, respectable. Her mother made the word 'respectable' sound so important it frightened Christine at times. All her friends wore make-up, went out with their mates and had a good time, but not her – she was monitored constantly. It was like living with a huge burden, the burden being that she must never make her mother feel ashamed of having her. But from the way Eileen talked, the way she acted, it was obvious Christine already had.

She felt that she had already let her mother down, so she always felt as though she was having to make amends, even though she had never intentionally done anything to make her mother feel like she did. As her friend Joanie said, it was her mother who had the problem, not her. It was Eileen who read filth into the most innocent of conversations, Eileen who was so convinced her daughter was already gone to the bad, as she so succinctly put it. Was it any wonder Christine lied and cheated to get away from her? All she wanted was to be a normal teenager.

Christine looked at her reflection in the mirror of her dressing table; she knew she was pretty, knew she was sexy even, desirable. Phillip Murphy made her feel like she was the only girl on earth, like a woman. He was the only person to ever make her feel she was worth something, other than her dad, of course, but he didn't count. He was her dad. He had to love her. But, like her, Dad was also under her mother's thumb, he couldn't have an opinion in his own home, it was more than he dared. Her mother would see that as tantamount to mutiny: it was her way or no way. How many times had Christine heard that over the course of her young life?

Chapter Three

Eileen Booth was angry. She was always angry. As she pushed her daughter's bedroom door open, she said in her usual demanding way, 'Are you deliberately ignoring me or have you suddenly been struck stone deaf?'

Christine sighed audibly. She wasn't going to take the bait, wouldn't bite back. That was what Eileen wanted, she always wanted a full-on row, a reason to ground her daughter. Well, Christine wasn't going to play into her hands.

'I'm sorry, Mum, I was miles away.' She was smiling at her, trying to look innocent, trying to make her leave her alone.

Eileen Booth narrowed her eyes in suspicion – was this a piss-take? She knew better than anyone that her daughter would need to be at least fifty miles away to block her voice out when she was at full throttle. 'Where are you off to again?'

'Round Joanie's, we're doing our history homework. The Elizabethan era, I told you last night.' She saw her mother looking her over, determined as always to find fault. But there was none. She made sure of that.

Christine had on the minimum of make-up, she wore a plain black dress that ended below the knee and American Tan tights. She also wore her school shoes – black, clumpy school shoes from Clarks. She looked awful in comparison to her contemporaries, and she knew it. She saw her mother battling inside herself to find fault.

'For crying out loud, I'm only going to Joanie's! When have

you ever had cause to doubt me, Mum? When have I ever let you down?' She had the hurt and misunderstood look down to a T.

'Well, make sure you're home by nine, and I'm ringing Joanie's mum so don't think you can pull the wool over my eyes, all right?'

'Why would I bother, Mum? Answer me that one, eh?' Picking up her schoolbag off the floor, Christine kissed her mother on the cheek dutifully and walked sedately from the room.

Eileen Booth listened to her daughter's retreating footsteps and sat down on the bed. Why couldn't her daughter see the danger her looks and friendly nature put her in? She was a nice girl, Eileen knew that better than anyone, but it was the nice girls who got caught out. She didn't want her daughter to have a life like hers, making do. Christine was worth so much more than that, but she was too young to see it.

One day, Eileen was convinced her daughter would thank her for her love and the interest she took in her life. Until then she consoled herself with the knowledge that not only was her girl too shrewd to be caught out, but that Eileen herself was far too vigilant to let her daughter get into any position that could ruin her future. Her Christine was going to have every advantage, every chance to make something of herself. Whether the ungrateful little mare wanted it or not.

Chapter Four

Breda Murphy opened the front door wide with a smile that was even wider and eyes that were merry. Christine liked her at once.

'You must be Miss Booth.'

Christine smiled shyly, she had got this far so she was determined to make a good impression. 'And you must be Miss Breda.'

Breda laughed, but it was a derogatory laugh. 'Oh Jesus, he'll eat you for breakfast. Come on in anyway. You're expected.'

Christine followed her, disconcerted by Breda's greeting.

Phillip's street, she hadn't been able to help but notice, was very run down. It was part of a typical council estate and it was alien to her. Her home was a large semi in a nice neighbourhood. It was quiet, and people kept themselves very much to themselves. Here though, there were kids hanging around in the street and curtains were left wide open so anyone could look in and see what was going on. See their lives as they really were without any kind of pretence.

Even Phillip's home, which she knew he was proud of, and was nicer than all the others in the street with its double glazing and obvious extension, would only fit into the ground floor of her own home. She saw the house as her mother would see it, and that annoyed her. These were nice people, friendly people, and they had invited her into their lives without hesitation. She knew her mother would have a full-on coronary if she knew where her daughter was, and she didn't care. For the moment, she didn't give a monkey's.

Christine had to admit, though, that walking up the road had been like walking a gauntlet. She was new, she was suspect, and the people there had made her aware of that. When she had walked in the gate that was the entrance to the Murphy home, she had seen the young lads hesitate, watch her closely. She knew they were wondering what she was there for.

But now she was inside, she was amazed at the warmth, the size and the sheer goodwill that seemed to emanate from everyone and everything around her. This was a home alive with people and sounds. There was noise coming from every room and, as she saw Phillip in the kitchen doorway, his handsome face smiling and his obvious nervousness at her visit, she felt herself relax. She knew then that he was as scared as she was, and that made it suddenly all right.

Breda pushed her gently from behind and, laughing, she walked through to the enormous kitchen that was so obviously the pride and joy of Phillip's mother. Smiling shyly, Christine looked around the table at his whole family but before she could utter a word his mother bustled towards her shouting, 'Jasus, Phillip, she's gorgeous and far too good for the likes of you.'

It broke the ice, and Christine Booth, for the first time in her whole life, felt like she had finally come home.

Chapter Five

'It's only twenty past nine, are you sure you have to get going, child?'

Christine smiled nervously, embarrassed at her predicament. 'To be honest, I'm already late, Mrs Murphy.'

Veronica grinned, her round face thrilled at the girl's obvious decency. Her Phillip had chosen a good girl and, in this day and age, they were few and far between. She only had to look at her Breda to know that. And if not her Breda, then the papers. Young girls were like men these days, sex was everywhere, and girls were bombarded with so-called choices. The world had gone shagging mad, as her mother would have said.

'My mum is a bit of a tartar about me being home on time. She worries about me.'

Veronica laughed easily. 'And who could blame her? Sure, you're a dote, that's what you are, Christine, a dote.'

Veronica glanced at her husband for support and he winked at the girl, as thrilled as his wife with his son's choice of mate. Like his wife he knew that his son was serious. Phillip had been attracting girls, and women, since he was a lad, and he'd got away with a lot over the years. Seeing him with this little one and knowing that if he had brought her to his parents' house he had to be serious about her, pleased Phillip Senior as much as it did his wife. He knew better than anyone what the wrong mate could cause in a man. His younger brother had married a whore of the first water, and he was doing life for his mistake. She had

18

escaped his wrath – you didn't hit women – but her fancy man had met a knife in the ribs, and none of them thought his brother had done the wrong thing. The whore had produced a child and the parentage had been very suspect. It had been blonder than a Swedish au pair, with nonexistent eyebrows and a harelip. As the old saying went, it was a wise child that knew its own mother, but it was a *very* wise child that knew its own father.

Who would take the chance on something like that? Why would you put yourself through it? If you chose wisely from the off, got them young and innocent, and never shat on your own doorstep, then you were guaranteed a happy marriage and peace of mind. Women were like horses, you stabled them and gave them a stud. If you did it right the first time and kept them close, you had a marriage that could only bring you children and lasting happiness. He had told his three sons that from the off, and it seemed his words had struck a chord. With this one anyway. His daughter, on the other hand, lay down for any man she liked the look of. His words of wisdom had seemed to send her in the opposite direction altogether; sure, she delighted in her loose ways. But she was his only daughter so he overlooked a lot in that respect. In any case, he saw it as his wife's job to keep Breda on the straight and narrow. And he wished Veronica good luck with that. Breda was like his own mother: strong, capable and able to have more fights than John Wayne in the course of the average day. Plus, if he was really honest, he felt a small iota of respect. Breda's voracious appetite for men, sex and adventure came from his side of the family. Strong women the lot of them and proud of it.

Phillip admired his daughter's sense of self. She was eighteen, full-blooded and full-figured – a real beauty, and every man knew that beauty *and* brains were a lethal combination. His Breda was as savvy as any man he had ever known, and therefore he wanted her to have the same chances as his sons. He knew

19

what was in store for his Breda if she wasn't careful, and though he was quite happy to see the likes of Christine get trapped by love, he still wanted a bit more for his own wayward daughter. She had already had one child, at fifteen no less. Who the father was no one knew – she refused to tell. He suspected she didn't know, but he didn't allow himself to dwell too much on that. Young Porrick was a handsome, strong boy and she loved him.

However she chose to love, Breda was his daughter, and that was enough for him. After all, if he didn't look out for his own who would?

The hammering on his front door broke Phillip Senior out of his reverie and, like his three sons and his wife, he expected the worst. It was what was termed in their street 'an Old Bill knock'.

As the Murphys crowded into the small hallway, Christine hung back in the kitchen, fearful of the way everyone had assumed it was trouble coming. In *her* home, a knock on the door was considered normal, no one would be worried about it or assume it was something dangerous. She was really scared. She wished suddenly that she was at home, and safely tucked up in her own bed.

This banging was sinister, and Phillip and his family's reaction made her fears seem valid. All the things she had heard about his family were crowding her mind: that they were dangerous, that they were Faces. That no one messed with them, they were a law unto themselves.

That they were capable of all sorts.

Veronica opened the door while the rest of the family stood together like a human wall; the Murphys knew instinctively to stand close to each other, and make sure that nothing or no one could get past them. Each was determined to protect the others around them no matter what.

But it was only Joanie, Christine's friend, and her presence on the doorstep gave rise to a general sigh of relief. She peered around the Murphys to see Christine.

'Your mum's looking for you round ours, Chris, you better get a move on.'

Everyone turned to look at her then, all amazed that this little girl could have been the cause of so much fear.

Grabbing her coat and bag, Christine slunk from the house with a muttered 'thank you' and a heartfelt goodbye to Phillip, aware of the tension her friend's presence had inadvertently caused them all. She hated her mother anew for making this night such a bloody abortion. She had been really enjoying herself but, as always, her mother had managed to ruin it. Christine was more determined than ever to get away from her.

467 501

Chapter Six

'Fucking hell, Phil, did you break into a nursery? She's jailbait.'

Phillip Junior, who was normally very good natured with his sister, turned on her then, and everyone in the hallway was shocked at his words. 'Shut your fucking trap, Breda, just because she ain't a dog like you. She's only fifteen, of course her mother is looking for her. We all looked for you at the same age if you remember. Not that it did us much good.'

Breda being Breda was not about to let that go. 'What do you mean by that, Phil? Are you having a pop at me then? I was making a joke . . .'

Phillip turned to her and, poking a finger in her face, said quietly, 'Well, I ain't in the mood for jokes. So take my advice, and keep them to yourself.'

They were interrupted by the sound of crying coming from upstairs. Phillip looked at his sister and said sarcastically, 'You better get up there, Bred, sort your boy out. Let's face it, it ain't like his father's gonna turn up and help out, is it?'

'You nasty bastard, how dare you talk to me like that! Just 'cos your little girlfriend done a runner with her mate. Don't take it out on me.'

James, the youngest of the Murphy boys, stepped in then, seeing the hurt that Phillip's words had caused not just his sister but also his mother.

The father of Breda's child was what was commonly known as a wonderer – everyone wondered who he might have been.

Breda had never let on, and now at two years old, young Porrick was the darling of the household.

'He don't mean it, Breda, he's on a love job.'

Phillip looked at his sister and felt ashamed at his words, even though he knew that there was a bit of him that believed she was in the wrong. Deep down inside he thought she was a fucking slag. A baby at fifteen, and no fucking answer to the who-did-it question? It was hardly rocket science. He knew what people were saying about her; it was only his reputation that stopped them saying it to her face.

His family loyalty, though, was stronger than his bigotry and, whatever he might really think, he would defend her to the death if necessary. Opening his arms wide in a gesture of forgiveness, he said seriously, 'Come on, Breda, give me a break, me bird's just run home to her mother, how do you think I feel? I'm sorry, mate, you know I don't mean it . . .'

Breda wasn't to be placated though and, shaking her head slowly, she said heavily, 'I'll give you a heads-up, shall I? Sister to brother. Christine is a lovely girl, but she will be trouble, Phil. You'll never believe that, you will only ever see the good girl, the wilting virgin. How you were *first* in, and *last* out. Well, do you know something, bruv? We women are not as different as you all seem to think we are. And that child up there will always mean more to me than any fucking bloke. You lot included. He is my flesh and blood, so fuck the neighbours, and fuck you for your narrow-mindedness. Unlike men, we women know exactly what we have produced, and we do not have to rely on someone else's honesty to convince us of our children's paternity. So, next time you have a go at me about my baby being fatherless, remember this much. *I* know and *he* will *always* know who his mother is, there can never be an argument about that. And he will also know that he was more important to me than my reputation. You see, that's something none of you ever quite got. At fifteen years old, I chose my *own* flesh and blood over

23

the neighbours and their gossiping. Over you lot, and your fear of what people might think. So anything you have to say to me is pointless. I made a decision against everything you all believed was right.'

'Stop this now, Breda, it's gone far enough,' Veronica interjected, visibly upset.

Breda shook her head again, her lovely face smiling amiably, the hurt she had kept inside for so long hidden, until she said sarcastically, 'Oh, Mum, how did it go when I told you I was pregnant? Oh yeah, I remember, "get an abortion, no one will ever know, you're ruining your life, no one will ever want you if you have a baby". And you hammering the door of the church down every Sunday. I nearly swallowed your crap and all. But you see, you never allowed for me and the love I already had for my child. None of you thought about me and what I might want. You *had* to get married, Mum. I chose not to.'

Breda pushed past her eldest brother, shoving him angrily out of her way. 'I had my baby, I kept my baby, and for you to give me a tug because your little schoolie had to go home to her mum and dad's . . . I ain't your whipping boy, and you better get your head around that. And now I am going up to settle *my* little boy, and you can go and fuck yourselves.' She walked from the room then, her back ramrod straight and her animosity almost tangible.

'What the fuck was all that about?' Declan, the middle brother, was genuinely shocked at the night's turn of events.

Veronica Murphy shook her head in despair.

Watching his sister mount the stairs, Phillip looked at his father and said honestly, 'She has a point, I suppose.'

Phillip Murphy Senior looked at his sons and, pushing them gently back into the kitchen, he said loudly, 'Well, that needed to be said. She did a brave thing keeping the child. These days you can flush the poor unfortunates away without a second's thought. If she had done that, sure none of you would have been any the wiser and she would still be like your one there tonight, who ran home to her mammy like a good girl. Can you blame your sister for feeling you all think wrong of her?'

Phillip looked at his eldest son in particular as he spoke, and Phillip Junior knew that his reaction to his sister had not only been uncalled for, but had also been seen for the hypocrisy that it was. He was suitably ashamed.

But Christine's goodness, her family's decent reputation, their standing in the small community they had to live in, had shown him just how other people really perceived them all. He knew that his sister's child had been a slur on the family. It was a stigma to have a child and not be married. It was still seen as a terrible thing. Not for the fathers of course, only the mothers of the children. Their lives were more or less ruined. He understood that Breda was telling him this night, without fear or favour, that her child was not going to be apologised for in any way, shape or form. Especially not to the likes of Christine Booth and her family. Breda had tapped into his fear of what Christine's family might think about his sister having a child out of wedlock. She had implied that *his* taking up with a fifteen-year-old girl who didn't know her arse from her proverbial elbow was the reason Phillip suddenly looked down on his own sister, on his own flesh and blood.

Phillip knew that Breda had perceived his real feelings towards her. He looked at his two brothers, and saw their sceptical looks. They were as aware as Breda of his worries that her child might affect the Booths' overall opinion of him and his family. Phillip was ashamed of his thoughts, and the fact that he had allowed Eileen Booth and her opinions to cloud his judgement.

But in his favour, he loved Christine with a vengeance. Realistically he knew that his family name alone would be enough for her mother to cause them aggro – on top of everything else, his sister's unmarried state would be another thing Eileen would use against him. Already this young girl had made him turn on his own sister, had made him want to be someone different, someone her family would be happy to welcome. Who her family would see as an asset, not as a liability. Christine was not like the Murphys; she was pure, she was good and decent and that meant the world to him.

Christine had never asked for anything in her whole life, not really, and he so badly wanted to be good enough for her he had nearly allowed himself to betray his own family. The strength of his feelings and what they made him do frightened him; he had never wanted anyone this way before, had never felt that kind of anger before. And it turned out Christine had not even told her family where she was going – that spoke volumes to him. That she had come to his home and lied to her parents about her whereabouts had really offended him, even though he understood the reasoning behind it.

But Phillip was going to get his girl, no matter what it took. He was obsessed with her, and he knew there would never be anyone else for him.

Chapter Seven

'I want to know where you were. And don't you lie to me, Christine, I already know the answer.'

'Then why ask the road you know, Mum?'

The two antagonists stared at one another, neither willing to be the first to look away. They were so alike physically – thick blond hair and dark blue eyes. Both were fine boned, with small hands and feet. Eileen saw herself in her daughter, a younger, prettier version, of course. Christine wouldn't waste herself on a no mark; unlike her mother, this girl would use her looks and her brains to her advantage. Eileen would make sure of that if it was the last thing she did in this life.

She was heartbroken that it had come to this with her only child. A girl who had always done what she was told, who had made her so proud deep inside. Christine couldn't see that her name being associated with a family like the Murphys was something she would one day regret with all her heart. She might be naïve, but she was certainly not stupid. Christine had seen the people who frequented their supermarket (Eileen never called it a shop, ever). She had *seen* how those people lived. She was nearly sixteen, she would be off to the sixth form soon and she would meet a different class of person. She would see that the estate was a dump for transients and no-hopers. She had seen them all her life, queuing up for their family allowance and their giros. She had to have seen that this was no life for the likes of her.

That the post office was a big part of their income Eileen never admitted. She looked on it with disdain as she did everything to do with the supermarket. With her husband's working life. With the place that kept her in the manner she was still not accustomed to as a result of it not bringing in as much money as she would have liked. Eileen was bitter; she had once pictured them with a chain of small supermarkets, and she admitted to herself that if she had been willing to work side-by-side with her husband, a second one would have been possible and then a third. But she was too proud. She had been to teacher training college and had become a part-time teacher at the local primary school. But she now understood that the supermarket should have been a joint venture. That boat had sailed a long time ago though, and she didn't plan to tell her husband he had been right. It was too late anyway, because he didn't want her there any more – she only put off the customers they *did* have. If it wasn't for him and the tick, the majority would leave and go to the new supermarkets springing up all over the place. Nevertheless, times were tough. They now *depended* on the giros, the family allowance and the car tax. They desperately needed another income, because they were finding it increasingly hard to make ends meet. The mortgage was crippling them, and Eileen was determined her daughter was going to contribute before she swanned off to marry and reproduce.

'Are you going to answer me, Mum?'

Christine was fed up now. Being questioned every day, every week, so aggressively was not something she was willing to endure any more. She knew her association with Phillip Murphy was now common knowledge, and she had accepted that her mother would eventually get wind of it. She just wished it had not happened so quickly, had not happened tonight.

'I was at Joanie's.' She knew she had said this to her mother too much recently, but it couldn't be helped. 'It's not a crime to go to a friend's, is it?'

'No one said it was, but if it was so innocent why didn't you say that in the first place?'

Christine closed her eyes and counted to ten; she had read a problem page once that said if you took a deep breath and counted to ten before you answered a question, it stopped you from blurting out things you might one day regret. That advice had stood her in good stead over the years with her mother. Not so much lying, as just not telling her the whole truth.

Her mother saw the bad in *everything*, in her eyes everyone in her daughter's orbit was a potential threat. Even her school-friends and their mothers. Joanie's mum had always sympathised with Christine, had seen the way her mother had demanded total control of her only daughter. Joanie's mum had told her many years ago that she was always welcome to stay there if she needed a break. It had been a watershed for Christine hearing those words. She had known then that her feelings for her mother weren't ingratitude, her mother was genuinely unreason-able.

'Why didn't I tell you? Do you really need to ask me that, Mum? You keep questioning me as if I have done something wrong, and the more you question me the more I don't want to tell you anything. You're supposed to trust me, trust what I say.' Christine was so upset she was visibly shaking, not so much with anger, though that was a big part of it, but with sheer distress. Why was her mother always trying to catch her out? She *had* been at Joanie's, on the night she was being questioned about anyway. She didn't get to see her friend much these days. Phillip didn't like her for some reason.

Eileen Booth took a deep breath, and looked into her daughter's eyes. Christine noted that her face was the usual mask of heavy foundation. She thought her mother's make-up made her look like a doll. Made her look unreal. She came down to the breakfast table every day in full war paint, and for as long as Christine could remember, she had never once seen her mother

29

without her face on. Eileen never looked natural, had never looked approachable or friendly even. From her blue eye shadow to her pink cheeks she looked like a stranger. Like someone else's mum. She was very attractive, Christine knew that, saw the way men looked at her. She knew instinctively that her mother's make-up was for their benefit, not her husband's. Eileen had disregarded Ted since Christine could remember. He rarely disagreed with his wife, she was far too aggressive, far too overpowering. Christine knew he had given up trying to make any kind of point long ago. He had been worn down by his wife's constant complaints. Christine was determined that she would not have a marriage like that.

As Eileen Booth looked at her lovely daughter she felt the urge to cry. She couldn't bear to see her lovely girl waste herself on a Murphy. And waste herself she would if Eileen didn't step in and steer her in the right direction.

'I've heard a rumour, Christine, and that rumour is that you are trailing after Phillip Murphy. The Murphys are the scum of the earth, darling. Now, put yourself in my position. If you had a daughter, and I want you to think about this seriously, would you honestly want her wasting herself on a no mark like that?'

When she was really angry, as she was now, Eileen resorted to the gutter speak. It showed her up for what she really was. 'No mark' was a common expression, and Christine knew that while her mother might believe she was better than everyone, she had been born over a newsagent's in East London. The shop her husband now ran had been bought with the proceeds of that newsagent's. That she still looked down on everyone around her was a constant source of irritation to her only daughter.

Looking squarely at her mother, Christine asked sarcastically, 'What's a "no mark", Mum?'

Her mother's hand shot out and physically knocked her across the room. Then, grabbing her daughter's hair, Eileen dragged her into the downstairs toilet. Pushing her face against the mirror, she screamed, 'Look at yourself, you stupid girl! You could have anyone, do anything with your life.'

Christine was not going to cry, no matter what, so, pulling herself from her mother's grasp, she said, 'What, like you did, you mean?' The words were quietly spoken, but the implication was there for anyone to hear.

'You nasty little mare. After all I've done for you . . .'

'That's all I've ever heard, Mum, all me life, what *you've* done for me. Well, I wish you hadn't bothered, because I want out of here. *Sooner* rather than later, and I know you don't like Phil, but that's half the attraction. I'd shag a tramp if it got me away from you.'

Christine knew then that she had finally gone too far.

Chapter Eight

Phillip Murphy was really angry, but as usual he kept his feelings to himself. He understood only too well the value of blandness; in his job, the less people could gauge about you the less they could put away for future reference. Consequently, no matter what he was paid to do, he did it quietly, quickly and, most importantly, without expressing any kind of opinion whatsoever. He was already getting a reputation as a good earner. As someone who took the job on offer and didn't ask questions either way and, more to the point, didn't feel the urge to discuss it with all and sundry.

His attitude was it wasn't any of his business and, for that reason, he had no interest in the history of the people involved. He wasn't in the market for hearing grievances or explanations. He wanted his poke, and he would happily carry out what was requested of him to get it without a prolonged discussion. He prided himself on his knack for not caring about the people involved – not the people who paid him, and *definitely* not the people he was paid to visit.

Until now, that was.

It didn't mean he wasn't aware of the situations he had been asked to deal with. He always knew exactly what the score was, he just never asked the person concerned why they wanted his services. The fact that he expected a very nice fee for what he did spoke volumes. His price told the person who needed his expertise that he knew exactly what was going on, but that he didn't let it cloud his judgement in any way. If he wasn't *told* anything it was assumed he did not *know* anything. It was simple economics. He just wanted his money, he was not a fucking agony aunt. This endeared him to people because they knew he never discussed his work, and never felt the need to prove himself by running off his mouth. And his brothers were the same. But most petty Faces were banged up because they couldn't resist opening their traps. They needed people to know who they were and what they were capable of. Liked to name-drop the people they were working for, liked the fact that they felt a bit of reflected glory. Real Faces were too shrewd to let anyone know anything, no matter how big or how small. It was enough for *them* to know they had done it and got away with it; they certainly didn't feel the need to broadcast it to the fucking nation.

Now here he was, standing before Stan Barclay, a man he had grown up respecting, a man his father had always spoken of in hushed tones, and he was asking Phillip to do something that was not only against the grain, but an insult to boot. There wasn't much Phillip wouldn't do, but even he had his limit. He knew that Stan was relying on his reputation for discretion, and he understood that it was that reputation that had brought him to Stan's attention. But he was not about to be used by him. Being given a job that Stan would be chary of giving to his regular workforce said it all as far as he was concerned. Even though it would enable Phillip to step up into the world of serious villainy, as Stan had repeatedly pointed out to him. What Stan didn't realise, however, was that Phillip knew that Stan would make sure what he was asking him to do was never made public. That meant that Phillip himself would be a target once the job was completed. Stan was betting on his greed and that he would be too dense to work out the bottom line. Phillip was young and he was hungry, but Stan Barclay had made a mistake in thinking he was also stupid. This was a poser, this was a real dilemma. But he had to ask the question.

'Are you sure about this, Stan?'

Stan Barclay nodded his huge head; he looked like an oversized shelf stacker, not a criminal mastermind. He had a huge workforce and a large slice of the pie that was London. He also had an Achilles heel, and now that Phillip knew what it was he knew he had to act quickly. Stan Barclay was not going to wait around for him to put two and two together. Even Phillip was secretly impressed; if Stan had him removed, who would even suspect he was a part of it? It would be assumed he had upset one of the powers-that-be and had been taken care of. It would not be seen as important. He was a young pup, and the word would be put round that he had upset the wrong person.

'This is not something I was expecting. How much *after* the job's done?' Phillip said the words with the arrogance he knew Stan would expect. He was well aware that Stan had no intention of paying him a fucking brass razoo. Any front money would be reacquired after his demise.

Stanley Barclay smiled slightly as he opened his arms in a gesture of open-handed generosity. 'Thirty grand after, ten in cash today.'

Phillip nodded, his face didn't betray his real thoughts. 'Where is she? Where's the best place to find her?'

Stan grinned, happy in the knowledge he had sorted out another problem with the least amount of aggro and the maximum amount of camaraderie. He was sorry in a way; this kid was good but, like all good generals, Stan had to understand the term 'collateral damage'.

Chapter Nine

Veronica looked at her son's girlfriend, saw the bruises on her face, and the sorrow in her eyes. If she was honest, she didn't blame Eileen Booth for her reaction; she was truthful enough to admit she wouldn't want her daughter to come home with men like her sons.

But Phillip loved this girl. Trouble was she was only fifteen. And now, she was on the doorstep refusing to go home.

Christine was battered and bruised, and she needed someone to look out for her. Eileen Booth was an eejit, she should realise she was driving the girl away. Everyone knew about Christine and Phillip. They were the talk of the estate.

Christine's parents were well known too. Ted Booth's supermarket was just down the road. Ted treated everyone with respect. He allowed tick to some people, and he had a knack of refusing others in a way that didn't cause them to retaliate. He had always had a Christmas Club, and everyone knew he was meticulous about the money that was paid in. She herself had been a part of it for longer than she cared to remember. It was his wife that people had the problem with. Eileen Booth made a point of lording it over everyone who came into what she referred to as 'her establishment'; she made sure that everyone knew she thought they were beneath her. So Veronica could be forgiven for finding a small measure of satisfaction in having Eileen's daughter in her front room, determined not to go home for love nor money.

She made Christine a cup of tea, and held her hand until Phillip came home. She knew this girl didn't have any idea of just how deep her son already was in the criminal world, didn't know how deep they *all* were in that world. Herself included. She also knew that, like her at fifteen, this girl looked like a woman but, unlike Veronica, Christine didn't have the brains she was born with. She had been too sheltered all her life, and as much as Veronica was fond of her, she knew Christine was far too naïve for her own good.

Chapter Ten

'Are you all right, Phil?' James was not the most vocal of men, but even he had sussed that Phillip was not right.

Phillip shrugged. 'No, not really, Jamsie. I think we need to talk to Billy Bantry, he's usually at his gym about this time.'

Jamsie started the car, uneasy now. Billy Bantry was seriously big time, and no one went to him unless they had an invitation. He was not known for his light-hearted banter or his friendly personality. He was, however, known for his short temper, and his unwillingness to suffer fools gladly.

As they approached the gym in North London, Phillip said gently, 'Park round the back, I don't want to be seen going in the front door. Then I want you to go home and wait for me there, OK?'

Jamsie parked the BMW neatly then, turning to his brother, he said, 'I ain't going nowhere without you, Phil.'

Phillip smiled, pleased at his brother's loyalty; Jamsie wasn't the sharpest knife in the drawer, but he was someone you could depend on and he appreciated that.

'This could all turn pear-shaped, Jamsie. I warn you.'

Jamsie shrugged easily. 'Whatever. You're me brother, I ain't about to let you walk in on your Jack Jones, am I?'

'I appreciate that, Jamsie.'

'So what's this all about?'

Phillip grinned then. 'I can't tell you. You'll have to trust me.'

Jamsie didn't even think about what had been said. He answered immediately, 'Fair enough.'

Phillip took a deep breath, then opened the car door slowly. 'Wish me luck, bruv.'

As he spoke the back door of the offices opened and two of Billy Bantry's minders walked towards him. He was impressed by their speed. They had to have been looking out for someone acting suspicious, or more to the point someone who had the nerve to park in the car park and, even worse, who wasn't invited, let alone welcome.

'Is Mr Bantry about?'

The older of the two men answered him with a sneer. 'Why, who are you, the fucking police?'

Chapter Eleven

Billy Bantry was not a big man, but he was heavy-set and possessed what was known as an uncompromising personality. He was frightened of no one, and that came across within ten seconds of meeting him. He was a dour, dark-eyed Irishman. Unlike his compatriots he rarely drank, and he rarely had a tale to tell. His life revolved around his work and his family. He was a dedicated family man. His eldest son was halfway through a degree at Oxford University, and his eldest daughter was married to an idiot on daytime TV. He had two more children by his long-time mistress, and they went to Ampleforth; unlike him, the mistress was a devout Catholic.

As he stared now at Phillip Murphy he seemed devoid of any emotion whatsoever, and Phillip realised that this man could teach him more in a week than most men could in a year. Billy Bantry was that rare breed, the serious loner. He needed no one at all, except the people he employed, and they were paid far too well to ever be tempted away. Plus Billy would never forgive them leaving him, no matter what the circumstances. He owned them.

Bantry regarded young Phillip Murphy through slitted eyes. He had heard good things about him, and he was intrigued as to why the boy had come to him like this. He was not known as an approachable man, he had made sure of that over the years. He had no interest in small talk or gossip. Anything he needed to know he found out with the minimum of fuss and, if necessary, the maximum of pain. So this boy coming to him like this out of the blue had to mean something. He hoped he wasn't going to waste his time asking him for a job, but from what he had heard about Phillip he was too shrewd to try that old fanny.

'Can I speak to you in private, Mr Bantry?' Phillip was nervous, and he was sure the others in the room would pick up on it.

Billy Bantry looked at the lad; he was a lump, no mistaking. But he also seemed a decent enough kid in many respects. He didn't sense any fear or skulduggery emanating from him. In fact, the boy seemed genuine. He was apprehensive, that much was clear. But Phillip was still there, and he had the balls to ask him for his time. That alone impressed Bantry. He waved his two henchmen away, and they left the small office quietly and unquestioningly. Phillip liked that, understood clearly they thought Bantry could take care of himself should the need arise. He knew he was lucky to get this far, but that was the chance he had taken.

'So what do you want, Murphy, and make it quick. I have a notoriously low threshold for boredom.'

'You know a girl called Lisa Mercer, right?'

Billy Bantry didn't move a muscle. 'So what, what about her?'

'She's five months pregnant by Stanley Barclay.'

'And?'

'He wants me to take her out, her and her baby. Offered me forty grand in all. Ten up front, I have that in the car, and thirty afterwards. But I know I wouldn't live long enough to get the rest of the money. I also have no intention of murdering a woman, especially not a pregnant one. I didn't know what to do, then I remembered that she had been rumoured to have had a friendship with you. Just a rumour, mind, and I wondered if you would be kind enough to give me some advice. I keep everything close to my chest and Barclay is relying on that. But,

Mr Bantry, I will do a lot of things for a lot of money, but murdering babies ain't in my résumé.'

Billy Bantry was nodding his head; Phillip hoped it was in agreement with what he was saying. Bantry sighed heavily. 'Barclay's scum, always has been. Five months gone? She tried her hardest, but was never going to score the big one. Good-looking girl, though. Nice natured. You did the right thing, Phillip. Women and children have no real place in our world. They are off-limits. So you assume your reputation for never questioning a job was what he was relying on?'

Phillip nodded.

'He must be desperate if he's giving you ten grand up front. Have you ever killed anyone before?'

Phillip shook his head. 'Not yet, no.'

'Do you think you could?'

Phillip nodded, which made Billy Bantry laugh. 'Keep the ten grand, you've earned it. I'll sort out Barclay, the treacherous cunt. Lisa's old man's in Dartmoor, she had no real father figure, so I've always kept an eye out for her in me own way. But you knew that, that's why you came to me.'

Phillip didn't say a word in response. Bantry liked that the boy didn't try and explain himself. He had heard good things about this kid, and he was happy to give him a helping hand.

'Report to me here on Saturday morning, seven o'clock and don't be late. I think you are worth a chance, son, but remember, with me, you only get the *one* chance.'

Phillip was thrilled at the turn of events. He had taken a big risk, and had known that it could have gone either way. But for all that, he was never going to kill a pregnant woman. Especially one who had friends in high places.

Chapter Twelve

Ted Booth heard the bell in his shop, and walked casually out of his small office in the back. As he entered the shop he saw Phillip Murphy locking the door and turning the sign round to 'Closed'.

'What are you doing? It's only six, I have another five hours yet till I close up.'

Phillip smiled at him as if he had known that all along. 'Sorry, Mr Booth, but I need to talk to you.'

Ted Booth felt his heart sinking inside his chest, and for one split second he wondered if he was on the verge of a heart attack. It wouldn't surprise him. He never felt one hundred per cent. His life was a series of minor irritations, the only things he cared about these days were his daughter and the shop. His daughter had her name up with this one here, and he wondered how long before it would all turn sour. He heard everything in this shop; it was part of his job to talk to the customers, listen to them, know their lives. He was frightened, but he tried not to show that. 'What do you want? Make it quick, I'm losing money.'

'It's about your daughter . . .'

'I worked that one out for meself.'

'She's round my mum's, refusing to go home. Mrs Booth gave her a clump; she's bruised and battered and determined that she ain't going home.'

Ted didn't know what to do. This boy, and he used that term loosely because he was a man in all the ways that counted, was the reason his wife was nearly out of her mind, and why his daughter was happier than she had been in years.

'She's a child. Fifteen.'

'She will be sixteen in three weeks and, Mr Booth, I need to tell you that she ain't in the frame of mind for going home. I told her to, me mum and dad have told her to, but she's adamant.'

Ted sighed. This man, this boy-man, had a hold over his daughter that he knew he would never be able to break. It had already gone too far. He could offer her freedom and excitement, and that was a heady mixture for his Christine. She craved love, craved attention, and the Murphys would give her that in abundance. He knew there and then that he couldn't compete with them on that score, but he had to try.

'I want her home, she's still legally in my jurisdiction.' Ted felt foolish even saying the words. He knew and Phillip Murphy knew that it was only a matter of weeks. Once Christine hit sixteen her life was her own. And the worst thing was that, in a strange way, he didn't blame her for what she'd done. Eileen had suffocated her all her life.

'Well, Mr Booth, that's your prerogative. But I just want you to know that she's safe. I would want to know that if it was my daughter.' Phillip smiled his amiable, friendly smile. Then, shrugging his shoulders in a man of the world gesture, he said to change the subject, 'This is a big space, ain't it? Just out of curiosity, where do you get your alcohol? Only I know a bloke, and he could guarantee you a much better return for your money. He supplies most of the pubs and clubs around here.'

Teddy Booth felt his heart sink even further; he knew exactly where this conversation was going.

Chapter Thirteen

'You're bright and early.'

Phillip was smiling at Billy Bantry, thrilled at the chance to work for a real crew. He knew he was on a winner; Billy didn't offer his time to wasters, he was a man who only employed the best. Well, Phillip wanted to be the best, and if that meant he had to be a gofer for a while then so be it. He was willing, more than willing, to learn at the knee of a master, and Billy Bantry was a master.

'I can't believe I'm here, Mr Bantry. It's an honour, and I mean that.'

He was sincere, Bantry knew that. He had done his homework on Phillip Murphy and had been proved right. The lad was willing and he was able, more than able, in fact, to take care of himself. He was a lump, but that in itself meant nothing to Billy Bantry. He had taken on bigger men than Phillip and won the war. It was never about size, physical strength, that is. It was about mental strength. The determination to harm your opponent no matter what. Bantry had always been possessed of a cold streak, even as a kid, and he had a big presence, which was more important in his line of work than anything. He was amazed to find that he actually liked this kid, liked his heart. He appreciated that he had come to him quietly and with the least amount of fuss. Lisa Mercer was a nice enough girl, but for Barclay to even think about taking out her and the child was beyond the pale as far as he was concerned. His own child and all! Barclay had had no qualms about offing his own fucking baby. Well, he was now the proud possessor of a pair of cement boots. His disappearance might cause a stir for a few weeks, but unless someone decided to dredge the North Sea, he wasn't likely to be turning up any time in the near future. It suited Bantry; Barclay was becoming a pest anyway, a nuisance, so a valid reason to remove him from the arena was always going to be handy. Plus he had the added bonus of doing his old mate a favour. Lisa's old man would never forget what Billy had done for him, and he wouldn't let him either. Everyone got out one day, and they were always welcome so long as they had something to bring to the table.

'Aren't you going to ask me what happened, then?'

Phillip was too shrewd to fall for that old fanny, but he kept his face neutral and feigned surprise. 'I don't care, Mr Bantry, it's nothing to do with me, is it?'

Billy Bantry laughed, a rare, real laugh. 'You'll do. I want you out collecting with Keith Kenton. He's big and quiet and he knows more about the grab than anyone else in the Smoke. He's expecting you at the Bricklayers' Arms in Hornchurch. Be there by lunchtime.'

He saw the confusion on Phillip's face and he laughed once more. 'Rule number one, son. Always sort business out on neutral ground. Never talk money on the premises. Demand the money, yes, but never drink in a place you're earning from, it causes bad feeling. Can often be misconstrued as a piss-take. Let's face it, going in and collecting is one thing, sitting around all day on the piss and reminding them of your primary function is something else entirely. That causes bad feeling. I like it all to be low key: in, collect and out. Now, have you any questions?'

Phillip shook his head.

'Good. Now fuck off and get on the earn.'

Chapter Fourteen

Veronica heard the hammering on her front door, and sighed heavily. This time she knew exactly who it was going to be. She walked up the hallway slowly and opened the door as if it was a normal caller, someone she wanted to find on her doorstep. Instead, she looked into Eileen Booth's face and smiled sadly. 'Come in quietly, let's leave the screaming and the shouting for the young ones. Don't be making a show of yourself for the neighbours. I'll make a pot of tea.'

Eileen Booth was so furious she thought her head would explode. This woman was acting as if this was *normal*, as if young girls walked out on their families and their lives every day of the week. Was she mentally deficient or something? Couldn't she see how her heart was broken with it all? Did she think that to lose your only child to a family of heathens was not something she should be worried about? Couldn't she understand the fear a mother felt when a teenage child made such potentially devastating decisions without realising the consequences of them? She rounded on the culprit standing before her, the person she saw as responsible. The woman she felt was taking her child from her.

'Have a cup of tea! Are you having a laugh with me? All I want is me daughter.' The refined voice was gone, all pretence washed away; she was showing her East-End roots. Eileen Booth wanted her daughter and was determined she was *not* leaving without her.

46

Veronica Murphy looked her antagonist over slowly, deliberately, and with hate in her heart at the woman's assumption that the Murphy family was not good enough to mix with her brood. She took a deep breath and said haughtily, 'Come inside, woman, for Christ's sake. Don't do this on the doorstep like some old slapper. My neighbours are very respectable people. They don't need to be subjected to this. Have you no shame?'

Eileen was so incensed at Veronica's words that she drew her arm back to strike. It was the worst thing she could have ever contemplated. Veronica grabbed her adversary by the throat, her hand like a vice, and dragged the taller woman into the hallway none too gently. She kicked the door shut behind her and, pushing the distraught woman roughly towards the kitchen, she shrieked, 'As God is my witness, you have driven me fecking demented! One more word and I'll annihilate you where you stand, lady. No wonder your daughter doesn't want to be around you! On the few occasions I've met you, it's took all me willpower not to knock your fucking brains in meself. You think you're better than everyone else, don't you? Well, I have news for you, you're not. Now, I think you had better relax, lady, before this gets out of hand. Believe me, I am two seconds away from giving you a serious clump.'

Veronica wasn't sure who was shocked the most, Eileen Booth, who was suddenly very quiet, or she herself at her reaction. She still felt the urge to wring Eileen's scrawny neck, really lay into her. This wasn't like her at all; Veronica had mellowed with age, there was a time when she would have wiped the floor with this one from the off and never given it a moment's thought. But it was good to know that she was still capable of a fight should the need arise.

'I want my daughter, and I am not leaving without her.'

Veronica was tired suddenly. She could see Eileen's dilemma better than anyone; after all, she had been there herself. 'Well, in that case you should have packed a bag, because you'll be here for a while. She won't go home, and it's not for want of us lot trying. I *know* she should be with you, I ain't a complete fool, but if you can't see how your actions have driven that child away then I don't know what to tell you.'

Veronica understood Eileen Booth's complete bewilderment. But she also knew that this woman had not exactly helped the situation. If anything she had only made it worse. If she had just tried to give a little leeway, but that was not her style. Like Veronica had believed with Breda, this stupid woman thought she could tell her daughter what to do. Well, those days were long gone, girls these days had choices. And like many a girl before them, their age practically guaranteed they would make the wrong ones. Always the wrong ones. It was a pattern that seemed to come with hormones and breasts. Overnight they looked like women, but that didn't mean they were.

The two women stared at each other for a long moment. Eileen Booth knew that she was beaten. Knew that this woman had her daughter's trust, her daughter's respect. Her face crumpled, her hurt and fear for her daughter shining through her heavy make-up. 'I only ever wanted what was best for her, that's all. I wanted her to have a chance in life. The chance to make something of herself. The way you all act you'd think I was trying to fucking hurt her. She's still a child.' It was the plaintive cry of many a woman before her. It was the cry of a woman who was not only at the end of her tether, but also of a woman who had finally run out of options. She was defeated, and she knew it.

Veronica brought her through to the kitchen and sat her in a chair. She made the pot of tea quietly, aware that the best thing she could do now was let this woman get it out of her system. Let her have her say, let her expend her hatred on her, a stranger. Veronica didn't care, knew this had to happen at some point, and personally she would rather it happened sooner rather than later. It was pointless delaying the inevitable.

As she listened to the vitriol of the woman before her, her mind wandered to her own feelings for Breda who had been uncontrollable at thirteen, let alone fifteen. It was hard to admit, but Veronica knew it was not something she could have ever prevented. It was just Breda's way, she had always been a law unto herself. She had seemed unaware of how her actions affected the people around her, nor had she cared how her behaviour was received. Whereas Eileen's daughter was only rebelling against her *mother* – nothing else – but Veronica wasn't about to say that just yet. With Breda it had been different, she had just wanted her own life, her own sex life anyway. Veronica placed a mug of tea in front of the woman she knew she would never find it in her heart to ever like.

Eileen was looking around the kitchen, impressed despite herself at the grandeur of the surroundings; it was the last thing she had expected, if she was honest with herself. In spite of her anger she felt a grudging respect for Veronica Murphy. The place was spotless, well decorated and had top of the range appliances. In Eileen's world that was all that mattered. Top show, as her mother used to say. Well, as far as she was concerned, how you lived was important; she knew that from years of being ashamed of her home, of her parents and their preference for drink, bingo and the attitude that it was enough just to make a living. She had wanted far more than that. And yet her dream of respectability had not made her any happier. How ironic was that?

'Look, Eileen – can I call you Eileen? – Christine is terrified of you and what you did to her. She's at school now, she hasn't missed a day, but you have to believe that this was her choice, not mine. I never wanted this on my doorstep, why the feck would I? My Phillip might not be what you want for your daughter, but he's what *she* wants, and she seems to be what *he* wants. If you want my advice, swallow your anger and try and talk her round. Try and see it from her point of view, like. Kids have all sorts of rights these days, didn't I find that out meself with my Breda? The shame and degradation of that one, up and pregnant and still at school, and the social workers behind her, all on her side, acting like what she had done was normal! I didn't even have a say in the end. I watched her nearly destroy herself, but my opinions counted for nothing. So you are preaching to the fecking converted. What I want is for you and Christine to sort yourselves out.'

Eileen felt she could sympathise with the woman now. She could hear the genuine sorrow in her voice. Coupled with the knowledge that Veronica was capable of giving her a serious clump should she feel the urge, Eileen Booth felt it best to retreat on this occasion and try and make some kind of concession. After all, this was the Murphys they were talking about, and their name was a byword for villainy and assertiveness around these parts. So sipping the tea she said sadly, 'I only wanted what was best for her, Mrs Murphy, and this is how she repays me? The treacherous little mare.'

This was more like it, this was language she could understand. Veronica flapped her hand in agreement. 'Sure, they all think they know what's best for them! But I tell you, if they only knew the truth of love and marriage, they would think twice about it. I know I would.' She was telling the woman what she wanted to hear.

Eileen Booth latched on to the woman's words as if they were a lifeline. 'That's what I've been trying to tell her. There's plenty of time for all that. She has a brain in her head, my Christine. She could make something of herself, make her life worth something. Ten years from now she could have the job of her dreams, the qualifications to take her anywhere she wanted to go in the world. But at the moment she just wants him, can only see *him*, him and his handsome face. And I mean that with no disrespect, but she wants him before she understands what life is *really* about. Before the disappointment and the regrets set in.'

50

Veronica sighed, suddenly sorry for this woman, so deeply sorry. 'Those two seem intent on doing what they want. He thinks the world of her, I can tell you that much. I've never seen him like this before.'

'She'll be tied down with a posse of kids before she's twenty, and by twenty-five she'll be worn out with child-bearing, and her future will be settled once and for all. But will she listen to me? 'Course not. When she's got a belly full of stretchmarks, and she's robbing Peter to pay Paul to get from one week to the next, she'll wish she'd listened to me, but by then it'll be too late.'

Veronica Murphy didn't answer her, she didn't know what to say. The truth, as she knew herself, often hurt. And this was one of those times.

Chapter Fifteen

Keith Kenton liked Phillip Murphy, and the knowledge surprised him. Not a man to be easily influenced, he normally took his time sussing people out. But this young lad had impressed him with his quiet demeanour, and his natural affinity for the work in hand. Every now and then, you were lucky enough to find a Phillip Murphy, and if you used your loaf you took them onside. Phillip had the rare ability to hurt people without a second's thought; he wasn't a fool, he just saw it for what it was, a job. Keith felt the boy's natural aptitude for the game, and he was willing to nurture it. Get them young, and you could shape them properly. It was the law of the pavement.

Keith was a big man, in stature and in personality. He was known for his ability to fight his way out of any situation, for being, like Bantry, a loner and, most of all, for his reputation as a ladies' man. Keith liked the fairer sex, and it was fair to say that they, for some unknown reason, liked him. Not the most handsome man in the world, he had over the years perfected the gift of the gab. He could talk a girl round in under fifteen minutes, and he had the respect of every man who knew him because of it. Women fell for him; his charm, his generosity, and his sense of humour never failed to get him an in. He was always on the lookout for a bit of strange. A new conquest. It was part of the game of life as far as he was concerned. Unfortunately, the *women* concerned all assumed they were the *only* ones in his life, and it was only a matter of time before they realised that he was a romancer. Until then, though, he made sure they had the time of their lives. Consequently, Keith was always trying to avoid some female. More often than not that person was his long-suffering wife Lorna who, for some reason, always ended up forgiving him and taking him back.

Phillip Murphy was impressed despite himself; some of Keith's birds were well fit, and so obviously out of his league looks-wise, you could only bow to the master. He could charm the proverbial birds out of the trees and, in his case, into his bed. Trouble was, once they had landed there, he lost interest in them. It was the chase that got him going. The capture, unfortunately for the girls concerned, was the beginning of the end.

So Phillip was getting an education that was two-fold: he was learning the pitfalls of juggling more than one bird at a time (something that in all honesty didn't appeal to him) and how to collect protection money with the minimum of fuss and the maximum of goodwill. Keith made the people he collected from feel that he was doing them a favour and, in his own way, he was. After all, if they still didn't pay up when he turned on his good-natured patter, he was capable of killing them if the need arose or if he needed to set an example. Any trouble in the premises he earned off was sorted within twenty-four hours, if not sooner. And the perpetrator was given a lesson that would stay with them for a lifetime.

Scars, according to Keith, did that to people – especially cowards. A cut face, or the loss of a few teeth, were a constant reminder of their stupidity and made sure that the offender never saw fit to repeat his actions. Keith had a way of making it perfectly clear that a second offence would not be tolerated. As he explained to Phillip, it was the principle as far as he was concerned; he would not allow anyone to cause him the aggravation of having to look for them more than once. By then all his goodwill was used up, and all that he had left was the need for retribution.

Phillip Murphy was soaking it all in like a sponge. This was a whole new world to him, and he loved it. Every second of it. As his father said, he had started at the top, with the best, and there was only one way for him to go, and that was up. He liked Keith and his attitude towards life, and he liked working with him. He knew that Keith respected him. He also knew that Keith understood his association with Bantry, and respected it. Keith did not suffer fools gladly, so his relationship with his mentor could only enhance him and his chosen career.

Life was pretty good. Things were going well with Christine too. This feud with her mother couldn't be better; he was sure that if he sat it out Eileen would drive her daughter even further into his arms, thereby giving him exactly what he wanted. It was criminal really, how easy it was. He had her dad onside now as well; he was providing him with certain alcoholic beverages that were making him a very good profit, which made Phillip indispensable to him.

She was going nowhere, his Christine, she was *his*, and he would make sure that everybody knew that eventually. She was the only one he wanted and he had his pick of strange. But he had no feelings for anyone else. Unlike Keith, now he only had eyes for his Christine. He mustn't hurt her, or chance driving her away. She was his all.

Christine was, in actual fact, like an illness with him; without her in his life he didn't know how he would cope. She was like a cancer, eating away at him, and he knew deep inside himself that it wasn't natural to feel so strongly, and so intensely, for another person. It wasn't natural to want someone so desperately, but he would happily kill to keep her beside him. His feelings for Christine were so overpowering they even frightened him at times. The thought of being without her was enough to make him feel suicidal, not that he let those emotions show. He knew only that she was his, would always be his, and he would ensure that she stayed by his side – no matter what.

Chapter Sixteen

Christine Booth was in her element. She was loving the attention she was getting from all and sundry. She was the envy of her friends, and she had been catapulted overnight into the role of most popular girl in the school. Of all the girls they would have imagined having had the guts to move into her boyfriend's house at fifteen, Christine knew she would have been classed as the rank outsider. Now it was common knowledge that she was actually *living* with Phillip Murphy, in his parents' house. And he was not just any young lad either, that would have been shocking enough in itself. But she was living with someone whose family was synonymous with villainy. Christine was suddenly being treated like a movie star. People wanted to be friends with her now, wanted to be *seen* to be friends with her.

Christine didn't give a toss who knew about it, it was like she had been let out of prison. She loved the Murphy family, even Breda, who was a hardcase. Loved the way they rallied round to help each other out. Loved the sheer enjoyment of life that his family seemed to embrace on a daily basis. Loved that Phillip was so protective of her, and agreeable to what she wanted.

But most of all she loved the way he crept into her room of a night, and made her feel like a real woman. The first time he had come into her bed was because she was crying and he had come in to comfort her. He told her he would always be there for her, and that he loved her. Now he came in because she wanted him to. Needed him to. It was as though she had been let in on this great big secret, and now she could cope with anything the world threw at her. She was without fear, she lived for Phillip, and his touch, his words of love, and the feelings she was now unable to do without. She knew instinctively that he wasn't using her in any way, that he felt the same as she did.

His taking her had given her a new persona: she was suddenly sure of herself, suddenly she was different. She knew what she wanted in life, and what she wanted was *him*. His name gave her cachet, made people treat her with respect. He wanted her and wanted to *marry* her, and marry him she would, as soon as possible. She was determined to shrug off the Booth name, and become a Murphy. She wanted to be a part of that family so badly, to be free of her mother's constant criticism and constant vigilance. She would finally be her own woman.

Woman being the operative word. Christine felt taller, slimmer, prettier now than she had ever felt before. She wore make-up, and the clothes that she liked, not what her mother thought was appropriate. She looked forward to going home, *to his home*, for the first time in her life. Having had this taste of freedom she knew she would never go back to being a nobody again. She was Phillip Murphy's intended, and becoming his wife was now the height of her ambition. If her mother didn't like it, then she knew exactly what she could do.

She hugged herself mentally, thrilled with the turn her life had taken when she had met up with Phillip Murphy outside the off-licence on that dark winter's night. It was fate, they both knew that then, and they had both accepted it. Now it seemed, her mother would have to accept it as well.

Chapter Seventeen

'You think she'll be all right then, do you, living with that scum?'

Teddy Booth looked up as his wife spoke and felt a deep sorrow for her. It was the same sorrow he felt inside himself. His daughter had been like a lamb to the slaughter, and it was because of this woman before him. She had forced them into this situation, and now they would pay the price for it, one way or another. This alliance his daughter had made would cost them all, and cost them dearly. He knew more about their daughter's future in-laws than Eileen did; he had watched Phillip Murphy grow up, as he had many of the boys on that estate. Ted had been there for over twenty years. Unlike Eileen with her part-time teaching job and her belief that she was too good for the estate that they earned their living from. Unlike her, *he* knew everyone's pedigree on that estate, it was how he had survived so long, if only the silly bitch had bothered to see that. Between them they could have really got on and made a real difference to their lives; all it would have taken was some effort on their part. Well, her part, anyway.

How the mighty had fallen, though! Ever since she had arrived home two weeks previously, scratch marks on her neck, and her head drooping with defeat, Ted had listened to Eileen's complaints, had comforted her as best he could, but he had known that she was beaten. Well and truly beaten. Her daughter's behaviour was now common knowledge and there was nothing she could do about that. In fact, she wasn't even asking him his opinion, she was simply talking out loud. She had never really expected an answer from him. Not for a long time anyway.

Ted wanted to help his daughter; he missed her and, even though she popped into the shop occasionally when she knew her mother wouldn't be there, he found the house empty without her. He loved his girl, his only child, and he wanted to see her happy. He understood why she was doing what she was doing, even though it broke his heart. So despite his true feelings he said brightly, 'He seems to be doing well for himself though, Eileen, he's already helped me enormously with the shop.'

His wife narrowed her eyes, suddenly interested in what he had to say. 'In what way? How could *he* have helped *you*?' It was an accusation.

Teddy took a deep breath before answering. 'Since the balloon went up, people who've been avoiding paying me have suddenly found the money, and he has put me on to a supplier for the off-licence that has doubled the profits. I don't have any aggro from the teenagers any more either, it's Mr Booth this, and Mr Booth that. They even put their rubbish in the bin outside. I don't have to sweep the pavement half as much as usual.' He smiled. 'Even the Martins are all sweetness and light. Now, I am not saying that we should forget what's happened, but in light of what *has* happened, we should think twice about pushing Christine further away.'

Eileen Booth was staring at her husband as if she had never seen him before. His words seemed to have penetrated her brain for once.

He carried on talking, determined to make her see the positives instead of the negatives. She needed to find a reason to embrace her daughter's new-found family and he was willing to give her one if it meant he could see his little girl again. 'For the first time in twenty years, we don't have to ask anyone to pay up, Eileen. I pulled in three grand this week alone in outstanding payments. It's like people can't be seen to owe us money any more. The off-licence pulled in another two grand profit, and people who normally go to the Tesco down the road are suddenly availing themselves of our little establishment. So all I am saying is that Phillip Murphy, love him or loathe him, is going places and we are feeling the benefit. If this carries on, we'll be out of the woods in no time.'

'Five thousand pounds in one week?'

Teddy smiled wryly at the incredulity in his wife's voice. He nodded, hating the avaricious glint in her eye as she worked out their potential earnings. 'He has a lot of contacts, Eileen, and they are people I wouldn't normally dream of being able to deal with.'

That much was true anyway, the money was nothing to him really. Ted wasn't happy that it took a thug like Murphy to get him all paid up, but that was how it worked in this world. Also the suppliers he had always wanted to deal with were now phoning *him* with lucrative deals, were now courting *him* as a potential customer, and he would be a liar if he didn't admit that it felt good to be so in demand.

'What, you think this is all because of Phillip Murphy?' Veronica demanded.

He sighed. 'Think about it, Eileen – in twenty years they ain't returned a call. Now I am being given produce on a sale or return basis. Fresh, frozen *and* processed foods. Phillip said he would put the word out and he has. He works for Bantry, and that means he has access to all the suppliers in the vicinity. Bantry controls everything that goes on round here, as we both know. So all I am saying is, it could be worse, Eileen. At least Phillip Murphy has the means to give our Christine a good life.'

'But she's only fifteen, Teddy. A baby.'

He nodded once more. 'A baby who has grown up and away from us. All we can do now is try and bring her back into the fold. If we aren't careful she'll stay away for good and I for one couldn't live with that. I could cheerfully strangle her for what she's done but, at the same time, I love her and I miss her, and I know that you feel the same. She's sixteen on Friday, we can make our peace with her then, if you will just calm yourself down.'

But Ted had already won Eileen over, he knew that; she was a slave to money and everything it could bring her. She had already forgotten that she was Mrs Respectable School Teacher, had conveniently forgotten her big fear about how her so-called friends would perceive her daughter's liaison with a budding criminal. She was now picturing the upside of being a part of the Murphys' world. He knew that the Murphy name would now be seen as an asset as far as she was concerned. Money-wise anyway. If it could give her everything she had dreamed of then so be it – even if that meant her daughter would be sacrificed to achieve it.

He knew Eileen better than she knew herself. She was looking for an out, an excuse to let her daughter have what she wanted without losing face. Now she had it, and he had given it to her, just to keep the peace. Just so his child could once more be a part of his life. He missed her so much – she alone had made his life bearable. Christine had made his marriage worthwhile, she gave him a reason to get up in the mornings and a reason to work late into the night. He would do anything to get his daughter back into his life, even if that meant he had to talk his wife into accepting the Murphys and all they stood for. He only hoped he didn't live to regret it.

Chapter Eighteen

Veronica loved it when the house was full of people, and tonight it was packed to the rafters. She had been baking for two days, and she stood happily watching all the food she had prepared being wolfed down by her sons and their friends. The music was loud and the chatter was louder, everyone was there, even that fucker Bantry, which showed just how much her son was esteemed. And why wouldn't he be? He was a man in the making. But for all that, he respected his mother and wasn't afraid to show it.

Young Christine looked gorgeous, and Veronica smiled sadly as she watched the girl being the belle of the ball. She wanted to tell her that she should enjoy it while she could. It wouldn't last. Life wasn't that good to females – once they produced children that was enough for the likes of her Phillip. She felt such a sorrow at the girl's inevitable demise. After all, Veronica had been Christine's age when she had married and, like this child, she had been happy about it. But a small part of her knew that Christine Booth would one day regret her alliance with her son, would live to rue the day she had snatched the chance of freedom, the chance to leave her mother's claustrophobic love behind her. But Veronica wouldn't say any of that, of course; this wasn't the time or the place. It was the girl's birthday party, and that was why they were all there in the first place.

She observed her son Phillip as he looked at his young lady, saw the desire that almost burned his eyes out, saw the way she affected him. It was unnatural, his need to be with her – it would result in his needing to control her. For the first time she admitted to herself that it wasn't healthy. Her son had always been far too determined for his own good, had always got what he wanted no matter what the price. Veronica had a feeling he would never change. She liked this little girl of his, but she was frightened for her because she sensed Christine wasn't strong enough to look after herself, especially now Phillip had set his cap at her. He was as controlling as Eileen, only the girl couldn't see any of that yet. All Christine saw was Phillip's handsome face and the novelty of her first sexual encounter. She was mixing up love and lust, and she wasn't the first girl to do that. She was enjoying her party and the freedom that being with Phillip now afforded her, but she didn't understand that this freedom was not real, that she only had it because he chose to give it to her, because it brought her closer to him and what he wanted. It would come at a price, a price she would eventually have to pay.

The doorbell went and Eileen Booth was welcomed into the house, followed by her husband. As she walked towards her daughter, all smiles and heavy perfume, an expensive present in her well-manicured hands, Veronica knew that the young girl's fate was well and truly sealed. Now that Eileen had accepted the situation, warning bells were sounding inside Veronica's head. She felt guilty though for the thoughts she was having about her son and his impact on this young girl's life. She watched the proceedings with a sick feeling inside her gut, but she knew it was far too late to do anything about it.

As her son slipped the diamond ring on Christine's finger and beamed happily at the people gathered around, she turned away abruptly and went out into the garden. Her lovely home was suddenly alien to her, she saw it for the pretence it really was, and she saw the truth of her own situation in stunning clarity. As she smoked a cigarette she wondered at what had come over her. Questioned her thoughts and the disloyalty of them.

'You all right, Mum?' Phillip's voice was quiet. She hadn't noticed him follow her out.

She forced a smile on to her face. ''Course I am, I'm just hot, son, hot and tired.' She could hear the forced joviality in her voice, and it saddened her even further.

'I'll look after her, Mum, don't worry about it. I know we're young, but this feels right. I'll never hurt her. I couldn't.'

Veronica smiled gently. 'Oh, Phillip, you're a good lad, but as my mother used to say, don't make promises you can't keep.'

Chapter Nineteen

'How can I be pregnant? It can't be right.' Christine's voice was soft and the fear was already making her light-headed.

Phillip laughed gently beside her in the bed. 'It happens, Chris, especially when you start having sex.'

'But we used protection, Phil, you said we were safe.'

Phillip sighed. Secretly he was over the moon at her news. He would never tell her that he had often slipped the condom off during their more passionate encounters. That he had deliberately set out to get her pregnant. He knew that she was not in the right frame of mind to understand his reasoning. So instead he said soothingly, 'It happens, love, and if you think about it, I ain't running away from the news, am I? I ain't leaving you to your own devices like my poor sister Breda was left. I am going to stick by you, Christine. I want to marry you and give my child a name. It'll just be sooner than we anticipated, that's all.'

Christine didn't know how to answer him, she was still terrified out of her wits. If he left her now she would be destroyed. But he was reassuring her of his devotion, so why wasn't she happy?

Phillip could feel her indecision, had expected it. He knew she would be disturbed by a pregnancy; although this was the eighties, she was still a girl who wanted to do things properly. But he wanted her for himself and this would guarantee that happened sooner rather than later. Her mother would have the marriage arranged in nanoseconds, she would not want her baby having an illegitimate child. By marrying Christine he would become a hero overnight as far as that old bitch was concerned. Inside himself he knew that he had forced this decision on her, but he overlooked that by telling himself this would have happened at some point anyway. His feelings for Christine overrode everything else in his life. He had taken her virginity and he had sworn to keep her beside him no matter what. No other female could make a dent in his heart, he didn't want or need anyone other than her. She was his all.

He hugged her to him again, almost suffocating her with the strength of his arms, his embrace. He understood her fears. She was only sixteen; a baby was a serious event at any age, let alone for someone so young. 'Look, Chris, I know you wanted to go to college, or university, whatever. But you are having a lovely little baby. Our baby. Like the Bible says, when I was a child I thought like a child, when I became a man I put away childish things. I have to look after you and the baby now, don't I? It's not like we can do anything about it, is it? We're Catholics, we have to make this into something good. I'll marry you, and we'll be happy and so will our baby. We'll have a great life, the three of us, you wait and see. We'll buy a little house and we'll show the world that we are meant to be together. That we can give our kid a good life.'

She nodded then, unable to speak with the emotion inside herself. The enormity of what had happened to her was suddenly crushing down on her. The knowledge that her life as she knew it was finished overwhelmed her. All her so-called independence had just been wiped out as if it had never happened. She was too young to have a baby, too young and too frightened. She wanted to have a life first, have some real freedom. She had wanted them to have a few years together, go abroad, experience the world. Now she was just another girl who had got caught out, another teenage mum dependent on everyone around her again. It was so unfair. There was no abortion for her, and she wouldn't, couldn't do something like that even if it was possible. She would never be able to live with herself; after all, this child had a right to life. It was what she had been brought up to believe, and believe it she did. Phillip's attendance at Mass was all her mother had ever found in his favour. He was a good Catholic, everyone in his family was, even Breda in her own way.

But Christine was not happy about this child at all. She had wanted to marry Phillip more than anything in the world until now, until this second. Now she felt trapped.

Maybe the hormones were affecting her already. After all, she had given up everything and everyone in her life for just this moment, and now it was here she was plagued with doubt. Her terror was so real it was almost physical. She actually felt sick with apprehension, but that could be the result of her pregnancy. Women felt sick in the early stages, that was how they knew they had a child inside them. It was the morning sickness that had alerted her to her predicament in the first place.

Christine felt Phillip squeeze her once more until she was almost melded into his body. He always held her to him with a strength that until now had made her feel safe and secure, but suddenly his embrace felt claustrophobic; it reminded her that she was now his, wholly and for ever. The intensity of his feelings for her felt wrong somehow, felt unnatural. She had a deep sense of foreboding that his love for her would overpower everything she wanted. And guarantee she would never again be her own person.

As if he was aware of her sudden reluctance, Phillip tightened his hold on her and she felt again the sheer power of his physical strength. His arms felt like a steel band. He and this baby had ensured that any hopes or dreams its mother might have been harbouring were long gone from her. A child growing inside you soon made you wake up to just how one-sided childbirth really was. Phillip's life wouldn't change, not one iota. Whereas her life on the other hand, would change out of all recognition.

She would be a mother before she was even legally eligible to vote. She would be tied to a child before she had left her own childhood behind. She almost hated Phillip then, for his maleness, for doing this to her even though she had been a more than willing participant. She hated her disloyalty towards him, but a baby, she knew, would ensure that she would never be able to walk away from him. Phillip Murphy would never allow that to happen.

But why was she thinking these things? Why would she even consider leaving him? What was wrong with her? She was crying, and she had not even realised it.

Phillip laughed gently in the darkness. The smell of him permeated the small room; the aroma of their bodies, of their joint sexual encounters was so strong Christine felt as if she would never get the stench from out of her nostrils. He seemed almost sinister to her now, and she knew at that moment that he had *wanted* this to happen, had *made* it happen. She had been too naïve to see what he was doing.

Yet, this baby had been created with love. *Their* love, which was real, and surely that had to mean something? As Phillip's lips found hers in the darkness and his tongue probed her mouth with its usual determination, she felt herself responding to him as she always had since the first time they had slept together. Christine forced away the dreadful thoughts that were crowding her mind, forced away the fear that she was already into something she couldn't control. She reminded herself that he alone had made her life exciting, and he alone had made her feel alive for the first time ever. Once he was inside her, deep inside her, she didn't have any doubts about him, all she had was the knowledge that she couldn't live without him, without this – his touch, his tongue, his physical presence. She loved him, and he loved her, that was what mattered at the end of the day. It was the pregnancy that was making her doubt him, doubt herself. She knew she had to get her head around what the child would mean to them both. She might feel scared at having a baby, but she had to grow up and, as he said, put away her childish thoughts. She mentally shrugged; she was being silly. They were going to get married anyway, and it was natural for a girl to feel overwhelmed about something so huge, so life changing at such a young age.

As she succumbed to his embraces, Christine convinced herself that her fears were just the result of her hormones. If she was being honest with herself, she wasn't looking forward to her mother's reaction once she heard the happy news either.

She would go ballistic.

Chapter Twenty

'I told you this would happen, didn't I, you stupid little mare!'

Christine looked into her mother's eyes and saw the disappointment there, as well as the pleasure her mother got from being proved right. That was how it had always been, ever since she could remember.

'Sixteen and already in the club. Do you realise just how bloody stupid you are? Do you understand what this really means to you? You personally? Your life's over before it's even begun – his ain't. Men never have to take any responsibility, not really. You're the one who'll be stuck at home with it. Not him, his life won't bloody well change. If you had any sense you'd get rid of it.' She put her hand to her mouth.

Eileen could cry with the shock, with the unfairness of it all. She had given this ungrateful bastard everything a girl could want, and for what? For her to be taken down by the first good-looking bloke who had given her more than a second glance. Eileen knew she had said something terrible, she was being unfair to her daughter, but she didn't care. This girl should have had it all. Now she had a belly full of arms and legs and the honour of becoming a Murphy. She wiped her hand across her face, as if the action could erase the knowledge of her daughter's spectacular fuck-up. And fuck-up it was, only this silly cow wouldn't realise that until it was too late.

Christine looked at her mother and marvelled at the woman's hypocrisy and her complete lack of loyalty, not just to her, but towards her future son-in-law. Phillip had made sure that her dad's shop was finally paying off. Her mother would be enjoying the benefits of his interference, of his putting money in their pockets. She had previously acted like she was, if not exactly pleased about their relationship, willing to accept it. Her duplicity was too much for Christine to bear. The fact that her words were a bit too close for comfort didn't help either.

'We're getting married, Mum, but I need your consent to do that. We love each other and we're going to make something of ourselves, whatever *you* might think to the contrary. Now, I have come round here to ask you to sign the papers. If you don't sign them, then my Phillip will be forced to come round here himself and, believe me, Mum, he won't be as amenable as I am, do you get my drift?'

Christine could see the fear that her words had caused, could feel her mother's discomfort and, despite herself, she found herself actually enjoying it. The two-faced old bitch was finally getting her comeuppance.

'Are you threatening me, Christine, your own mother?' Eileen's voice was low, almost inaudible, as she realised that her daughter now held all the cards, was the stronger of the two, and all through her liaison with Phillip Murphy.

'I'm not threatening you, Mum, I'm just stating a fact.'

'Well.' Eileen shrugged, resigned to her daughter's fate. 'You know what they say don't you, Christine? Be careful what you ask for, you just might get it.'

Christine grinned then, and for the first time she felt superior to this woman. Placing the papers that would allow her to get married on the kitchen table, she said happily, 'I've got exactly what I asked for, Mum – I got away from you, didn't I?'

Eileen sighed. Seeing her husband's signature already there she swallowed back the urge to cry, and said brightly, 'Well, whatever you might think of me, Christine, I only ever wanted what was best for you. One day you will understand that. When that baby you're carrying comes into the world, you'll finally understand why I was like I was. You always want better for your kids, better than you had. It's called being a mother.'

She turned away from her daughter, and busied herself making a pot of tea. Christine watched her quietly, saw the drooping of her shoulders, heard the defeat in her voice, and wished with all her heart that things could have been different. Her mother was an avaricious, demanding and deeply unhappy woman; this, coupled with her snobbery and her unwavering belief that she was better than everyone around her, had guaranteed that she would always be incapable of ever experiencing any real happiness. Consequently, those within her orbit were also denied the chance of any real happiness as well. If Christine had any doubts left about marrying into the Murphys, this woman had just removed them. She would rather die than become like her mother. Her discontentment with her lot, and with her family, had eventually bled into every aspect of all their lives until none of them knew how to be happy. The Murphys had welcomed her with open arms and she saw that, no matter what, they were there for one another. They loved each other, and it showed.

Thinking of the life inside her, she put her hand on her still-flat belly, and for the first time since she had found out she was pregnant, she actually welcomed the child. She was young and healthy, she had a man who loved her, and a new family who had taken her into their lives and made her feel welcome and wanted.

Just ten minutes in the house she had grown up in had made her realise how lucky she was.

Chapter Twenty-One

The pub was packed, and the heat was overwhelming. It was noisy and it was scruffy, and Christine loved everything about it. The pub was their local, this was Phillip's domain now. People came here to pay him money owed, or to ask favours from him, and it was where he showed the world he lived in how much his reputation had grown and how his name was becoming synonymous with Billy Bantry's and Keith Kenton's. In this world he moved in, reputation was everything, as was the female beside you.

As Christine saw Keith and Phillip talking together across the other side of the room, she felt a surge of pride. People were deferential to them, to her as well. It was a whole new world. Joanie was smiling at her happily – Christine could tell she'd had a few drinks; she made a point of having them frequently. But Christine couldn't begrudge her that; if she wasn't pregnant, she'd be doing the same. Unlike her friend though, she wouldn't have drunk so much so quickly – Phillip would have made sure of that. He wasn't a drinker, not really. He didn't like the feeling of being out of control, he had told her that on more than one occasion. He believed that alcohol, like drugs, was for mugs. He said that when people were drunk they opened themselves up for stupidity. He only drank with her, and that was because he trusted her enough to let himself go. He didn't like to see a woman in drink, and his arguments with his sister Breda over her drinking were frequent and passionate. Breda was the antithesis of Phillip;

72

she drank, drugged and fucked with a passion that was almost unbearable to witness. She was like a man in that respect, she did what she wanted without any thought for the consequences. She didn't even attempt to try and get herself a steady bloke, she went out, she got drunk, and she got laid. End of story. Christine knew that it bothered Phillip. Even though it was what Breda wanted, was what she enjoyed. She made no secret of her lifestyle, and even though it wasn't unusual in this day and age for a girl to live her own life in her own way, Christine knew that Phillip saw his sister's antics as a reflection on him personally. Breda was an exemplary mother to her son, and she adored him, but her attitude was that when she went out, she went *all* out, and there was nothing anyone could do about it.

Tonight Breda was hanging all over a heavily built Greek-looking man, with cheap shoes and thick curly hair. Christine was aware that her Phillip was keeping an eye on his sister, only he was watching her antics surreptitiously. Breda was pretty, but she was already hard faced, her delicate features obscured by her heavy make-up and her constant frown. She talked too much and too loudly. Her conversation was peppered with profanities and innuendo. As Phillip had screamed at her one night, she was one step away from charging for it. And Christine understood his fears. Breda was self-destructive once she had a few Bacardis, she seemed to almost enjoy the reaction she got from her brothers and the people around her. The worse she behaved, the happier she seemed to be. It was like a game she played, as if she was just seeing how far she could push them. But tonight Christine sensed a new undercurrent to Breda's behaviour, this man she was all over was a stranger, he was not her usual type of conquest. Breda had a few blokes on the go, and she made a point of seeing them on the quiet. She didn't usually pull total strangers in full view of her brothers and their assorted friends and acquaintances. That was a definite no-no in anyone's books.

The man in question was with two other Greeks, and all three were happily hitting on Breda. Breda, for her part, was loving the attention she was getting from them. Like a lot of the Greek men in East London, they were only in England to get out of their national service. They came over and worked as waiters, or attended college, until such time as they could go back home. Their families paid for them to come over, and that money guaranteed that they could swerve the army, and at the same time learn a trade. These men were obviously so new to the area they didn't realise the girl they were all so enamoured of was far more dangerous than anything the Greek army might have thrown at them. All they saw was an available English girl and, in their limited experience, most of the English girls they had met were not only available, but happy to oblige in any way they could. For Greek men from small villages, this was heady stuff indeed.

Christine, young though she was, knew all of this instinctively and she could feel the animosity coming off Phillip in waves. She saw the nervousness of the people around him. How they were waiting to see his reaction to his sister's outrageous behaviour. She looked around for Declan and James, but they were nowhere to be seen. Declan was one of the only people capable of talking Phillip round, one of the only people Phillip would listen to. She moved closer to Phillip, pushing her way through the throng of people until she was by his side. He looked at her and smiled happily. She knew that whatever people might say about him and his temper, he was not a lecher, she knew deep inside that she was all he wanted or needed. He was so staid in that respect. His sister's antics were all the more unsettling to him because he had no understanding of why she could be like she was. Christine knew that Phillip would never betray her, as well as she knew he would kill her before he would let another man into her bed.

Breda was so drunk she was unaware that her dress was

slipping off her shoulders and that, consequently, she was showing a lot of breast, and her loud raucous laughter was even drowning out the jukebox. The three men seemed mesmerised by her abundance of naked flesh, and the promise in her eyes for all of them.

Perry Croft, the landlord – a short stocky man with a bald head – had the unenviable task of having to serve the men he knew were aggravating the life out of his most important customer. As Breda demanded another drink, he looked over at Phillip, and Christine saw him nod almost imperceptibly in response, his handsome face dark with barely suppressed anger, but unless you knew him as well as she did, the true extent of his annoyance would not be evident at all. The landlord served the drinks without a word, and Christine sipped at her orange juice, worried for Breda and what she was doing.

'How you doing, Chris?'

She smiled at Phillip, at the genuine concern in his voice. 'Fine, Phil. You OK?'

He shrugged nonchalantly. Then, taking her elbow, he steered her through the throng of people and behind the bar itself. She walked through to the back room with him happily, glad of the quiet once the door was shut behind them. It was a heavy oak door, specially designed to keep the noise of the pub out, and any noise made inside the room inaudible to the pub's clientele. It was a very expensive but very necessary fixture. It also had some serious brass work: two mortice locks, two heavy-duty bolts and a steel bar that slipped easily into the wall cavity. It would take a battering ram to open it should the need ever arise – for example, if the police came sniffing around or a rival of some description took it into their heads to come visiting mob-handed. Neither of these scenarios was unheard of in Phillip's world, and he was ready for them.

'Are you sure you're all right, Phillip?'

He sat her down on the black leather sofa and, placing himself gently beside her, he said honestly, 'No, no, Christine, I'm not all right. Breda's gone too far this time.'

His voice was flat, there was no emotion in it whatsoever. Christine searched his face for some kind of clue, for something to tell her what he was feeling inside. He had placed his arm around her shoulders and, though the gesture was a loving one, she knew that as far as he was concerned, she didn't exist for him at this particular moment in time. She turned into him, forcing him to look into her eyes. 'She doesn't mean it, Phil, you know that as well as I do. She just likes to have a laugh, likes to get out and be a young girl again. Please don't fight with her, not tonight. I'm having such a lovely time.'

He looked at her, and she knew it was no good, he would only humour her. His eyes were hard and his handsome face was expressionless. She knew the signs now, knew his moods. When he was like this he scared her, even though she knew without a shadow of a doubt that he would never hurt her.

'I can't swallow this, Chris, she's undermining my credibility by the day. If I can't fucking control my little sister, how can I be expected to control the people who work for me? It's not about her, mate, it's about how her actions affect the people around her. She's out there, out of her fucking nut, with three fucking chancers. This ain't about her any more, it's about me.'

Christine knew he really believed that. In a strange way, she even understood where he was coming from. She understood that his world was a dangerous and unpredictable one. That he was only as good as his reputation. He was young and on his way up, and, for the moment, he had the backing of some serious names. She had learned an awful lot, things she had never thought she would have to know about. But she was with him now, for better or for worse. He would be the father of her child, her children, and she had accepted his way of life because she had no other choice. She guessed that he shielded her from a lot of it but seeing him like this was something she wasn't used to. This was the Phillip Murphy people talked about, not the Phillip Murphy who she was going to marry in one week's time, who treated her like a queen, and smothered her with his love.

'Please, Phil, don't start. Leave her alone, she doesn't mean any harm.'

Before he could answer her, the door opened and Perry Croft popped his head inside. 'Breda just got in a cab, Phil, I thought she needed to get off home.'

Phillip smiled. 'Thanks, mate. We'll be out in a minute.'

Perry was gone without another word. Christine felt her body relaxing, felt the tension leaving her and the lightness of the relief as it washed over her.

Phillip hugged her to him, kissing the top of her head. 'See? You were worried over nothing.'

'I'm sorry, Phil, I overreacted. I just didn't want you to start a row with Breda, she thinks the world of you. And those blokes she was with, they didn't know she was your sister, they didn't know the score. They couldn't believe their luck that she was giving them the time of day!'

Phillip laughed with her then, and she instinctively rubbed her hand across her belly; she was just starting to round out a bit, as Phil's mother so succinctly put it. Her normally flat belly was beginning to grow outwards, and she caressed it happily. She was inordinately pleased that Phillip had listened to her, had taken her feelings into consideration. She knew that Breda's performance had made him angry, angry and ashamed. Her behaviour was anathema to him. But the fact he had put her feelings first really meant a lot to her.

Christine was becoming more comfortable with her situation by the day, she was growing up fast, and that was not a bad thing considering she would be a married woman in one week's time, and a mother in six months' time. Instead of fearing the change a baby would bring to her, she now welcomed the child. It was already the love of her life after Phillip; now she had accepted its existence she felt a deep and abiding connection to it. She hoped it was a boy, because Phillip wanted a son so badly. He didn't actually say that, but she just knew that was the case.

As she settled once more into his arms, she wondered at how she could ever have questioned her feelings for him. She was lucky, a very lucky young woman. Who would soon be a bride and a mother, and who was not yet seventeen. But as Phillip had said to her on more than one occasion, they were young all right, but they were still old enough to have kids and they would enjoy them. Give them a good life, and love them with a vengeance.

Chapter Twenty-Two

Breda walked into the kitchen to her father shouting merrily, 'The dead arose and appeared to many.'

They all laughed at his words, especially Christine.

'Jesus, Breda, you look like you've just been exhumed,' quipped Declan.

Breda didn't say a word, but she looked at Declan and her expression told him everything he needed to know. She poured herself a cup of tea and, sipping the hot liquid noisily, she sat down heavily at the kitchen table. Her son was sitting on his grandmother's lap, and he grinned saucily at his mummy as she put out her hand and caressed his hair.

Christine looked around her. She had never experienced anything like this in her life. Breakfast in her house had always been a solemn affair – no chat, no camaraderie, no radio blaring in the background. She loved the mornings now, looked forward to them.

'How's the morning sickness, Chris? Shall I get you a couple of cream crackers?' Veronica's voice was filled with concern for her. She had been great about the baby, about the wedding, about everything in fact.

'I'm fine. Really, I feel great.'

Veronica lifted her grandson from her lap and placed him on her chair. Going to the cooker, she put the frying pan on to the hob, saying cheerily, 'How about a bit of sausage and egg? Could you manage that?'

Christine shook her head, pleased at the attention she got from this kind and caring woman. 'Honestly, I couldn't eat a thing yet. I still feel a bit queasy. I'll have some toast later.'

Veronica frowned, her eyes almost disappearing inside the sockets as she surveyed the young girl with mock severity. 'Mind that you do, that child you're carrying needs fuel. Food is fuel for humans. It's what keeps us going. I reckon you've a boy there. Morning, noon and night sickness usually means a son. Girls are easier to carry. No trouble at all really.'

Breda laughed then, a scornful, hateful laugh. Christine saw that whatever ailed Breda, it was much more than a hangover. 'Is that so? Your boys have never caused you any trouble of course, have they, Mother?'

Christine looked at her soon-to-be-sister-in-law's bloated face, and saw the way she looked around the table at her brothers. She watched as Phillip stood up abruptly and walked out of the room, his back ramrod straight and his hands clenched into fists. Sometimes she hated Breda for the way she casually lashed out at her family, her cryptic sarcasm delivered with such venom it made everyone around her as unhappy as she was. Christine picked up her mug of tea and sipped it anxiously; the atmosphere was heavy with dread now. Breda's son was looking at his mother intently, even he was aware that something was suddenly amiss.

It was Declan who spoke first, playing the peacekeeper. He rounded on Breda, not allowing for her son's presence as they usually did. Pushing his face almost into his sister's, he spat at her, 'You're a bitter pill, Breda. You are a vicious, bitter bitch of a woman, and one of these days you'll go too fucking far.'

Veronica walked quickly to where her son sat and, slapping him heavily across his shoulders, she said in a low voice, 'That's enough, Declan. I won't have another word said.'

Declan stood up then and, looking down at his mother, who at just five feet tall was over a foot shorter than him, he answered her, with a loud and angry sneer, 'That's right, Mum, you keep defending her. But she needs to know that all any of us are guilty of is looking out for her. Whore that she is.'

Christine was shocked at the turn the morning had suddenly taken, but this kind of confrontation was par for the course in this house. The rows were as easily forgotten as they were easily started. These people said what was on their minds and, as much as it could be upsetting, like it was now, it was also their way of getting things off their chests and out into the open. After all the years in her own home, where nothing was ever really resolved, she loved that the Murphys felt comfortable enough to say what they needed to without fear or favour. They cleared the air and then forgot about it.

Spandau Ballet were playing on the radio, and Jamsie was eating his breakfast as if nothing was going on around him. Breda was staring at her son, Declan's vitriol for once subduing her usual argumentative personality, and Veronica was shaking her head sadly in despair at her children's need to fight each other.

Declan walked from the kitchen, and Christine knew he would be going to Phillip, would make sure that his brother was OK. Phillip often seemed to take the brunt of Breda's disaffection with her life, and Christine admired him for the way he accepted it from her. Breda, though, was rarely cross with her. In fact, Breda was very kind to her personally. But that could be because she wasn't a blood relative.

Christine waited a few minutes and then, picking up her tea, she excused herself and left the kitchen. She hoped the house Phillip was buying for them went through soon. She decided they needed to put some space between him and his sister.

As she went up the stairs to the bedroom she shared with Phillip, she heard the low murmur of Phillip and Declan's voices coming from the small front room.

Chapter Twenty-Three

'He's a bruiser all right, Chris. Just like his brother.'

Christine grinned with pride at the praise. Breda was genuinely thrilled with her nephews. Phillip Murphy the third was a handsome child, who delighted everyone around him. Even her own mother had succumbed to his charms; the woman who had taken her daughter's pregnancy and marriage as a personal insult to herself was mad about her grandsons, especially the first-born. His thick, dark hair and his sparkling blue eyes which were so like his father's hadn't put her mother off him one iota. In fact, everyone worshipped the ground he walked on.

And walk he did; at ten months he had taken his first tentative steps and by thirteen months he was running around the house like Roger Bannister on speed. He was talking by eighteen months, not just words, but whole sentences. Now at nearly three he could chat with the best of them. Even the arrival of his little brother a year earlier had not fazed him; instead of the jealousy predicted by everyone around her, Philly, as they referred to him, had taken one look at his new-born brother, his handsome face concerned and rapt with interest, and declared loudly and confidently, 'I like him, Mummy, can we keep him?'

The newly born Timothy Murphy had taken to his older brother with the same zeal. Christine was thrilled at their closeness, it made her life much easier because they were so happy in each other's company. Each kept the other amused and they thrived on the closeness that being together brought to them. They looked alike, had the same mannerisms, and they were both possessed of an easy-going nature, that is unless they were crossed about something: a toy another child wanted, or being denied a favourite sweet. Even then, they tended to gang up together, the one-year-old Timmy following his brother around like a faithful puppy. Young Phillip would charge around the house, his loud voice cutting through all the adults' conversation. He was a natural leader; even Breda's child Porrick didn't have the strength to overpower him, or his dominant personality. Philly, as they called him, had the knack of making older children bend to his will. Christine was thrilled to bits with her two handsome sons, and at how easily she had slipped into the role of a mother. All the fears she'd had about being responsible for a small human being had turned out to be groundless in the end. Even though she'd had a bit of a hard time with Timmy, she was a natural nurturer, a born mother, even *her* own mother remarked on it, and coming from her that was high praise indeed.

Veronica had, as always, given her the support she needed, but without butting in too much. From the very beginning she had praised Christine loudly and often for the way she cared for her children. She blossomed with the birth of her sons. All the fears that she had trapped herself with her pregnancy and had lost the chance to make something of her life had disappeared with her first glance at her elder son's angry red face. From the moment she had delivered each of her boys she had been besotted with them.

Phillip was proud of her and of his new family, and she knew that he adored them with a passion. She was aware though that he saw her as the primary carer, but it was a role she was more than happy to fulfil; after all, Phillip made sure they wanted for nothing. She simply had to mention something she desired, and it was provided for her. She knew that her mother envied her the easy life she seemed to have fallen into. Her mother's warnings about Phillip and his family were silenced, she now seemed to think he was the dog's gonads, as Phillip himself would say. It was a real pleasure to prove her mother wrong, and she knew she would be a liar not to admit how *good* it felt to see her mother proved so spectacularly wrong about everything. It was odd just how much her mother had changed towards her husband, she treated him like visiting royalty these days and Phillip, for his part, found her about-face amusing. As he said, money did that to people – either the lack of it or the offer of it. He made sure her parents had the means to live in a way they had only ever dreamed of. The boys had been like the icing on the cake for her parents. Phillip Murphy had become a man to be reckoned with and she was proud of that.

Christine thanked God every day for her idyllic life and her beautiful home. At nineteen years old she had not only two perfect sons and a husband who was as attentive to her now as he had been when they first met, but she also had a lovely detached farmhouse in two acres of land, which they were gradually renovating to ensure they had the home of their dreams. It had been hard to find the money at first, but they had managed it. Now they were like any other young couple, saving up every spare penny, and then when they had enough, they would get another room finished, or another bathroom brought up-to-date. It was a labour of love, and indeed she loved this house. Had done since the first time she had seen it. Heavily pregnant with her elder son, she had stood in the entrance hall with her husband's arm around her shoulders and the new-found confidence of a married woman, and known that this was the house they would grow old in together.

It didn't occur to her that her husband's presence had made the owners of the house nervous, that the price they eventually paid had been well under the market value. That she was living in a house that was only theirs because her husband had wanted it so desperately for them. She was still naïve enough to believe everything he told her. She didn't understand property and its worth, didn't see the acreage and the potential that Phillip recognised. All she saw was somewhere they could build a life together and bring up their rapidly expanding family. All she thought of were her and the kids' wants and needs. And if there were any whispers about the intimidation and the paying of gambling debts, she ignored them. That was none of her business. She honestly believed that it was all meant to be, that she and Phillip were meant to live in this house. She was so contented with her wonderful life, so happy and involved with her perfect family and her adoring husband, she wasn't ready when the truth first came knocking at her freshly painted front door.

'Poor old Declan, eh, if it wasn't for him these boys of yours would be fatherless now.' Breda was speaking to her.

Christine refused to get into this conversation. 'Come on, Breda, you don't mean that. Not really.' Christine's voice was soft, determined to ward off any arguments that Breda might decide she wanted to start.

Breda picked up little Timmy and she hugged him to her again for a few moments before she said frankly, 'Are you for real, Chris? Are you telling me you honestly don't know the truth about the court case?'

Christine shook her head; her pretty face was well made-up, her thick blond hair was cut so it framed her face, highlighting her high cheekbones and deep-set eyes, yet still hanging down her back like a curtain. It occurred to Breda suddenly that Christine was seriously beautiful; she was also, it seemed, seriously thick.

'Don't you read the papers, Chris, or watch the news?'

Christine shook her head once again, she didn't want to pursue this conversation any further, in fact she was determined not to hear any more about it. 'I don't care what the papers say. I don't care about any of it. So can we just drop the subject, Breda?'

Breda snorted in annoyance, her eyes searching her sister-in-law's for some kind of reaction. The exasperation in her voice was evident as she said, 'You can't keep burying your head in the sand, mate. One day you are going to have to accept the truth of what's going on around you. My advice to you is to do it now, sooner rather than later. Declan is going away, and Jamsie and Phillip, your husband, are only out and about because Declan took the can for them. He was grassed – they were all grassed up. If it wasn't for Declan the whole fucking lot of us would be in clink. Me included. None of us are exactly choirboys, or girls, as the case may be. Getting nicked is what's known in our world as an occupational hazard. The difference is, we accept that as a truth, and so should you.'

Waves of fear washed over Christine. She refused to listen to anything that might have a detrimental effect on her and her world. As Phil had always promised her, it was her job to look after the boys, and he would look after everything else. She didn't want to hear her sister-in-law's poison. Breda was a troublemaker, everyone knew that, she found aggro in the unlikeliest places. This wasn't the first time she had hinted at Phillip's involvement in serious criminal activity. It was as if Breda was trying to force Christine to admit that her husband was a villain. Well, her Phillip *wasn't* a villain, not a real one, not like Breda was trying to insinuate anyway, and she would not allow her to force that opinion on her, in her own home. Breda didn't really frighten her any more, not like she had in the beginning. Since the birth of her boys, Christine felt she had become tougher, had become hardened to the outside world and all its dangers. Phillip looked out for her, he always looked out for his own, and that included his sister. Though the treacherous bitch was forever trying to undermine him at every opportunity she got. Christine heard the rumours about him, and she had dismissed them for the crap they were. He had explained to her that people were always going to talk about him and his lifestyle. That she was to expect it, while at the same time ignore it. As he had told her from the off, he wasn't a choirboy, and he would never be a nine-to-fiver. But he would never put her or his children in any danger. They were his priority and they always would be. All the talk about him was nothing but exaggerated rubbish, and she would not listen to any of it. Especially not when it came from his own sister.

Christine had already had her mother on the blower that day, asking her what the truth of it all was and, predictably, questioning if her father's usual deliveries were going to be affected by the court case. Declan was the one who ensured her father's shop was filled with cheap merchandise, and consequently that her mother had the wherewithal to live her life in the luxury she had quickly become accustomed to. She had finally put the phone down on Eileen, angry at being pulled into things she had no intention of getting involved in. Now here was Breda trying to do the same thing. Trying to make her be a part of Phillip's other life.

'Stop it, Breda, and I mean it. I won't hear another word about it.'

'Jesus, Christine, you can't not know the score . . . Declan has taken the can for everyone. He's put his hand up to keep the Filth away from everyone else. But whoever grassed him in the first place is on a death wish; they won't last the fucking week, and right and all, the treacherous cunt.'

Hearing the hate in Breda's voice, Christine felt the fear overwhelm her once more and she was sick with apprehension. She despised this feeling that she was walking on quicksand, that her life, and her sons' lives, were hanging in the balance. That at any moment her world would disintegrate before her eyes. It was her nightmare, the truth was more than she was willing to bear. Couldn't Breda see how the knowledge terrified her? Couldn't she understand that her constant insinuations only served to make Christine feel more and more paranoid about the foundations of her marriage, and her relationship with her husband and his family?

Breda looked down at the child she was holding in her arms and, sighing gently, she handed him back to his mother. Christine grabbed him as though she was rescuing him from imminent danger. Almost snatched him from her arms.

Breda spoke softly now, her words full of genuine remorse, sorry for the distress she had caused this young girl. 'I ain't trying to hurt you, Christine, I'm trying to help you, love. You're not a fool, you can't honestly think all this comes from legitimate means?' She waved her arms around, encompassing the house. 'I'm just trying to prepare you. God knows we all have to face up to reality at some point. Even you, love.'

Christine didn't answer her, instead she busied herself with little Timmy. She could feel herself beginning to shake, her whole body trembling so violently it had to be apparent, even to someone as thick-skinned as Breda, the effect her words had caused. She was already taking antidepressants, had been since the birth of Timmy. The second pregnancy had exhausted and overwhelmed her towards the end and now she needed the tablets to keep her on an even keel. They helped take the edge off her fears, convinced her she could cope with her life.

Breda watched her silently, and her heart was heavy for this girl's stupidity, she couldn't understand why Christine deliberately chose to overlook what was, in essence, right under her nose. It wasn't that Breda wanted to hurt her in any way, she just wanted her to understand the reality of her situation. Phillip had walked away from it this time, but it had been at the expense of his brother's freedom. Christine had to accept that her sumptuous lifestyle came with consequences. All Breda really wanted was to make sure her brother's wife wouldn't crack if she came under any undue strain. Phillip might think she was too delicate to know the score, but he didn't see the big picture.

His wife needed to understand that if the worst happened she would be expected to keep her trap shut, and if she didn't know what she was meant to keep quiet about, then that could only make her a liability. Plus, Breda, if she was honest with herself, resented the way Christine was treated by everyone; they acted like she was made of fine china, as if she was too fragile to be told the truth about her life. Phillip was a dangerous fuck, and that was being polite about him and his business tactics. He was not going to swallow his brother's incarceration without a serious amount of violent retribution, and that could well lead to them all being dragged even further into this mess. She felt Christine should understand the pitfalls of being a Murphy as well as enjoying the perks. The trouble with the Christines of the world was they were the ones who eventually suffered more through their chosen ignorance. Because if and when the bomb dropped into the middle of their existence they were the least able to cope.

But now, looking at Christine's terrified countenance she suddenly wondered if she was right; she felt the same need to protect her as the rest of the family did. Breda lowered her voice, trying to make the silly girl understand the seriousness of what was going on around her. 'Look, mate, I'm not trying to hurt you deliberately, I just think you should be aware of what's happening around you. I think you deserve to know the truth.'

Christine shrugged her shoulders, and turned away from her sister-in-law as if the action would negate what she had been trying to tell her. 'You can see yourself out, Breda. I have to get my kids ready. We're going to your mum's for dinner. She'll need us there with Declan being away.'

As Christine walked up the newly decorated stairway, with its expensive wallpaper and freshly painted woodwork, to her baby's bedroom, she could feel her body rebelling against her sister-in-law's words. Her younger son was crowing with contentment in her arms, unaware of what was happening to the people closest to him. The complete devastation his uncle's incarceration had brought on the rest of his family.

Breda was always trying to undermine her, and make her feel like her life was not as rock solid as she believed it was. She felt that Breda took pleasure in making her feel insecure and nervous that her idyllic life could be over with at any moment. She was always trying to force that point home, as if it would make some kind of difference, would make her accept it as a truth. Breda terrified her with her truths. She didn't want the truth, didn't need it.

As she opened her blouse and settled her son on to her swollen breast, she forced herself to calm down and focus on her boys. As the terror of her situation slowly abated she looked around her at all they had achieved, and reminded herself once again just how lucky she was to have her Phillip.

Chapter Twenty-Four

Veronica Murphy was heartbroken about her son's situation, but she was also a realist. She knew that it had had to happen to one of them and, really, it had to be the son with the least to lose. Phillip had a family and he was the main earner, so even though she was upset about Declan's situation, she accepted it. What else could she do? Whoever had grassed had to be a name of sorts, otherwise the Murphys would have found out who it was before it had come to this. She wasn't a fool, she knew that Phillip had probably tracked down the person responsible by now, he would have their name, address and social security number. She knew him better than most. Even though he was seething, he would not make a drama out of a crisis. Unlike the police, he would make sure he had all the facts and the correct culprit before meting out any kind of punishment.

Her husband was, as always, without any real opinion on the subject, and Phillip had assured her that he would see to it that Declan was well taken care of. In effect it was all over, and now they all had to carry on as best they could.

It was Breda who worried her. Breda was very upset about it all and, typically, was being very vocal about it. She could *never* keep her trap closed. It would be the ruination of her eventually. Not that she would listen to anyone's advice. But one day her big trap would bring her trouble of Olympian standards. She never considered how her actions might affect the people around her. It would always be her weakness, and it would surely be the thing that would eventually lead to her own downfall. She didn't have the brains to keep herself and her business private.

As Veronica opened the oven door, and took out the huge forerib of beef she had been roasting for the best part of the day, she heard the front door open. She was basting the meat when her youngest son came into the kitchen. He smiled craftily as he said to her, 'That smells handsome, Mum. How long until dinner?'

Her James, her Jamsie, was big and good-looking, and had the brain capacity of a gnat. She could see that it was better for Declan to go away than this eejit, even though she knew that Declan was worth ten of his little brother. Unlike Declan, Jamsie wasn't cut out for prison, though in reality who was? But the difference was, of course, that Declan could cope with the confinement, would do his time in relative comfort, and with the minimum of fuss. He would get himself settled, and make use of his time there.

None of them thought that much of poor Jamsie. He was a bit of a loose cannon. Unpredictable. He had been like that since a small child. Jamsie wouldn't have been able to do the time quietly and patiently. It wasn't in his make-up; he was a brawler, unable to control his emotions, or contain his temper. Without one of his brothers guiding him, he would make a serious fuck-up within days. She smiled at him sadly. 'Not long now, Jamsie, go and get yourself washed up. I'll make you a cup of tea.'

He nodded absent-mindedly, and she realised he wasn't thinking about his brother's confinement; all he was interested in at this particular moment in time was filling his belly. The knowledge disturbed her more than she would ever admit. She busied herself with the meal, but her heart wasn't in it any more. She made a pot of tea and waited patiently for the rest of her family to arrive. She knew that they would descend on her as usual; it was Friday night, and that was family night in this house. Normally she lived for these occasions, it was what kept her going. Tonight though would be the first real Friday night without her Declan and she was feeling his absence acutely. He was her second son, the sensible son. He was away, really away, not on remand any more, but with a proper prison sentence hanging around his neck. All hope of an acquittal was gone now.

Seven years he had been given, seven long years for the possession of firearms; it should have been much longer she knew that but the knowledge didn't help her any. It broke her heart to think about it. She knew he wouldn't do the whole stretch, only two thirds of it, and with his time on remand it wouldn't even be that long. He would be out in less than three if he didn't play up or, more to the point, have a tear-up with someone in there and add to his sentence. But it still hurt her deeply; she hated that her child was locked away from society, locked away from her. Whatever the courts might think about him, he was still her boy, her flesh and blood. He would always be her baby. That was the cross that women had to bear; no matter what your children did, they were still your children, and you loved them no matter what.

Unlike her husband, who had gone to the pub as usual, who saw his son's prison sentence as an occupational hazard, Veronica felt Declan's loss deeply. But for all that, she also knew she had to carry on as usual; they were a family, and as a family they were stronger. As a family they would cope with Declan's absence, and ensure that he was well looked after. Phillip would see to that. He was the main earner and the one they turned to for guidance. It was what he did, looked out for each of them one way or another and, in all fairness, he did it very well.

Chapter Twenty-Five

'Come on, Chris, get a move on. Me mother will be panicking. You know how she loves the Friday night dinners, how she depends on the boys coming round. Now more than any other time.'

Phillip was trying to act as if nothing had really changed, as if everything was normal. Christine watched him as he changed his shirt, and combed his hair. She knew he wouldn't let his real feelings show, he would see that as a weakness. He was holding it together for all their sakes. Especially hers. He still had the power to make her want him more than anything or anyone in her life. Except for her boys, though even then she wouldn't want that to be put to the test. But she couldn't escape the fact that Breda and her words had depressed her, frightened her. There was a naked truth to them that couldn't be denied.

'I don't really feel like it tonight, Phil. The boys are tired, and your mum must be devastated about Declan. I think we should give it a miss.'

She saw Phillip smile, but the smile had no real warmth to it. She had encountered this smile before, every time that she had gone up against him. Not that she had done so often, there had never really been any need to. But the few times she had that smile had told her that he was humouring her until she backed off and did exactly what he expected of her.

'My mum will need us there tonight, Chris. Think about it – she's just lost one of her sons, she'll want her family around her tonight more than ever. The kids will take her mind off her loss. She adores them.' He stared at her for long moments before saying quietly, 'I need my family around me as well, I've lost me closest friend, as well as me brother.'

He sounded so sincere, and looked so inoffensive and surprised at her demeanour and her refusal to accompany him to his mother's house, that she knew anyone witnessing this exchange would not think he was being at all unreasonable. And he wasn't, not really. He had every right to expect her to go along to his poor mother's with him. So why did she feel she was being coerced into going? Because she knew, deep down inside, that if she didn't do as he wanted, he would not let it rest. She was expected to do as he wanted; refusal wasn't an option. She knew that somehow he would make sure she accompanied him to his mother's house. She could see the confusion on his face, his shock that she might even contemplate defying him, and she knew she was already beaten.

'You're right, Phil. What was I thinking? You've lost Declan.'

She saw him physically relax and, realising that he was under immense pressure because of his brother's prison sentence, she felt ashamed at her actions. Breda had once more made her doubt her husband's loyalty. Breda might think she was a fool, but Christine knew she needed this man and all that he stood for. He had given her his name and his children. What more could she ask of him?

'Me mum is the one I'm worried about, she'll be bereft. It was a gutter, but we can't change it, we just have to swallow our knobs, and get on with it.'

That would be his last word on the matter. Like her, he felt the less said at times the better.

'Come on, Christine love, chop chop. We ain't got all night.'

Phillip was laughing as he hurried her along, but she could still feel a slight atmosphere between them. It always appeared when she questioned their lives, when she felt the uncertainty of

95

their future. She knew he saw it as a reflection on him, on his ability to take care of his family. And she hated herself for doubting him. But it was at times like this, when real life forced its way into their home, that she sensed just how precarious their life and all it entailed really was.

Ten minutes later, as they were settling the boys into the back of the Land Rover, Phillip grabbed her around the waist and pulled her into his arms. She felt his tongue forcing its way into her mouth, and she accepted the kiss willingly. He held her tightly to him, whispering into her hair, 'I feel bad enough as it is, Chris, me mum's fucking destroyed with it, don't you make me feel worse. I'll sort this, darling, I'll sort this before you know it.'

Her heart went out to him. She could hear the desolation in his voice, knew then that he was feeling the loss of his brother far more than he was letting on. She was thrilled that he was willing to show that to her, and her alone. He would never let anyone else see how he was really feeling. She wished Breda could see this side of him, could understand that this was why she didn't need to listen to gossip or know too much about what went on in her husband's life. She was just glad that it wasn't her Phillip doing seven years, she would rather it was anyone but him. Now they had to go and face poor Veronica, and that was going to be very hard for Phillip to bear. He felt responsible; they all worked for him in one way or another. He kept each of them financially, even his father was on the payroll now.

She saw little Philly watching his parents closely; his handsome face seemed to understand exactly what was going on around him and, for a split second, the fear gripped her once more. It was as if he had inherited his father's ability to look inside her head and pick out her thoughts. Breda always made her feel like this too, with her friendly warnings, and her insistence that Christine should know more than was good for her always left her nerves in tatters. She knew that she had to be strong for Phillip now, knew that he needed her. Anyway, what was a few years in the grand scheme of things? Declan would be out and about before they knew it. Phillip had done everything he could to help him, and he would have to look out for them all on his own now Declan was banged up. He needed her to be strong for him. She was determined not to let him down.

Chapter Twenty-Six

Eileen Booth sat at the table and watched her daughter warily. She knew that having slammed the phone down on her earlier in the day, Christine might well decide to continue the argument in front of her in-laws.

It was the first time Eileen Booth had ever felt nervous of her daughter, in fact she couldn't remember ever feeling this nervous about anything in her life before. She was determined to make her peace with Christine, she was not about to let anything ruin the life she had become so fond of.

Eileen felt almost ashamed at how grateful Veronica had been at her coming round. Veronica had been touched because she had truly believed Eileen was coming over to show her support at this awful time when, in reality, she had not even thought about how Declan's going away might affect anyone other than herself. She was only there because her daughter had finally had enough of her, and she was desperate to try and build some kind of bridge between them in case she and Ted were cut out entirely from the Murphys' orbit. Even Phillip seemed to think she was here to show her solidarity, and that told her that Christine had kept their argument to herself. She was unsure what she was supposed to say, but she was not going to leave until her daughter was once more back onside. Ted might not feel the need to be here, but she did; someone had to look out for their future earnings.

Other than James, who had wolfed down his dinner as usual,

the food Veronica had prepared had pretty much gone uneaten. It sat on the plates, gradually drying out as they all discussed the day's events. Phillip was putting a good spin on it, and no one was brave or foolish enough to contradict him. Breda was keeping a low profile tonight, and Veronica Murphy was secretly glad about that much anyway. She wasn't sure she could have coped with any kind of conflict this night. And God Himself knew, her Breda wasn't exactly renowned for her tact. She was heart-sorry for Phillip, he was obviously as distraught as she was at the turn of events. Getting up, she went to the cupboard above the sink and she took out a bottle of Paddy. Opening it with a flourish, she said loudly, 'Get the glasses out. All this moping around isn't going to get our Declan home.'

Christine watched as her mother-in-law tried to make the evening almost bearable, and was impressed at how the woman suddenly lifted the atmosphere until it was almost jovial.

'Before we know it our Declan will be back amongst us, regaling us with stories about his exploits inside.'

It was as if Veronica had given them all permission to stop worrying. Christine knew that this was how things were dealt with in this family, you accepted the bad and you made a point of not letting it get the better of you.

Phillip Murphy Senior looked at his wife and smiled for the first time in days. 'Pour me a shot, love, it's not the end of the world. He's lucky he hasn't been captured before this. Fuck me, he's lucky it was only a seven! Three sawn-off shotguns and an assault rifle in his boot! They could've thrown away the fucking keys.'

Breda chipped in then with, 'Not to forget the conspiracy to murder charge that was miraculously dropped at the last minute. Fucking Filth couldn't pin the tail on a kiddie's donkey with a miner's lamp and a detailed map!'

Everyone was laughing now, joking about it, the whisky was flowing and the tales of Declan and his exploits over the years were coming thick and fast. The evening had taken on a party mood. Declan's brothers and sister were all pleased to celebrate him and their obvious love for him. They could pretend he was with them now, a part of them once more. Now that the shock of his sentence had worn off they were able to see that in actuality he had got off lightly. He would do his time, and be back among them soon enough.

Christine was pleased at the change in the atmosphere, and she felt herself relaxing; this was what had made her want to be a part of the Murphys, this love that they had for each other. This loyalty that they all had in abundance. The way they could be fighting one moment, and in the next lined up together against the outside world.

Eileen Booth was frankly bewildered. How could they laugh and joke about something so awful? How could they not see that they should be ashamed of their son's predicament? It was as if they thought what had happened was acceptable. Normal, even. But, then again, she supposed it was to people like them.

Philly ran through the kitchen then, pretending to shoot his little brother. He screamed out at the top of his voice, 'Bang! Bang! Bang! Bang!'

Jamsie shouted out, 'He's a fucking Murphy all right!'

As Eileen watched her only daughter laugh along with them, she knew then that she had lost Christine to this family, and she would never get her back.

Chapter Twenty-Seven

Christine was aware that whatever her husband was up to was serious. He had closeted himself in the office block he had created for himself in what had originally been outhouses and stables, and now there were men she'd never seen before visiting him at regular intervals. Normally he had the same people come to the house, and even they didn't come often enough for her to really notice their presence. The last few days though, the drive was like a council car park, and men were coming and going at all hours of the day and night.

It made her feel nervous, but she knew this was all part of Phillip's world, and that she had to stop worrying about it. She felt it was her youth that let her down; she didn't understand the economics of her husband's lifestyle, and she was annoyed with herself for worrying about what he might be up to.

As she made a pot of coffee she heard the back door open and she smiled as her husband came into the warmth of the kitchen. The seriousness of his expression vanished as he saw her and she felt the pleasure his presence always brought her.

'They're going home, darling, you'll have peace and quiet in a minute.'

She smiled at his words. He knew she hated the constant noise of the cars on the gravel drive. It was loud, and it often woke the kids up as it could go on into the night.

'That grub smells handsome! You're really getting to be a good little cook – even me mother said that you're a natural and she don't like anyone else cooking for her lot.'

Christine almost beamed with pride at his words; if Veronica had actually said that, then it was high praise indeed. 'I try, but I've a long way to go yet!'

She knew she was doing well, she liked cooking these days, enjoyed the simplicity of it. The chopping, the peeling – she liked the combination of manual labour and the unknown. She was forever trying out her own recipes, new combinations of herbs and oils. As they had an orchard and plenty of land, she was learning about growing her own vegetables, and had even planted a small herb garden. The gardener Phillip had employed had been more than happy to explain the intricacies to her. She was surprised at how much she enjoyed it. And the boys just loved being out in the dirt trying to help her dig and sow.

Phillip laughed, then, looking into her eyes, he said seriously, 'I got rid of everyone for a reason, Chris. I've got a couple of blokes coming to the house – they're Old Bill, and I want to see them in the front room here, not in the offices. Is that OK with you?'

She smiled happily, deliberately overlooking the serious tone of his voice. ''Course. You don't need to ask my permission.'

He always looked too big for the kitchen, too tall and too wide. Though it was a large room, it had a low ceiling, and that made him seem huge in the confined space. Today he looked almost sinister in the late afternoon twilight. She knew he was gently warning her about something, and that he expected her to understand and comply with whatever he wanted to do.

'They're here on the quiet, Chris, they are going to tell me who served up my Declan. You can't ever let on you saw them here, or spoke to them, to anyone. Do you understand that? Not even to your mum, or *my* mum, not to *anyone*. 'Specially not Breda.'

Phillip could see the confusion in his wife's eyes, and he was genuinely sorry for having to do this to her, but he had to make sure she understood the importance of what he was saying to her. But she was a good girl, his Christine, she understood the value of keeping her nose out of things that didn't concern her. Unlike most women he knew, she didn't feel the need to be involved in every second of his life; she accepted him without questions of any kind.

She was a wonderful wife, a wonderful mother, and a fantastic lover. She kept his home spotless, and she still had a good body. He was thrilled with her, and he hated having to bring her into all this aggravation. But she needed to be aware that what occurred this day had to be kept as quiet as possible. He knew he needed to impress this information on her, but that she would heed his warning. She was nothing if not sensible.

'When you find out who it was, what are you going to do, Phil?' Her voice was quiet, matter-of-fact.

He shrugged, his smile once more without warmth. 'I'll mark their card, Chris, that's all, darling.' He opened his arms in a gesture of innocence, as if he was completely unaware of what she really meant by the question. It was like a game they played where he told her blatant lies and she accepted them as truths. 'What do you think I'm gonna do? I need to know for the future. Fuck me, Chris, this is my brother we're talking about. Even the Filth think he was stitched up. That's why they are coming round here, to set the record straight.'

She turned away from him, and poured them both out a mug of coffee, the strong aroma of the freshly ground beans heavy in the air. She knew he was bullshitting her but, then again, that suited her down to the ground. Someone had once said that knowledge was power, but, as far as she was concerned, in this world she lived in, knowledge caused nothing but trouble. So she turned the other cheek as always, pretending she was happy to go along with her husband's lies and subterfuge.

'OK. Whatever you say, Phil. I never discuss anything with anyone anyway, why would I?'

He slipped his arms around her slim waist and hugged her to him, enjoying the slightness of her frame, and the familiarity of her body. He felt himself getting hard, and she smiled at his reaction to her.

'You're a blinder, Chris, do you know that? Together me and you will go places. We'll fucking own the world.' He spoke to her in a hoarse whisper, but she could hear the determination in his voice, and she wondered briefly what the price would eventually be for their good fortune. Everything they had they got at someone else's expense, so there had to be a price eventually, she was convinced of that much. It kept her up at night, was the reason she popped her happy pills as Phillip called them.

But she didn't answer him, instead she turned and pushed herself tighter into his embrace, kidding herself that what she didn't know couldn't really hurt her.

Chapter Twenty-Eight

Breda was angry. She had heard the chatter about Phillip and his cronies, had seen that he was more than aware of his brother's incarceration being through a grass, and knew that he was moving heaven and earth to find out who the said grass might be. She also wondered why she was not party to the investigation – that really rankled. She understood Jamsie being sidelined, he was a prize cunt in most respects. But she saw herself as a valid and important member of the family businesses. After all, she brought in a serious earn, and that alone should be enough to include her in everything that was going on; if she was a bloke, of course, there wouldn't be a problem. So being overlooked like this pained her. She worked as hard as any of the men around her, harder in some ways because she had to constantly prove herself worthy of her position. Well, she was determined that this time she would prove her real worth.

She had never wanted the married and pregnant life, she had too much go in her to settle for some bloke. She wanted to be someone in her own right, achieve things through her own graft. It was the eighties, women were running the country now, and were more than capable of making their own lives, their own luck. She knew she should have moved into her own drum by now. But, in all honesty, her mother's house suited her these days. She had a babysitter on hand, as and when she needed one, and she had all the perks of a family life and none of the hassle of the bills and the loneliness living alone would incur. Besides, her mum needed her at home – Veronica Murphy had trouble letting her daughter go, and Breda knew that worked in her favour. She was still blessed with an almost-single life; her parents allowed her the freedom she craved, and in return she allowed them unrestricted access to their first grandbaby. That was something no one could put a price on. That her son took second place these days to Phillip's offspring she didn't let bother her too much. She had what she wanted and that was enough for her.

As she drove along a dark country lane in Upminster, she looked out for a dark-green Land Rover. Spying it, she slowed down and then parked neatly behind it. She sat in her silver BMW and waited patiently for the man she was meeting to slip into her passenger seat. Smiling slightly, she watched him as he walked slowly towards her – this was a man she had bedded on more than one occasion. She hoped that there might be a bit of sexual palaver after they had talked. She remembered he was well endowed – not exactly possessed of any finesse in that department, but what he lacked in technique he more than made up for in willingness, and that, as she always said, more than compensated for the lack of small talk.

As he slid into the seat beside her she was aware of him in every way. The excitement of what she was about to find out only made her feel more powerful sexually. It was about power with her. Always about the power.

Chapter Twenty-Nine

Peter Knolls was dressed for work. As a nightclub doorman, he wore an expensive suit and hand-made shirts, and God help anyone who came within two feet of his attire. He was big in every way and he knew it. His sheer brute strength had made him feared and that was a big help in his chosen profession. The rougher clientele of certain establishments were much less likely to kick off when Knollsy, as he was known, was on the door. He was also a dyed-in-the-wool racist, and unafraid to use a firearm. He had all the natural accoutrements his job required, and then some. Add to that his fascination with the female form, and his reputation for shagging till the crack of dawn if he could stay up late enough, and his job was made for him. He spent all night watching strange and collecting phone numbers, while deciding who could deal in his club and who couldn't. He earned a serious wedge and he loved hurting people; all in all it was his dream job. He also listened to everything around him, and his natural quietness made people forget he was there. This stood him in good stead; he was happy to pass along information for certain monetary rewards. Which was what he was about to do now, only this time he was worried about what he had heard whispered. Not that it affected him as such, but because it was such an explosive bit of knowledge, worth a good deal to the right people.

'All right, Breda? You look well, love.'

He was staring at her ample breasts as he spoke and she laughed at his audacity. She lit a cigarette, the blackness around them was comforting somehow. It was funny but the dark didn't bother her, she had always embraced it. It hid a lot, and it encouraged you to think. The darkness of this lane was enveloping them, making them invisible to the world. Peter Knolls opened the window; he hated smoking, especially women smoking. It was a filthy habit and he loathed the way his suits stank after a night in the clubs. Breda, knowing this, blew cigarette smoke right into his face. 'What you found out, Pete?'

'How much you got on you?'

She sighed. 'Enough. Or would you rather I got Phillip to talk to you? Only he's the one who is moving heaven and earth to find out the score about our Declan. It's up to you.' She was cold towards him now, the hardness of her eyes evident even in the dimness of the car.

'All right. Fucking relax. No need to get out of your shopping trolley.'

He was offended and she knew that. It was a calculated gesture. She wanted him annoyed, she was making him aware of who was boss. She knew he could play the game, so she wasn't bothered about it. She had rattled him more than she thought and that was evident when he said quietly, 'You swear that you'll never let on I told you this, not to Phillip, Declan, anyone?'

She frowned slightly at his words. 'Phillip will give whoever spills his guts the fucking Victoria Cross. I don't know where you've been hiding but he's given word that anyone with any kind of knowledge only had to let him know.'

Peter Knolls shook his head sadly. 'He might not want to know though, have you thought about that? Neither might you when you find out, did that ever occur to any of you?' He was looking at her face now, staring into her eyes. 'I'm only talking to you now because we're mates.'

She didn't answer him, she was already working out what he

was actually saying to her. Or more to the point, what he was *trying* to say to her. It wasn't rocket science. She looked him in the eye as she said, 'Before we go any further, how did *you* come by this information?'

Peter sighed again. He wished he had never come now, he was in well over his head already. Breda was one thing, but Phillip, he was a different entity entirely. Whereas Breda was all action, quick words, and hasty decisions, Phillip was the opposite. He thought things through, so not only did he make the right decisions, but he also made them at the right time – generally a time that was very advantageous to himself. Always his justice was swift and without any preamble. It was all very easy to Phillip Murphy. He never troubled himself with what ifs, or if onlys. You fucked up, you paid the price.

Peter's worry was that Phillip might turn out to be one of those people who felt the need to shoot the messenger; after all, this wasn't something he would want broadcast to the nation.

'You've come this far, you must know you can't go back now. Is it Jamsie, is that what you're trying to tell me?' Breda was screwing up her eyes at the incongruity of it. James was a fucker, a fool, but he wasn't a grass – was he?

Peter Knolls shrugged. 'Jamsie was caught with three keys of cocaine and a fifteen-year-old girl in his car; he was out of his nut. He was caught over by Heathrow, and the Filth there were convinced he was part of an importing ring. You know how thick they are on the airports, like anyone would try and bring it that way! He offered a deal to get out of it. Sorry, Breda, he might be your brother, but he's a fucking waster. Anyway, the Filth took it and one of them is on my payroll, he bounces for me on the side. A big cunt, all brawn and no brain. He let it slip one night when he was in his cups, so to speak. Jamsie was playing up and they had a bit of a confrontation. I heard the gist of it, and now I don't know if I'm doing the right thing or not. On the one hand, if he was my brother I would want to know,

109

on the other hand, if he was my brother I'd rather *not* know. So there you have it.'

Breda was quiet for long moments, her heavy breathing the only sound in the car. 'Who's this Filth? What's his name and where does he live?'

'What are you going to do, Breda, go round there and knock on his front door?' His voice was slightly mocking and that fuelled Breda's already gathering anger.

'I ain't scared of the Filth, I ain't scared of no one, and that includes my brother Phillip. He'll want to know what you told me, you do realise that.' She threw the last bit in to frighten Peter, to pay him back for his disrespect of her and her reputation, a reputation that was gaining momentum by the week. She would not be treated like a second-class citizen by anyone, especially not nightclub doormen whose only job requirements were a broad chest and a penchant for fighting drunks. She wasn't going to let him have his wicked way either. He could kiss that goodbye and all.

Chapter Thirty

Jamsie was stoned – not just mellow, he was stoned out of his nut. As he rolled himself another joint he wondered at how easy life could be if you just had the good sense to plan everything down to the last detail.

June Pines was lying in the bed watching him languorously. Say what you liked about Jamsie, he could fuck for England, stoned or not. He was a waster, as her mother was constantly reminding her, and she knew that well enough. It didn't stop the attraction though, in fact it only enhanced it for her. He was good-looking and she liked the danger of him. She liked the knowledge that his name was feared around their way, and she got a kick out of the fact that her mother was more than aware of it. If she was honest, she would admit that it had been a big part of his initial attraction for her; now it was developing into a genuine romance, at least she hoped it was. She had been round the turf more times than a greyhound, and she knew that there were not many who could satisfy her like Jamsie Murphy. Christ Himself knew, she had tried out enough blokes in her lifetime. In fact, she was considering a move if this thing with Jamsie didn't work out. Her reputation was preceding her these days and only being with someone like Jamsie could hold the remarks in check. She had a cousin who lived near Birmingham who said that she was welcome to come and share her flat with her; she had a baby and, by all accounts, the talent up there was for the taking. It was something to think about anyway.

She took the joint gratefully from Jamsie and pulled on it deeply, letting the grass envelop her mind and iron out any problems she might foresee. She loved the feeling of floating above herself. Feeling the fluidness of her own body. Jamsie was noisily trying to clear his throat and, as he coughed over and over again, his eyes caught hers and they both started to crack up laughing, as if it was the funniest thing they had ever heard. *Really* laughing, their eyes running with tears.

The peculiar buzz that grass produced had reduced them to hopeless wrecks of laughter, but now they were quiet again, both engrossed in their own thoughts. Jamsie was lying beside her, and she was tucked under his arm, enjoying the feel of him, the smell of him. Somewhere outside a car went past and the familiar sound of Bob Marley was wafting up the stairs. 'Redemption Song' was one of her favourite tracks. She closed her eyes and let the music wash over her, she felt so relaxed again. The sound of feet on the stairs didn't bother either of them at first, but the door being kicked in alerted them both to the fact that something serious was about to occur.

Breda Murphy's red, furious face told them that it was trouble. As Breda and her henchmen dragged Jamsie bodily from the bed, screaming obscenities at him all the while, June was relieved that the woman hadn't come looking for her. She looked angry enough to commit murder.

As June scrambled into her clothes and ran terrified from the chaos in the bedroom, she decided there and then that Birmingham was suddenly the high spot of the universe. She was packed and on a train north within two hours. She had a feeling she should get out of Dodge, as her father was always remarking, his penchant for the cowboy films of his youth always spattering his daily conversations. She liked Jamsie a lot, but his family, especially his sister, seemed to feel differently about him. She didn't know what had caused the commotion but she was sensible enough not to hang around to find out.

She didn't know that much about the gangster lifestyle, but even she knew that when your own sister and three men with baseball bats set about you, it was a serious breach of familial etiquette. She repaired her make-up, got herself a coffee and sat back in the train seat with a sigh of relief. This was just the push she needed to start her young life anew. She had no intention of being pulled in as a material witness by the Old Bill. As far as she was concerned her life in the Smoke was well and truly over. She sighed with relief; it had been a close shave all right, and she wanted to put it as far behind her as possible. She wondered briefly if Jamsie was OK, then she forced him from her mind. She knew that whatever happened, she would be the furthest thing from *his* mind, and she was determined to return the compliment.

Chapter Thirty-One

Phillip was seething, only now the anger was directed at his sister. How dare she take this matter into her own hands! Who the fuck did she think she was?

As he drove towards his mother's house he could feel black fury consuming him. Not that anyone looking at him would see that of course, at least no one who wasn't really close to him. He knew his biggest strength was the fact he never look harassed about anything. He always looked cool, calm, and, as his mother often joked, collected. But inside he was a writhing mass of hate and that hate was right now directed at Breda. She had gone too far this time. Fucking baseball bats in public, letting the world know their fucking business. He had already received three calls about it before he had left the house. What did she think, that her little escapade would be overlooked? She had just advertised to the world that their brother was a fucking grass, and she thought that would help them in some way? Why not go the whole hog and have it advertised in the fucking *Romford Recorder* and the *London Daily News*? The silly, stupid bitch. And as if that wasn't bad enough he now had to go and sort out his fucking mother, who was terrified of what was going to happen to her only daughter, let alone her fucking battered and bemused son! It was like living in a circus, they were all fucking clowns of one type or another. He was already trying to minimise the damage that dozy mare had caused; the Filth were being weighed off, and that wasn't fucking cheap at any time. Breda

114

had made them look like a bunch of muppets. Incapable of getting their own house in order in a private and dignified manner.

Well, he was going to take her down a peg, and she would remember this fuck-up until the day she died.

Chapter Thirty-Two

'What possessed you, girl? Your own brother!'

Veronica's voice was thick with tears, she was still unable to comprehend what had taken place in her own family.

'He grassed up Declan, how many fucking times, Mother!'

Veronica screamed back at her daughter, her thick Irish accent even more pronounced with her anger. 'I don't believe it! I won't believe it! James Joachim Murphy might not be the brightest star in the constellation but he wouldn't be that fecking stupid. Use your head, Breda! He'd have to be halfway to the county home to even *dream* of doing something that fecking stupid.' She looked to where her husband was sitting at the kitchen table drinking a large Scotch. He shook his head at her then, refusing to get involved.

'Will you talk some sense into your daughter, Phillip, not just sit there like the fecking village idiot.'

There was dread in her voice now, fear that all she had heard was true. If it *was* true her Jamsie, the biggest eejit this side of the Irish Sea, would indeed be safer in a mental institution than in his own home. Breda was bad enough, but Phillip, her eldest, he would be like a man demented. There was no way he would let Jamsie walk away from something like this; it was inconceivable that it could even have happened. Surely they had it wrong and some begrudger was telling them lies to try and cause trouble between them all? Wasn't it bad enough she had lost her lovely Declan without them taking her Jamsie away from her as well?

116

'Phillip will kill him stone dead.' Her voice was higher than ever, the terror making her feel faint.

Phillip Murphy Senior got up slowly and went to his wife. Veronica allowed him to pull her into his arms, to hold her – she knew she needed holding at this moment. She had to calm down, get herself sorted so she could talk to her eldest son, make him see that it was all a load of old shite. That his brother wasn't capable of such skulduggery, that he wasn't bright enough to do something so underhand, so treacherous.

For the first time ever, Veronica saw her family as other people saw them: violent criminals with no scruples whatsoever. She could hear the talk now as if the voices were in the room with her. '*Look at them Murphys, even their own flesh and blood aren't safe. Their own brother!*' It would never be forgotten. It would be dragged up and remembered on regular occasions. They would be seen as animals, wild animals with no care for anyone – not even their own. She knew that they were talked about now – their lifestyles, their way of going on, but that was normal, that was just gossip. There was even an edge of respect for them in it, but there wouldn't be any more. The tight-knit Murphys were no more. They would now be seen as people who turned on their own.

Breda had caused more trouble than she realised with her actions this night. And now they had to wait and see what the upshot was going to be, because it was Phillip who would decide the outcome, and Breda should have understood that from the start. As she watched her daughter, trying to pretend she wasn't bothered about the aggravation she had caused, she was filled with regret for what her family had been reduced to. No one knew her children's faults better than her; after all she had birthed them, each one, she knew their weaknesses, as well as their strengths. But for all Jamsie's stupidity, unlike this daughter of hers, he honestly didn't have the sense to work out that every action had a consequence. Her Phillip, on the other hand, had known that from a very young age, he didn't shit unless he had planned it down to the last detail. Breda should have used her loaf, thought about what she was doing. Her youngest son was fighting for his life in hospital and she couldn't even go to his side until she had sorted out the situation here first. She daren't leave Breda alone with her brother – otherwise the chances were she would be visiting two of her children in intensive care instead of one. How had this happened to them? It was as if overnight her family was being decimated before her eyes; their closeness which she had been so proud of was gone and her children were suddenly enemies. Everything she had worked for since their births was destroyed.

Breda was sitting on the kitchen chair defiantly, looking at her mother as if *she* was the one who had done something wrong, as if this was *her* fault somehow. Veronica left her husband's embrace and walked slowly over to her. Then, taking her arm back, she slapped her daughter's face with all the energy she could muster. It said something for Breda that she didn't retaliate, that she took the blow without a word. She looked at her father, but he didn't react in any way. He had sat down again quietly, and resumed sipping his whisky. As if he knew exactly what was going to happen and there was nothing he could do about it. Or wanted to. And it was that, her father's reaction, or rather his lack of it, that finally convinced her how much trouble she was actually in.

'I did it for our Declan, for his being banged up. I did it for the family!'

Veronica shook her head sadly; the fight had left her now. 'No, you didn't, Breda, you did it for yourself, like you have always done everything for yourself.'

Breda looked at her father again and, when he deliberately avoided eye contact, she said with bravado, 'Phillip doesn't scare me, the man ain't been born who can scare me.'

Veronica laughed mirthlessly. 'I wouldn't be too sure about that, Breda. I think that man just pulled up outside.'

Chapter Thirty-Three

Phillip stood outside his mother's house for a few moments to gather himself together. He knew that he was still angry enough to let his sister have it. He could really hurt her badly if he wasn't careful.

This was the first public problem he'd had to face where the family was concerned. And it didn't come more fucking public than this. All his hard work keeping them on a low profile, making them part of the inner fabric of their world quietly and unobtrusively, was gone now. Thanks to Breda they were like the local fucking bully boys. He could hear his heartbeat crashing in his chest, even though outwardly he looked perfectly calm. The evening air was welcome, he gulped it into his lungs, enjoying the darkness and the solitude for another few moments before all hell was let loose.

The worst thing was that this confrontation with his sister had been on the cards for a long while – he just hadn't thought it would be over something this serious, over something so personal. He was frustrated that he hadn't seen something like this coming; it was, in reality, typical Breda, sticking her nose in regardless of the consequences. He knew she was stupid enough to think that people knowing what she had done to her own brother, and why, could only be good for the family. That's how fucking far from reality she actually was. Breda thought they should live like some kind of gangster film; she walked the walk, talked the talk, and looked a complete prat because of it. The reason he was so successful was because he didn't feel the need to become a parody of himself. He had his businesses and they were legitimate – any moody enterprises were well hidden from the public face of the family. It didn't suit him to have Jamsie and Breda tearing around like the Krays on amphetamines, it drew unwanted attention to him. It was the old guilt by association – the fact the whole neighbourhood knew didn't augur well for the future. It was simple logistics. He had sussed all that out at an early age having worked for people with a measure of decorum and sense. He had learned and learned well, that people only knew what you told them – ergo, keep your trap shut and you'll be safe.

Now he had Declan to protect, and as for Jamsie – well, he knew exactly what was going to happen there. Thanks to Breda it had all come on top a bit too soon. Breda had gone too far – how dare she take this on herself. How dare she think she could get away with this as if it was nothing! As if he would not have anything to say about her actions. Who the fuck did she think she was?

There was a large part of him that believed she needed a serious fright, to understand, finally and irrevocably, that her behaviour was totally unacceptable. She needed a kicking, a real fucking hiding to show her just how serious he was. He automatically smoothed his hair, wiped his hand over his face, and straightened his clothes. He liked to be in control but, more to the point, he liked to look it.

As he made his way into the family home he felt the atmosphere and he was glad of it. He walked into the kitchen quietly, the reassuring smells of his childhood reminding him that this was his family and, no matter how great his ire, he had to keep this as low-key as possible. The raw terror on Breda's face told him that his sister finally understood the enormity of what she had done. It was a shame the silly bitch hadn't worked all this out earlier – none of this would have been necessary. But that was by the by now, he had to sort this and then get to the hospital, try and smooth over the cracks as per usual.

His instinct was to take Breda by the scruff of her neck and throttle her. But, of course, that wasn't an option. Not at this particular moment anyway. He could feel her eyes on him, feel the arrogance mingled with fear, as she stared at him.

Veronica ran into her son's path, her arms held out as if to stop him in his tracks. 'Now come on, son, calm down, she realises she's been a fool . . .'

He knew that his mother was terrified for her daughter; the fact she wasn't at the hospital with her son who was lying in a coma spoke volumes. Like any mother, she was trying to protect her young no matter what they might have done. He frowned at her then and, moving her gently from his path, he addressed his father. 'Get her down the hospital, to Jamsie. He needs his mummy at a time like this. Also, it will be damage limitation when the Filth start sniffing round.' He looked at his mother and, smiling gently, he said seriously, 'And they will start sniffing, Mum, so we have to box clever, eh?'

He was stroking her down, they all knew it. His father was already out of the chair and putting his jacket on.

'Listen to me, Phil,' Veronica tried one last time. 'I've lost Declan, and Jamsie never means the half of it, you know what he's like . . . He's a coward. And as for her . . .' She flicked her head towards her daughter. 'She's sorry. She knows she did wrong.'

'Come on, Mum, get yourself off, I need to talk to Breda alone.'

'You won't . . . Promise me, Phil . . .'

He could hear the tears in his mother's voice and was shocked to realise that she actually thought he was capable of killing his sister; seemed his mother knew him better than he thought. That was certainly something he needed to think about at some point. The main thing now though was to get his mother and father out of the house, and off to the hospital as quickly as possible. Only then could he talk to his sister without hindrance, and he used the expression 'talk' very loosely.

Chapter Thirty-Four

'Mum, will you just watch the boys for me? I promise I won't be more than an hour or so.'

Eileen Booth was astounded; for her daughter to turn up out of the blue with her sons bundled up in blankets, white-faced and obviously agitated, was a first by anyone's standards.

'What's happened, Chris?' Eileen's voice was all interest now, and thick with feigned caring and worry. 'You can tell me, darling.'

Christine sighed heavily. 'Look, Mum, I don't ask you for much, do I? Now will you just take the boys for me? I don't need a fucking government White Paper on it – a simple yes or no will suffice.'

If Eileen needed any more proof this was serious then her daughter swearing provided it. 'Is this about Breda and Jamsie? Everyone's talking about it . . .'

Ted Booth took his daughter's arm and, walking her to the front door, he said quietly, 'Do you want me to drive you, love?'

Christine nodded gratefully and they left the house then and there, much to the chagrin of Eileen who was hoping for some first-hand gossip on what was, after all, going to be a nine-day wonder.

Chapter Thirty-Five

Breda had always understood that Phillip was dangerous, only a fool could have failed to see that over the years. What she had not seen, however, was that he was as dangerous to people inside his family as he was to those outside it. As she looked into his handsome face now she saw, not for the first time, that he had dead eyes. He looked at you, he spoke to you, he interacted with you, but it was all calculated, an act.

Phillip had never done anything he didn't want to, not even as a kid. His mum used to laugh at how stubborn he was. They had all laughed. It occurred to Breda now that it wasn't funny really. He wasn't stubborn at all. He was single-minded, selfish, and without empathy; he had no real care for other people's feelings.

'Well then, Breda, looks like it's just the two of us, eh?' He sounded calm, almost relaxed. He took a step towards her and she instinctively stepped back. Phillip grinned, and lit himself a cigarette. 'Oh, what's the matter, Breda? You tired after your energetic endeavours? By the way, Jamsie's in a coma – not that you'd notice, considering he's hardly fucking Einstein, is he? But, by all accounts, you nearly killed him, so you must be really fucking proud of yourself about that. Breda Murphy, the Ma Baker of London.'

'He's a grass . . .'

Phillip laughed then, a low sarcastic laugh. 'So I heard, before you actually – but then I would, wouldn't I? Considering I was entertaining half the local Filth at my gaff, seems only natural that might have come up in the general conversation, don't you think? You know me, Breda, why smash my way through half of London for what I want to know when I can find it out over a nice brandy in the comfort and safety of my own *fucking home.*' He bellowed the last two words and Breda was almost brought from the floor with the force of his anger.

He pulled on his cigarette once more, physically calming himself down. 'You are a prize cunt, Breda, do you realise that? You're a laughing stock, but then you always have been. You only get what you get because I *choose* to let you have it. Blood is thicker than water and all that old fanny. But this, this fucking abomination, has changed everything. I always thought you acting like you do was a good front, local PR, kept the natives in check. But what did you go and do this time, you publicly hammered your own brother, denounced him as a grass – a fucking grass! An accusation anyone else would have had the sense to keep fucking quiet about, because accusations like that tend to be remembered. But not you, eh, Breda? You couldn't fucking use your loaf of bread just once. You should have brought that information to *me*, you should have had the sense to realise that it was something *I* needed to know, and *I* needed to decide what we were going to do about it. You see, you forgot the main rule of being a Murphy, and do you know what that rule is, Breda?'

She was incapable of answering him, the calmer he spoke the more the fear was growing inside her.

He grinned genially now. 'The main rule of being a Murphy is you don't shit without asking *me* first. You don't ever have an original thought without running it by *me* first. In short, Breda, *you* wait until *I* decide what you're going to do. It's pretty easy, *I* tell you what to do, and then *you* fucking do it.'

Breda was watching him warily, wondering what his next move was going to be. For the first time in her life it occurred to her that Phillip was quite capable of really hurting her, she also realised that it wouldn't bother him to have to do it. In fact, she felt he relished it, wanted the excuse. She was not about to give it to him. She watched as he poured them both a large Scotch, and when he held the glass out to her she moved towards him cautiously. As she opened her hand, the contents of her glass were thrown into her face, and she felt the burn as the neat whisky found its way into her eyes. Two seconds later she was laid across the kitchen table and a serious beating began. It started with slapping, a heavy forceful slapping that after a few seconds had already caused her lips to swell; she could feel the sheer strength of him as he held her down. But she knew the last thing she should do was struggle – that is what he wanted her to do. Phillip wanted an excuse to let rip, and she knew that once he got it she would be lucky to leave the room alive.

The quiet of the house gave the proceedings an almost surreal feel. When she felt his hand in her hair, and her body being dragged up off the table she didn't know whether to be relieved or not. The kick that sent her across the room was vicious, and when she collapsed on to the floor, she curled herself into a protective ball. She could hear him moving around, pouring himself another drink, smelt the smoke as he lit another cigarette. So taut were her nerves she even heard him pull the smoke gently into his lungs. The waiting was the worst, because she knew he wasn't finished with her. He hadn't even started. For all she had heard whispered of her brother, she never realised until now just what a dangerous fuck he really was. The more so because he had no real care for her. This was something he was enjoying and it occurred to her that he had been storing up this anger with her for a long time, it was her own foolishness that hadn't had the sense to understand that. She knew that everything she had ever done to aggravate this brother of hers had been taken onboard and filed away for the moment. She had played right into his hands with her antics over Jamsie.

She saw her own arrogance, heard herself as she talked the big talk, remembered with a terrible dread and fear the times she had spoken disrespectfully about Phillip to his contemporaries. She lay there, hands covering her head and terror enveloping her, finally understanding that everything in life has to be paid for, every time you hurt someone it came back to you at some point, and it bit you right on the arse. She thought of her own son, and wondered if she would see him grow to a man.

Breda finally understood that the world didn't start or finish with her, her wants and her needs. And, more importantly, she finally understood you could push certain people much too far.

Chapter Thirty-Six

Jamsie Murphy was in a bad way, but it was obvious to his mother that he would survive his injuries. As she had always said, no brain no pain, and that was her Jamsie all right. Her husband was refusing to sit in the room with him; as far as he was concerned it would be better if the boy did die, for he was dead to him already.

Veronica sat by her son's bed, listened to the monitors and the night sounds of the hospital ward and wondered what the hell had happened to her family for all this to come over them so suddenly. It had been bad enough with her Declan going away but that, at least, she could understand. He'd had a capture, he'd do his time and come back home none the worse for wear. But all this? Her Jamsie at death's door, her daughter responsible for it, and Phillip, her golden boy, capable of killing them all.

She was worried for Breda. Phillip was not a happy bunny. Oh, she saw his acting for what it was, she knew him better than he knew himself. That was the half the trouble. Phillip thought he had fooled her like he had everyone else, but he hadn't. Not that she had ever let on, of course, but she had guessed even when he was a child that the way her Phillip acted was not the norm. She had watched him struggle to fit into any kind of situation, he had no idea how to react to the most mundane things. She had seen then that he had a distinct lack of feelings; he loved in a way, but it was not love as most people understood it. Phillip loved what he possessed. It was his, he owned it, therefore he loved it. He had no empathy, had never had any.

She remembered years ago, when they were all small, a man had leapt off a local tower block. Other kids had seen the result and, in their own ways, had felt ill, shocked, everything you'd expect. Phillip had not even batted an eyelid – he had been fascinated more than anything. It had been then that she had started to watch him. She had seen him stick up for his brothers and sister, but more because they were his family than because he cared what happened to them. It was as if to disrespect them you were disrespecting *him*.

When the family's pet rabbit had died he had watched the others crying, and she knew he had tried his hardest to cry with them, but it just hadn't happened. It couldn't happen, because he didn't know how to care. It was as if he was missing something in that department. She had always thought him a strange child, even as a small baby he had not reacted like the others. Quiet, rarely crying and never smiling. He was always detached somehow, and she had done what many a mother before her had done; she had made excuses for him. She had rationalised his behaviour and made it seem normal. Told the school he had always been quiet, that he didn't understand that if you cut someone then they would bleed – it wasn't that he wanted to hurt the other child, it was just that he was fascinated at how things happened. He had always had an inordinate interest in blood and death. He had devoured horror books as a teen and she had seen that as somehow proving her right, he wasn't *odd*, he was just fascinated by the macabre. His teachers had questioned his behaviour; he had fought like the other boys but, unlike them, he had never known when to stop the fight, had always had to be pulled off the offender before he killed them – and she had no doubt that kill them he would should they provoke him enough. Phillip lived by a completely different set of moral and ethical codes. Codes that made sense only to him.

But over the years he had given himself a polish of sorts; he had learned how to be a part of society, how to blend in. And this had given Veronica a measure of peace – until all this, of course. Now the old fears were back with a vengeance. The terror that he was without real feelings of any kind. She wiped away the tears of frustration and terror that rolled down her cheeks. Now his amazing temper was focused on his own family, and she was not sure how this night was going to end. That her own child frightened her was bad enough, but that she had no real control over him bothered her even more.

She took her rosary beads from her pocket and started a decade of Hail Marys, praying that Our Lady, the Mother of God would see it in her heart to ease the burden of her pain, and save her family for her this night.

She didn't hold out much hope.

Chapter Thirty-Seven

Phillip looked at his sister as she lay on the kitchen floor. She was curled up in the foetal position, her whole demeanour now one of fear, repentance – and pain.

He had been holding back his true nature for years now. He knew that his haphazard brand of violence was not seen as the norm by most people, but he felt that his natural instincts were what gave him the edge in his world and he used them to that end. Now, this excuse for a fucking female had made him step out of character; she had forced him to retaliate, and now the genie was out of the bottle he was seriously considering killing her. Get her off his fucking back once and for all.

That she would dare to make a fool of him in front of the very people they relied on for their livelihoods was extremely stupid, and enough to bring the fucking authorities down on them. The Filth would have a field day seeing the Murphys implode, and in spectacular fashion at that. All killing each other, and doing it in full view of anyone who cared to have a gander. That she thought she could get away with it told him he had made a grave error of judgement in trusting her. Well, that wasn't going to ever happen again. He had given her far too much leeway, had let her believe she was in control of her own life, and she had done what all fucking idiots eventually did – she had believed her own press. She thought that her silly little local reputation gave her some kind of fucking swerve where the real world was concerned. She played to the gallery, while he

131

took the money on the door. It was the difference between them and it always would be. Well, now he had to show her just what a mega fuck-up she'd made, not just for herself, but for him and everyone they knew. She needed the lesson of all lessons.

Walking towards her he kicked her, with all his strength, in the small of her back; so great was its power that it forced her two feet across the floor, and she slammed into the bottom of the cupboard doors. The thud was loud in the quiet of the kitchen. He was grudgingly impressed that she didn't cry out, that went a small way towards abating his anger slightly. He admired people who were strong, who were able to take what was coming to them. It was this part of his sister that showed she was a Murphy.

He spat at her. 'I could kill you, Breda, for the grief you've caused me.'

She wasn't about to answer him, she knew he needed to talk now and she was happy to let him. Her eyes were tightly shut, and her instincts told her not to make eye contact with him in any way. Just let him run off his steam. Let him get it out of his system. She could hear him smoking again, the click of the lighter like a gunshot in the quiet of the room. She was in the most precarious position of her life, but there was nothing she could do about it. She had to let this run its course; even her mother had walked away from it, and that alone told her everything she needed to know. But she swore to God and all the saints that if she survived this she would never again take anyone or anything for granted as long as she lived.

Phillip smoked his cigarette slowly, sipping at his whisky occasionally. Sometimes, when he was very angry, like now, he had difficulty keeping his mind concentrated. He pictured himself doing things, right now he could picture himself boiling the kettle and pouring it all over her fucking greasy head. The thought made him smile – that would get a reaction from her all right. That would get her on the move.

He began laughing gently, almost chuckling, and this sound was far more frightening to Breda than anything else she had heard.

'All my fucking hard graft, out the door in five minutes because you couldn't resist showing off could you, eh, Breda? Had to be the hard bird, hard Breda Murphy. A bloke with tits.'

The anger was building in his voice once more. She knew she had to keep quiet and as still as possible, but her back felt like it was broken, and her face was stinging, the swelling was so bad on her lips she was having difficulty breathing. She could taste blood every time she swallowed. Breda knew she was in a bad way, and that she would be much worse before the night was through. She was praying in her head, over and over, begging the gods to help her get out of this situation. She was bargaining with the Lord like many a coward before her, only she feared it was all too late.

As Phillip walked back over to her she held her breath in anticipation, expecting another blow of equally ferocious proportions. As she tensed her body, ready, she thought she was hallucinating as she heard her sister-in-law's voice calling out loudly, 'Phil . . . Phillip, are you in there?'

Breda heard her brother swearing under his breath, and knew that Christine really was there, had turned up at the house to save her. Breda could feel the tears breaking through her closed eyelids; the relief was palpable now, and her body started to shudder as shock set in.

Phillip Murphy was looking at his wife as if she had just grown a separate head on her shoulders in front of his eyes as he registered the shock and the disgust in her face. He knew that his mother was behind Christine coming here, shaming him further. Oh, would this fucking day never cease to surprise him? Would this day never fucking end?

Christine walked tentatively into the kitchen, and he could

sense the fear emanating from her, almost smell it. His wife's fear affected him in a way Breda's failed to, he needed her goodwill, needed her to think well of him.

'What's going on, Phillip . . . ? Come on, Breda, get up off the floor, love, did you fall over or something?'

It sounded silly even to her own ears, but Christine knew in her heart that she had to pretend she had no real idea what was going on here. She knew that her husband was not only volatile, but that he'd had some kind of break with reality. She had sensed this only a few times before, and she had been loath to explore her feelings then. She was even less inclined to think too much about it now.

She bent over Breda offering her a hand, and trying to smile reassuringly at her. The situation was so surreal she wondered briefly if she had stumbled into some kind of twilight dream world. There was whisky all over the floor and Breda looked like she had been flattened somehow, her whole face was swollen and already bruising. But it was Phillip who was worrying her – he looked vacant, unaware of what was happening around him, but she knew that he was more than aware and was watching them both with an intensity that made her feel he could see into their minds. She was pulling Breda's hands from around her head, making her let go, silently trying to impress on her how important it was to get up off the floor and away from Phillip as soon as possible. Once she was out of his sight she would be safe, for a while anyway.

'Come on, Bred, get up, will you? I'll make us a nice cup of tea and we'll all sit down and have a chat. I'm freezing, I need a hot drink.' She could hear the desperation in her own voice, hated herself for her weakness. She knew she needed to be strong tonight in order to get Phillip out of that house without doing his sister any more harm. But she was shaking with terror. This was the father of her children, and the thought that he could have passed this vicious trait on to the boys, along with his good looks, was weighing heavy on her mind.

Breda finally seemed to realise she had to move, and she slowly and gradually pulled herself up into a sitting position, all the time avoiding her brother's gaze and concentrating on Christine's eyes. Eyes that were telling her to keep calm, and do as she was told.

Phillip watched the display as if it was the singularly most fascinating thing he had ever witnessed in his life. His wife, his little Christine, helping foul-mouthed Breda, it was an incongruous situation, and it should never have happened. It *wouldn't* have happened if Breda had not been the catalyst for all the ills this day had brought him, and now this last humiliation was almost too much to bear. He pictured himself taking the bread knife from his mother's drawer, slicing it into his sister's liver over and over again, saw the pool of blood as it spread pleasingly across his mother's lovely floor.

But he knew that Christine couldn't see that, could never see anything like that. Christine didn't understand the real world, the world she lived in, and he didn't want her to. He didn't want her tainted with it, like the others were tainted. Christine was too good for this, she was far, far too good. In every way.

Phillip turned abruptly and walked out of the house, unable to tolerate the scene before him any longer without retaliating in some explosive and frightening way.

When the front door closed behind him, Christine felt her sister-in-law start to cry. She held Breda to her as she cried loudly, and with absolute abandon.

Chapter Thirty-Eight

In intensive care, Jamsie opened his eyes to find his mother sitting by his bed. It took him a few minutes to remember what had happened to him; when he did, he closed his eyes again, wishing he had never woken up in the first place. He heard his mother praying softly, could hear the gentle clicks as she passed the rosary beads through her fingers at the end of each prayer. It was comforting for him, reminded him of when he was a kid and she'd make them all say the rosary in May for Our Lady, Queen of Heaven.

He felt the sting of tears then; everything he had ever known was gone now, everything he had thought would always be there, that he had taken for granted, was gone. He had pulled some stunts in his time, and they were legion, but they were nothing compared to getting Declan put away. He had crossed a line, and there was no going back.

His mother leant towards him; he could smell the mints on her breath and, opening his eyes, he looked at her sadly. 'Mum?'

She stared into his eyes for a long moment before she said gently and forcefully, 'You should have died, Jamsie, you treacherous little bastard.'

Chapter Thirty-Nine

Veronica was worried. Phillip had been missing for five days, and she was once more sitting in her daughter-in-law's kitchen, watching her grandsons' antics, and hoping against hope that her boy would walk in the front door as if nothing had happened.

That was how these things usually panned out – after a bout of violence when he was young he would go off somewhere, and she would have the heart across her until he came back home. She wasn't frightened of anything happening to him, she was more worried about him hurting other people. He wasn't able to calm himself down, that was the trouble, and anyone in his path was easy prey. She knew from experience how he could get, knew that he was dangerous and incapable of controlling himself when things went too far. He had to hide away and try to wait out his immense fury. She knew the score, she was only nonplussed now because it was so long since he had experienced an episode like this one she had secretly hoped they were a thing of the past.

Yet if she was honest with herself, she doubted whether it was possible to grow out of that kind of anti-social behaviour. Phillip was, as her husband had once remarked, a complete nut-bag. She had laughed at the epithet at the time, but now it seemed to sum him up perfectly. She had seen Christine as his saving grace, had believed that his feelings for the girl proved he was at least normal enough to love on some level, and the same with the boys she had produced for him. Around his wife, he was a different person, the person Veronica knew he *wanted* to be. It was all a pretence, of course, she realised that now – his whole life was one big game. She looked around her at the lovely home he had provided for his family, and knew that, like Christine and his boys, this was his proof to the world that he was successful, that he was different to his peers. He saw himself as above everyone else and she knew how much store her Phillip put on how other people perceived him and his.

Now, thanks to Breda and that piece of shite Jamsie, he was back to where he was ten years previously. Between them they had destroyed their own family. She would never forgive either of them.

Her son might not be all the ticket in comparison to most other people, but he was her first-born and she loved him more than all the others put together. He needed her more than they did, even though he didn't actually realise that himself. Phillip was broken: it wasn't anything she had done, he had been born that way, and as such he was her responsibility. That, as far as she was concerned, was what being a mother was about.

Chapter Forty

Breda was like a caged lion. She sat in her mother's house and waited, feeling like she had the Sword of Damocles hanging over her head. She knew that Phillip would be back at some point, but when? And what kind of mood would he be in when he arrived? She could kick herself for forgetting just how dangerous her brother could be. She had really believed he would have thanked her for her actions towards Jamsie, and she saw now that it was this belief that had caused this terrible retribution to come down on her. She had really overestimated her own strength, and her brother's capacity for coping with serious aggravation. It was years since he had gone off on one; like her mother, she had believed he had, if not grown out of his rages, at least managed to control them.

Seeing how wrong she was had knocked her confidence completely. It reminded her of when they were kids and they had all been terrified of upsetting him. It was an unwritten rule in the household that Phillip and his strange moods, as her mother referred to them, were always given precedence. Her mother had almost made them seem normal, because she had learned to cope with them in a way that caused the minimum of fuss. They all knew, though, that Phillip was her mother's boy – especially her father, he had taken a back seat to him since he had thrown his first violent tantrum.

That Phillip could walk in at any moment and throttle her without a second's thought was forefront in her mind, night and day. Breda looked at her son and wondered if he was to be left motherless. Phillip was more than capable of seeing to that. Veronica would cover for him as per usual, they all knew that. Even if he murdered his own sister, her mother would see it as an aberration, not as a serious event. Where Phillip was concerned her mother could, and would, paper over any cracks, no matter how monumental they might actually be.

Christine had certainly gone up in her estimation, but then she *had* tried to warn the girl about her husband's capabilities. Still, Breda couldn't help feeling sorry for her; judging by the shock and the horror on her face as she witnessed her husband's handiwork, that night had certainly been a learning curve for her.

Breda had been aware of her utter incomprehension of the scene in the kitchen. It would have forced Christine to rethink her whole life, and she would now be realising she was absolutely trapped. That she had, in effect, married a nutter – a handsome, charming nutter, but a headcase all the same. Christine was sensible enough to understand now that she could never leave Phillip, that he would not countenance it, would see it as a personal affront. He was more than capable of turning on her should she displease him, and the fact that Christine was having to take that onboard saddened Breda. That night she could almost feel the girl's dismay as she saw what she had tied herself to. People wondered why Breda was so set against being tied to someone for any length of time – well she had been brought up with three brothers and she had learned one important thing: men were basically scum.

She watched as her father poured himself another cup of tea and carried on happily reading the racing form in the *Sun*. She envied him his complete acceptance of his way of life. He had not been affected one iota by recent events – in fact he seemed to hold her entirely responsible for everything. As he said, over and over, you ask for something often enough, and you'll get it tenfold. Like her mother, he felt that Phillip could do no real wrong, and any trouble he caused was because other people didn't understand him. So this was all *her* fault now, even Jamsie had not suffered as much flak as she had over it all. King Phillip had been upset, and that would never do. For as long as he brought in the wedge her father would see no wrong in him.

Well, perhaps she *had* asked for this, even she was aware of that much. She had pushed him too far, and that was not a mistake she was ever going to make again. If she survived this she would ensure she never again gave her brother reason to doubt her.

Chapter Forty-One

Jamsie awoke to see his brother looking down at him; the eyes were cold and the smirk was clearly evident. He was leaning over him in the bed and, to anyone outside their family, he looked genuinely concerned.

'How are you feeling, bruv?'

Jamsie's mouth was dry, and his heart was crashing in his ears, he was hoping he was imagining this. He looked around to see if Phillip had a knife or box cutter on him, something that could do the most damage in the quietest way. Phillip seemed to read his mind and he laughed softly. Pulling up a chair he sat down easily, his long legs crossed neatly and his arms lying carelessly along the sides of the upholstered chair. He looked for all the world like a man without a care. He grinned. 'She gave you a serious old battering, didn't she?'

Jamsie watched his brother warily, he knew that anything could happen when Phillip was like this, and anything often did.

'Cat got your tongue? Seems a pity considering you can't keep your fucking trap shut normally. A very chatty little fucker by all accounts, especially when it comes to family business or getting yourself out of schtook. All this over a few keys of coke. Amazed there was any left for the Filth to find – you tend to Hoover it up in vast amounts, don't you? Trouble is, bruv, if you'd come to *me* I could have sorted it, and it would have all gone away, but not you, Brain of fucking Britain. Now, thanks to you, and your grassing, we're *all* in a fucking muddle. Poor Declan, stuck in stir, as stoic as always, doing his time with the minimum of fuss – can't wait till he hears the latest, can you? His temper isn't as epic as mine, but he can come a pretty close second, don't you think? But I digress. I have sorted it for you and Breda, so all's not lost, as they say. Now what's left for me to do is to decide how best to pay you out, and I can assure you I will be thinking about it long and hard. You will have my undivided attention, not just for the piss-take with Declan, but because you made my wife see a side of me that I would rather she had never known about. You made me look a mug in front of her, and that is a cardinal sin where I am concerned. I deserve to be canonised for the saintly way I have treated that girl, and now, thanks to you, she's frightened of me. She's wondering what she's lumbered herself with. Bless her heart, she doesn't understand the world we inhabit, and I never wanted her to. So, as you can imagine, all that damage is going to deserve some serious retribution, and revenge is basically my middle name.'

Phillip was talking rapidly, his tone friendly, but the manic look in his eyes was enough to tell Jamsie that he was in a very precarious position. Phillip was capable of taking him out *now*, in full view of everyone. Jamsie kept his mouth shut and waited fearfully for Phillip to make a move.

Phillip was looking on at his little brother as if he was a fly struggling in the bottom of the toilet pan. He was enjoying Jamsie's discomfort immensely, but was sensible enough to know now that he mustn't give rein to his true feelings, not yet anyway. This ponce needed to stay around for a while, just for appearance's sake if nothing else. Plus, he would enjoy making him wait – it would add to the torment.

'Don't worry, bruv, you're safe enough for the moment. I promised your mummy I wouldn't harm you. She's worried about you, see, but then she should be, shouldn't she?'

Jamsie still didn't answer him, but he felt a small surge of relief at his brother's words. His mother would fight for him, he was sure of that, and Phillip would listen to her.

'Oh, cheer up. You really do have a reprieve, bruv. The only proviso is that you never ever find yourself in the same room as me. As far as I am concerned, you're dead. If I go to Mum's – which I will, often – you make yourself fucking scarce. You keep as far away from me as is physically possible and that way me and you will be all right.'

His mocking tone was all too evident to Jamsie and he knew he was getting off lightly. Phillip was warning him in more ways than one, was telling him he was finished with him completely, not just as a brother. He had no job and, without his brother's protection and goodwill, he had no chance of getting one either.

'For all Breda's a cunt, she's a *loyal* cunt, and that counts for something at least. Overnight, you have helped to destroy not only your own family, but also everything I have worked for, and that is something I will *never* forgive, Jamsie. I'll get my own back one day, remember that. You are living on borrowed time, you treacherous cunt, and that time is running out every second of every day. But, mark my words, *bruv*, you're a walking dead man.'

Standing up, Phillip winked at him jauntily and, turning, walked quickly away. Jamsie watched him as he left the ward, his clothes perfect as always, his demeanour friendly to everyone around him.

Jamsie was aware that he really was living on borrowed time. Closing his eyes, he felt the weakness wash over him again, and was frightened that the tears in his eyes were about to spill over and shame him even more.

Chapter Forty-Two

Christine looked at her sons in their beds and felt the panic rising inside her once more. It seemed impossible that she was looking at such normality, when her life as she knew it had ceased to exist. Since the incident at Veronica's house she had been living on her nerves. Every time she closed her eyes she saw Phillip as he had been that night, but it wasn't the Phillip she had fallen in love with, it wasn't the man who had fathered her children; she saw a monster who had no control over himself whatsoever.

Since that night she had felt that she was slowly sinking into the quicksand that her whole life had been built on. When his mother had rung her and begged her to get to the house, she wasn't sure what she had expected to find – a family argument obviously, but nothing like what she had been confronted with. She kept seeing Breda on the kitchen floor, battered and bruised and, more frightening than anything, allowing it to happen to her. Breda, who normally had a row like other people had a cup of tea, had been terrified and, worse than that, she was completely accepting of her brother's outrageous behaviour. Christine felt that her whole life was a lie; everything she had believed in, and her future, had disappeared overnight.

She thought of the few times she had disagreed with Phil; he would smile at her somehow, nothing violent or intimidating, but something in his face had told her to back down, and she always had. She understood now that a small part of her must have already realised that to oppose Phil wasn't something anyone in his orbit did lightly. That even *she* was dependent on his good humour, his being happy.

He had looked absolutely demonic, like something from a horror movie; the devil himself could not have been more frightening in the flesh. When she thought of him in church beside her, taking Communion, smiling at the people around him, proud of his family and his beliefs, it was like she was thinking about a completely different person, someone else entirely. She couldn't equate the loving husband and father with the bullying maniac she had seen with her own eyes.

That Phillip Murphy was someone she had never really met, but she knew now that the manic-eyed, vicious man she had encountered was the *real* Phillip Murphy. He had hidden it well, she had to give him that, he had known how to suppress that part of his personality. But it still didn't change the fact that that was who he really was, and she knew, without a shadow of a doubt, that she was stuck with this stranger for the rest of her days. And, more to the point, so were her sons. She had given her boys a father who was capable of literally anything and now she had seen him in his true light, fear was bearing down on her like a lead weight. A part of her hoped he had done something, had been arrested and locked up, and that was why he was missing now. She didn't want him back in her life or her sons' lives. She wanted nothing more to do with him.

Christine Murphy wanted out of her marriage, out of this life, but she knew that would never be an option for her. Phillip would make sure of it.

'Come down and have a cup of tea, child.' Veronica's voice was quiet, and Christine automatically turned and followed her from the room. She had made her mother-in-law promise to stay with her until Phil came back, as she couldn't face dealing with him alone. Veronica had readily agreed, which told

Christine just how much danger she and her boys were actually in.

As she followed her mother-in-law down to the kitchen, her beautiful home didn't interest her any more. Now it felt like some kind of prison, somewhere she was being forced to reside, even though she hated it with a vengeance. She felt a wave of sickness wash over her, and knew that if something didn't happen soon she would snap. It was like waiting for a bomb to explode, only this bomb was flesh and blood, and he wasn't going to disappear after the explosion. The boys were laughing and playing, the radio was on in the background, and the smell of chicken casserole filled the house. All these things, such normal, everyday things, just made the days seem more and more surreal.

As Veronica said frequently, like some kind of mantra, life, such as it was, had to go on. You got up, and you got on with it. Well, Christine wasn't sure she was capable of going on. Only time would be the judge of that.

Chapter Forty-Three

'Fuck me, Phillip, you scared the life out of me creeping in like a fucking burglar!'

Phil Senior had turned and seen his son standing in the kitchen doorway, and it had given him a serious fright.

Phillip grinned, and his father was relieved to see he looked more or less back to normal. 'Sorry, mate, any chance of a cup of tea?'

Phil Senior was already putting the kettle on, pleased his son was back and even more pleased to see him acting normally. Phillip could be the proverbial handful, but he was a good boy for all that, he just needed to be handled gently; if you respected his nature you were all right.

'Where's Breda?'

Phil Senior looked at his son now and, sighing, he said gently, 'Not again, Phillip. She's took it on the chin, she's been waiting to see you, but think of your mother . . .'

Phillip chuckled. 'She upstairs?' He walked out to the hallway calling loudly, 'Come down, Bred, Dad's making a cup of tea.' He sounded jovial, full of the joys of spring. It was as if nothing had happened. Phil Senior made the tea happily now; the storm was over, for the time being anyway.

Breda came down slowly and, as she walked into the kitchen and faced her brother, she was white-faced with fear. Phillip looked at her for a long moment, as if appraising her, then, opening his arms widely, he said in a choked voice, 'Come here,

Breda. Fucking hell, girl, what the fuck has that Jamsie caused us . . .'

He was being magnanimous, the big man, he was all forgiving, all loving. This was benevolent Phillip; she had experienced this man before, it meant he was over his ire, he was going to let it all go. Basically she knew she was safe, and that meant the world to her. This was Phillip at his best, this was the Phillip she loved more than anyone else in the world, even her own child. She went into his arms without hesitation. She was so relieved she started to sob, her whole body shaking with the intensity of her emotions.

Phillip held her to him tightly, as if protecting her from harm. She could smell the particular smell he had – a mixture of healthy sweat and expensive aftershave. It was unique to him and, at times like this, it made her feel safe, made her feel needed, wanted. Cared for. She was still part of the family, and that meant more to her than anything.

'I've seen that treacherous cunt Jamsie, and put the hard word on him. I appreciate you were only doing what you thought was right, Bred. I see that now.' He pulled her away from him and looked deep into her eyes as he said seriously, 'You caused me a lot of fucking hag, but I forgive you. You thought you were doing good and I see that now. I've smoothed over the Filth and sorted out everything. We'll talk no more about it. But, in future, you don't ever take anything like that on yourself again, do you understand me?'

She was nodding furiously now. 'I'm so sorry, Phil, I lost it a bit . . . I didn't think it through . . .'

Phillip smiled and hugged her. 'You were doing what you thought was right, and I appreciate your loyalty to me and the family. As will Declan when I tell him. You are a fucking diamond, Breda – a bit quick off the mark, but a diamond all the same.'

Phil Senior poured the tea, filled with relief. It was over,

149

Phillip had decided he would allow his sister to carry on in the family business. Phillip wasn't a fool, she was a grafter old Breda, they all knew that. He was just relieved it was over. He wasn't too worried about Jamsie – he would have to swallow whatever came his way now – he had asked for it, and he had got it. He was on his own now.

'Where's the little fella? Go and get him, I ain't seen him for ages. Any cake to go with that tea, Dad? I'm fucking starving . . .'

Breda went upstairs to get her son, she could feel her legs buckling underneath her with the relief. As she picked up her son and hugged him to her, she thanked God that she had escaped her brother's wrath, and she swore that from now on she would never take him or his moods for granted again. It was all about Phillip now, and that suited her down to the ground. She had come close to losing everything, and she was not about to make that mistake again. As for Jamsie, he had made his bed, he had better get used to lying in it. Now that Phillip had blanked him, he was as good as a dead man. No one in their right mind would give him the time of day without Phillip's say-so. Jamsie was out, and she was back in; life was suddenly good again.

Chapter Forty-Four

'He'll be here soon, Christine, go and tidy yourself up, child.'

Since the call from her husband, Veronica had been like a young girl. Phillip was back home, happy as a sandboy, so all was right with the world. Christine actually found that even more unnerving than anything else, if she was honest. They seemed to think that because Phillip was happy that was enough. No one appeared to take onboard what he had done, what had happened that night, as if his behaviour didn't warrant discussion.

Veronica looked at the troubled countenance of her daughter-in-law and her heart went out to her. She understood how hard this had been for her, but Christine was going to have to learn how to tackle this husband of hers the hard way. Because he was not going to change, and she needed to accept that.

'Look, Christine, I love you like me own, but you have to understand that Phillip . . . well, he's not like other people.'

Christine laughed derisively then. 'You don't say! I would never have worked that one out for myself.'

Veronica immediately felt worried. Christine was about to make the mistake of a lifetime, and she had literally thirty minutes to get her into a different frame of mind. Phillip would not tolerate any kind of criticism, especially not from his wife. If he loved anyone, it was this girl. Her questioning him while he was vulnerable would only set him off again. If Christine would just use her loaf, she could have the life that most young women dreamed about. Veronica knew it was time to get tough.

'Listen to me, Christine, and listen good. When my Phillip walks through that door, you smile and you looked pleased to see him – act like you were worried something had happened to him. *Do not*, and I repeat, *do not* ask him where he's been for the last five days. Do not question him about anything. When he's like this, it is all about him. You feed him, you love him, and you accept whatever he tells you without any kind of questioning. That is the main thing here – you ask him nothing. Now, I know how this sounds, darling, but believe me, if you *do* question him, you really won't want to know the answers. I've lived with this side of him since he was old enough to crawl. He's strange, but he's still a good man, and he loves you. He adores you. But for all that, if you push him, he'll retaliate, and I know what I'm saying when I tell you you do *not* want that in your life.'

Christine was staring at her mother-in-law; she knew the woman was deadly serious, that Veronica thought she should hear all this about her husband and would meekly agree with her and her home diagnosis about the lunatic she had given birth to.

'Strange? He's strange you say? I mustn't question him, so what exactly am I to do, then? Come on, Veronica, I'm fascinated now.'

Veronica closed her eyes tightly, and shook her head in sheer desperation. 'He's your husband and there'll be no divorce, he won't countenance that – you know it, and I know it. What you do now, darling, is what many a woman has done before you. You learn how to live a good life, you learn how to overlook his foibles, and make the best of what you've got. Look at me – I married a fucking waster, but he's my husband, and I made a life as best I could.' She grabbed Christine's hands in hers then and, pulling them to her chest, she said sadly, 'Listen, Chris. People like my Phillip can't cope with being crossed in any way. When he's like this you *have* to humour him. These episodes don't last long, and it's been years since he had one. He'll feel bad that you witnessed it. You have to act like you don't care about it all. You have to pretend that everything's fine. You don't want him fretting, and you certainly don't want him going off again. Think of the boys, think about your lovely life – and you have got a lovely life, darling. Look around you at your home, at how well you're doing, how well you two are doing together. When he comes in, you treat him like visiting royalty. I promise you, that's how you cope with Phillip's nature.'

'But he frightens me . . . I'm frightened of him . . .'

Veronica could see the terror in her daughter-in-law's face, and her heart genuinely went out to her, but she also knew that this was not something the girl could show her husband. He wouldn't be able to cope with it.

'And so he should! You wouldn't be human if you didn't feel afraid. But I'm trying to tell you, darling, you *have* to act like you're not scared of him. He needs you to try and understand him now, and that's what you are going to do.'

They heard the car pull up on the drive and Veronica hugged the girl to her tightly. 'Now, remember what I said and take my lead, OK?'

Christine nodded, her heart hammering in her chest; she felt almost faint at the thought of facing him. It felt as if she was about to welcome an axe murderer into her home and, in many ways, that was exactly what she was doing.

The front door opened and his voice boomed out towards them. 'Where are my best girls, eh?' His voice was full of fun, sounded so natural and happy. Veronica winked at her then, and Christine could see the relief on her face.

'The wanderer returns! Come away in, son, and let us get a look at you.'

Christine couldn't believe how relaxed Veronica's voice sounded. It was as if she had forgotten everything that had happened. It was so surreal that Christine wondered briefly if she was caught in a waking nightmare.

Then Phillip was there, in the room with them and she could hear the boys making their way to their father from the playroom. She wanted to run – pick the boys up, and leave the house, but she knew that wasn't an option. Phillip looked wonderful, he was clean, smartly dressed, his hair was freshly cut. He had his handsome smile turned on full beam, and she knew this was a definitive moment in her young life.

'She's been worried out of her mind, Phil, but I told her you had a lot of things to sort out. There's a chicken casserole in the oven – I'll serve it up, while you two get reacquainted.'

Veronica bustled from the room, taking the boys with her. It didn't escape Christine's notice that Phillip had ignored the boys, he was concentrating on her, and her alone. She was amazed to realise that she was crying, the tears rolling freely down her lovely face.

Phillip went to her and, as he put his hand out, she felt herself flinch. She saw the horror on his face at her reaction and, looking into his eyes, she said brokenly, 'Oh, Phil, I was so scared something had happened . . .'

It was the right approach, he shook his head slowly and, taking her in his arms, he enveloped her in a hug that almost took the breath from her body.

'Oh, darling Christine, I'm sorry, babe. I had a lot of things to sort out. I didn't want to bring any of it here, into our home. I knew my mother would take care of you.'

He pulled her away from him and kissed her deeply on the lips. She could feel his tongue sliding into her mouth, and had to stifle the urge to gag. Pulling his face noisily away from hers, he looked at her seriously. 'Don't ever be frightened of me, Christine, I could never hurt you, babe. Outside in the real world, I have to be a different person to survive. But in here, in our world, it will always just be us.'

She knew somehow that it was a veiled threat, but following her mother-in-law's lead she forced herself to smile at him. 'I'm just glad you're home safe and sound, Phil.'

Then the tears began again, and he held her and comforted her until eventually she calmed down.

Book Two

Tell me what company you keep and I'll tell you
what you are

Miguel de Cervantes (1547–1616)
Spanish adventurer, author and poet

Man, biologically considered, and whatever else he may be
into the bargain, is simply the most formidable of all the
beasts of prey and, indeed, the only one that preys
systematically on its own species

William James (1842–1910)
American philosopher

Chapter Forty-Five

1998

'Come on, boys, it's time we got going.'

Christine smoothed some lipstick on her lips, as she hunted for the keys to the Range Rover. She could feel Phillip's eyes on her and, turning, she smiled at him. 'All right?'

He answered her truthfully, 'Very, especially as you seem a lot better in yourself, mate. Are the new tablets any good?'

She nodded. 'I feel much better inside meself, Phil. It's like the doctor says, depression is an illness, and it can happen to anyone at any time so, like any illness, I have to get it treated. But these new pills make me feel a million dollars.' She was telling him what he wanted to hear, she always told him what he wanted to hear. For years she had lived beside a man she was terrified of, and the fact that he treated her like a queen just made it all feel worse.

'Well, don't forget tonight we've got Ricky Thomas and his wife coming to dinner. I have a bit of business with him. Are you sure you'll be OK? We can get a chef in, or me mother will cook for us.'

She laughed then. 'I've got it all in hand, Phil. We're having crab cakes to start, roast lamb for the main, and I've already knocked up a lemon posset for dessert. Lastly, we've got a fuck-off cheese board for the wine and brandy. I'll be fine – I love cooking, it relaxes me.'

He grinned, relieved that she wasn't under any undue

159

pressure. 'Well, you're a blinding cook, sweetheart. How lucky was I, eh? Beautiful, clever and a wonderful wife. Fantastic mother, and still the only woman who interests me.'

She turned away from him then, unable to look him in the face. When he spoke like that all it did was make her panic inside. She felt as though he was constantly reminding her she was his.

Philly came into the kitchen; at thirteen he was already big for his age, and he had the dark hair and the blue eyes of his father.

'All right, Dad? Can I come to the arcade again this weekend?'

Phillip smiled. ' 'Course you can, you can work the change booth for me. At least I know I can trust you!' They laughed easily together.

Just then her younger son wandered in to the room. Philly and Timmy were so similar they were like twins born a few years apart and it was uncanny how like Phillip they were – she saw nothing of herself in them. Little Timmy was quieter than his brother though; they all joked that he was deep waters, but, if she was honest, she worried that he seemed to have a bit too much of Phillip's nature in him. Philly had a temper too, but it was quick to flare and just as quick to die out. Timmy, on the other hand, had a temper that was phenomenal in its intensity. She had been forced to remove him from his first playgroup over it – he fought the other kids like a tiger for almost no reasons at all.

'Come on, you two, get in the Range, and no arguing who sits where, OK? Mummy has to have peace and quiet while she's concentrating on her driving, so don't let me hear any fucking stories today about you two rowing, and I mean it.'

Both boys nodded; when Phillip swore they knew he meant business.

'See you later, Dad.'

Christine ushered them from the house and, as she pulled

160

out of the electric gates, she saw Declan on his way in. He waved at her, and she automatically waved back. She liked Declan; he had been good to her over the years, and she had come to rely on him. He was the voice of reason, and strangely Phillip listened to him and respected what he said. These days Declan was the only person on the planet who her husband listened to. Somehow he kept Phillip from going overboard, and for that alone she would be eternally grateful.

Chapter Forty-Six

Ricky Thomas was a big man in his early fifties. He had a young, new wife called Deandra – she had given him two new kids, a boy and a girl, and he had given her a lovely house, new tits and all the clothes she could buy. It was strange because they actually *did* care about one another. Deandra had been brought up on a council estate, with a piss-head for a mother and an errant father. Ricky was everything she had ever wanted in a man; he was a father, a lover and a friend and she adored him.

'Look, Dee, Phillip Murphy can fucking whistle – he's not getting anything from me and I'm going to tell him that tonight, so stop worrying, will you?'

'He's weird, Rick, he scares me.'

'Well, he don't fucking scare me. I've been around the pavements a bit too long for all that old fanny and, besides, he's a businessman at heart. He'll understand I don't want to get rid and that'll be it.'

'Everyone he falls out with either disappears, or has a bad accident – look at his fucking mate Bantry, he's like the poor relation these days. Phillip Murphy is the fucking main face of that operation.'

'Oh, Deandra, will you put a fucking sock in it, girl, it's too early in the morning for aggravation of the ear drums. Go and help the au pair or something.'

She laughed despite herself, he could be funny, could her Ricky. But she had a bad feeling about this business with Murphy.

He had taken over most of the seafront in Southend; buying people out, running them away. She knew how much money there was in the games – after all, it was their livelihood – but she felt that Murphy wanted the whole thing and would stop at nothing to get it.

Ricky lit one of the many cigars he would smoke that day; he was worried all right, but he wasn't about to let Deandra know that. Tonight he had to keep his wits about him and, in the process, stop his livelihood from slipping into Murphy's clutches. He would sit in his house, chat with his Stepford wife, who always looked like she was about to bolt from the room, and eat his grub, all the time being a jovial and congenial guest. He would then tell him in as nice a way possible that he had no intention of selling his arcades, and that there was more than enough room for the two of them. He knew Phillip Murphy had moved in on two clubs recently, and was making a play for everything on the front, even the hot-dog stalls and the fast-food outlets. It seemed he wanted to be king of the seafront. Well, Ricky was fine with that but he was not going to add his own little bit of Essex to Phillip's pile.

He was nervous though, and that annoyed him. It wasn't in his nature – he was a big, gregarious and, sometimes, hard man. This young Phillip Murphy was an anomaly to him, part of the new breed of young Faces – all money and violence, no finesse and certainly no real intelligence. It was the nineties for fuck's sake, all that threatening and posturing went out with the ark. That was for the drug dealers and the foreign fucks, not the locals; they stuck together to make sure the new breed of eastern Europeans didn't infiltrate their patches. Phillip Murphy was a grade-A cunt, and that was his last thought on it. Unfortunately, Phillip Murphy was on his mind all that day, and Ricky knew he was playing a dangerous game with him. The only thing left was to find out who was going to be the victor.

Chapter Forty-Seven

Declan sipped his coffee and listened to Phillip's new game plan. It amazed him that he really believed Ricky Thomas would roll over without a fight, and he said as much. 'Hang on a minute, Phil, Ricky's family have had that arcade since the nineteen twenties. It's a family business – his grandfather started it, and it's all he's ever known. I think you're being a bit premature assuming he's going to swallow without a fight.'

Phillip listened intently to his brother, let him have his say. He was always polite with Declan, he was the one person whose opinion he was even remotely interested in. But he had made up his mind and this was made evident by his next remark. 'The thing is, Dec, I ain't giving him a choice here; he either sells to me at a decent price, or I'll get it by fair means or foul. It's what I want, it's perfect.'

Declan sighed heavily. There was no more to say and they both knew it. It was futile labouring the point; Phillip had made his mind up and that, basically, was that. Declan felt a pang of sorrow for Ricky. He was a nice bloke, out of his league of course, but a nice fella all the same.

'What about this place? How's the pig farming going?'

Phillip grinned. 'Fucking lovely, we decided on Old Spot, a real English pig. Come and have a look at them, they are fucking phenomenal, Declan. Do you know pigs will eat literally anything? Bone, skull, you name it. The only thing they don't eat is the teeth of a carcass – well, they do eat them but shit

164

them out afterwards! And the chickens are amazing. It's like watching a soap opera – one of the cockerels gives each hen a quick shag first thing every morning, randy fucker he is.'

Declan laughed. 'How's the old boy Sammy working out?'

Phillip was pulling on his wellies as he spoke. 'Come and have a looksee. The cottage is finished and I think it's the best digs the poor old fucker ever had. I had Sky put in for him, he's over the fucking moon. But there ain't a thing he don't know about farming or animals. He's like having me own personal Jack Hargreaves, I could listen to him for hours. I've got a couple of the lads working for him too. The kitchen garden is three times the size now, and the polytunnels are all bursting with produce. Honestly, the difference in the taste of the food is amazing. And even more amazing is that young Timmy is turning into a right Farmer Giles – he loves the land. Reckon it must be the Irish in us, eh?'

'Farmer Giles, he got piles then!'

They both laughed as they crossed the yard towards the new piggery. The sounds of the smallholding were wholesome and innocent, pigs snorting, hens clucking and, in the distance, the sheep were dotted about the top field; it was idyllic, it was beautiful and well looked after. Nothing was too good for Phillip's livestock. He had created an oasis for himself, they were more or less self-sufficient now, and this farm was Phillip's number one priority. He fed the whole family on his produce and he was rightly proud of that fact. He had added to the land over the years; through threats and intimidation he had taken on all the surrounding houses and fields. He was like the lord of the manor, and he took his place as the head of the community very seriously indeed.

It was yet another facet of Phillip Murphy's weird and wonderful personality.

Chapter Forty-Eight

Breda was tired. She had had a very late night with a young Jamaican fella with bushy dreads and arms like legs of lamb. She was sated, happy and late for a meeting.

Breda had changed a lot in ten years. She had taken to wearing power suits and expensive shirts, and she ran the clerical side of the games enterprises, sorting out the staff, the wages and other mundane matters that Phillip saw as beneath him. She loved every second of it. She kept a beady eye on everyone, made sure no one was making any money for themselves, and the few times she had found thieving among the staff she had meted out a swift and painful retribution. She had everything she wanted really – respect (her number one priority), money (her second priority) and a job that was interesting, exciting and gave her the chance to show off her skills. Phillip was thrilled with her, and that was the main thing.

Today though, she was having a meeting with a gun specialist who she had come across through a favourite pastime of hers: looking for men of a certain age and disposition. Her criteria were pretty basic: young, healthy, muscular and black. This particular man was called Daniel, and he was a gun runner for the Jamaican Yardies. He could get the best quality guns on the pavement for a fraction of the usual price. They were brought in quickly and safely by boat, and they were distributed with the minimum of fuss. As all the guns were preordered, there was no need to stash them, or find the buyers. It was a pretty neat little operation, and Phillip was pleased at her acumen in getting them all in on the ground floor. The Jamaicans were notoriously difficult to work with, having an inherent distrust of the white Anglo-Saxon male. Somehow Breda had inveigled herself into their world, and she fitted in perfectly where a man wouldn't have been given such a chance. She got on well with Daniel on all levels; they were two of a kind, so understood each other perfectly. The guns she procured were clean, of a superior nature, and didn't have any local bodies on them. She was selling them on for a good profit, and that was as always the bottom line with Phillip.

She was also well in with her mother at the moment because, after all these years, she had talked Phillip into letting Jamsie be her driver. Phillip had never spoken a word to Jamsie since he grassed on Declan, had never even looked directly at him. He always removed himself from Phillip's presence as soon as he heard him enter the house. Even on Christmas Day, as soon as Phil turned up with his family, Jamsie had to go upstairs out of his sight. No one commented on it, it was surreal almost. It was stranger still because Declan had long forgiven him. But it was better than the alternative, and that was Jamsie being murdered by his brother. Jamsie hadn't touched a drink or drugs since he had came home from hospital. It was as if he didn't trust himself to be out of control; he needed to be in his right mind. Now, because of that, he was the perfect driving material, and he was grateful, *so* grateful, to be even a small part of the family firm. It was a thawing of sorts on Phillip's part, but there was still a very long way to go. Breda thought he was humouring her to please their mother but, either way, it was seen by everyone as a coup on her part, and that pleased her very much.

These days she was a really big part of the family firm and, because of that, she had utter respect. Everyone in their orbit treated her with the reverence she felt she deserved. Like Jamsie, she had learned a valuable lesson about how best to get on in the family, and that was by listening to Phillip, taking onboard what he wanted from her, and making sure any orders were carried out to the letter. Having Declan there was an added boon. When he came home, he took up the reins with Phillip, and his presence was a much-needed buffer between them all and Phillip. Forever the voice of reason, Declan was the only person alive that Phil would even entertain being questioned by.

All in all the Murphys' lives were good, and they could only get better. Breda couldn't be more pleased to be an integral and important part of it all.

Chapter Forty-Nine

Veronica was thrilled to bits. The house had just been redecorated from head to foot, courtesy of Phillip and Declan, and it looked amazing. She had enjoyed the whole experience of having the decorators and carpet fitters in. Now the place resembled something from a magazine and she knew the neighbours were impressed, and that alone was enough for Veronica. People saw the esteem her kids held her in and how well they looked after her, and that meant the world to her.

She was also pleased that poor Jamsie was driving for the family firm; that was a huge burden lifted because she had worried over the years that Phillip would hurt him one day. She knew it was only Declan who'd stopped his older brother from taking his retribution and she was grateful for that.

'Hey, Phil, would you look at those curtains! They look like they could be in a stately home with the swags and tails. Did you ever see the fecking like of it!'

Phil Senior sat at the new dining table that now dominated the kitchen-diner and, as usual, he had a racing paper, his fags, and a pot of tea in front of him. He didn't even look up from his perusal of *Sporting Life* as he said quickly, 'They done you proud, girl, no doubt about that.'

'Do you remember when they were all small, Phil, and we'd struggle for a few quid? You out breaking arms for a living and me making meals out of nothing.'

He laughed with her. 'Those were good days, Veronica, we

169

had some good times, love. But the most important thing is that we brought up a crowd of great kids, really great kids. Our Phillip is a fucking diamond. In fairness, he's come on leaps and bounds but he still comes here every day and he hasn't forgotten where he came from.'

This was the kind of talk Veronica loved and her husband knew it. He could spout that shit all day if it kept her happy and he frequently did. The secret with Veronica was making the family, especially Phillip, sound normal, sound like other people. Personally, he had accepted that Phillip had more than a few screws loose when he had used a nail-gun on another boy's elbow when he was fourteen. But, for all that, Phillip was Phillip and he kept them all living like kings, and that, for Phil Senior, was what really counted. He had a nice wedge delivered to him every week, they ate like frigging royalty, all the bills were taken care of, and anything Veronica wanted she only had to mention and it appeared. He drove a nice little BMW all paid for courtesy of his kids, and he knew that no one in their world would ever fall out with him – it would be more than they dared. He owed money to every bookie within a ten-mile radius, but there wasn't much chance of them asking for it – Phillip's rep made sure of that, and Declan wasn't what you would call a walkover. Life was good, all right, it had never been better.

'Do you think Christine's looking better these days?'

Phil Senior just stopped himself from rolling his eyes in annoyance. Christine and her fucking so-called 'nerves' were all Veronica thought about. Personally he couldn't understand it; the girl had everything her heart desired, Phillip had not so much as looked at another bird since he'd married her and the boys were perfecto mondo. She had a drum that most young women could only dream of, a villa in Marbella – a big fucking villa and all, a pool, the lot. Her old man was the reigning king of the seafront, but apparently she still had her 'nerves'. Phillip had dragged that ungrateful little mare to every fucking shrink with letters after his name and they all said the same thing. She suffered from depression. Well, what that silly cunt had to be depressed about he didn't know. He wished he had her problems. Not that he would ever air those opinions out loud, of course; he made all the appropriate noises, he wouldn't queer his pitch with his Phillip for all the tea in China. But, in all honesty, Christine got on his tits; he thought she was an ungrateful little whore and, if it was left with him, he would have given her a kick up the jacksie and told her to fucking grow up.

'She looked lovely yesterday. Them pills are miracle workers apparently, so stop worrying about her, she'll sort herself out.'

Veronica nodded, feeling better now. 'You're right. She's looking happier I think, so that can only be good.'

'Oh yeah, much happier, darling. I saw her smiling yesterday, a real smile and all. Not one of those weird ones she does, when she's off her box on the pills . . .'

Veronica turned on him instantly. 'Don't talk about her like that! She's delicate natured. That loony of a mother is the reason she suffers from her nerves.'

Veronica always blamed Christine's mother, the truth was too much for her to bear. That her son had destroyed that lovely little girl was what kept her up some nights, along with the fact she had talked her into staying with him. Consequently, she took a deep interest in her daughter-in-law's mental state. She knew that Christine Murphy was like a time bomb, and when she finally went off, the reverberations would be felt throughout the land.

Phil Senior decided to retreat on this occasion, so he deftly changed the subject. 'Well, you know best, love. What time are the neighbours in for the grand showing? Are you feeding them as usual?'

Veronica smiled brightly. 'Don't worry, there'll be plenty of food and drink to go round.'

Phil Senior grinned then. 'I got meself a good one with you,

Veronica. You can read me like a book.'

They laughed easily together. 'Yeah, well, we've weathered the years, Phil, not many can say that these days, eh?'

'That's true, my love. Now, how about making me a cup of tea and a slice of cake.'

Veronica went about the chore happily; she was a lucky woman, and she appreciated that. If only young Christine was properly on the mend her life would be just about perfect.

Chapter Fifty

Ted Booth was serving a young man with purple hair and the whole shop reeked of the smell of cannabis emanating from him. Still, the boy was very respectful, and said please and thank you.

Everyone on the estate did now. They used the litter bins provided for their rubbish, even from the chippy, and they all made sure they cashed their giros, pensions and family allowance in his post office. He made a fortune every week, especially since Phillip had got Breda to set up the loan scheme – the profits were all his and Eileen's, so that was another lucrative earner. Yet Ted was a very unhappy man. He did what he was asked and he made a lot of money, but it was wrong in his eyes; they were taking money from people who could barely afford it, who were forever in their debt and often ended up borrowing more money to pay off their existing loans. Unlike his wife, who thought it was great and very appropriate, he thought it was taking advantage of people less well off than themselves.

They had three more shops now, all on similar estates and all doing the same kind of business. What should have made him happy only emphasised to him how deeply he was now enmeshed with Phillip Murphy. If his daughter was happy he might have been able to swallow it all, but she was wasting away before his eyes, there wasn't an ounce of fat on her, and her nerves were terrible.

Yet in fairness to Phillip Murphy, he treated her like a queen; you could see his love for her and them boys. As far as Ted

Booth was concerned that was his only saving grace. He made sure they had a good earn, and he was grateful for that in some ways – it got Eileen off his back anyway. But none of it sat right with him, it was all smoke and mirrors, skulduggery, everything was a con, a scam. He would rather be back where he was, his own man and owned by no one, owing his livelihood to no one but himself.

As he looked out the door and saw the beat copper salute him, he felt the usual amazement that even the police were too frightened to question the fact that his shops were making money hand over fist on an estate that was made up mostly of unmarried mothers, the unemployed and the unemployable. But, as Eileen had pointed out, it suited the Filth, as she now referred to them in her street patois; they were glad they weren't forever having to turn up mob-handed in riot gear. If you listened to her, Phillip Murphy was the South East's answer to Henry Kissinger. Ted waved back at the young plod, and went back to perusing the stock lists; even shoplifting was unheard of these days. So why couldn't he sit back like his wife and enjoy the ride?

Chapter Fifty-One

'That smells fucking handsome, Chris.'

Christine smiled tightly at Phillip's praise, she knew he meant every word of it as well. She had dressed the lamb with rosemary and garlic the night before, covered it in fresh herbs and horseradish butter, and left it to infuse overnight in the fridge. It did smell spectacular. It was their own lamb, slaughtered in their own small abattoir, and hung until it was perfect. Every vegetable was home-grown, and almost every ingredient was from the farm. She was proud of her skills and she loved the whole concept of cooking. When she was in the kitchen she could forget about everything else; she concentrated on the recipe, on preparing her ingredients. She felt a sense of worth when she saw her sons gobbling up her food. She prided herself that they didn't eat shop-bought cakes or biscuits, that she even made the bread they ate. It was how she coped with her life, small things like that made it bearable.

'Well, Ricky and that stick insect he married will be thrilled at the effort, babe, and the table looks wonderful. You were right to serve them in here; the kitchen's a nice informal setting, the dining room would have been a bit overpowering.'

The kitchen table seated twelve; the kitchen was now forty by thirty feet, mostly encased by a huge Victorian conservatory. It was still a kitchen, but one that wouldn't look out of place in *Homes & Gardens* magazine. She liked eating in the kitchen – the five-oven Aga was warming, and she also had an island with a state-of-the-art cooker that had cost more than her car. The kitchen had lovely views of the farm as well, and her herb garden always gave the room a wonderful homely smell, especially when she was baking bread. Everything her little heart could desire she had, and the irony wasn't lost on her. She knew that Deandra envied her the beautiful surroundings, and the wonderful life she had. Everyone she knew did. They couldn't understand her being plagued with her nerves and depression and if she told them everything, they wouldn't see it as a problem like she did. They would see it as Phillip being strong, and being a *man*.

Her father had warned her she was not right for the Murphys and their way of life, and she knew that he hated being a part of it all – that only added to her guilt. She had dragged him into her mess, and that played on her mind a lot. As her sons were growing older she worried about what their lives would become too.

'Are you with us, babe?'

She literally jumped at her husband's words. She had forgotten he was there; it was the new pills, they were strong and she often went into little worlds of her own. 'Sorry, Phil, I was miles away.'

'That's all right, mate. You sure you're all right for tonight? I can easily take them to a restaurant.'

She sighed heavily. 'Please, Phil, I'm fine, and I'd be even better if you stopped asking me if I was all right all the time.' She was looking into his eyes, pleading with him silently to just let her get on with what she was doing.

He shrugged resignedly, and then smiled gently. 'I just worry about you, Chris, the doctor said it was all about not getting overwhelmed, remember?'

'I know that, and I'm sorry I can't be like everyone else, Phil. But I'm all right, I swear. Now go and get changed – they'll be here soon. The boys are staying at Breda's tonight so let's enjoy the quiet, shall we?'

Phillip pulled her into his arms and hugged her close. 'You are perfect to me, you're my world and don't you ever forget that. We'll get you back on your feet, that's a promise, darling.'

She smiled her usual smile, but it was almost a grimace. 'I know, Phil. Listen, that's the gates, Declan must be here. I'll pour him a glass of wine while you tidy yourself up.'

Phillip left the room. She could see she had calmed him – as long as she told him she was OK he was fine. He would move the earth for her, and she was aware of that, but it still didn't change the fact that she was living and sleeping with a man she was terrified of. A man who she knew loved her in his own weird way. She opened the wine and poured two glasses; she had already drained hers when Declan came in the back door. One good thing with wine was that the pills she took worked much better with a few drinks in her. Then she could even stand Phillip making love to her, which he did nearly every day.

'That smells the nuts, Christine.' Declan was rubbing his big hands together in anticipation. 'I'm starving. I ain't eaten all day because I didn't want to ruin me appetite.'

She gave him the glass of wine with a small smile and went back to her prepping. The best thing about Declan was she didn't feel the need to talk to him. Instead he had the knack of talking to her, and making her feel included without her having to force herself to join in the conversation.

Declan watched her work, and marvelled at how Phillip couldn't see what was in front of his face; the girl was living on the edge. She was thinner than Twiggy, and her movements were either jerking all over the place, or she looked like she was walking through water. She was not right in the bonce, and he was sorry for her. In fact, he was sorry for them, because this way they lived surely couldn't go on for ever.

Chapter Fifty-Two

Deandra was watching Christine Murphy as she served the cheese plate. She had cleared the table quietly and unobtrusively, and had then placed the port and brandy in the middle before deftly taking away the wine glasses and the water pitcher and placing a plate of home-made chocolates centre stage. The table still looked wonderful, from the white damask tablecloth to the expensive white lily centrepiece. Deandra was very impressed, you could see this all came naturally to Christine Murphy – she assumed it was her upbringing. Everyone knew her mother was a snob of the first water.

She liked the way Christine worked though; she was quick, and she made it look effortless. The food had been spectacular, and even Deandra, who usually needed a government White Paper before she consumed one calorie, had found herself having seconds. Until tonight she had thought a lemon posset was a small American rodent, so she had learned something new as well. The talk around the table had been good – funny stories, and serious subjects, mixed with the usual innuendo and spattering of gossip about people they knew. All in all, she had really enjoyed the evening. She had been worried about the business, but it seemed she had been wrong there. The subject had not even come up yet and, the way it was going, she felt that Ricky's refusal would be accepted and forgotten about.

She asked Christine again if she wanted any help, and she was politely turned down, as she had hoped she would be. There was nothing worse than going to someone's house for dinner and having to wash up afterwards. What the fuck was all that about? You could clear up at home!

Christine sat down and picked up her wine glass. Deandra had been counting all night and this was her sixth glass. Christine Murphy could certainly put it away, and she looked as sober as a judge, well, as sober as a prescription junkie could look, anyway. Go Christine! Deandra wished she could drink like that. Christine was certainly a dark horse in more ways than one. Two glasses and she herself was pissed and talking bollocks, at least that was what Ricky always told her anyway. He said it was because she drank so much wine all day she was just topping herself up on a regular basis. He could be funny could Ricky, and she took it in good part; after all, nine times out of ten he was spot on about her.

She eyed Phillip and Declan and, in her wine-induced happy state, decided they were both worth a second look – not that she would do anything, but she was a young woman and she could still dream.

Phillip sat back in his chair comfortably. He poured himself and Declan a large brandy, then one for Ricky that was even larger. He was pleased with the evening so far. It had been a very congenial gathering, and he had not detected any undue undertones coming from his guest, so all in all he was a very happy man. But now it was time for the real business of the night. He would do the deal, toast their success, and everyone was a winner.

'Cheers, Rick. Now, I know business isn't fit talk for the dinner table, but we ain't Tory politicians, are we, so have you thought any further about my offer?'

Ricky was lighting one of his huge cigars, and he puffed on it for a few moments before blowing out the smoke lazily and saying in a very forceful but jovial way, 'I have, young Phillip, and I'm afraid the answer's no. I can't see what I'd do with meself if I didn't have the arcades, and there's plenty of room for all of us.'

Phillip was nodding as if in agreement, but the atmosphere in the kitchen changed dramatically. Deandra saw Declan filling up the brandy glasses, and she felt a second's panic shoot through her body.

'But the thing is, Rick, what you don't seem to understand is that I *want* them.'

Ricky heard the determination in Phillip's voice. But the mixture of wine and brandy was already affecting his usual excellent judgement and, laughing, he said, 'Well you can't fucking have them, can you?'

It was meant as a joke, but it came out as a challenge, and everyone around the table was aware of that. Especially Christine Murphy. She knew the signs better than anyone, and Phillip would not take something like that without a fight. She finished her wine quickly, and poured herself another glass; she had a feeling she was going to need it.

Chapter Fifty-Three

Veronica's long-time neighbour and friend Jeannie Brown was admiring the newly decorated house, and her praise was loud and sincere. Jeannie benefited from her friend's good fortune in that she always inherited her old furniture and fittings, and Phillip would send the decorators in to her to give her place a quick lick of paint as well. Like many people, that made her a fan of his for life. She counted herself very lucky to be in with the Murphys, and she never tired of telling anyone and everyone what good people they were. That she had hidden guns and money for them over the years she kept very much to herself. In fact, she was honoured to help them out; after all, they had repaid her a hundredfold.

'You're glowing, Veronica, positively glowing!'

As she spoke Breda came in the back door with Porrick. 'Can I leave him here for a few hours, Mum? I have to meet someone.'

' 'Course you can. He'll have Philly and Timmy for company too. God, Breda, you look lovely.'

Breda grinned. She did look wonderful, and she knew it. 'Well, don't sound so shocked about it. And don't let my Porrick have anything rich, he's been sick as a dog today.'

Her teenage son was white-faced, and his eyes looked sunken in his head. Veronica was immediately concerned. 'Come away in, Porrick love, I'll make you a nice boiled egg, shall I?'

Philly and Timmy laughed. 'Don't forget the soldiers, Nan, he loves his little soldiers.'

Veronica's world was complete. She had her grandsons and her family around her, she had the neighbours all agape at the wonderful home she had been provided with, and her husband had not even gone to the pub. All in all, life was really good.

As she saw Breda out to her car she said happily, 'How's Jamsie doing?'

Breda shrugged. 'All right. Phillip still won't acknowledge his existence, Mum, but it's a start, I suppose.'

Veronica grabbed on to that and held it to her like a charm. 'Well, you know Phillip, he does everything in his own time.'

'Listen, Mum, don't get your hopes up. Jamsie done a fucking terrible thing, and our Phillip's memory is long, and his anger never burns out. So just wait and see what happens, OK? Don't push the issue.'

Veronica nodded sagely, she knew the girl was talking the truth. But her daughter's words saddened her all the same. She hated seeing poor Jamsie so destroyed and, after all, blood was thicker than water. But she would keep her own counsel for a while; as Breda said, Phillip didn't forget easily.

She wandered back into the house but the shine had gone off the night for her.

Chapter Fifty-Four

Ricky was annoyed. He had drunk too much, and a warning voice was telling him that he should leave it. But he couldn't back down in front of Deandra, she was his wife, he couldn't act like a frightened schoolboy, and he didn't want to anyway. Why the fuck should he? There was no law that said he had to sell to Phillip Murphy; that was his choice, and he chose not to. What the fuck was the big deal? He had a lot of mates, Faces, who would stand behind him on this. Word on the street was a lot of people were fed up with Phillip Murphy anyway. He had trampled on a lot of people, and made a ton of fucking enemies over the last few years.

'You've disappointed me, Ricky. I assumed this was going to be a very convivial arrangement because me and you both know that it's the right thing to do. I was even going to offer you a percentage for ten years to sweeten the pot.' Phillip was shaking his head now, as if he was the victim of the most outrageous skulduggery imaginable and he did not look happy about it.

Ricky noticed that Declan was avoiding eye contact with him, Deandra and Christine were both mortified, and somehow Ricky felt it was all his fault. This just incensed him even more; he felt like he was the bad bastard now and all he was doing was trying to protect his earn, that was hardly a fucking crime. He was looking out for his own, it was a natural reaction.

'I'm sorry you feel that way, Phillip, and I'm sorry it's come to this, but I own the arcades and I don't want to sell them. End of. You've got more than enough to keep you occupied. You've walked away with most of the fucking front as it is.' He started to poke his finger towards Phillip now, all common sense gone. 'And let me tell you, there's a few people who think you've already got too much.'

Declan got up suddenly and the scraping noise as he pushed back his chair was loud and threatening in the room. 'That's enough, Ricky, shut the fuck up before you go too far. Why are you making this so personal, eh? What have we ever done to you for you to treat us like this?' He was pointing his finger right into the man's face and it was evident to everyone that he was barely holding his temper together. What he was really doing though was taking the onus off Phillip, because Phillip could quite easily get out of his own chair, pick up the boning knife, and gut Ricky like a fish over what he had just said.

Ricky sat back in amazement. All caution gone now as the anger enveloped him. 'Oh, so we've got muppet number two now, have we? You fucking listen to me, the pair of you. *I* own the fucking arcades, *me*. And I ain't aiming them out for you or anyone else, and that, my friends, is called *my* fucking prerogative. *Mine*. Not yours, not your big brother's or fucking King Street Charlie's, it's *mine*. Now I came here to tell you no, and I thought that would be that. All grown-ups together, a big so what, and see you around. I never expected to have you demand what's mine, because you can demand till the cows come home, you ain't fucking getting it.'

Declan was watching Phillip closely now; he hoped he would keep it together, for all their sakes. Phillip was a wild card at the best of times, and it wasn't sensible to front him up like that. Ricky should know better. Declan was aware that it was only Christine's presence that was stopping Phillip from killing this mad cunt like a rabid dog.

Phillip wiped a hand across his face; he looked hurt, devastated and like a puppy who had been kicked by a gang of glue-sniffing skinheads.

'I am amazed at you attacking me like this, Rick, and please, who are the people who think I've got enough? Who the fuck are they to tell me what I can and can't own, eh? You know where to come when you get strong-armed. Phillip Murphy will sort it out. "Oh, Phil, someone's threatening me, or they're selling drugs on my premises." I'm all right then though, ain't I? When I am doing you all fucking favours. I am trying to build myself an enterprise, I never made a fucking secret of it. That front has never been run better – there's less violence, less fucking scamming, the punters feel safer and return with their families again and again. How you can accuse me of pushing in, I don't know, I have done every cunt there a favour in some way or another. *You* especially. You've got a short memory, Ricky. I bailed you out last year when you were being forced out of business by Micky Driscoll. I sorted him for you and, if I remember, you were more than grateful to get that mad cunt off your back. Well, if you don't fucking sell to *me*, I'll let him know you're open for business again, and you can fucking deal with him on your own, or with the fucking big mates you've suddenly acquired from somewhere. Now, get your coat and get out of my drum before this all really does go too far.'

Christine was still staring at the tablecloth, her heart hammering in her ears, fear spiralling up inside her. She knew Phillip was using all his considerable willpower not to physically attack Ricky in front of her.

Deandra was in outright shock, she couldn't believe what she had witnessed. Getting up unsteadily, she picked up her handbag and left the kitchen as quickly as possible, squeezing Christine's shoulder gently as she passed her.

Declan gestured for Ricky to go.

Ricky was like a man in a trance; he knew he had caused something bad, and he knew it was something that could never be resolved. Not now. He had, in effect, fucked himself from here to Barnsley, and the more that thought broke into his drink-filled mind the more the fear consumed him. He couldn't understand how this had happened. All right, Phillip had helped him out before and he had been grateful. But now he felt he was the one in the wrong because he should somehow feel honour bound to give Phillip Murphy what he had not wanted to give Micky Driscoll. What the fuck had occurred here? Why did he feel like he was the one in the wrong, and why was he suddenly convinced that he had just signed his own death warrant?

As he drove out of the electric gates, he was still reeling from the night's events. And it didn't help when Deandra said angrily, 'And you've got the cheek to say that *I* talk bollocks when I'm pissed!'

Chapter Fifty-Five

Christine was loading both her dishwashers, but her mind was still on the conversation at the table. She could hear Phillip talking as if he was amazed at what had taken place. He might be playing the innocent but she knew that Phillip would take those arcades by fair means or foul. He wanted them, and that was enough justification for him.

She was sad; she liked Deandra, and she was sorry that the night had descended into chaos. Still, the food had been blinding. Kind of like a last supper; well, for poor Ricky anyway. She allowed herself a small smile at that. She was cleaning up like a woman possessed; it was strange, but cleaning made her feel more in control of everything around her. Every drawer in the house was tidy, every wardrobe, every cupboard. The shrink said it was her way of coping with the chaos in her mind, the need for complete control over her environment. She thought he talked shite, but she wouldn't say that to him. She cleaned and cooked because it stopped her from thinking too much. She was done in no time and, pouring herself a large glass of port, she kissed her husband gently and said goodnight to him and his brother.

Phillip grabbed her arm, and kissed her hand. 'I'm sorry about that, Chris. All that work, that handsome grub, fucking too good for the likes of them.'

She shrugged, resigned to the inevitable. 'Well, you'll sort it all out, Phil. I'm going to have a nice bath and go to bed. See you tomorrow, Declan.'

She walked from the kitchen, and in the large entrance hall, she stopped by the antique bureau, opened the large leather address book and crossed out Deandra's home and mobile numbers. After all, she wasn't likely to be seeing her again in the near future, was she?

Chapter Fifty-Six

Breda was in a small drinking club; she was already well oiled, and the young Jamaican with her was keeping her supplied with rum and Coke. She knew she should leave but she was enjoying herself. She had already concluded her business, and meeting this young man, with the smiling eyes and the ready grin, was a nice diversion. It was a smart little club, well attended and only open to people with something to offer. It was a meeting place for the movers and shakers of the criminal underbelly and, as such, it had a decent clientele. Breda knew most of them and was making the most of the social aspect as well as the business contacts.

Phillip left her to deal with a lot of the day-to-day stuff, and she knew that he appreciated how well she handled it. She was thrilled about them acquiring the two new arcades, because that would mean they had the seafront at Southend basically sewn up. If they didn't own it, then they were paid a percentage by the renters to trade. It was a very lucrative and easy market. She had it well under control – she could run it in her sleep.

She was very surprised to get a text on her phone telling her to get round Phillip's immediately. Declan was not a drama queen so she knew something serious had occurred. She left immediately, regretting her drinking bout already, and determined to sober up before she got to Phillip's. But not before taking her young Jamaican's number and filing it away for future reference.

Chapter Fifty-Seven

'Will you come to bed, Ricky? Sitting here in the dark ain't going to change the night's events, is it?'

Deandra was worried, she had never seen Ricky like this before. He was usually so strong, and that was what had initially attracted her. She would never forget meeting him in the pub all that time ago. She had been seventeen, and he was in his forties. She had been bowled over by him. He dressed well, had money, and an interesting face; when he smiled he was almost handsome. He had talked to her, *really* talked to her, and the attraction between them had been instant and electric. She had fallen for him then and there, and she had fallen hard. He had kids older than her, and grandchildren older than her own kids. But it had worked because over the years even his daughters had realised she genuinely cared for him. He had been divorced a long time, and they had not believed he would ever marry again, especially not to a young girl like her. But they had weathered it, and now they were a big happy family. She was terrified now that this was all going to end because Ricky had fallen out with Phillip Murphy.

Her initial reading of Phillip had been right, he was the poison that would infect their lives. Her husband had basically thrown down the gauntlet to a man who was capable of literally anything. Now there was a threat hanging over them, and she feared it was going to crush them no matter what Ricky did to try and stop it.

'Please answer me at least, Ricky, I'm frightened.'

Ricky sighed in the darkness and, leaning forwards, he switched on a lamp. The light was soft and the room looked beautiful. Deandra had made the house lovely, their lives were wonderful, he had never been happier in his whole life than during the years he had spent with her. She had given him something he had never dreamed of: peace of mind, and the joy that comes with being with a woman he loved, admired and respected. And he did respect her, and he knew that she loved him wholeheartedly, and now, through his own fault, through his own vanity, he feared he would have to leave her and the children to cope without him. Because he had a terrible feeling that Phillip Murphy was not about to let this lie. In fact, he knew that the only way Phillip Murphy would be placated would be by his complete obliteration. His only chance was a massive grovel, and that was what he was now willing to do.

He had already decided that he was going to go back to the farm first thing in the morning, go straight to Phillip and apologise. But a little voice was telling him that it was too little too late. He was willing to do the biggest about-face since the Germans had conceded the war and, as hard as it would be, he knew he would do it to protect his family, and his way of life. Phillip Murphy already owned the arcades, that was a fact, all that was left now was giving them to him with the least aggravation and trying to get a decent price, because Phillip would want them for nix now. Ricky would be forced to sweeten the pot at the expense of his own lifestyle. It would be the only way he could walk away with any chance of retaining his life. The saddest part for him was that once he had sobered up, he couldn't think of one person he knew who would be willing to front Murphy up and stand beside him in his hour of need. That in itself was a sobering thought.

'I'm sorry about tonight, babe. I was pissed, I'll sort it all out tomorrow.'

She slipped on to the sofa beside him, and he automatically held her in his arms. He loved her so much. He could kick himself for worrying her like this. What the hell had he been thinking?

'Let him have them, Rick, nothing is worth all this, and anyway, we talked about you retiring and now seems the perfect opportunity. We could finally move to Spain, we've talked about it long enough. And I understand if we have to tighten our belts a bit, that won't bother me, as long as we're together, that's all that matters.'

He knew she meant every word and he felt the sting of tears at her utter loyalty to him and their marriage. 'We ain't going to be on our uppers, love, but I appreciate the sentiment all the same.'

He squeezed her to him again, and felt some of the tension leave her body. He knew she had mentioned Spain so he would have a legitimate reason for leaving the country and his problems behind. She was a good girl all right, bless her. He could only pray to God that he could salvage something from this mess, but he honestly didn't hold out much hope.

Chapter Fifty-Eight

'Calm down, Phil, getting aggravated ain't going to help us out now, is it?'

'All I've done for that ponce, and he shames me in me own house.'

'Well, I think that tomorrow in the cold light of day he will be on the blower, all contrite. We'll get the arcades, and at a song. I mean, let's face it, Phil, he's going to have to really fucking grovel after tonight's little fiasco.'

The thought cheered Phillip, and he finally broke into a smile. 'Yeah, you're right. He'll be at panic stations now, won't he, wondering how best to talk himself out of the trouble. I really thought he was going to go for it, though. And what was all that about other people thinking I had too much? I want to know exactly who *they* are.'

Declan had wondered how long it would be before the real nub of his brother's ire came out. Ever since that idiot Ricky had said those words he had known that Phillip would not let it lie until he had all the names, addresses and phone numbers of the people he would now see as his mortal enemies. He would then feel honour bound to let them know what he thought about them, and that could never be good for business. Declan knew that it was normal to be cunted when you were in the position they were, it was a natural reaction on the part of the people they were pushing aside. It always caused a bit of jealousy and resentment, it was better people let off steam with words than actions. After all, as their old mum had always said, sticks and stones.

Phillip, however, took what people said about him a bit too seriously, his whole life was about how he was perceived, about what people thought of him, and what he had achieved. Success meant a lot to Phillip, not just the money side of it, but also the lifestyle that came with it. He had always cared far too much about other people's opinions. Even poor Christine had become a casualty of Phillip's striving for perfection; no one could live up to his expectations, least of all a girl who was terrified of her husband, and had to pop pills just to get out of bed in the morning.

As much as Declan loved his brother, and he *did* love him, it was this part of his make-up that Declan always felt made him weak. A lesser man wouldn't care what people said about them, it would be enough to know they were feared *and* revered. Not Phillip though, he had to be feared, respected, and *liked*, and with the best will in the world Phillip was a lot of things, but likeable wasn't one of them.

Breda came in and broke the tension. She was red-faced from the biting wind, but Declan was pleased to see she looked up for anything, even at this late hour. He wondered which little Rasta's sex life had been interrupted by his summons.

Phillip nodded at her, and she sat down at the table quickly.

'Tomorrow, Breda, I want you to start asking around the front about people's opinion of us, especially me. It's come to my attention that we're being cunted up hill and down dale. I want to know who the culprits are, and then I want them dealt with. If we start letting people get away with insubordination we lay ourselves wide open to being mugged off. I want this nipped in the bud.'

Breda nodded sagely, wondering what the fuck Phillip was on about. She wasn't going to ask him though – Declan would fill her in on the score at a more appropriate time. She could see

Phillip was on one, and she knew the best thing to do was keep quiet, keep her head down, and agree with whatever he said to her.

Declan passed her a cup of coffee and she sipped the hot liquid gratefully. 'I'll get on it first thing, and see what I can find out.'

Phillip went on, 'Yeah, it pays to keep people on their toes. By the way, we're taking everything Ricky's got, and we're taking it for a third of its value. You need to find out exactly what that is. He'll accept, don't worry about that. But I want you to deal with him, OK?'

She nodded once more. Seems the big party night all ended in tears. Still, she would find out everything soon enough. 'I have the figures on me desk, I'll let you know first thing.'

'You're a good girl, Breda. How's that treacherous bastard Jamsie doing?'

She smiled sadly. 'All right. Mum's thrilled anyway. But, in fairness, Phil, he don't even drink a shandy these days, let alone snort anything. I think he's a changed man.'

'He would fucking need to be, wouldn't he?'

She didn't answer him, she knew he was looking for a reason to take his ire out on someone and Jamsie was not going to be his whipping boy tonight. Not if she could help it anyway. 'By the way, I got the firearms, they get delivered next Thursday. I've taken the liberty of renting some garages in Chigwell. They are down a little lane, and it's not somewhere the Old Bill frequent. They're owned by a retired colonel who's fallen on hard times. Basically he owes Benny the Bookie, who owes me a favour. I'm getting them all delivered there, OK?'

Phillip and Declan laughed together at her front.

'Fuck me, Bred, comes to something when even the Colonel Blimps have to resort to a bit of honest skulduggery to make ends meet.'

'I thought you'd appreciate the irony, especially as his

195

daughter is married to the Chief Super's son.'

They were all really laughing now, and Declan could have kissed Breda – she knew just how to work Phillip, and bring him round to a better frame of mind. Even if they got a capture, the fact it was so close to the Filth would work in their favour. She was a shrewdie was Breda and she could find out anything about anyone, which she frequently did. Then she worked out how best the information could work in their favour. Declan knew he would have to put the hard word on her about not letting Phillip know too much about what was said about him. But he'd sort that as and when he had to.

'Suppose I'd better go up the wooden hill to Bedfordshire.'

As they all got ready to say goodbye, Phillip said thoughtfully, 'Shame really, ain't it?'

Declan slipped his overcoat on and said calmly, 'What is, Phil, what's a shame?'

'Ricky killing himself. That'll cause a ripple through the manor.'

Breda and Declan didn't say anything, both were digesting what he had said.

'Being so well liked, especially by all his *mates*, it'll come as a big shock to the local community, I can tell you that.' Turning to leave the room Phillip said over his shoulder, 'Lock up on your way out, Declan.'

Breda shook her head sadly, and Declan shrugged in frustration. They both knew poor Ricky was living on borrowed time.

Chapter Fifty-Nine

Phillip looked good, as if he had slept the sleep of the just and the righteous, which of course, in his mind, was exactly what he had done.

As Christine placed a large Aga-cooked breakfast before him, he was all smiles and camaraderie. The boys were being dropped off at school by Jamsie, which had pleased his mother no end as she saw him becoming what she insisted on calling indispensable, and Declan was on his way over to sort out the day's business. Christine had slept well too, at least as well as you could sleep on three Valium and nine glasses of alcohol. Not even groggy, she had slipped out of bed, showered and dressed by six thirty. Phillip had a habit of wanting early morning sex which she didn't share so she was up and about as soon as, making him his breakfast, and preparing to give the already-spotless house yet another good cleaning. She made it seem important, and she knew Phillip was proud of her cleanliness, and overlooked her reluctance to lie in bed with him. She had told him the doctor had said her lack of libido was due to the meds, just as she blamed everything on the meds. Deep down Phillip had to know the truth but he wouldn't challenge her, because he wouldn't want to admit it. He knew what was really wrong with her, and he knew *she* knew. It was like the old song.

She laughed gently to herself, and noticed Phillip watching her intently. She was flying higher than a Boeing 747 and she liked it: she felt carefree, loose and almost happy this morning and, after last night's fiasco, that could only be a good thing. She would have to double up on the pills more often if they made her this energetic and happy. And later, she would have a nice cold glass of vin; whoever had invented wine was a fucking god, and that would set her up for the evening.

'You all right, Phil? You're staring at me.'

'I was just thinking how beautiful you are when you're happy – not that you ain't beautiful when you're sad, but when you smile, Chris, it really lights you up inside.'

She shrugged. 'The new pills are working, I think, they make me feel happier than I have in a long time.'

He nodded. 'I can see that. Shall we go out tonight? Have a meal, a few drinks and a laugh?'

She nodded. She knew it would please him, and she would be glad to get out of the house for a few hours. 'That sounds lovely. Get all dressed up, and paint the town red.' She could see how happy she had made him, and for a split second she felt guilty because it took so little to please him.

'I'll show you the new club later on. You will love it – it's really upmarket and the décor is superb, like something out of a fashion magazine. Really tasteful.'

He loved showing her how well he had done, it was important to him that she understood how hard he worked for them all. She knew that what he really wanted was her approval, and that it would make her life much easier if she just gave it to him. But it was hard at times, playing a part, pretending every minute of every day, it got her down. She felt the depression looming again, like a dead weight, and forced herself to stop thinking too much about her life.

'I'll look forward to it, Phil.'

She would dress up for him and wear her best jewellery; it made him proud when people admired her. He loved to see people gasp at their obvious wealth. She decided she would raid the safe and really go to town. Even get her hair and nails done.

She was surprised to find she was actually looking forward to it, and she saw that as a step in the right direction.

She heard someone pressing the electric gates, and automatically opened them, assuming it was the postman, so she was surprised to see Ricky pulling up in his top-of-the-range Mercedes. She saw him get out with a huge bunch of flowers, and a very contrite expression on his face; she had to admire his guts, if not his common sense.

'It's Ricky, Phil.'

Phillip shrugged and carried on eating his breakfast.

Ricky came through the back door all false smiles and obvious embarrassment. Christine went to greet him and, giving her the flowers, he said loudly, 'For you, Christine, an apology for my boorish and drunken behaviour last night. I have been getting serious earache off Deandra over my actions and I can only blame the surfeit of wine and brandy. Can you ever forgive me?'

Before she could answer Phillip said loudly, 'She might, but I fucking won't.'

He was wiping his mouth with his napkin, and sitting there, in his tracksuit bottoms, bare chested and needing a shave, it struck Christine just how very good-looking he actually was. His deep blue eyes were focused on Ricky, and she could feel the power of his gaze herself like a physical thing. It was accusatory, showing how upset he was at what had happened last night, and it was also devoid of any sympathy or pity for Ricky's obvious discomfort. Taking the huge bunch of flowers she left the kitchen, and made her way through to the utility rooms, shutting the heavy baize door behind her. She didn't want to hear any of this conversation, not today. She couldn't cope with any of it.

Ricky was on his own.

Chapter Sixty

'Look, Phillip, I can't fucking apologise enough, mate . . .'

Phillip was leaning back in his Carver chair, relaxed, with an interested look on his face. He was secretly pleased that Ricky had been so worried he had come round his drum first thing; it appealed to his sense of honour and respect. It showed just how worried the man had been. That appeased him in small measure. He appreciated it when people put their hand up – as far as he was concerned, it showed true strength of character. To be able to admit your mistakes was something all the powerful generals had been willing to do throughout history. It was a sign of good leadership, it was also a sign of shrewdness, because anyone with half a brain knew Phillip wasn't the type to swallow last night's events without some kind of retaliation.

'I bet you can't. But the thing is, Ricky, you not only mugged me off, you mugged me off in my own home in front of my wife. Now everyone knows how I feel about my wife – she is a very fragile girl, what with her delicate constitution, and last night's outrageous behaviour on your part upset her deeply, as it did me.'

He still hadn't offered the man a seat and, as he resumed his breakfast, Ricky felt like an errant schoolboy in front of the headmaster.

'I realise that, Phil, that's why I'm here first thing. I don't know what came over me. I feel like a right cunt and, on my life, Phil, I'd do anything to put it right. Get it all sorted. Of course

I'll sell the arcades to you, we had a good deal there, and I know that better than anyone. So can we put this behind us?'

Phillip was mopping up the last of his egg yolk with a slice of home-made bread and, popping the food into his mouth, he chewed on it thoughtfully before washing it down with the last of his tea. Then, standing up, he sniffed loudly and looked Ricky over as if deciding what to do about him. Finally he said, 'Talk to Breda, she'll know what to do.' Turning casually he left the kitchen, and let the door shut behind him loudly, leaving Ricky standing there like a fool.

Ricky felt somehow that he had got off quite lightly. He had expected a real hammering this morning, and he was pleased he was still in one piece – at least he could go home now and put poor Deandra's mind at rest. She was like a cat on a bonfire, so this should calm her down some.

Chapter Sixty-One

Breda was already at the offices in Southend which she loved as they were so palatial and conducive to work. Everyone looked smart, and the place was more or less legit, which was even better. This was where they did all their real business and the accountants and lawyers were put at their ease by the atmosphere here. She glanced out the window. The sea was quite calm today. Usually, when the waves were crashing in she liked to open the windows to enjoy the sound of the sea. She found it soothing, it made her feel at one with herself. She was in her own little world here, and she liked it that way. When Phillip was here everyone kowtowed to him, and she respected that; after all, this was his at the end of the day. But once he left, it became her domain once more, and she could relax and rule in peace.

She had the figures ready for Ricky, and she had discussed the events of last night at length with Declan. She couldn't help feeling sorry for the man, he had to have been off his trolley to try and front Phillip like that. But she still felt a twinge of guilt at what she was going to offer him, and the reasons why. She waited patiently for him to arrive, her pulse racing at the thought of what she was going to do, but the need to do it overriding any guilt she might feel. Phillip was her main priority, as he was anyone's with half a fucking brain in their head, and that was something that Ricky Thomas should have thought about before he opened his big flapping trap.

As she saw him stroll through to the outer office she took a deep breath. She hated being Phillip's axe lady, but it was what kept her in designer clothes, and a fuck-off house, so she was willing to do whatever she felt was needed to keep her livelihood. But she liked Ricky Thomas. In fact, she had had a fling with him many years before, and he had treated her well, very well. Still, that was then and this was now and there was no place for sentiment in business – Phillip was always reminding her of that.

Chapter Sixty-Two

'All right, Sammy Boy, how are the girls?'

Samuel Gardiner grinned his toothless grin. He liked Phillip Murphy, the man had an instinct for the land that wasn't often seen in townies. Phillip reckoned it was the Irish in him; personally Samuel thought any Irish in him would have been from a navvy, a road builder, but he kept that gem of wisdom to himself. No, Sam believed that you either got the land or you didn't. Look at his own boys – neither of them had taken to it. Both had factory jobs, whereas this lad here could almost smell the loam. It was all instinct, and this lad had it, wherever it had come from.

'They're good, Phil, happy as the proverbial pigs in shit!'

Phillip looked proudly around the new building. The pigs were settled, and the place had the rich smell of the earth about it. Sammy was over the moon with all the new equipment, and a free hand with the whole place. Phillip was learning from him, and he loved it, couldn't get enough of the old man's wisdom and common sense. Phillip actually respected very few people, but Old Sammy was top of his list. His own father didn't come close, but when all was said and done he was his father and that was that. Phillip kept him, as he was honour bound to, but it galled him at times that his father had never done a real day's collar in his fucking life. Sammy, on the other hand, had worked since he was twelve, out in all weathers, and was a better man than most for it. Phillip felt relaxed around him, as if he was with a kindred spirit. He wanted to learn everything this old boy had inside his head, and only then would Phillip feel he was good enough to run this place by himself. He had already made provision for Sammy – he would have the use of his cottage on the farm until he died, then it passed back to Phillip. Sammy knew this and was grateful, but he was also a proud man so, after an initial grunt of thanks, it had never been referred to by either of them again. That was how Phillip felt things should be.

'She'll litter soon, the fat bitch, and we'll see some life come to this place, I can tell you. She's low, Phillip, so I'd say she has a good brood there. Look at her, she knows you. Clever bastards, pigs – people don't realise that.'

The sow was already holding up her head for a scratch, and Phillip obliged her, pleased at her trust and her recognition.

'She's getting extra feed, bless her, and I keep me ear out of a night in case anything occurs, like. But, to be honest, son, she's a Brahma – she'll shit them out without a second's thought.'

Phillip laughed; he loved the old boy's colourful descriptions. 'You reckon?'

'I know so. Been doing this for nearly sixty years, I know a troublesome pig when I see one. She's got a lovely nature, this one, and she'll have good porkers, I guarantee it.'

Phillip was pleased. He walked to the top field and looked at the sheep. They were happy enough. Christine liked a hogget at the end of the year as she preferred the stronger meat, though he liked the spring lamb himself. But then, she was such a good cook he happily ate whatever was put in front of him. He enjoyed his food, he loved everything about it: the presentation, the pleasure in eating and, now they grew both meat and vegetables, he liked that they all ate organic and wholesome produce. He was obsessed with the environment, going so far as to have erected huge greenhouses for the growing of the more exotic fruits and veg he liked. He conveniently forgot that he imported drugs from South America, and the effect that had on the local ecology there. He was good at justifying himself, in fact he could completely separate his two lives at will. It was a necessity that most people in his world had long learned to do.

This was his little bit of England, and he walked his land with the knowledge he was doing something worthwhile with his time. He supplied a lot of the local restaurants with his produce, and he made sure that they got the best of the best. After all, they were paying top dollar for it, as they should. The chickens were happy, the farm made a profit, and he felt he had achieved something that most people never do: complete oneness with himself, and the animals around him. Sammy had taught him early on to feel the land, and he had laughed at first, but now he understood what the old fucker was talking about. He could smell the rain in the air, and feel when it was going to snow, he knew whether a day would be bright or heavy with showers.

All this made him feel, for the first time ever, a real part of something. All his life he had felt an outsider, now he didn't feel that quite so much, and for that alone he would always thank Sammy Boy. The farm gave him peace of mind, and that was something he had never really experienced before. Seeing things grow gave him such a sense of worth, and, even now, every time he picked up an egg, he felt the same thrill as he had when he had found the first one all those years ago. Sammy told him that all farmers had to be naturally ruthless – you grew it, you slaughtered it and you ate it; there was no place for sentiment on a farm. That was no problem for Phillip whatsoever.

He glanced at his watch. Breda would be arriving soon with her update on Ricky Thomas and the acquisition of his arcades. Then he was taking Christine out later. All in all, he felt he was the lucky recipient of a very good day.

Chapter Sixty-Three

Christine was manicured and blow-dried to within an inch of her life, and she knew she looked good. Not that it was going to help her now. As she drove through the gates with her elder son beside her, she felt the urge to cry.

'He is going to go ballistic, Philly, what the fuck was you thinking of?'

Philly was white-faced with fear; he knew he was in big trouble, very big trouble indeed. It wasn't often his father went off on one, but when he did it was always over the top and something you remembered for a long time.

'Have you got to tell him, Mum?'

She looked into her son's strained face and, shaking her head sadly, she said, 'They've expelled you, I think that is going to warrant an explanation of some sort, don't you? Think yourself lucky they didn't get the police involved. His car's there. Get indoors and go straight to your room – you'll know when he's been apprised of the situation, they'll hear him go off on one from the next county.'

She watched her son run into the house and her heart broke for him. But at the same time what he had done was so awful she felt that he needed to be taught a lesson and she was going to make sure he got one.

Chapter Sixty-Four

Phillip was looking at Christine as if he had never met her before in his life. His wife, his Christine, had just informed him that his elder son had been expelled from school. Just like that. No warnings, nothing. Out the door like a fucking nothing, a nowt, and after all he had paid them bastards to educate the child.

'Sit down, Phillip, and let me explain.'

'Was he fighting again?'

She shook her head quickly, wishing it *was* fighting, at least they knew how to cope with that.

'Well, what then? What the fuck's he done, Chris?'

She looked at his handsome, bewildered face and said loudly, 'He was drug dealing, fucking drug dealing at St John's, the best, most expensive school in the fucking county, run by Jesuits, and attended by the children of the great and the good.'

Phillip was absolutely shell-shocked at her words. 'Drug dealing? My Philly? Are they sure?'

She nodded almost imperceptibly. 'They were watching him for ages, caught him on a hidden camera in the boys' toilets. He's been selling cannabis and Es. Nice state of affairs, isn't it? All that fucking money, and for what?'

'Did they call the Filth?'

She shook her head. 'No, thank God, they don't want this out there any more than we do. But I was so ashamed, Phil. I mean, where's he getting it from? You'll have to find that out because he won't tell me. If people hear about this he's finished for any other school . . .'

'What about Timmy, is he involved?'

'No, that's one thing we can be pleased about. He's not involved at all.'

Phillip finally sat down and, grabbing his wife's hands, said confidently, 'We'll nip this in the bud, Chris, I'll sort the school out, get him back there, and I'll make sure he never does anything like this again. So stop worrying, all right? We can sort this.'

He got up and walked out into the entrance hall, bellowing loudly up the newly carved, curved staircase that was his pride and joy, 'Get your fucking arse down here now, boy!'

For the first time ever, Christine hoped that her husband's phenomenal temper would be used to make her son realise the seriousness of what he had done. She knew he needed a short, sharp shock, and Phil was just the man to deliver it. If it made sure Philly never sold another drug in his life, she was willing to see him hospitalised if necessary. Because this was not a boyish prank, this was dangerous, adult behaviour that could one day see him put in prison. For once she was relying on her husband's volatile nature to do some kind of good, because if the boys went to the bad, she would be finished.

Chapter Sixty-Five

'He offered you what?'

Ricky Thomas was still reeling from the morning's events. 'He ain't offered it, Dee, that's what we've been *given*. The bastard certainly got his pound of flesh, and I have to swallow me knob and wipe me mouth. Nothing else I can do, darling.'

Deandra wasn't a businesswoman, but even she knew this was a paltry sum of money, and she was upset about it; after all, this was their earn they were talking about. 'The rotten cunt, he wants to see us crawl, that's what this is all about.'

'Breda explained that the less we took, the more Phillip was liable to forget the insult. As she pointed out, he is known for holding a grudge longer than a Freemason. She also pointed out that he has businesses in Spain and Portugal, where he could make it very difficult for us to settle there on a permanent basis. Look, it ain't all bad news. Once we sell up here we'll still have a good wedge, and we can start again with that.'

She nodded slowly, still taking in the fact that their life, their lovely life as they had always known it, was well and truly over. 'You had to fucking get drunk, didn't you? Now look what we're left with. No money and our lives in ruins.'

She burst into tears, and Ricky went to her; he had never felt so bad in his life before. At least he had escaped with a life of some sort, but this wasn't the time to mention that. Instead he held her as she cried and wished, like Cher, that he could turn back fucking time.

Chapter Sixty-Six

Father Theobald was not used to being interrupted by irate fathers and, as he looked at Phillip Murphy, he realised that this was not a man who could be fobbed off without what the Americans liked to call a full and frank discussion. Sighing in resignation, he offered the man a seat and then, sitting opposite him at his large antique desk, he waited for him to say his piece.

Phillip sat down heavily. Lighting a cigarette, he slowly and deliberately blew the smoke at the old priest before saying, 'When I have said my piece I am leaving here and going straight to the police. I am telling them that my boy was offered drugs to sell by the Right Honourable Ian Halpern's son who, at sixteen, is three years older than my boy. It seems he gets the drugs from his older brother, who grows the grass himself in the grounds of Yardley Hall. I can only wonder where they get the Es from. I am also going to see my legal people about suing you, Halpern and everyone else I can think of, including the fucking *Pope*, because my boy is being used as the scapegoat here. I wouldn't mind, but that cunt Halpern ain't even a fucking *Catholic*! You must think I am a right fucking pushover, *Father*, if you believed I was going to swallow this lot without a fight. Well, you picked on the wrong boy here, mate. My son was *forced* to sell that stuff. He's thirteen years old. Thirteen! When this hits the fucking papers, I am going to tell everyone how shocked, how disgusted, and how distraught I am at this school's lack of security, lack of moral fibre, and I will explain how my boy was fitted up because we're just Irish nothings to you people. You protect the rich and the well known at the expense of the children they are exploiting. And, furthermore, you had no right to terrorise my *wife* – you know how fragile she is. I'll give you fucking expulsion without further ado. I'm going to take your words and shove them right back up your jacksie. I can buy and sell Halpern, the man relies on me for his daily bread. Bet you didn't know that, did you? I bailed him out two years ago, and I own the Hall – they rent it from *me* now. But not for long now that I know they are growing drugs on my premises. So you backed the wrong horse today, didn't you, Theobald me old china plate. You treacherous bastard, you. Now what you got to say about that, eh?'

Chapter Sixty-Seven

Christine was stoned out of her head after drinking three glasses of Chardonnay and taking two more of her pills. As Phillip walked back into the house, she was waiting expectantly in the hallway for him, her hand to her throat in a gesture of naked fear. Philly was hanging back behind her.

Phillip smiled at her widely. 'Sorted.' He pushed his son towards the stairs. 'You get yourself up there and I'll deal with you in a minute.'

Christine saw the boy run up the stairs as if he had the hounds of hell on his heels.

'He's back to school tomorrow, Chris. I gave the priest a few home truths, and we came to an understanding of sorts.'

Christine followed him into the kitchen, her face registering her shock at his words. 'What kind of home truths? You didn't threaten the priest, Phil!'

Phillip laughed at her incredulity. 'I simply pointed out the downside of all this becoming public knowledge. Do you know what, Christine? All the money we've weighed out to that old cunt, and he looks down at us like we crawled from under a stone. Well, he had a fucking shock today. Philly's back at school tomorrow, and Halpern's boy's out and, incidentally, I have good reason to evict the slippery fucker from the Hall now. Turns out it was his boy doing the dealing – our little fella just got caught up in the crossfire. So, all in all, it was quite a productive day. Oh, there's one last thing. I'm going to be

213

cancelling the direct debit for the school fees, because they are both going there for nix from now on.'

Christine couldn't believe what she was hearing. She had really thought her son would be expelled and ostracised; that Phil had sorted it like this made her want to kiss him. He had saved her boy from having to change schools, make new friends, and she was so grateful to her husband at this moment, she almost loved him again.

'Oh, Phillip, I was so worried, something like this follows a kid all their lives!'

He grinned at her and held out his arms, and she ran into them happily, without the usual hesitation, and he kissed the top of her head. 'I said I'd sort it, Chris, and I have. Now get your glad rags on. I still have to talk to that little fucker, and remind him of the error of his ways before we go out.'

'We'll celebrate, eh?'

He nodded, smiling, and went upstairs to talk to his son.

Chapter Sixty-Eight

Philly couldn't believe his luck; he had got a complete swerve and all because he had given his father enough ammunition to keep old man Halpern in his pocket for the rest of his days.

As his father came into his bedroom they smiled at each other in complete accord and, winking, Phillip said quietly, 'Your mum thinks you're grounded, and we have to play along with that, OK? But now we've got a few minutes I want you to tell me how much you were shifting, and how much you were making a month.'

Philly took a deep breath before saying carefully, 'Well, it depended really, Dad. You see, we mostly sold five-pound bags and, as it was home grown, it was bright green and plentiful. Laughing gear, the boys called it. Anyway, I averaged about sixty bags a month, and I was getting it for two quid a pop. The Es were a different matter, they varied on price by how good they were. But I suppose on a good month I could rake in about four hundred quid.'

'What did you do with the money you collected?'

Philly bit on his lip before replying truthfully, 'You're standing on it. That floorboard's loose, it's underneath the floor.'

Phillip watched as his son knelt down and lifted the floorboard up. The whole space underneath was packed out with money.

'How much is down there?'

'Six grand.'

Phillip could hear the pride in his son's voice and, pulling him into a gentle headlock, he held him tightly as he said laughingly, 'You are a chip off the old block, no doubt about it. But remember what I told you in the car – you could have got us all hammered for this. You never shit on your own doorstep. But this wisdom will come in time. Until then, keep your head down, your nose clean, and apply yourself to your schoolwork. OK?'

Philly nodded happily. 'What about the money?'

Phillip shrugged. 'What about it? You earned it, it's yours. You wanted a trail bike, now you can get one.'

'Really? Can I really?'

'Give it a few months. You'll have to act all contrite for a while and then, when I deem it's the right time, I'll talk your mother round for you, OK? But I want *good* grades, and *good* reports, or the deal's off.'

Philly shrugged, the living image of his father, as he said cheerfully, 'Fair enough.'

Phillip left him a little while later, proud of his son's obvious business acumen, and thrilled that he had such a son to teach and develop in the years to come.

Chapter Sixty-Nine

'Christine looks amazing, really great, Phil.'

Breda was genuinely happy that her sister-in-law was enjoying herself so much out on the town tonight. She worried about her at times – when she looked so down and depressed it was tragic to see her. But tonight she looked like the girl she had been years ago, before Jamsie and all that trouble.

Phillip gave her a small breakdown of the day's events, and he grinned in delight at how obviously impressed she was with Philly's little enterprise.

'The little fucker! Six grand! He's a chip off the old block, all right. I take it Christine thinks he's been punished big time?'

Phillip tapped his nose sagely. 'Well, you know my Chris, the less she knows about the real world the better.'

'Does Declan know?'

He nodded happily. 'He thinks we should bring Philly into the firm when he's a bit older. I tell you, when you find out the whole story you'll fucking freak, girl.'

Breda was loving this Phillip, this was the Phillip everyone responded to. He was upbeat, charming, and she chose that moment to give him more good news. 'I got both the arcades for under four hundred grand, Phil, we signed this afternoon.'

Phillip looked at her with undisguised glee. 'Oh, Breda, you have made a happy man even happier.'

She preened at the praise, this was what she lived for. Phillip's opinion of her was more important than anything.

'I'll tell you something else, girl, you're looking good and all – almost as good as my Christine!'

Breda laughed. 'She is a looker, Phil, there's no doubt about that, mate.'

Phillip was pleased that Breda wasn't jealous of Christine's obvious charms. He watched his wife as she chatted to Declan, and saw the looks she got from the men around her. She had class did his Christine, real class. In her diamonds and expensive black dress, she looked like she'd stepped from the pages of a fashion magazine. She dressed like a real lady, her high-heeled Jimmy Choos made her long legs look shapelier. He had never wanted her more than at this moment.

'We've done well, us lot, and we're just starting out really. Once I've finished we'll have the whole south coast. No one saw the potential here like I did. Look at this place, Breda, it's fucking buzzing.'

The pride in his voice was evident, and she understood how important achieving was to him. Unlike the others, she felt the same in many respects. She craved the respect money and position could guarantee. It was like Phillip said, a lot of the old-money people were wasters, they never understood the economics of how you made your fortune, all they understood was how to spend it. Like Breda, Phillip wanted his kids to understand the actual earn, so they would appreciate how hard money was to come by in the first place. It was about making your mark, your own personal mark on the world, and that was something Declan, Breda and Phillip were determined to do. Jamsie was like their father, he would take whatever fell into his lap – he had no ambition, therefore he was worthless to them all in more ways than one.

'It's a triumph, Phil. This place was dying on its feet until you took it over, and now it's *the* place to be seen. It's been heaving like this every night.'

Phillip nodded, he was more than happy with his new investment. Kissing his sister's cheek, he pushed through the crowded bar to his wife's side and then, taking her arm gently, he led her through to the VIP bar, stopping to say hello here and there to friends and acquaintances. All were hailing him like the new king of the turf, and that is exactly how he saw himself. This was his manor now, he owned it, and if he didn't own it, he had a stake in it.

Christine was having a great time, and that pleased him no end; seeing her happy made it all worthwhile. When she sparkled like this there was no one in the world like her. No one could touch her. This was the girl who had ensnared him all those years ago. This was his Christine at her finest.

In the relative quietness of the VIP bar, he kissed her on the lips. 'So what do you think, Chris? Like it?'

He looked around him, at the newly refurbished club, and she smiled genuinely. 'It's beautiful, Phil, really fantastic. Well done.'

She meant every word she said. For the first time in years she was seeing things from Phillip's perspective, seeing his world as it related to him. The new pills were making her old fears seem groundless somehow, and her life suddenly looked much better than she had believed it to be. Tonight she felt strong enough to venture out of her protective shell. 'Let's have a toast shall we, Phillip? To us, and a new start.'

He went behind the bar, and opened a bottle of Cristal champagne and, pouring two glasses, he handed one to her saying, 'I only keep this in for the footballers, fucking wasters the lot of them. But they give the place a certain cachet, so I can swallow them when I have to. Now, for that toast. To us, and to our boys, our sons, both of them blinding kids with great futures ahead of them, just like their parents.'

Christine looked into her husband's deep blue eyes and said sincerely, 'I'll drink to that.'

She was happier than she had been in years; she knew it was a combination of the drink, the meds, and the relief at her boy being saved from expulsion. But just for a few hours she wanted her Phillip again, to feel the love of him, and remember why she had fallen for him all those years ago. If it made him happy to see her so happy, then all the better. At the end of the day she realised that whatever he was, he put them all first. When the boys had needed him he had come through for them, and that proved to her that whatever he might be, he loved them in his own way. She had been drowning in her fear of him for so many years that she hadn't seen what was staring her in the face – the fact that he would do anything for his family. She was stuck with him no matter what, so why not make the best of it? Why not do what countless other women had done for generations – see his good points, play up his kindnesses. Appreciate what she *did* have; a lovely home, two fantastic sons, and a man who loved her to death. All of that had to count for something? Surely?

Tonight she felt a desperate need to be happy, just happy for a little while. And she felt there was a chance that she might finally achieve just that. God Himself knew she had prayed for this for years, it was about time He remembered she existed.

'I love you, Phil.'

Phillip felt like all his Christmases and birthdays had come at once and, kissing her deeply on the lips, he said huskily, 'You don't know just how much those words mean to me, Chris.'

But she did, she knew exactly how much they meant to him.

They were interrupted by the bar staff coming through to open up and, entwined in each other's arms, they greeted the guests who were lucky enough to get into the VIP bar and, therefore, an audience with Phillip Murphy. This was his seafront now, and everyone knew it. Christine stood beside him and accepted the praise and the respect he had worked so hard for and which, for him, was the icing on the cake. He was happier than he had ever been and, for once, it showed.

Chapter Seventy

'Are you all right, Christine?'

Christine laughed, a loud, brash laugh. 'Bloody hell, Mum, what is it with you? I'm either too depressed or too happy. Can't you just enjoy being here with us and stop questioning me?'

Eileen was concerned, her daughter was not right. She hadn't been right for years, of course, but she was almost manic today, like a film on fast-forward.

Christine continued, 'I've got these new meds, and they make me feel a bit odd, but they are helping me, Mum, really helping me. So don't spoil it all by having a big court case about it in me own kitchen.'

She was talking in riddles, but Eileen thought it better not to mention that. 'All right, keep your hair on. I just worry about you, darling, you are me daughter, after all.'

Eileen was grieved as usual, it was always about *her*, she was a two-faced, vindictive old bag. Christine felt the urge to smack her mother right in the face. But she resisted, she knew it would cause too much trouble. It was easier to listen to her, and wait patiently until she had talked herself out and then, finally, went home. Christine resented the way Eileen always came into her house and, without saying a word, made her feel inadequate, made her feel as if she was failing everyone because she didn't have the same strength her mother had to face everyday life. She knew Eileen looked down on her, looked down on her lifestyle, even though Phillip had made sure that her parents were doing really well. They were coining it in with the four shops, as her mother remarked to anyone within earshot. Yet she knew that this woman, who professed to love her, also saw her as a failure of sorts. She felt her disapproval like a physical blow and yet as Phillip added to the house and the land, she saw the naked envy on her mother's face that her daughter had gained so much from her liaison with Phillip Murphy. She was convinced her mother had prayed for them to crash and burn.

'Do you want a glass of wine, Mum?'

'Bit early, even for you, Christine.'

'Well, as Phil always says, if I want it, I should have it. Unlike you, Mother, Phil knows how to enjoy his wife *and* his life.' She was laughing, she felt that she was being clever, witty even.

Eileen wondered how long before this child of hers cracked up; she was like a fart in a colander, flitting here there and everywhere and going absolutely nowhere. You could almost feel the charge coming off of her. All her movements were jerky, off-kilter, and her eyes were too bright, burning in her face like hot coals. It wasn't natural and it was frightening to see her like this.

'Should you drink on those meds, Chris?'

Christine rolled her eyes in an exaggerated fashion. 'Will you fucking give it a rest, Mother! I like a few drinks sometimes, there's no law against it, is there? Fuck knows I'm entitled to a bit of relaxation, surely . . .'

Eileen swallowed down her usual waspish retort and said instead, as pleasantly as possible, 'Go on then. Just a small one, mind, I'm driving.'

She knew it wasn't worth saying any more, and she could see she was distressing the girl, so she changed the subject. 'The new club's been in all the papers, I bet Phillip is well made-up.'

Christine smiled happily. 'Oh, Mum, it's really fantastic, really upmarket. We were there the other evening. Honestly, it was the best night I've had out in years.'

Eileen could hear the pleasure in her daughter's voice, and was torn between sorrow and relief, because it was a long time since she had seen her daughter so animated. Even if she was manic, at least it was better than when she was desperately sad and almost monosyllabic. Sometimes the girl looked so sad it would break your heart and, as much as her daughter could irritate her, she was still her daughter and, in her own way, she loved her.

'I'm glad you're going out again. You're a lovely-looking girl, and you have a great lifestyle, it'll do you the world of good to get out there and have a bit of a boogie!'

Christine grinned then. 'No one says "boogie" any more, Mum!'

'I do!'

Eileen took the glass of wine and sipped it cheerfully; maybe she was worrying too much, at least the girl was chatting, trying to be a part of life. Surely that was a step in the right direction? She knew she got on her daughter's nerves; Christine always seemed to think she was criticising her and, at times, she knew she was doing just that. But she genuinely wanted to help her – it was hard seeing your child drowning in her own sorrow and not being able to do anything about it. Not know how to make them better. Sometimes Christine frightened her, especially when the depression was dragging her down, and she didn't get dressed for days on end, or just sat staring at the walls. She hoped these new tablets did the trick; Christine was too young and too beautiful to be plagued like she was.

As Christine downed her wine in record time and poured herself another large glass, Eileen made a conscious effort to bite her tongue. Everyone seemed to drink wine like water these days – half the soap operas on TV had piss-heads who practically lived in the pub, and every drama you watched had people drinking like it was going out of fashion, so maybe she worried about it too much. But, mixed with the pills the doctor prescribed, she was concerned that Christine might be doing herself or her body untold damage.

Sighing gently, she sipped at her drink and listened to her daughter as she talked excitedly about anything and everything that popped into her head, barely pausing for the frequent gulps of wine and completely unaware of how odd her behaviour seemed to those around her. Even the boys couldn't wait to leave her presence, and that alone spoke volumes. Christine was like an accident waiting to happen, and it was just a case of *when* it would happen, because Eileen knew her daughter couldn't carry on like this for much longer.

Chapter Seventy-One

Ricky Thomas was sitting in his Mercedes alone, watching the sea as the tide came in. He loved the seafront and he knew he would miss being there. Now that his arcades were truly gone the enormity of what he had lost had come crashing in on him. But he was a realist, and he knew that he had to let it go, which is why he was so pleased to get this chance to meet with Phillip Murphy. If he could smooth things over then maybe he could still salvage a little piece of his old life. After all, this was the only thing he had ever known: the games, the machines, the beach. Like his father before him, he had never thought he would leave. Now his kids were without an inheritance and his life was without any structure; he hadn't understood just to what extent the seaside had been the backbone of his everyday existence. He missed it, missed it all dreadfully. The days seemed to stretch out into nothingness. He sighed sadly, turning up the heat as the autumn chill was already settling in for the winter. There was a deep, damp cold on the seafront, and it took what his father used to laughingly call hardy perennials to cope with it year in and year out. But Ricky *had* coped, and furthermore he had loved every second of it.

He heard Phillip crunching across the shingle beach towards his car, and opened the passenger door for him. Phillip settled himself down in the leather seat, blowing on his hands for warmth. 'It's fucking freezing out there, mate.'

Ricky laughed softly, then busied himself lighting one of his huge cigars. Phillip took out a small hip flask and took a deep gulp of brandy, before handing the flask to Ricky, who did the same. They sat in silence for a few moments watching an old fishing boat as it sailed in the distance.

'I love this place.'

Phillip coughed softly before answering him. 'I know you do, Rick. But you'll get used to your new life, it's all about how you perceive yourself. That's what my wife's shrink says anyway but, between me and you, he's fucking nuttier than her at times. A right fucking lumpfish he is – all glasses and bad breath. You could imagine him picking his nose, right dirty-looking oik.'

Ricky laughed at his description, and Phillip laughed too. 'Honestly, I love that girl but she worries me, she's not right in the head, Ricky. Do you know what she was doing at five o'clock this morning? Not sleeping like normal people, oh no, she was Hoovering the downstairs of the house. She had already polished the furniture, washed the skirting boards and scrubbed the floors, so she was Hoovering as if it was the most normal thing in the world. Woke the boys up. They think she's slowly losing her mind, and I have to agree with them this time. But the good news is, she's regained her sense of humour and her energy, so that's something, I suppose.'

Ricky didn't know what to say; in all the years he had known this man he had never once spoken out of place about his wife before, and this was talk that was not for the likes of him. This was private, family talk.

'She cut her wrists once,' Phillip continued quietly. 'I've never seen so much blood before in my life. Funny though, the doctor said it always looks more than it really is. She hadn't cut deep enough, see, to do any real damage. Scared my Philly though, he was only ten and he was the one who found her. That was the one time I could have happily topped her meself. But I love her and I always will.'

'My mum suffered with her nerves, Phil. It was my dad's fault

– he was a womaniser, they used to joke that he had fucked every woman on the seafront, *and* their mothers.'

Phillip laughed loudly at Ricky's jocular tone. 'He was a lad, all right. Do you miss him?'

Ricky nodded in the darkness, the light from his cigar giving his face a warm glow. 'Yeah. He was an old cunt at times, but he was still me father.'

'True, Ricky. We can't choose our relatives unfortunately – look at my brother Jamsie.'

They were quiet for a few moments before Phillip broke the silence asking dangerously, 'Who are the people you said thought I had too much?'

Ricky was shocked at the sudden vehemence of the man's words; they were dripping with malice, and he suddenly understood what this meeting was really about. 'That was just talk, Phillip, stupid drunk talk . . .'

Phillip grinned then, and his face looked almost demonic in the dimness. 'Stupid talk, yes, but there was also more than a grain of truth in it, and you and I both know that. Now, names.'

Ricky felt his heart sink down to his boots. This was not just foolish, it was hopeless.

Phillip opened the hip flask again and, handing it to Ricky, he said menacingly, 'Get that down your Gregory Peck, might loosen your tongue.'

'Look, Phillip, I don't know what this is about, you got what you wanted, you've fucking cleared me out, and you've made sure I am persona non grata to all me old mates. I ain't got a pot to piss in, and I am having to move to Spain to start a new business and a new life. Now I am not going to sit here and gossip with you about every bit of tittle-tattle I have heard spoken over the years, all right?'

Phillip took a sip of the brandy himself before answering, 'Fair enough, that is a very fair statement. I liked the tittle-tattle bit, because that just about sums it all up really. A load of wankers tittle-tattling.' He laughed at his own words. 'So, it looks like we need to get to the main business of the night.'

Ricky felt the cold fingers of fear inside him now. 'And what's that, Phil?' he said with forced calm.

Phillip wasn't fooled by Ricky's bravado, the fear in the car was so real it was almost tangible. It had finally dawned on Ricky that this wasn't a social visit of any kind, it was a payback.

'You see, Ricky, I can't let you go to Spain. You mugged me off big time, and that is something I know I would not be able to live with. I'm a funny fucker like that, my mum says I take things too personally. In fact she thinks it's my fault my wife's stoned out of her nut on pills all the time – that's when she ain't pissed, of course. A lot of people think it's my fault apparently, is that what you thought too? Was that something else for you all to tittle-tattle about, eh, my private life?'

The truth was people *had* discussed it and at length. Christine had seemed very strange at times over the years, and it was noticed; it was only human nature to discuss it occasionally. Deandra had talked about it many times, and he had to admit a lot of people did, on the quiet.

'You shouldn't be talking about Christine like this to me, it's wrong, Phillip, and you know it.'

Phillip laughed as if he had heard the best joke ever. 'But who better than you to talk to about it? After all, Ricky, you'll be taking this conversation to the grave with you. It ain't like you'll be tittle-tattling to your big mates about it, is it? You'll be dead and gone, won't you?'

Ricky heard the words, and the inevitability in them; he should have known that Phillip wouldn't let him walk away. He thought of Deandra and the kids, waiting for him, not realising that he would never come home again.

'Don't do this, Phil, I'm begging you . . . I've got two little kids . . .'

Phillip shrugged. 'You should have thought of them when you made a cunt out of me. You should have thought of them when you were talking about me with your fucking hard-nut mates, laughing at me behind my back. Well, I'll see they get taken care of, no worries on that score, Ricky. I hope you're well insured though. Deandra will need all the poke she can get – it ain't cheap bringing up kids these days, I can tell you.'

For Ricky it was all over – there was nothing he could do now to change anything. He looked out at the sea, and a small part of him was glad that if he was going to die it would be here, in a place he loved, where he had experienced so much happiness. He wouldn't fight, it was pointless; there was no going back now so best to get it over with. He thought of Deandra, and was sorry he would have to leave her at the mercy of the world. He genuinely loved that girl. Tears filled his eyes, and he felt a great sorrow wash over him at what might have been had he made a few different choices in life. You couldn't win when you were up against someone like Phillip Murphy, because they didn't play by any accepted rules. All he could do now was die with dignity, and hope that it would be short and sweet.

The waves were crashing into the shore now, and they both watched, mesmerised, as the sounds gathered momentum, and the darkness swallowed up the last of the light. It was calm now in the car, and they sat side-by-side, each lost in his own thoughts. Phillip was glad that Ricky had taken it so well, and he admired him in a strange way for being so stoic about it all. He had always liked Ricky, and if the man had used his loaf he could have been on to a good earn now, and in a position to see his family grow and thrive. Pride was a terrible affliction, there was no doubt about that.

The knife was long, slim-bladed, and when it slipped between Ricky's ribs, it didn't really hurt that much. It was only when Phillip pulled it out and started to stab Ricky over and over again that the pain and the shock set in.

When he was finished, Phillip sat beside the man, and smoked a cigarette calmly, looking out at the sea, and waiting patiently for Ricky Thomas to bleed out. He was humming to himself the opening bars of 'Gangsta's Paradise', and made a mental note to get the music changed in the arcades.

He was sick to death of hearing that bloody song.

Chapter Seventy-Two

Declan was in the new arcade, making sure that the staff were all aware of the new regime. He found it best to be on-site for the first few weeks, that way you got a real working knowledge of the people you had around you.

So far, so good. In fairness to Ricky Thomas he had gathered a pretty decent team around himself, and that made their job that much easier. Because it was a cash business the potential for theft from within was astronomical, so certain measures had to be put in place. But the name Murphy was usually enough to see that honesty prevailed. Still, it helped to let the employees know you were watching them all the same.

Declan walked through to the office at the back of the hall; he liked it in there, it had a nice bar and comfortable chairs. It also had a large TV that often came in handy for the racing – he liked a bet and had a flutter every day. He also had his eye on a young blonde who was one of the floor walkers; she was pretty but, more importantly, she was intelligent. He thought she would be worth keeping an eye on for the future. She had great tits as well, and that was always a bonus as far as he was concerned. She had already given him the glad eye, so he reckoned he might be in there before too long. He wasn't after a serious relationship; he felt he was still too young, and too enamoured of a bit of strange to tie himself down. The prospect just didn't appeal to him and, in his line of work, he had an endless line of females all dying to drop their flimsy little drawers for him, so it was a pretty good deal all round. As Declan poured himself a large Scotch, Phillip came into the room, and he was surprised to see him tonight.

Phillip locked the door quickly, saying, 'Pour me one, Dec.' As he slipped off his overcoat, Declan saw he was covered in blood, and was immediately worried.

'You all right, Phil?'

Phillip laughed, pleased at his brother's concern. 'Yeah, had a bit of unfinished business with Ricky Thomas.'

He was already stripping off his clothes and placing them in a black bin bag. When he was naked he picked up his drink and swallowed it down, holding out the glass for another. Declan obliged, but he was annoyed. There was no reason to take out Ricky – they had got what they wanted, this was just petty and juvenile and he said as much. 'You had to do it, didn't you? Everyone will know it was us, Phil . . .'

'They'd better. This is my message to the whole fucking seafront: don't fuck with the Murphys. Especially this fucking Murphy.'

He walked through to the small bathroom and turned on the shower, then, coming back into the room, he said happily, 'Oh, by the way, I promised him I'd look out for his kids, and you know me, Dec, I am a lot of things but I always keep a promise. So we'll get a few quid together for his old woman, and make sure everyone puts in a decent wedge. She'll need it now they won't be going to Spain.'

'She'll be devastated, she loved him you know.'

'Oh, I wouldn't worry about her too much. Six weeks after the funeral she'll be sweating her arse off underneath some young ponce, who's as interested in what she's got as he is in her fake tits. Hardly *Gone With the* fucking *Wind*, is it?'

Declan laughed despite himself, he knew what Phillip said was true. But it was still a shame – he had liked Ricky Thomas, he was a nice geezer. But the damage was done, and there was no reason to keep on about it. Phillip had done what he felt he had to do, and that was that. While his brother showered, Declan tied up the bin bag ready to be burned in the incinerator at the farm.

Ten minutes later Phillip was washed, dressed and ready to go to one of the clubs for a few drinks.

It was over with, finished, done.

Chapter Seventy-Three

Christine was making the boys their breakfast. She was happy again, but she still wasn't sleeping much. In fact, she was hardly sleeping at all. She would mention it to the doctor on Wednesday when she went for her appointment. She had hardly slept for ten days now, and even she knew that it wasn't right. She was manic again, and she was afraid that meant she was due one of her brain storms, as Phillip so succinctly put it. She was too frightened to go to sleep, because when she did, she was plagued by bad dreams, about blood, and death, and suicide. She saw herself drowning in a sea of thick, hot blood, could taste it as it forced its way down her throat and into her body; the smell was heavy, cloying, and she knew it was never going to stop. She shivered at the thought as she opened the Aga and took out the boys' huge breakfasts. They had a full English every morning, it was what they needed to get them through the day. They were growing like weeds, and they were both heavy-boned and tall like their father.

As she placed the plates on the table, she listened to the news on her local radio station and, for a few seconds, she thought she had imagined what she had heard.

'Shut up, you two! I'm trying to hear.'

The boys immediately became quiet, listening with her.

'The man was found brutally stabbed to death on Southend Seafront at five o'clock this morning by two young fishermen who saw the car abandoned in the small lay-by near the sea. Mr

Richard Thomas was a well-known face in Southend, his grandfather had opened his first arcade along the front in the nineteen twenties and his son, Richard Thomas's father, had opened another one in the late fifties. Police say they are treating the death as murder, and urge any witnesses to come forward. Anything they have to say will be received in the strictest confidence. Mr Thomas leaves a wife and two young children.'

Philly and Timmy were both open-mouthed with astonishment.

'Is that Uncle Ricky? Someone murdered Uncle Ricky?' Philly's voice was drenched in incredulity and shock. Timmy was near to tears, and Christine sat down heavily in the nearest chair, her mind whirling at the news. She was already shaking with fear and, standing up quickly, she ran from the room. She was holding her hand across her mouth as if to stop herself from making any sound. A voice in her head was screaming that it wasn't true, what she was thinking couldn't be true. Phillip wouldn't do that, he had got what he wanted, so surely there was no need for him to do that . . . But something inside her knew that she was wrong, was convinced that Phillip was involved somehow.

As she retched over the sink in the downstairs toilet, she heard the door opening behind her. She could feel Phillip's presence even before she looked in the bathroom mirror and stared straight into his eyes.

'I just heard, Chris. Fucking hell, it's unbelievable, ain't it?'

She nodded slowly, not trusting herself to speak.

'Come on, a cup of hot sweet tea for you. You've had a terrible shock, and so have the boys. I'm going to keep them home today.'

He walked her gently back to the kitchen and, sitting her down, he poured her a cup of tea and, after he laced it liberally with Courvoisier, he did the same for the two boys. Christine gulped the liquid, and watched her husband's reaction to the news.

'You all right, Timmy?'

The boy was crying silently, and Christine knew she should comfort him, but she couldn't move from the chair.

Phillip poured her another brandy, not bothering with the tea this time, and he also went and got her a couple of her pills. She took them gratefully, uncaring of the way the boys were watching her in disgust.

Just then, Breda and Declan came through the back door. Christine had never been so grateful to see anyone in her life before.

'I take it you've heard?' Breda went straight to Christine and hugged her tenderly. 'He was such a bloody fool, he made so many bloody enemies in the last few months, and he owed money everywhere. Even Phillip bailed him out, tried to help him, but he wouldn't be helped.'

Christine was listening to her sister-in-law as if what she was saying was gospel. She couldn't believe that the man who had come to her home for dinner, whose only crime had been wanting to keep his business, had been murdered by her husband, by the father of her children. But she knew whatever anyone said it was true; deep inside she knew this was Phillip Murphy at work.

Declan was pouring tea for him and Breda, and she saw Phillip filling up her brandy glass again. It suited him to get her pissed because he knew that she suspected him.

'But why would they kill him, Auntie Breda, what reason could they have to stab him?' This was her Philly now, he was shrewder than they gave him credit for.

She saw her husband shrug, all innocence and bewilderment, and she felt the urge to get out of the chair and fell him, take her arm back and just fell him to the ground.

'Look, boys,' Phillip replied. 'Uncle Ricky had a lot of

problems, and he turned on a lot of his mates. People he had known for years. That was why I took the arcades off his hands, to try and help him out. But he had got in with some right villains, and they must have had it in for him.'

Christine watched as the lies tripped off his tongue but, looking at her Philly, her first-born, she saw that he wasn't swallowing any of it. Somehow he knew, and she felt like he approved of what his father had done. Her boy was so young, he shouldn't know the ways of his father's world just yet, but then how could he be oblivious to it? The Murphys were treated like visiting royalty on the seafront. Philly must have realised that it was his name that gave him so much attention. Phillip walked around with his sons like a king visiting his subjects. The boys were given free rides, money for the machines, free drink, free food. They had to know their father was a Face of sorts, they weren't fucking stupid.

The pills were kicking in, and she could feel herself detaching slowly from the people around her. She kept seeing Deandra's face as she had left their house that night, could still feel the squeeze she had given her on her shoulder as an apology for her husband's boorish behaviour. Poor Deandra, and those two little children.

Breda was watching Christine closely, and she motioned for Phillip to get the boys out of the room. Then she knelt in front of her sister-in-law and said kindly, 'Come on, Christine, let's get you back to bed, love, this has been a big shock for all of us.'

'Breda, tell me the truth and swear on your Porrick's life, was this anything to do with Phillip?'

Breda shook her head and sighed deeply as she said, 'I swear to you, on my boy's life, that this is not anything to do with us lot.' She sounded shocked at the accusation, and suitably offended as well.

Christine grabbed at her hands and held them tightly. 'I'm

sorry, Breda, but just for a split second there . . . I can't help it, I get these thoughts.'

'Come on, mate, let's get you to bed, eh? We've all had a terrible shock, and it takes everyone in different ways. You're not well, love, and you need to rest.'

Christine went to bed obediently, glad to be away from the family, glad to be away from her husband.

When Phillip slipped in an hour later, she pretended to be asleep and, as his lips touched her face gently, she was only just able to stop herself from screaming out loud.

Chapter Seventy-Four

Veronica was at Phillip's house, as she had been for the last five days, taking care of the boys. It was something she had done many times over the years when Christine wasn't herself, as she liked to put it. The boys loved her looking after them, and usually that bothered Christine, but right now she was glad of the woman's company. She knew she couldn't be alone with Phillip yet. She was still reeling from the events of the last few days.

The police had questioned Phillip in front of Christine, and she had known then that they too suspected his hand in all this, but they couldn't prove it. He owned most of the police around here anyway. It was how their world worked – she had cooked for them and their wives enough times over the years. Phillip had always looked after them, had joked that if you looked after the Filth, the Filth would look after you. And it seemed he was right.

Veronica placed a cup of coffee in front of her and said gently, 'Shall I make you a nice omelette, Chris, something light and tasty?'

Christine sipped at the coffee obediently, but shook her head in refusal. 'I should have kept that doctor's appointment, was he all right about me changing it?'

Veronica smiled at her. ' 'Course he was. Phillip explained you had received a terrible shock, and you were taking it easy for a while, and the doctor said that was the best thing for you. He said there would be a prescription for sleeping tablets at the surgery, and Phil's going to pick them up later on, so stop worrying. Once you get a good night's rest you'll feel much better.'

Christine nodded, she was tired out. 'Any news about Ricky? Have the police found out who did it yet?'

Veronica shook her head sagely. 'Sure, they'll never find out. It's like Phillip says, whoever did it is long gone. He thinks it was someone come over from Spain – apparently Ricky had ripped off a lot of people over there with a timeshare scam. So, it looks like there could be a few culprits in the mix. What a foolish man, eh? And I always liked him. He seemed pretty genuine, like, but then you never really know anyone, I suppose.'

'Were Phillip and Declan really round your house that night, Veronica?'

'How many times, child! They were there sorting out with Breda about the clubs and the new arcades. I wouldn't lie to you about something so important, I swear to you before God and man. Now stop asking me for Christ's sakes.'

Christine didn't answer her, instead she sipped at her coffee and chain-smoked Marlboro Lights.

Veronica went about the business of the house, and wondered if Phillip realised that his own wife thought he had murdered Ricky Thomas. She could see it in her eyes, could see it in her demeanour. Had almost heard the accusation from her lips. The trouble was, she thought exactly the same thing but, unlike this girl here, she knew better than to dwell on it all. She had learned very early on that knowledge wasn't power – that was a crock of shit. Knowledge was actually added aggravation, and there were some things you were better off never knowing the truth about, for sure.

She was aware that her Phillip wasn't an angel, but she also knew he wasn't wired like other people and, because of that, she overlooked a lot where he was concerned. Blood *was* thicker than water, and family was all that really mattered in the end. She didn't ask questions, because she didn't want to know the answers, and if this poor young woman could only learn to live by that credo she would be a much happier person. Veronica would lie for her kids until the day she died, and she would do it happily. That was what mothers were for.

Christine would find that out for herself one day, because those two lads she had produced were their father's sons all right. They would be a big part of this family in years to come. Maybe then this silly girl would open her eyes and see the world as it really was, count her blessings, and thank God her sons were safe inside a family that loved them, and would protect them no matter what.

Chapter Seventy-Five

'Everyone knows it was Phillip, but no one is going to accuse him, are they?' Ted Booth was worried to death about his daughter and cursed the day she had captured the interest of Phillip Murphy. 'Doesn't it bother you that our daughter is tied to a murderer? Her nerves are shot, and she is like a fucking wraith, she can't weigh more than a few stone, and you don't seem bothered about it at all.'

Eileen sighed heavily, sometimes this man was like a broken record. 'All right then, I dare you, *I dare you*, to go round Phillip Murphy's house and bring her home. Go on! If you're that worried about her, go and get her. Go and save her from her husband.' She laughed then, a nasty vindictive laugh. 'Didn't think so. Now, this is the last time I am going to discuss this, Ted, and I mean it. She made her bed years ago when she fought us to marry him. Now she is stuck there and, like you, I hate seeing what it's doing to her, but what the fuck can we do about it? Phillip ain't the type of person you could discuss it with, is he? He won't *allow* us to take her away from him, he actually loves her in his own way. That's half the fucking trouble, if he would dump her she'd be halfway home. But the worse she gets, the more he seems determined to keep her beside him. Until he outs her, there is nothing we can do without bringing his wrath down on our own heads, and none of us want that, do we? Well, do we?!' She was screaming the last words now, her anger and frustration overwhelming her. 'He gives us a good living, and he gives her a good life. Until he allows her to leave him, there is nothing anyone can do. So either grow a spine and go and get her, or shut up about it.'

Ted Booth knew she spoke the truth, and that hurt him more than anything. Because he knew he would never have the guts to go and front up Phillip Murphy – the man terrified him. As he would any normal person. But Ted was scared for his daughter; he could see her drowning in her own mind and it was killing him.

Eileen felt a moment's sympathy for her husband; she understood exactly how he felt, but she also knew it was useless trying to do anything about it. She took what they were given, and she was grateful for it, and she made sure Phillip Murphy knew that.

'Look, Ted, I feel the same as you but, in reality, what can we do? He ain't a person you can cross. This latest should remind you of exactly what we are dealing with here. So just let it go, eh?'

He nodded sadly.

'Like my old mum always said, Ted, be careful what you ask for, because you just might get it. We fought Christine every step of the way with him, and she married him regardless. Now there's no more we can do for her. I wish it was different, but it ain't. He loves the bones of that girl, and she's got his kids, and she's got his name. What we want doesn't matter any more. She's tied to him until one of them dies, because he won't ever let her go without a fight.'

Teddy knew the truth of his wife's words, and hoped God might be good to them and see that maniac Murphy murdered sooner rather than later. It was his constant prayer, and he begged that it would be answered one day.

Chapter Seventy-Six

'Are you sure you can do this, Chris?'

Christine nodded silently, aware that they were all amazed to see her up and dressed, ready for the funeral. Breda went to her sister-in-law and put her arm around her shoulder. 'You look lovely, Christine. Deandra will appreciate you paying your respects.'

Phillip and Declan exchanged glances, and Breda nodded her head almost imperceptibly to let them know she would babysit her sister-in-law.

When the boys walked into the kitchen sad-faced and dressed in their black suits Christine felt her eyes fill with tears. 'Are you sure they should go today, Phil?'

Phillip nodded and said firmly, 'Ricky was a part of their lives, and now they are growing up they need to learn to respect people who have passed away. He thought the world of our lads, and it's fitting they should be there to see him sent on his last journey.'

He sounded so reasonable, so normal. Christine couldn't find an argument against it.

'You all right, Mum?'

This from Timmy, he was the most kind-hearted of her boys. Philly she knew resented her because she wasn't what he termed 'normal', like his friends' mothers. She had heard him telling Timmy he was ashamed of her, and that people at school said mental illness ran in families. His words had cut her to the quick, but she didn't let on she knew what he thought about her. She hoped that one day her sons would understand why she acted as she did.

Timmy came over and gave her a little hug, which touched her. Phillip had to force his elder son to do the same, and that hurt her more than he would ever know. Every day Philly was growing closer to his father, and there wasn't a thing she could do about it. Both the boys adored him, and with her being like she was, she knew they both depended on him far too much. It was a vicious circle, and she couldn't tell where it started, let alone where it would all finish.

Chapter Seventy-Seven

Deandra was in bits. The funeral had been huge, with people coming from all over the country and even Europe to pay their respects. The funeral car had driven slowly along the seafront at Southend, and the traders had lined the streets, hats in their hands, suited and booted, as they saw off one of their own. It had been very emotional and fitting. Every Face imaginable had turned up for Ricky; the newspapers were loving it, as were the film crews. It was a big event, and even the Mayor had turned out in full regalia to say goodbye to a man who had been well liked, and whose bloody murder had sent shock waves through the tightknit community.

Christine watched as Phillip was fêted by everyone. Even Bantry waited in line like a schoolboy to see the man he had given his first job. He had shaken his hand and told him all he wanted to hear, because that was the only way to show the proper respect Phillip Murphy demanded. She watched Breda too as she stood beside her brothers, and accepted all the handshakes as her right.

The funeral proved to Christine just how far her husband had come. He had escorted Deandra into the church and passed her over to Ricky's older daughters, all nice-looking girls, all feeling the loss of their father acutely. They knew that the man who had killed their father was talking to them and condoling them, and they were unable to do anything about it. She watched her two sons being chaffed by all; they were enjoying themselves even

247

though they were at a funeral. Christine knew then that she had lost them, and she wondered at how much pain a person could take before they just lay down and died from it. She saw her mother and father, standing with Veronica and Phillip Senior. She knew her mother was probably loving every minute of it, and that her father was only there for appearances' sake. Phillip would want him there, would want them to look united as a family. She saw all the people who worked for the Murphys, all in black looking suitably sad. She knew that her husband employed literally hundreds of people now, and that they depended on him for their mortgages, their car payments, the bread they ate, and the lives they lived. He was bigger than he had ever dreamed, and he was more or less untouchable now. She saw it all, and she accepted it all. Phillip had won, as she had always known he would, and there was nothing she could do about it.

Back at the house, she talked to people, said all the right things, until eventually she had a chance to catch Deandra alone. She was repairing her make-up in the big bedroom she had shared with her husband and, slipping inside, Christine shut the door behind her. Deandra was watching her warily in the dressing-table mirror; she was already well pissed, and she had also been given a couple of lines of coke by a well-meaning friend.

'I'm so sorry, Deandra, I can't imagine what you must be going through, love.'

Deandra didn't answer her. She was remembering the night of the dinner party; that had been the beginning of the end for her and Ricky, though she had not known that then, of course. But she had put it all together soon enough. What Ricky had told her had given her a good idea of what had occurred. As she looked at Christine Murphy she felt the hate and the anger spiralling up inside her, and the drink and the coke made it all the more raw. 'You're sorry, are you, Christine?'

Christine nodded, knowing what was coming, welcoming it almost.

'You know who killed my Ricky as well as I do, and you know why. Because he wouldn't sell him his arcades. My kids are fatherless because *your* old man wanted to expand his empire. How you've got the front to come in here . . . it's bad enough having to swallow that cunt pretending he's doing me a favour, but *you*, Christine, I thought you were a bit better than that.'

Christine shook her head as if clearing it and, taking a deep breath, she said honestly, 'I am sorry, Deandra, genuinely sorry. Whatever you might think.'

Turning, she left the room, walked down the stairs and out of the house. Getting into Breda's car, she said to a surprised Jamsie, 'Take me home.'

'Does Phillip know—'

Closing her eyes she bellowed, 'Just fucking take me home! Believe me, he'll thank you for it, because if I go back in there I'll cause a fucking war!'

Chapter Seventy-Eight

Phillip looked around him at the carnage and wondered how she had managed it considering how little she weighed. The whole place was wrecked; Christine had systematically gone through the house and destroyed everything with a hammer. As Phillip stood in the kitchen he felt the cold anger boiling up inside him, and he swallowed it down. His mother had taken the boys home; he had insisted on coming back by himself to see what had occurred. Jamsie had come up trumps anyway; he had called him and the ambulance, so at least she had not had too long to harm herself. She was now heavily sedated in a private mental hospital. The doctors were talking about electric-shock treatment this time. He would gladly plug her head into the national grid himself if it sorted her out once and for all.

He turned as he heard the back door open and, seeing Old Sammy standing there in his pyjamas and dressing gown holding a bottle of Scotch, he felt a moment's gratitude that this old man had waited for him to come home.

'I thought you might need a stiff drink, son.'

Phillip nodded sadly and welcomed him into what remained of the kitchen.

'She certainly had a good go anyway, I could hear her screaming from my cottage.'

Phillip found two mugs that had escaped Christine's wrath,

and poured two large whiskies. Sitting at the kitchen table they toasted each other in silence.

'What was she saying?'

'Just swearing really, screaming obscenities and smashing anything that came in her path. Swearing and talking rubbish.'

Phillip knew Sammy was trying to warn him, and he appreciated that more than he could ever express.

'I told the ambulance people she was delusional, but they said they knew that. I stayed with them until they gave her a shot, like, until she went to sleep.'

Phillip digested the information. 'She has a lot of problems, Sammy.'

The old boy nodded in agreement. 'My mother was the same, mad as a March hare most of the time – went to my school once in her nightdress, I hated her for that. But me father always said, women ain't got the mental ability of the male. He was right.'

Phillip watched as the old man sipped at his whisky and tried in his own way to comfort him. It was strange, but he did feel better for him being there. Sammy had a quiet way with him that made the people and animals around him feel calmer just by his presence.

'Jamsie said you came in and talked her down. Thanks for that.'

The old man shrugged. 'It wasn't hard, she was spent by then. I just said that maybe she had better quieten down because she was frightening the pigs!'

Phillip laughed ruefully.

'She's a very sad girl, Phillip. The madness takes them like that sometimes. Had a horse once, well bred, high spirited, but she had the madness in her. All you can do is leave her in the hands of the professionals. They know what they are doing, see. She'll come out of that place better than ever, you mark my words. I think that funeral was a bit too much for her, it's been on the news and everything.'

251

'I hope so, Sammy. I love that woman, she's my world.'

'Do you know what, Phillip? She just needs to find out how to cope with life in general. She's not the first to be afflicted by it, and I daresay she won't be the last. Now then, I have a bit of good news for you: the boar did his job, and the sows are all in farrow. So that'll keep us occupied for a while, eh?'

Phillip smiled gently, pleased at the news despite everything.

'He got stuck in there, I said he was a good 'un, didn't I? Knew his way around a sow that one did, God bless him.'

'Thanks, Sammy, I appreciate you doing all this.'

Sammy shook his head in denial. 'Listen to me, son, you've been better than my own boys to me, and I would do anything to help you out, in any way I could. You remember that.'

Phillip understood what he was saying and he also was under no illusions that the old boy knew far more about what went on in this house than he let on. Tonight was a real eye-opener, that was for sure.

As Phillip lay in bed a few hours later he wondered what he was going to do about his Christine. Because there was one thing he knew now for sure: this couldn't go on. It was all getting a bit too dangerous now, for all of them, himself included.

Book Three

Don't get mad, get even

Late twentieth-century saying

Never say that marriage has more of joy than pain

Euripides (c. 480 BC–406 BC)

Chapter Seventy-Nine

'Don't talk to me like that, Philly. I'm not deaf, I *can* hear you.'

Philly looked at his mother and felt a moment's shame at his words. But she was acting weird, and he had some mates coming round. She wasn't as bad as she had been before, but she was drinking again, and that made her talk shite, as his father so nicely put it. He wasn't like Timmy – he couldn't laugh it all off. He thought his mother was an embarrassment. 'Eccentric' was Timmy's word for her, 'out-and-out nut-bag' was his. Look at her now – seven in the evening and still in her dressing gown, half-pissed and already slurring her words. Still, at least she wasn't morose and depressed; that was something to be grateful for he supposed.

'Go and get dressed, Mum! I've got Graham and Billy coming round.'

Christine laughed. This son of hers was so bothered about appearances, he was like a fucking woman at times. 'All right, son, keep your wig on. I'll slip on a pair of jeans, is that good enough for your mates? Or shall I wear a designer suit and diamonds like Billy's mum does? She's the weirdo, not me. She'll never see forty-five again and if she has one more face-lift she'll have a beard!'

Philly had to laugh at that, because it was true. Billy's mum was always in hospital having 'procedures' as she insisted on

255

calling them. Billy said he had planned to get her an electric blanket for Christmas but was frightened his mother might melt during the night. But at least Billy's mother didn't go into hospital because she was a fucking loony. Though, in fairness, his mum hadn't been away for a few years now. But both he and his brother expected her to lose it again at some point. It was the pattern of their lives.

Philly hated that his mother was like she was, and he thought his father was a saint to put up with her. Any other bloke would have outed her a long time ago, and who could have blamed him? Not Philly – he would have understood his father's actions better than anyone. After all, he had to live with the stigma of her illness as well, and it wasn't easy tiptoeing around her all the time. Depression was one thing, and he appreciated that, but she was way past all that now. He felt sometimes that she played up her illness just to get on their nerves, or get what she wanted. He felt bad thinking like that, but she was always upset about something, and it bored him. She didn't give a thought to how her behaviour affected their lives, her sons' lives. And if she stopped drinking so much, maybe she wouldn't act so fucking stupid and show up herself and her family. Her breath was disgusting, sour and vicious. You could smell it from across the room sometimes, and it was rancid.

He saw her pour herself another Jack Daniel's and Coke and sighed heavily. 'Do you really need another drink, Mum?'

She mimicked him then. 'Do you really need a slap across the face, son?'

He walked out of the kitchen before he said something they both regretted. Anyway he had other things on his mind. He had made a monumental cock-up, and he wasn't sure how to sort it out. He knew he had to tell his father though – if he didn't and Phillip found out another way he would go ballistic. But the issue was *how* Philly would tell him, he needed some way to sweeten the pot.

As he worried about his father's reaction to this latest gaffe, he heard his mother singing along to Simply Red's 'Holding Back The Years', and knew a crying bout was on the cards. She cried at films, she cried at songs, sometimes for no reason at all she just cried. Any sympathy he had for her had long ago disintegrated.

Frankly, she just got on his fucking nerves.

Chapter Eighty

Phillip and Declan were in a favourite pub in Wapping. They had just finished a lunchtime meeting with an old mate who wanted to offload his arcades in Soho due to the recession and a very hefty tax bill he was hoping to avoid by disappearing off the face of the earth. He had a wife who was well past her sell-by date, two sons who were about as much use as a stripper in an abbey, and a girlfriend who had thighs like a Russian shot-putter's and the face of an angel. At sixty-three he felt it was time he had a bit of fun, and he was determined to get it in South America, where the dollar ruled, and the sun shone all year round.

Phillip was pleased; he had already made a few inroads into the West End, and this man's proposition confirmed that he was considered a serious player in the games world – he always got first refusal. Declan ordered them another couple of vodkas and Phillip looked around the small pub with interest. It had the usual smattering of city types and workmen which was why he liked it.

'So what do you really think, Declan?'

Declan shrugged. 'We can afford them, but they are pretty run down, and for every pound that goes in, another pound is coming out. Plus, it's a haven for the runaways; he never gets them moved on, and that can only bring trouble. From what my spies tell me, the young lads use it as a pick-up joint. But then, me and you have always known the arcades are a paedos' paradise. We've all but stamped it out on the front, but that's because we keep a wary eye out. The West End's different; it's a hunting ground for them with all the transient kids, and the free warmth attracts them like flies.'

'Well, we'll keep a few walkers on the floor – that's the best way to deal with them – and the Old Bill give us a pass because they know we make their job easier for them. Any problems with the building?'

Declan shook his head. 'The flats above are rented by prostitutes and the whole building is in need of renovation, but I think if we did the flats up as offices we'd get a much better return on them.'

'Fucking right and all, we ain't pimps.' Phillip had an abhorrence of anyone or anything to do with the sex industry; in fact, his attitude was almost Victorian. He hated it with a vengeance, and made sure they never had anything remotely to do with it. In all the years he had been married to Christine there had never been a hint of him being unfaithful to her, though no one would have blamed him if he *had* been. Her problems were well known and well documented. People thought he was a saint for the way he had stood by her. It was like his church-going, every Sunday come rain or shine they were all there, sitting in the front row; if Christine was indisposed Phillip still made the boys attend. It pleased Veronica no end, because that meant his father had to go as well, as did Declan and Breda. Jamsie was a regular anyway – he took Communion at five a.m., every morning, seven days a week.

Phillip was already bored and it showed; all he wanted was to do the deal and get on to the next thing on his agenda. It was what made him so successful – they did what needed to be done, and they moved on. Declan loved the excitement of it and, even though it was hard at times, constantly playing second to Phillip, he still knew how lucky he was to have the life he had. The Murphys were doing really well, all of them, and now that young

Philly was on the firm Declan had someone to mentor, someone to look out for. Phillip had more or less passed the boy on to him, told him to show him the ropes from the bottom up, and he was enjoying doing just that. He had a certain longing for children lately; seeing the boys becoming men had made him realise what he had missed out on all these years.

Trouble was, Declan still didn't want the permanent female presence that came with having a family. He liked his solitary life. He had a nice penthouse in the Docklands, he entertained as and when it suited him, and he liked living alone. Observing the marriages around him had never given him the urge to take the plunge himself. His mother had had a raw deal for years with that lazy bastard she had married, and seeing Phillip and the nut-bag that he had to contend with every day was not exactly a shining example of marital harmony either. Most of the men he mixed with juggled wives, girlfriends and one-night stands, or were caught up in affairs that, while they burned brightly, could only go the same way as their marriages at some point in the future. Men never changed, and it was a pretty safe bet that if they fucked about on one wife they would fuck about on the next. It was the nature of the beast. He thought it was best to stay on your tod, at least that way you had no one to please except yourself. Breda and him were the same in that way; she, like him, enjoyed her 'singledom' as she called it, and thought women who tied themselves to a man for life were mugs.

'I reckon we can wrap this up in an hour, Declan, and be home in time for afternoon tea!'

Declan laughed at his brother's obvious good humour. 'How's Christine?'

Phillip shrugged, the laughter gone now. 'Still the same.' He motioned for two more vodkas and then said gamely, 'I hear you're trumping that little dark-haired girl from the club.'

Declan grinned. 'You hear right. Nice girl, Bernice, clever and all.'

'Oooh, is it finally lurve!' Phillip was smiling again, he had heard already that it *was* love, from the bird's point of view anyway. It was the talk of the clubs – apparently she adored his brother and told everyone she came across just that. 'She's been talking you up, bruv, telling everyone how great you are. How well you treat her, how much she likes your penthouse.'

Declan could feel himself blushing, and that annoyed him.

'Oooh, Declan's doing a cherry. What's the matter with you, man, you could do worse. She's good-looking, she's willing. Knock yourself out a couple of kids with her – if you don't start soon you'll be too old to play with them.'

'Fuck off, Phil. You know my thoughts on marriage. It doesn't appeal to me.'

Phillip laughed, but it was hollow now. 'Can't say I blame you. I love my Christine, but she's fucking hard work. If I could just get her back to her old self – to how she used to be before . . .' He left the sentence unfinished.

'Come on, Phil, let's get going. The sooner we get this over with the better.' Declan had no intention of getting into a big conversation about Christine, because they had been over this time and time again, and there was nothing anyone could do for her. Personally, he thought that she might benefit from Phillip divorcing her, but he kept that little bit of wisdom to himself, knowing that Phillip might not appreciate the sentiment. But it was obvious to everyone around them that Christine's problem was her husband, and *his* problem was *her*. It was something that could never be resolved to the satisfaction of either of them – they were like a circle, a wedding band, they didn't know where they began, and they certainly didn't know where they were going to end. One thing he knew for certain though – with Phillip and his beliefs there would be no divorce. He was in this marriage for the duration, and he believed that he had to cope with whatever was thrown at him, because Christine was his wife, and they were married in the eyes of God. Even though their marriage was destroying her on a daily basis, they would only part in death, and that was what was so tragic about it all. He had a feeling that when it happened, it would be Christine's death that released her, not his brother's. Even if that meant she achieved it with her own hand.

Oh no, marriage was a mug's game all right, and he was well out of it. As his mother always said, there was more ways to skin a cat, and many ways to scratch an itch. And that was exactly what women were to him – an itch that you scratched for momentary relief.

As they drove along the embankment they were both quiet, each filled with his own thoughts. The good humour they had shared seemed to have evaporated, and they were both aware of that.

Chapter Eighty-One

'What will your dad do, Philly?'

Philly shrugged nonchalantly; he didn't want his friends to know how worried he really was about what had happened. 'Well, suffice to say he won't be happy about it.'

Graham Planter laughed nervously. 'It was funny at the time, but now I ain't so sure.'

'We were out of order, Graham, and my dad will be more annoyed about that than he will at us being pissed. He's funny about respecting the people who work for us. He says that the least we can do is treat the employees how we would like to be treated ourselves – it's something he has hammered into us all our lives.'

Billy Jameson said sadly, 'I wish we'd just gone home, don't you?'

Philly wasn't even going to dignify that with an answer.

The front door slammed, and the boys heard someone taking the stairs two a time. Within seconds the bedroom door was banged open and Phillip Murphy stood there like some kind of avenging angel.

'You fucker! You rude, arrogant little fucker!'

All three boys were tense with fear, the man looked like a maniac. You could almost feel the rage seeping out of his pores.

'Get out, you two, and don't let me see your faces here again.'

The boys were rooted to the spot in fear, and didn't move

until he bellowed, 'I said, out!' Then they scurried from the room as fast as they could, leaving poor Philly to face his father's wrath alone.

Phillip slammed the bedroom door behind him, and stood in front of it, his arms crossed and his face set like concrete. 'Now, I want your version of events, and make sure you tell me the truth, boy, because I know exactly what happened – I watched it on the CCTV cameras.'

'I'm sorry, Dad—'

'Bit late for that, son. Now, either tell me what happened in graphic detail or kiss goodbye to the next six months of your life, because I'll ground you like an errant dog, as big as you are.'

Even at nineteen it didn't occur to Philly to remind his father that he could vote, get married, or drink in any pub he chose to. His father was the law, and that was a fact of life in this house.

'I was drunk. We went to the arcade and I asked the old boy for money to use on the machines. He said no. So I went in the booth and took it. He tried to stop me and I pushed him out of the way, and cunted him. He fell over, and I kicked him.'

Philly's summary was short, precise, and told the main facts of the story without over-dramatising it or making excuses for himself. He knew that it was the only way he would get out of this with his skin intact.

'He's sixty-seven years old and he's worked that booth for over fifty years, and you think because you're *my* son you have the right to treat him like garbage? Is that what this was all about?'

Philly was shaking his head now in utter despair because, in reality, that is *exactly* what he had thought at the time. 'No, Dad, I swear. I was drunk, I know I was out of order. Fucking outrageously out of order, and I know you have every right to be annoyed. I can't make any excuses for my bad behaviour because there ain't any. I just want to take me punishment like a man.'

Phillip laughed nastily. 'A man you ain't! Nineteen and bullying pensioners, a nice old bloke who would lay down his life for me. An old man who was just going about his own business. If a stranger had done that to him, I would have hunted them down and flayed them alive.'

Philly closed his eyes in distress, knowing his father spoke the truth. Phillip Murphy looked after all the people who worked for him, and he made sure they were safe, even getting the women cabs home if they worked late shifts. He was a good employer, and that paid off because his workers were loyal; he remembered all their names, and asked them about their families, and their kids or grandkids. He never forgot them at Christmas, and they knew they could come to him with any problems, major or minor, and get a fair hearing. It was all part of Phillip Murphy's big 'I am' act, but Philly wouldn't say that to his father either.

'Old Donny didn't tell me about it. He wasn't about to grass you up, but one of the girls ran it by me. She was so disgusted at how you behaved she kept the CCTV as evidence. Marvellous, ain't it? Me own son hasn't got the decency to tell me, but a seventeen-year-old college student felt I should know what my son was capable of.'

'Like I say, I was drunk . . .'

The fist when it shot out, got him square on the chin, and knocked him backwards over his bed, until he landed in a heap on the floor under the window seat.

'Drunk. So that's your excuse, is it? You treacherous little cunt. Well, you can get up, and get down to the car, because me and you are going to do some serious apologising, then we are going to have a long heart-to-heart about the perils of drink, and the treatment of people less fortunate than ourselves.'

Philly pulled himself up from the floor and, rubbing his chin, he felt the lump already forming there. It was the first time his father had hit him in years, and he had forgotten just how strong the old bastard was. He understood his father's fury – he wasn't so much annoyed at *what* Philly had done, but was more concerned with how it looked to people outside of the family. Appearances were everything to his father, he lived for his reputation, not just as a serious Face, but as a man. Philly had worked out years ago that it was all an act, his father's whole life was an act, from his church-going to his philanthropic enterprises. He was a fucking fake, and on every level. Philly knew this because in many ways he was just like his father, he was learning the ways of their world, and this would be a lesson for the future.

He wouldn't fuck up like this again, of that much he was sure. He needed his father's support and favour if he was going to get where he wanted to go in life. And that was further than this ponce, of that much Philly was determined.

Chapter Eighty-Two

Donny was embarrassed and it showed. He took the apology well, and shook hands with the lad. Everyone who witnessed Philly's humiliation was secretly pleased to be there and see it. He was an arrogant little fucker, and it was very satisfying to see him cut down to size. Phillip Murphy was a hero to these people, especially now, making his elder son apologise to Donny in full view of everyone. That was how it should be; Philly had treated the man appallingly, and it was right he should pay for it. This scene would be the talk of the seafront for weeks, and that was something the lad had to know, and it only added to his humiliation.

'I'm so ashamed, Donny, that one of my boys could act like that. Well, you and I both know that drink and youngsters don't mix.' Phillip was making the old man laugh, being affable and friendly, the big man. Philly wished he had a gun, because he would happily blow the fucker away at this moment in time.

'He's a good lad, Mr Murphy, and I've never had a problem with him before. I blame those mates of his, they were egging him on.' Donny was trying to make excuses for his employer's son and that was not lost on Philly, who finally had the decency to feel a sliver of remorse.

'Well, Donny, I can guarantee I won't be drinking again for a long time. I really can't apologise enough, it was out of order. Every time I think about it I could die of shame.'

'We're like one big family here, Donny,' Phillip added. 'And if anyone hurts my family, no matter who they are, they pay for it.'

It was what they all wanted to hear, and Philly had a sneaking admiration for his father's spin on what had been, after all, a terrible act of arrogance on his part. Phillip looked like the big benevolent employer, but Philly knew that he would climb over their dead bodies if it got him what he desired.

Back in the office Philly waited to be asked to sit, he knew the protocol by now. Phillip was still incensed at his son's behaviour, and how it reflected on him.

'You done good, kid, but I warn you, one more incident like that and you're on your own.' Phillip saw the shock on his son's face and smiled at Philly's stupidity. 'You're out next time on your arse. Fending for yourself. You've got a bit too much of my brother Jamsie in you, and I intend to make sure that gets knocked out of you sooner rather than later. Bullying is easy, anyone can be a bully. But in this game, you get on a lot better and a lot quicker by looking out for the people who handle your money on a daily basis. This is a cash business, and goodwill goes a lot further than a good hiding, remember that.'

Philly nodded.

'Now, about the drinking. I am going to arrange for you to have a blood test every week, and if I find any drugs in it, I'll brain you where you fucking lie. This wasn't about drink and we both know that, so what had you taken?'

Philly had been expecting this; he could never get one over on his father. 'I'd had an E. I was out of me brains.'

Phillip nodded almost imperceptibly. 'Drugs are for the dimlos, not for the likes of us. Drugs make you stupid, make you forget what you're doing. They make you a cunt in my book, and everyone else's. So make sure that's the last time you do anything that stupid.'

Philly nodded again, seeing his whole social life dissolving before his eyes. He was nineteen for Christ's sakes, not a little kid.

'And one last thing. You need to start treating your mother with some respect, or I'll rip your fucking head off and use it as a football. You have been acting the cunt for a while now, and I think it's about time you grew up.'

Philly didn't answer that. He honestly didn't know what to say.

Chapter Eighty-Three

'Come on, Christine, you know it makes sense.'

Christine was laughing loudly and Breda was pleased to see her so happy. They were having lunch on the seafront at a smart little fish restaurant where the food was only surpassed by the view. Christine ordered herself a large dessert; even though she didn't really want it, she knew it would please Breda. It was strange but the two women had become very close over the last few years. Since Ricky's funeral, Breda had made a point of visiting her almost daily, and they had found that in actuality they had quite a lot in common. Christine knew that Breda did what she did out of genuine caring, but she also knew that she reported back to Phillip. Phillip had been uneasy that she might talk about Ricky's murder to the doctors, but he had not realised that if she had been going to tell anyone the truth about her life, she would have done it long ago. Too many people depended on Phillip for their livelihoods, her own parents included, and she would never do anything to jeopardise them or their safety. She wouldn't trust her loving husband as far as she could throw him; he would take her father out just to get even with her. He was like God in many respects – he could be kind and loving, or he could be vengeful. She knew he saw himself as the nearest thing to God on this earth, so the simile was quite apt.

'I bet Philly's not happy, Breda, he's like his father in many ways. He worries too much about other people's opinions.'

Breda nodded in agreement. 'That's true, Chris. But I think Phillip was right to make him apologise in public. What he did was bang out of order.'

'He's a bully, he talks to me like shit half the time.'

Breda didn't answer her. She knew that Philly was ashamed of his mother, and that it made him feel guilty. But she understood the boy's dilemma in a strange way. He had his father on the one hand – a respected and well-liked man – and, on the other hand, he had a mother who was a drunk, a prescription junkie and the apple of said father's eye. She knew how hard it was for the boys.

'Shall we get another bottle of wine, Bred?'

'If you like. Jamsie's driving, bless him.'

'Has Phillip spoken to him yet?'

Breda shook her head in consternation. 'Never a once. In all these years, Chris. It's unbelievable really.'

Christine signalled for another bottle of wine and said resignedly, 'No, it ain't. You and I both know he's more than capable of worse than that.' She said the words without any malice whatsoever, as if she had finally accepted the way of her world and could live within it. It showed Breda just how far her sister-in-law had come.

'Why don't you leave him, Christine? I know he wouldn't like it, but he loves you enough to let you go. He only wants what's best for you.'

Christine grinned; her white, even teeth were expensively capped, and her make-up was as always perfect, she looked like any other rich woman who lunched their days away. Except her eyes were dead, they held no real life behind them. 'Now, you and I know that he might love me, but he wouldn't let me leave him – he would see that as a failure and you know my Phillip. He doesn't cope well with failure. Poor Philly failed him with his bad behaviour and look where that got him. No, Breda, I'll never leave him, love, and when I do it'll be because one of us is in a body bag.'

Christine laughed at her own wit, but the truth of her words stayed with Breda for the rest of the day.

Chapter Eighty-Four

'You ready, Dad?'

Phillip nodded and, finishing his cup of coffee, he kissed Christine on the cheek and then stood up, yawning widely. 'You and your rugby, Tims, fuck knows where you inherited that from.'

Christine didn't even look up from her *Daily Mail* as she said quietly, but forcefully, 'My father – he's always loved the rugby.'

Timmy saw Phillip's jaw tighten in annoyance, and wondered why his mother had to antagonise him all the time. It was as if she had come full circle, from the timid wretch to this woman who goaded her husband at every opportunity.

'He has sat on his granddad's lap and watched it since he could first walk, Phillip. Philly was football, like *your* family, and Timmy was a rugby boy, like *mine*.' The inference being, how could he have not known that?

'I wasn't really asking that as a question, it was more of a statement, Christine.'

She shrugged nonchalantly. 'Well, I'm glad we sorted all that out.'

Phillip threw the car keys at his son and said quietly, 'Go and get in the car. I want to talk to your mother in private for a minute.'

Timmy did as he was asked without questioning it. At seventeen he was a big lad, hence his being a rugby prop but, like his brother, he did what his father asked him without question.

When they were alone Phillip knelt down by his wife's chair and, putting his index finger under her chin, he forced her face round so he could look into her eyes. 'Now, Christine, I love you very much, but you are starting to get on my fucking nerves. If you challenge me once more in front of the boys, or anyone else come to that, I am going to get very angry indeed. Now, I'm pleased you are feeling better, and I am over the fucking moon that you are much chirpier, and chock-full of banter and chat. But one more crack like that and I'll put my hand right across your lovely face. Do you get my drift?'

Christine was shaking with suppressed anger, but she was also pleased that the fear of him wasn't paralysing her as it used to when she offended him in some way. But she knew not to push him too far; after all, this was Phillip Murphy and she must never forget that, or what he was capable of. She nodded her under-standing and he smiled at her then. That wide, all-encompassing smile that told everyone that all was right with the world.

'Good. I'm glad we got *that* sorted out.'

It was the first time he had ever come back at her like that, and she knew she had to have pushed him too far at last. That he had spoken to her like he had proved to her that even he had his limit, and she knew she would have to be careful in the future.

When he left the house she felt the anger returning once more, and wondered at a man who could still want someone who so obviously loathed him. She took an extra few pills, and washed them down with her first drink of the day. She liked the numbness of booze; it evened out the edges of the world and made her forget for a while that she was like a caged bird. The cage was lovely, there was no doubt about that, but it was a cage all the same.

Chapter Eighty-Five

Ted was sad to admit that he had gone off his elder grandson, and the knowledge grieved him. The boy was a sullen, rude little oik, and that was being nice about him.

As he watched the lad walking around the shop, he could almost feel the resentment coming off him at even having to be there. But this was one time when Ted Booth agreed with his son-in-law. Philly needed a lesson in respect and dealing with the people from this area should give him just that. These were plain-spoken people who said what they thought, and who often possessed a certain rough dignity, even though their surroundings weren't exactly conducive to the finer things in life. But they had something this boy desperately needed – the advantage of being streetwise, and that counted for a lot in this neighbourhood. Maybe seeing how other people had to live might make him appreciate just how lucky he actually was. Ted could only hope so anyway – from what he had heard the boy had been asking for this for a long time. People protected him because of Phillip's reputation, Christine especially. It seemed to him she couldn't see what the boys were really like; but then half the time she couldn't see what was in front of her face she was so out of it. No, this time he thought Phillip had done the right thing by his grandson, and he would help him sort the lad out with pleasure. Young Philly, for all his swaggering, posturing and bravado, wouldn't last ten minutes on this estate, and that was something he needed to learn, and learn fast. Philly had had it too easy, and it was making him weak and vulnerable. Phillip would not tolerate weakness of any kind in his family.

Ted was pleased that Phillip had entrusted the boy to him; it told him that Phillip respected him in a way he had not realised before. And even though he would never like this son-in-law of his, he was willing to do the best he could for his grandson.

'Come on, Philly, start filling those freezers. That stuff will be defrosted before you even open the bloody boxes!'

Philly sighed heavily, but he started the job as requested. He knew his granddad had to give his father a rundown on his behaviour. It was laughable – he was nineteen and still being treated like a kid. But he also knew he had got off lightly in many respects. At least this got him away from the seafront for a while; he was still embarrassed to be seen there, and he would appreciate the chance for everything to calm down and be forgotten about before he showed his face again. He knew it was cowardly, but that was how he felt. But his granddad's shops were the pits; all Happy Shopper teabags, old people and processed foods. The young blokes looked like armed robbers, and he was fascinated at how respectful they were to his grandfather. He wasn't a fool though, he knew it was because of his father – everyone he knew was scared of him, himself included. His dream was not to be like him, but *stronger*, *better* than him. Philly intended to show them all what he was made of, and then no one would ever be able to push him around again.

He opened the box and started to unpack the cheap pizzas and frozen lasagnes. Growing up on a farm he had developed a healthy disgust for this kind of food, and he was glad he had not been brought up on it. Especially if the kids he saw every day were anything to go by – most were already overweight before they started school, and ate crisps and sweets as if they were staple foods instead of treats. It had certainly been an eye-opener all right.

The door opened and Philly automatically looked over to see who it was. He was very pleasantly surprised to see a tall, slim blonde, with killer boots and a come-get-me smile swagger on to the premises.

As she picked up a loaf of bread and a pint of milk, he rushed to the till, saying loudly, 'It's all right, Granddad, I'll see to this young lady.'

Tiffany White looked at the young lad with the handsome face and expensive jeans and decided the day was not going to be a total wipeout after all. Smiling at one another, the two began the ritual mating dance of the young, and suddenly things were not looking so bleak for Philly Murphy. In fact, he was already looking forward to coming back to work in the morning.

Ted Booth smiled in exasperation; he could see the attraction, but he had a feeling that this young hussy might turn out to be a bit too knowing for his grandson, not least because she was already the proud possessor of a nine-month-old daughter. But he knew it would be pointless trying to give the lad advice; after all, he'd only worked here a week and apparently he already knew everything. This was the kind of situation where only experience would be of any real use, and Ted Booth knew for a fact that Tiffany White had enough experience for the both of them; she had been at it since she was thirteen. Ted should know – he had chased her from the backyard of the shop enough times. He had a feeling this grandson of his was about to get his initiation into the real world, especially when he saw Tiffany writing her mobile number down on the back of his grandson's hand.

He went through to the back of the shop, and allowed himself a little chuckle. She'd eat him for breakfast and spit out his balls, without even pausing for a breath. This was going to be fun to watch for a while, and he could do with a laugh.

Chapter Eighty-Six

'Is everything OK, Phillip?'

Declan had not seen Phillip like this in years, he seemed preoccupied and far too quiet for anyone's good. There was definitely something bothering him.

Phillip shrugged, the shrug that he used when he couldn't be bothered to talk. He was chewing his thumbnail, a definite sign of aggravation.

'Is it Christine?'

Phillip nodded. 'She is really pulling my chain lately, and it can get a bit wearing, if you know what I mean. She's always ready to argue with me, and I don't want to fight with her. I just want her to be happy.'

Declan could hear the exasperation his brother's voice. 'Well, look on the bright side, at least she ain't all quiet any more.'

Phillip laughed then. 'Didn't know when I was fucking well off, did I? Do you know, I was about two inches from clumping her today, that should tell you how annoyed I was.'

'Fucking hell, Phillip, that is serious, mate.'

'Precisely. I think we're together too much and that is never good in any relationship that entails the opposite sex.'

He lit a cigarette; he was smoking a lot lately and it wasn't like him. But his perfect life wasn't so perfect any more, and he was restless; he had everything he needed and yet he still didn't feel he had enough. He was unhappy in a way he had never been before, and he wondered if it was because he had gone as far as he ever could, and there was nothing left for him to achieve. It was a sobering thought. Even the other businesses, the guns and the betting were running so smoothly he barely thought about it all. Breda was good at what she did, exceptionally good in fact, and Declan took the main load off his shoulders here so really, other than the farm, he was without any real purpose. It occurred to him that he was bored. It was a concept he had never experienced before, and it intrigued him.

'We need a new project, Declan.'

Declan grinned. He had been expecting this for a while; he could sense that Phillip was getting restless, and he knew what that meant.

'Such as?'

'I don't know yet, but I'm sure I'll think of something.'

Chapter Eighty-Seven

Sunday lunch at Veronica's was now a fortnightly event, and she loved it. As she spread out the pristine white tablecloth and polished the wine glasses, she marvelled at how far her family had come. Jamsie didn't have to jump up and leave the room any longer, though Phillip still didn't throw a word in his direction, but at least he was once more a part of the family, so that had to count for something. Even Eileen and Ted Booth seemed to enjoy themselves these days, and she knew Christine liked having her parents there, well, her father at least. She watched her husband as he half-heartedly read the *News of the World*. She knew he would rather be down the pub, but he couldn't go because Phillip would have something to say about that. Her Phillip knew the importance of family, and she was proud of him for that much as well as for everything else he had achieved.

Sometimes she could cheerfully light a bonfire under that husband of hers; he was so lazy it was unbelievable. He would shite in the chair if they swapped it for a commode. Good job his kids hadn't inherited that from him, they had thankfully got all their energy from her. She was a 'doing' person, her husband on the other hand was a 'do I *have* to do it' type of person. Chalk and cheese, really.

She was cooking a huge piece of pork – from her son's farm, as always – and she had to admit the smell was magnificent. Christine had planted her a few tubs of herbs years ago, and shown her how to look after them, so Veronica had them fresh all year round. It had completely revolutionised her cooking, and she enjoyed the little bit of effort needed to keep them healthy. It pleased her no end to see her herb garden flourishing.

As she laid the table, she surveyed her kitchen and, satisfied that everything was going to plan, she poured herself out a nice cup of tea. They would be descending on her soon and she couldn't wait. She lived for the family all together, enjoying each other's company. She loved to see her kids around her table, chatting and laughing. It made it all worth it, the years of struggle to bring them up, the feeding them on fuck-all, and washing them in the same bath water. She missed those days sometimes, when her kids were small and she was their whole world. But they grew up, and they grew away, and you thanked God for the times they descended on you, and made you feel like you had done something with your life.

Family was all you really had in the end.

Chapter Eighty-Eight

Jamsie was happier than he had been for a long time; he had stopped feeling like his days were numbered, and started to enjoy his life a bit. He had met a girl called Linda Best, and he really liked her – the only bugbear was she had four kids, by two different fathers.

His mother would not be too thrilled about that, but he knew that Breda liked her, or at least she said she did anyway. Breda was all right really – she had looked out for him, and he would always be grateful for that. He knew how much it took for her to defy Phillip and he also knew that she genuinely cared about him, and what happened to him. He still wondered at what had possessed him all those years ago, and he could only say it was the drugs. The drink was one thing, but the drugs were something else entirely. He knew how much Phillip hated them, and that was a point they now both agreed on anyway. His only real goal in life was for Phillip to forgive him; even though Jamsie hated his brother at times, he knew that if Phillip would only give him a chance he would more than prove himself.

He sighed at the thought; all he had left was hope, and that saddened him. People were nice to him – he was a Murphy after all – but they didn't respect him the way they did the others. They took their lead from Phillip, as did everyone around his brother. But it would be nice to have something to look forward to in life. Breda paid him a good wedge to drive for her, but it wasn't a real earn, not a proper wage like the others got. Not enough to buy a decent house, though he did get the use of the car and, in fairness, that was a nice piece of machinery. But now he had Linda in his life, and her ready-made family, he had discovered that he wanted a bit more. Not too much, just enough to give her the things he felt she deserved. Linda got a bad press really, she was a victim of her own niceness. She believed every word said to her, and for the men she'd gone out with before him, that meant she had believed they would stand by her and take care of her. Of course, that had never happened. But he wanted to change that for her. She had given Jamsie something he had never thought he would get again, and that was pride in himself. She made him feel wanted, needed; she made him feel like a man. Not just sexually, but in all ways. She was a good mother too, her kids were nice, well spoken, polite and she made sure they ate well, were in bed at a reasonable time, and kept them spotlessly clean, as she did her little flat.

He would happily marry his Linda, and he would be proud to call her his wife. But he needed a better job and better prospects, because four kids didn't come cheap. So he was going to take the bull by the horns, and ask to speak with Phillip. His brother could only say no, and if you didn't ask then you didn't get.

Chapter Eighty-Nine

Phillip was watching his family as they all sat around the table; there was no doubt about it, his mother understood the need for families to spend quality time together. Christine looked happier today than she had for ages, which was strange considering at home she was like a bear with a sore arse. But he found her spunkiness exciting. She was still a looker too, for all her boozing; her face was relatively unlined and she had a great figure. She was the only woman he had ever truly wanted, and that would never change. But now the boys were more or less grown up, she needed something to *do*, as did he. That was his next step, sorting out his wife, and his life.

He eyed his father, saw him leaning back in the chair, bored already by the conversation and the people around him. He was a useless ponce, but his mother wouldn't have a word said against him, and that was how it should be. He was her husband and she stood by him no matter what. It was the law of the pavement, and it worked in a funny way; it kept people together who actually had fuck-all in common. That was what marriage was all about – you kept at it, you didn't run away at the first sign of discord.

He could hear Philly talking about the people who came in the shop, and he was pleased to hear his disbelief at the abject poverty he saw around him. That would do him the world of good, seeing how the other half lived. He sat forward and looking at his son he said easily, 'That was us lot once.'

Philly looked at his father in consternation. 'What was?'

'The estate. This house is a part of all that. I couldn't get your grandmother to move away, she loves it here. But we didn't have a lot when we were small.' Phillip looked at his father then. 'No disrespect intended, Dad.'

'None taken, son. It was a different world then.'

Philly was still unsure; he couldn't imagine his father like the young blokes he saw every day with no schooling, no interest in anything. 'But you got away from it all, didn't you?' Philly thought he had said the right thing, and was shocked at his father's reply.

'Not really, it never leaves you, Philly. I had a fight every day of my life. I was already breaking bones for money at your age, and making mc mark. You take a good long look around you, and you might realise just what a charmed life you really have.'

'Hear, hear.' It was Ted speaking and everyone stopped eating to look at him in amazement. He rarely said much at the dinner table. 'He's had it too easy, Phillip. You've done the right thing planting him in there, he will finally see how most people really live.'

Philly wished the old fucker would shut up but he was too shrewd to voice that opinion, of course.

'That was the idea of it, Ted. The thing is with those people, it's the old chicken and egg – what came first, poverty or debt?'

'Too right, my son.' This from Phillip Senior who loved reminiscing about the good old days and how hard they had it. He looked at his three grandsons and said loudly, 'You lot don't know you're fucking born.'

'Oh, get the violins out.' Everyone laughed at Breda's words, and it broke the tension that was falling over the table.

Changing the subject, Phillip asked, 'I think we need to start up a new enterprise, anyone got any ideas? I need a new project.'

Jamsie put his hand up like a schoolkid and, to the amazement of the whole family, Phillip looked at him and said gently, 'What, Jamsie?'

Jamsie smiled uneasily and said in a low, quivering voice, 'Car fronts, prestige cars.'

Phillip digested the words for a few moments before saying with interest, 'What, selling them, you mean?'

Jamsie nodded. 'I already buy the cars for us all, don't I? I know the people to deal with, where we can get the deals et cetera. But there is also a hidden market, especially on the seafront, and I don't mean ringing motors, that's for mugs. Terry Dedham is coining it in, he nicks cars to order for the Arab states. Rollers the fucking lot, and he ships them there himself.'

'How do you know all this, Jamsie?' Phillip was genuinely interested in what he was hearing.

'I went to school with him, didn't I? I saw a fuck-off Bentley in one of his workshops, and I asked him if he was taking on the higher-end cars, and he laughed and told me the score. I thought then it was a good scam, because everyone's a winner really. People actually approach him to nick the cars when they can't fund the finance any more. It's a good business, I've had a little investigate, like. I was going to run it by Breda. I could sort that with me eyes closed, you know me, Phil, there ain't a car been built that I can't get into within seconds. But the thing that interested me most was, there's more car fronts in Southend than anywhere else in the country. People come from all over the country to buy their motors from there, so it's a perfect front operation. You expect to see cars on a car front. If you do it properly, you can turn the cars around in less than twenty-four hours. Nicked, logged and in a container from Tilbury docks before the fucking insurance company has sent out the forms.'

No one had heard Jamsie say so much in one go in sixteen years, and the table was shrouded in a deadly hush for a few seconds after he had finished. He was so nervous he was breathing through his mouth.

Phillip digested his brother's words for a few moments, before he broke into a beatific grin, saying happily, 'What a fucking good scam, Jamsie my brother! You have just redeemed yourself in one fell swoop. What a blinding little business for us. And while I think about it, why ain't that cunt Dedham been giving me a touch? If it's on the front then it comes by me. So that will be your introduction to becoming his business partner, Jamsie.'

Declan wasn't as sure as Phillip that it would go so smoothly; he knew for a fact that Dedham dealt with a serious firm from Liverpool, and they might not be as amenable as Dedham to sharing their operation. But he wasn't going to piss on anyone's firework just yet. This was Jamsie's moment.

Phillip picked up his wine and, holding the glass up to his little brother, he said generously, 'To Jamsie. I knew there was a Murphy in there somewhere, just dying to get out.'

Jamsie was red-faced with happiness, even his ears were glowing. And Veronica was so choked at the turn of events she was nearly in tears. What she had prayed for all these years had finally come to pass. Her boys were together again at last, Jamsie was back in the family again. God love him, he had paid a heavy price. And now it was finally all over, and her family was united again.

Christine poured herself another glass of wine and, laughing, she said to Jamsie, 'Good on you, Jamsie. See if you can get me a nice little Bentley Sport, I've always fancied one of them.'

Ted Booth hated that his daughter seemed to be accepting their criminality without a thought. He knew too, as well as his Christine did, that now she had mentioned wanting the car, she would be given it by her husband. And considering the amount of alcohol she put away on a daily basis, a powerful car was not something she should be in charge of. All the same he kept his own counsel; after all, what say did he have over a husband and wife? Phillip would give her whatever she wanted just as he had always done.

Chapter Ninety

'What a turn up, eh? Jamsie having a bright idea is like MPs telling the truth – it's a great concept but you can't imagine it really happening.'

Declan laughed out loud at the truth of Phillip's statement. 'It is a good idea and, in fairness to him, he had a good little root about before voicing it. And as he says, there's not a person alive who knows more about motors than our Jamsie. Remember when he was about thirteen and he nicked that squad car? I thought Mother would kill him that night.'

Phillip grinned. 'Fuck, I'd forgotten about that. He drove it into the pub and parked it up next to my motor. I thought I was seeing things.'

They chuckled together, then Declan said seriously, 'Remember, Dedham was away with me, I was in Parkhurst with him. He was a good mate in there, Phillip. Because we came from the same manor we sort of teamed up. You know what it's like.'

Phillip didn't actually because he had never gone further than remand, but neither of them mentioned that.

'Well, he got good mates with a Scouser called Jonnie Piper, you've met him a couple of times. He's been to the club.'

Phillip nodded. He had liked the geezer, he was sound.

'Well, the Pipers are a big force in Liverpool, and if they are behind the cars then we have to deal with them gently.'

It was the wrong thing to say and Declan realised that immediately.

'So what are you trying to tell me, Declan? We have to write to some cunt in Liverpool and ask for permission to trade on our own fucking turf? Or shall we invite him down for the day, and ask him why he has been having an earn on *my* front and not giving me a piece of it? Only, that is normally common courtesy – no one can sell a fucking hot dog without me knowing about it and getting a little touch. I personally think this a diabolical liberty.'

Declan sighed in annoyance and it wasn't lost on Phillip. 'All right, Phillip, calm down. All I am saying is, the Pipers are like *us*, they are serious businessmen, and they deserve our respect.'

'And they will get it, bruv, as long as they do what I fucking want. Fucking Scousers dictating to me, what next! The Welsh turning up mob-handed and taking over the nightclubs? Jesus wept, I've heard everything now.'

Declan laughed but he was still worried. Unlike Phillip, who had an infallible belief in himself and getting what he wanted, Declan knew that sometimes it was better to negotiate than it was to demand. But he had planted the seed, and he would leave it for now – that was the best way to deal with Phillip. Let him work it out for himself, and then act like it was his idea in the first place. But Declan was genuinely perturbed, because Dedham wasn't without his own little back-up. He was a shrewdie in his own way; after all, you didn't get where he was without a few Faces in your corner.

Declan would start his own inquiry first thing in the morning; in contrast to Phillip he liked to know everything there was to know about his adversaries. There were times when guns, anger and the belief in your God-given right to take what you wanted from who you wanted just wasn't enough.

Chapter Ninety-One

Linda Best was pleased to see Jamsie so happy. He was almost overflowing with good humour and camaraderie. He was, without doubt, the best thing that had ever happened to her, or her kids. He was a really decent bloke, and she was lucky to get him.

As she dressed the kids in their best clothes she felt nervous once more; she was finally meeting his mother, and she was terrified at the prospect. Veronica Murphy was a legend around the streets, although she had a good rep. She'd help out anyone but was very protective of her kids. Well, Linda could understand that – she was the same about her own. She knew she wouldn't be a catch as far as Mrs Murphy was concerned; she already had four kids and she had been round the turf more than a few times, but Jamsie assured her his mother was looking forward to meeting her. But then, blokes were thick as shit about most things, so that didn't really give her much confidence.

She checked her make-up and gave her outfit – black trousers and a white fitted shirt, bought especially for the occasion from Next – a final once-over. She hoped she passed muster. As Jamsie ushered them out to the car, she felt a wave of sickness wash over her, and prayed that she didn't fuck up somehow.

Jamsie, for his part, was proud of his new little family and, picking up her two-year-old daughter, he said jovially, 'You looking forward to meeting my mum, Julie?'

The little girl grinned happily; she loved him like a father, and he felt it as acutely as he would had she been his own child. He loved all four of them; and they made him feel like he had something to work for, made him feel he had his own family. As they drove off, he began singing at the top of his voice, and the children delightedly joined in with him.

Chapter Ninety-Two

'Fucking hell, Mum, Linda's all right. So she's got four kids? That's Jamsie's business, not ours. I think she's good for him. I mean, let's face it, I've never seen him so happy, have you?'

Veronica had to admit there was truth in her daughter's statement. 'But four kids! What the shag would he take on four kids for? He should find a nice girl and have some of his own.'

Breda rolled her eyes at the ceiling in annoyance. 'Well, promise me you'll make her welcome and give her a chance. This must seem like some kind of torture for her, meeting all us en masse.'

'Nice-looking girl, young. Saw her in the pub with him, she has a nice smile,' Phillip Senior piped up from his armchair.

Veronica didn't even bother to answer her husband, everyone in the pub was nice to him; God Himself knew, he spent enough fucking time there.

Breda jumped out of her seat quickly. 'They just pulled up. Porrick, answer the door.'

Porrick pulled his large frame from his chair and ambled towards the hallway. He was a nice kid, Porrick, but he would never get further than a strong arm; everyone agreed he wasn't the sharpest knife in the drawer. But he was a good kid nonetheless, and his wild streak was an asset in his profession.

Veronica looked around her kitchen, making sure there wasn't a thing out of place, and then, forcing a smile, she waited to meet her youngest son's girlfriend.

Jamsie walked in carrying a little dark-haired girl, with huge eyes and long eyelashes, almost glued to his neck. Veronica's heart went out to her. Then Linda walked in with her older children. Good-looking kids, all well dressed and very quietly behaved.

'Mum, this is Linda Best. Linda, my old mum.' Jamsie spoke with obvious pride and love.

'Pleased to meet you.' Linda almost curtseyed and for that alone Veronica couldn't help but like her on sight.

'How do you do, Mrs Murphy.' The older children spoke as one, and Veronica was thrilled at their obvious good manners, and the fact they were spotlessly clean. But what Veronica couldn't believe was the change in this son of hers – he looked almost ecstatic with pride – and she knew then that this girl was good for him, was just what he needed.

Smiling widely she said pleasantly, 'Sit yourselves down, and I'll make some milkshakes, shall I?' She spoke to the children and they all nodded in unison.

'Yes, please, Mrs Murphy.'

'Jesus, they're gorgeous, Linda. Can I get you a glass of wine, child? I expect you need one coming here like this, it must be awful for you.'

Linda practically cried with relief.

Jamsie was thrilled and, walking over to his mum, he said quietly, 'Thanks, Mum, I knew you'd love her once you met her. Oh, and this is the youngest, Julie.' The little girl grinned shyly, pushing her face further into Jamsie's neck. 'She's the shy one. The older girl is Cindy, the middle boy there is Lewis, and the little girl beside him is his twin sister, Leona. This lot are hungry and ready for one of your lovely roast dinners, aren't you?'

They smiled and nodded in agreement. He watched as they were introduced to the rest of the family, and he sighed in relief. It was going to be all right. For the first time in years he felt his life was worth living.

As Veronica saw the way her son and Linda Best looked at one another, she resigned herself to the situation. It was wonderful to see her son so happy, and this girl seemed to be the reason for that. He was a natural father, and watching him with those children made her realise just how stunted his life had been until now. That was Phillip's fault, but she would never admit that out loud, of course. Still, her heart was sore knowing her youngest son's life had been blighted for so many years. The guilt tore at her then, and she determined to do the best for him and his new-found little family. At least the girl wasn't a whore, she had a bit of something about her anyway. She settled the children down in front of a DVD of *Mary Poppins* in the lounge, and then made a point of chatting to Linda about herself and her family as she finished cooking dinner for them all. Within the hour they were old friends.

Chapter Ninety-Three

'She seems nice, Jamsie.' Phillip's voice was quiet; they were smoking in the garden, and Jamsie was inordinately pleased at his brother's words. If Phillip liked her she was in.

'She *is* a nice girl, Phillip. Had a rough time of it, but she makes me happy, so what can I say?'

Phillip was amazed at his brother's demeanour. Jamsie was like a different person around Linda Best. It reminded him of when he had met Christine, he had wanted to be a better man for her. She had made him want more from life, so he could give her the world. 'The kids are nice and all, really well brought up, polite and that.'

Jamsie nodded in agreement. 'She's a good mother, I can't take that away from her. She's done a good job considering she's been on her Jack Jones with them.'

'Who're the culprits then?'

'The eldest girl's father is some bloke from West Ham, and the other three are by Robbie Foyle, the treacherous ponce. Never given her a penny towards any of them, and do you know, he fucking robbed them one Christmas. Nicked his own kids' presents! Fucking scum.'

Phillip looked suitably scandalised at his brother's words. 'I hope you had a word, Jamsie.'

Jamsie nodded. 'I done him one night in Canning Town, with a baseball bat. Told him if he went near them ever again I'd kill him. She don't know that, like – Linda ain't the type of person who can handle trouble. She's more of a keep-your-head-down-and-hope-it-goes-away kind of girl.'

Phillip laughed softly. 'Well, she's certainly won Mother over.'

Jamsie paused a moment, before saying, 'Look, Phillip, I know me and you have had our differences, but I swear to you, I'll make it up to you and Declan. My life is finally on some kind of even keel, and I want it to stay like that. I have been finding out everything there is to know about the motors and, when you're ready, I'll take you through it.'

Phillip nodded thoughtfully. He was staring at his brother in that vacant way he had sometimes and Jamsie found he was holding his breath with nervousness. Then, offering his hand out, Phillip shook his brother's hand, squeezing it tightly as he said genuinely, 'Good luck to you, bruv, she's a nice girl. Even Christine seems to be getting on with her, she ain't stopped talking since she came in. Are you going to marry her?'

Jamsie nodded happily. 'Yeah. Be a mug not to. She's my world now, Phillip, her and them kids.'

Phillip nodded in absolute agreement. 'They are your family now, mate, and family is *all* that really matters. Do Mum good to have some more little ones to dote on, she needs all that.'

Jamsie was thrilled at the turn of events, and smiled happily at his brother.

'Come in to the office tomorrow, and we'll get the ball rolling. There's a nice house I own not far from here, Jamsie, four bedrooms, large semi-detached. Just needs a bit of TLC. It's yours. Call it an early wedding present. I'll have the people renting it out by the end of the week.'

Jamsie was shocked and overcome at his brother's generosity. 'Oh, Phillip, what can I say?'

Phillip waved his thanks away quickly, and went into the house. Jamsie was going to be a lynchpin for their new business, so that meant he needed to be treated as one of the family, and he now needed to be *seen* to be treated as an integral part of the business. Hence the new house, and the new wage. Personally, Phillip still hated him for what he had done, but he wouldn't let on about that. It wasn't going to gain him anything, whereas being nice would get him everything. As always there was an agenda and, as always, Phillip kept the real agenda to himself.

Jamsie was over the moon to be invited once more back into the fold, and he privately toasted his brother's generosity before rejoining the others inside.

That Linda was amazed they were being given a four-bedroom house, in a nice road, was an understatement. She almost fainted with the shock and, when she looked at Veronica Murphy and saw the woman's obvious pleasure at her good fortune, she burst into tears of happiness and relief. Phillip put his arm around her shoulder and said loudly, 'I think I am going to be my brother's best man, Linda, so you and the girls had better start planning the wedding. After all, that house was a wedding present.'

Linda was speechless and, when Jamsie nodded at her, she started to cry once more. Veronica was happier than she had been in years – Linda had potential, and Jamsie was back in the family proper. She saw Christine hug the girl and wish her the best, and she felt that her family was finally growing and evolving again, and that was what families were meant to do. Veronica loved her family to death, and that was not an overstatement. No matter what, you protected them, each and every one of them.

Chapter Ninety-Four

Jonnie Piper was a small man, but he was still not someone you would look at and dismiss. He had an air about him that said he could be a bit of a menace if crossed and, from what Phillip had heard, it was a reputation he had earned fair and square.

Phillip was surprised to find that he genuinely liked Jonnie. He had a good sense of humour and a catalogue of stories that were as funny as they were interesting. So he was well pleased with this initial meeting. Especially as Jonnie had come down to see *him*, and not vice versa. It was the little things that pleased Phillip Murphy, and the fact this man had travelled down to see him without question went a long way. If the meeting was on his turf, then he had the natural advantage. Piper also seemed impressed with the farm, and that told Phillip that he was a man of a discerning nature. He had treated Old Sammy with respect too, and listened to what he had had to say, suggesting that he was a gentleman. Scally or not, Phillip was pleased to be dealing with someone of such calibre. He saw no reason why they couldn't all earn together and enjoy the partnership, for the time being at least. So, all in all, Phillip was a very happy man.

Piper's wife had been his companion for over twenty-five years, and over the course of this first meeting she and Christine were already like bosom pals; both were first wives, and each still adored by their partners. In fact, the similarity between the two men in some respects was uncanny. They were like two peas in a pod in every way except looks. They had a natural affinity that seemed to give them a really solid understanding of each other. Both had fought to get where they were, and both had set ideas about how they conducted their private lives. Like Phillip Murphy, there was no scandal to be heard about Jonnie Piper. No little birds in the offing, or errant kids on the local housing estates. Phillip saw that kind of behaviour as disgusting; disrespecting your wife and kids was something he found anathema. Chasing skirt when you should be chasing the dollar was a mug's game and left you open to all sorts of situations decent men avoided like the fucking plague. To Phillip, it showed a weakness of character and inherent untrustworthiness: if you could swindle your own close family, then you were capable of anything.

Jonnie had his wife Mary and family and that was enough. Like Phillip, he was a good Irish Catholic boy, and he knew the importance of family. But, unlike Phillip, he didn't enjoy the violence, or feel the need to pretend every second of every day. In reality, he was the person Phillip wanted to be.

Phillip was fascinated by this man; he was observing him at close quarters, and he liked what he saw. He knew that he had the same effect on people as Jonnie and that pleased him. That Phillip also knew he could buy and sell Jonnie was even more satisfying, because he knew that he had the edge. He had seen the man's utter respect for the way they lived, he had felt his admiration. This was going to be a really good call.

Phillip was also pleased with Jamsie – he had researched the ins and outs of the cat's arse where this con was concerned and, if Phillip was honest with himself, he was pleasantly surprised. It seemed Jamsie had a natural flair for the job that was as surprising as it was welcome. He still hated him with a passion, but he could put up with him while he was bringing in such a good earn. It wasn't hard pretending; after all, he was the master at it. The thought brought a smile to his face and Jonnie, seeing it and mistaking it for bonhomie, smiled in return. Pouring them all large malt whiskies, Phillip said jovially, 'A toast, mate, to a good business partnership.'

Jonnie and the women raised their glasses, and Jonnie answered genially, 'Now you're onboard we can really make this fly. I can see that you and your brothers have put a lot of thought into this, and it can become much bigger. But what I wanted to ask you about as well is if you are interested in the money laundering? I've had a touch recently with the euro, and I'm looking for an investor.'

Phillip had heard wind of this euro scam, and he was intrigued. If Piper already wanted to talk other business, then the car fronts were basically sewn up. He had laundered money many times – it was how most people cleaned their wages. But this was seen as a necessity rather than a business deal. The tax were shit-hot on it these days and that, as always, just made the average bloke more determined to keep as much of his dosh as possible. It was a disgrace what Labour had done to the working man, more interested in the lazy cunts. Let's face it, no one who wanted a quality of life was going to vote for them. Phillip was disgusted with the country. As far as he was concerned, any man, especially someone like Tony Blair, who couldn't even admit to being a closet Catholic, who wouldn't admit to something so personal and important as his religion, wasn't worth the proverbial wank. If you couldn't stand up for your beliefs you were scum in Phillip's book. Religion taught you a way of living. It taught you that there was something *bigger* than you, something out there that knew the real you. It gave you a set of guidelines and, if you lived by them, you lived well. People without a good grounding didn't make the most of their lives. That was what he thought, and as much as he hated the priests at his sons' school, they had given the boys a good grounding and that was the most important thing.

'I would love to discuss the laundering further with you,

Jonnie Boy, but I think the ladies have had enough business tonight, don't you?'

Jonnie laughed in agreement, but knew he had piqued Phillip's interest. He couldn't believe his luck really; this bloke was pure class, and he knew that any association with him could only better himself. He needed someone on the ground this end, and he knew he couldn't refuse this man what he asked without a war, so he was willing to compromise. That he had every intention of leaving him out of the main earn though he wasn't about to admit.

Jonnie, as much as he liked Phillip Murphy, knew in his heart of hearts that the next step Phillip would make could only be towards taking complete control. But he kept his own counsel; after all, as the Bible said, sufficient to the time thereof, and when it happened – and it *would* happen – he would have all his soldiers in a row and ready to go. Jonnie Piper was a lot of things, but a fool wasn't one of them.

As they chatted about nothing, Christine watched her husband surreptitiously. She saw he was playing the big 'I am', and she knew that Jonnie and Mary were mugs if they thought this was the way they would always be treated from now on. Once Phillip had his in, he would go for the jugular, and she wondered what they would say if she let that little gem out of the bag. But she wouldn't – she was too tired, and too shrewd these days. Plus, she liked her way of life, and she knew that she had already pushed this man as far as he was willing to go. She had to watch her behaviour for a while, and enjoy the fruits of his labour. After all, what else was there for her? Her sons were off her hands, and her husband would once more be fully occupied all day and all night. He always was when he was setting up a new business, so she was going to lie back and enjoy the peace and quiet. They were all still chatting and laughing when she saw the car lights coming down the drive. She glanced at the clock, it was twenty past twelve.

'Who's that at this time of night?' Christine sounded worried and, getting up, she heard her husband laughing. 'What's going on, Phil?'

He grinned at her. 'It's your new car, darling, straight off the M1. I ordered it from a geezer I know in Manchester.'

She heard the intake of breath from Mary, and they all got up and made their way out to the drive. It was lit up like Battersea Power Station, and the Bentley convertible was gleaming in the halogen lights.

'Oh, Phillip, it's lovely.' Even though she knew it had been delivered at this particular moment for no other reason than to impress Jonnie and his wife, she was still thrilled with it. Because she had mentioned it she had got it; these days that was all she had going for her, so she would use it to her heart's delight.

Declan was out of the car and handing her the keys.

'I wondered where you'd got to tonight!'

'Enjoy, Chris, it's a fuck of a motor.'

'Thanks, Phillip. I love it.'

'Your wish is my desire, babe.' He smiled amiably at her and walked into the house with the two men.

She knew she and Jonnie's wife were to ooh and ahh over the car while the three men talked the serious business of the night. It was strange though, now she had the car, she wasn't even that bothered about it any more. But the boys would love it, and that was something to look forward to; she saw so little of them these days. Her life was even emptier than before, and she knew that wasn't going to change. The boys had grown up and grown away, and she didn't know how to bring them back to her.

'Are you all right, love?'

Christine smiled at her new friend – she had few people she could call that these days – and said sadly, 'I'm feeling a bit emotional, I think.'

Mary put a friendly arm around her waist and said seriously, 'I'm not surprised, love, you don't get much change out of a hundred and twenty grand for one of them. You are a very lucky girl.'

Christine smiled, but she didn't answer her – she didn't know what to say. It always came down to the financial rewards, that was the trouble. But her life had cost her something far more precious – she had compromised her sanity. She was trapped, and she accepted that, because she could never leave her husband and, if she did, she would have nowhere to go. Phillip owned her, like he did this car, and everything around her.

Chapter Ninety-Five

Christine had taken the new Bentley for a spin, and ended up at her mother-in-law's. She often went round there when she was at a loose end; Veronica understood her better than most people. As much as she resented her mother-in-law at times, Christine knew that the woman would always fight for her in any way she could. In her marriage that was important, because Phillip listened to his mother, and that was only because she *was* his mother. Like most men, he had a romanticised image of her and she also knew that, in Phillip's mind, the woman lucky enough to give birth to him *had* to be fucking special.

'Hello, love, you look well. I heard about the car, it's lovely.'

Veronica had never driven in her life, and had literally no interest in cars of any kind. But she knew this was a seriously expensive motor, and she also knew the neighbours would see it; that was her way of enjoying her daughter-in-law's good fortune.

'I love it. How're the arrangements going for the wedding?'

'Good, she's a very nice girl that Linda, and those children are really great kids.'

'I liked her. She gets on well with Breda and all. Even Phillip likes her!'

Veronica laughed with her then. 'I know, and he can be so fucking funny about people and their lifestyles, if you know what I mean.' It was the nearest she would ever get to criticising him, and they both knew it. But Veronica was amazed at her son's

305

acceptance of a girl with four kids by two different men, and never a wedding ring on her finger.

'Jamsie's happy, that's what really matters. At the end of the day it's fuck-all to do with Phillip, isn't it?'

Veronica didn't answer the girl, she wasn't comfortable with this kind of talk about her son. 'Can I get you a cup of tea?'

Christine grinned. 'I'd rather have a drink, to be honest, but it's a bit early even for me! Tea will be fine.'

Veronica bit her lip, but she smiled anyway. 'Don't drink and drive, you know how I worry about you, child.'

Christine hugged the woman with genuine affection, she knew she really did care about her. Now her loving husband, on the other hand . . . It had occurred to her that the way he let her drink, he must harbour a hope she would wrap the car around a convenient lamp post. Yet she knew in her heart that wasn't true. In his own way he still needed her, whatever it was she had, whatever had attracted him to her in the first place, still kept him by her side. Because if any man had reason to walk out, he did. She knew if she had pushed a normal man like she had pushed him, they would have left long ago. But then he wasn't normal, was he?

She pushed the thoughts from her mind again, she had to stop dwelling on everything. The doctor said she had too much time to think, too much time on her hands. You had to laugh at men, it was all cut and dried for them. They knew nothing.

Veronica placed the teapot on the table and Christine got up and opened the biscuit tin. She ate a couple of digestives noisily – if you ate in this house you were all right. If not, you got a lecture about healthy eating and she wasn't in the mood. Plus, it pleased Veronica to see her eat, not that she ate very much these days. She still cooked, but she never had an appetite for what she produced. She enjoyed seeing the boys eat her food though, it was all they let her do these days, that and their washing and ironing, and the way things were going they wouldn't even need that soon.

'Are you all right, Chris? You were miles away again.'

Christine brought herself back to the present with difficulty; she was losing a lot of time lately, she would sit down and the next thing she knew hours had passed. It was the pills, she blamed everything on the pills. 'I'm fine, just a bit tired. I don't sleep that well, as you know.'

'You've seemed better in yourself lately, love, more lively, like.'

'Feel sick a lot of the time, to be honest. Tired out, and sick.'

Veronica grinned and said mischievously, 'Not pregnant, girl, are you? It's often the late ones that cause the trouble.' Veronica laughed in delight at the idea. She would be thrilled to have a new baby to fuss over.

But a cold hand of fear clutched at Christine's heart. Because she knew then, without a shadow of a doubt, that Veronica had identified *exactly* what was wrong with her. And that couldn't happen, she couldn't have another child. Not by *him*.

Veronica watched the blood drain from her daughter-in-law's face, and she was saddened that what her generation would have classed as good news was seen as something to fear by this new generation. This girl had money and time, the two things a child needed in life to thrive, yet the prospect of a new life filled this girl with horror. What else had she to do with herself? She had a life that was crying out for some kind of meaning, she did nothing of value from one end of the week to the other, except drink, take her meds and shop. If she didn't have her urge to clean, she would be pissed all day long. For the first time Veronica felt a twinge of resentment for this girl who she knew was not right, not right at all.

'Don't bloody wish that one on me, for Christ's sake!' Christine was trying to make a joke now, but her mind was whirling. If she was pregnant, then no one must ever know about it. Especially not this woman, she would see it as a gift from God. Not what it really was – a punishment from Him. Because there would be no getting rid of it, not in this family anyway. All of them breaking their necks to get to Mass every Sunday, telling themselves it cancelled out their actions in real life. She was suddenly sweating, because she knew as sure as she knew her own name that she was pregnant. She felt too old to be pregnant. By a man she knew would see it as a wonderful event, as something to celebrate, to enjoy. Who would make her stop drinking, make her stop the pills, a man who would see that his child had the best start in life, and whose child would be tainted because it bore his name and his DNA.

Christine left Veronica's as soon as she could and drove for two hours to a chemist where no one knew her, where she bought three pregnancy tests. Starting up the car, her brand-new, lovely car, she contemplated her situation. She was still crying when she got home, but the house was empty and the kitchen was warm. She opened a bottle of Barolo and drank herself into a stupor. She would do the test first thing the next morning.

She was asleep at the kitchen table when Philly came home to change his clothes. He walked by her, his nose turned up in disgust. She was nothing but a drunk, and how his father put up with her he didn't know. He left her there, knowing that Timmy would put her to bed. Personally, he thought she was a disgrace. After changing his clothes he left the house quietly; he was on a promise again, and he couldn't believe his luck. Tiffany White had thighs like a pair of nutcrackers, tits you could lose your whole face in, and she was up for anything, anything at all. She was filthy, and he was loving every second of it.

Chapter Ninety-Six

Phillip was bored out of his brains, and Declan knew that when he was like this he was dangerous. He recognised all the signs – when things went too smoothly Phillip wanted out. He needed to prove that he didn't need anyone. He very quickly gravitated from having a new friend and business partner to convincing himself that the same person was out to take what was his. It was a pattern that repeated itself far too often. Declan would never use the word paranoia out loud, but it was there at the back of his mind nonetheless. Most people were happy when things were going well, didn't feel the urge to stir everything up and cause ructions. But then most people weren't Phillip Murphy.

It occurred to Declan that he was getting fed up with playing the peacemaker all the time. For all his talk, one of the true reasons why he deliberately kept himself from any real relationships was because he needed to keep Phillip on track. It was a real eye-opener when he finally admitted that to himself. Here he was, well into his thirties and still having to pat down a man who was becoming increasingly unstable as the years wore on. Now he had a wife who was off her face, and two kids who were basically being left to do as they pleased. Phillip was ignoring his boys just as he did his wife, and her wants, her needs. Feast or famine as usual – either controlling their every move, or acting as though they didn't exist. Declan loved his brother, he loved all his family, but he was not blind to Phillip's faults and anyone who really knew him was wary of him. Phillip had a kink in his nature that it wasn't wise to ignore; he was dangerous. He could turn on a coin, and no one was immune.

Phillip was becoming more and more outrageous in his actions and his beliefs, and Declan knew it was only a matter of time before he went too far. In the past he had been able to head him off at the pass, so to speak. Keep his brother reined in – only he could talk him out of some of the more lunatic actions. But that was getting harder and harder lately. Phillip was fixated on Piper, and Phillip fixated on someone was not a good thing, for *anyone* concerned.

Phillip was now on a mission, and that was to take the car fronts from Jonnie Piper. He hadn't actually admitted it yet, it was still all about how great Jonnie was, how wonderful it would be to work with him, but Declan knew the signs. Just as he knew that there was much more for the taking if they used their combined loaves of bread. He sighed inwardly; initially in for the proverbial penny, he was now in for the pound. Or in this case, euro.

'Have you thought about the other business yet, Phil?'

Phillip pretended to be considering his brother's words, as if he had only just realised what the real potential of the scam was. It was all Oscar-winning stuff, if you didn't know him like Declan did. 'Let me put that back to you, bruv. What exactly do *you* think about this money laundering, Declan?'

Declan shrugged. He knew how to play the game. 'It's not the laundering I'm interested in, we already have all that in place. Like you, Phil, I am more interested in the counterfeiting. Jonnie didn't talk too much about that side of it, I noticed. But this new five-hundred euro note is supposed to be well worth the aggro. It's so neat, right, you can fit over twenty grand in a fag packet. It's perfect for moving large quantities of bogus cash around Europe. They are literally a piece of piss, Phillip, easier to copy than a twenty-quid Rolex. We sell them for three hundred a pop – that way we don't have the hag of passing them on; the buyer takes the real risks.'

Phillip shrugged in annoyance. His anti-European stance was well known to everyone around him. He saw England as an island, and if he had his way he would personally brick up the Channel Tunnel. 'Fucking euro! Mickey Mouse money, Monopoly money more like. But I can see where you're coming from – the most we've got is a fifty pounder. So a five-hundred euro note has to be worth it. I think you're right, bruv, me and you will have a touch there. See what we can get on the go. We'll shoot out to Marbella, see a few faces out there, do the usual, find out who the real players are in the game. Then we'll aim Jonnie Piper out of it; after all, he needs us, we don't need him.'

Declan nodded; that was his thought on the subject entirely. Piper was out either way. Unlike Phillip, Declan had not really taken to Jonnie. There was something off-kilter, and he wasn't sure exactly what it was. But Declan's shit-detector was on red alert, and it bothered him. He still didn't want the man dead though, which he had a feeling would be the upshot where Phillip was concerned. When Phil destroyed people, he liked them gone for good. They literally disappeared off the planet. No body meant no Filth, meant no forensics, meant they could all get on with their lives. It was another one of his brother's many little foibles. The trouble was, Declan had a feeling that Jonnie Piper had some serious clout behind him, he was big in his own way. But maybe not big enough to take on Phillip Murphy.

So it was now a case of finding out who was the real sponsor, and why they were so determined to keep their name out of the loop. Declan knew a few people who, though they liked Phillip, drank with him, socialised with his family, would not enter into a partnership with him because they knew it was a fruitless enterprise. Phillip wanted all or nothing, and that was never going to change. That meant one of two things: one, the people, or person concerned, were on the run (fair enough, but hardly something you would be comfortable keeping from people who you needed, and who would know the score anyway) or two, this was a set-up to take what they had. Personally, he was for the latter option. Phillip had pissed off a lot of people over the years, but even then it would take one brave fuck to try and have him over. So it was pretty much just a process of elimination really, in more ways than one. Finding out who Jonnie Boy had met with, where he had met with them and, most importantly, *why* he had met with them. Jonnie was a nice enough bloke, but he was obviously a cunt as well. Phillip was like a wild animal, he could smell skulduggery and treachery like a wolf could smell its own arse on a windy night. Declan had a feeling there was going to be murder, and the knowledge depressed him.

He hated real murder, it always brought you to the attention of the wrong people. Even when things were done properly and nothing could ever be proved, it didn't stop people being suspicious. It was the suspicion that caused a lot of the aggravation, was why certain people wouldn't partner them. It was why the Pipers and others of their ilk eventually signed their own death warrants.

Kill or be killed. But what no one realised was that Phillip *always* got his kill in first.

Chapter Ninety-Seven

Eileen Booth was amazed to see her daughter on her doorstep so early in the morning. 'Bloody hell, Christine, you been up all night?'

The sarcastic reference to her early morning visit was ignored. Christine followed her mother through to the kitchen, opened the fridge and took out a bottle of white wine.

'Christine, it's only nine fifteen!'

Christine looked at her fleetingly and said quietly, 'I'm pregnant, Mum.'

Eileen Booth's eyes were stretched to their utmost as she said quietly, 'Oh, for fuck's sake, Christine, pour me one and all.'

As they sat at the table together, Christine wondered why she had come here. Her mother wasn't the most reliable of women when it came to keeping secrets, and suddenly she was frightened.

As if reading her daughter's mind, Eileen said earnestly, 'It'll have to go, love, and Phillip can never find out about it. You couldn't cope with a baby, and who would want to at your age! Didn't you take any precautions?'

'Obviously not, Mum, or I wouldn't be here. Now, listen to me. You can't tell a living soul. If Phillip thought I'd had an abortion he would kill me, Mum, and that ain't a joke – you know that. He would fucking lose it, and he would take me out permanently.'

Eileen Booth was sorry to hear her daughter's language, she

even spoke like a criminal's wife. Even though she lived off her son-in-law's largesse, and enjoyed the proceeds, she still hated that this lovely girl of hers, who could have had the world if she wanted to, had tied herself to a thug, and for all his money and his possessions, Phillip Murphy was still just that. A vicious and violent thug. Even though Eileen would admit that she was often envious of her daughter's lifestyle, she knew exactly what it had cost Christine in more ways than one. 'You can get it done now without even telling your GP. We'll go away and do it somewhere, and I wouldn't tell a soul. Let's face it, Phillip would see me as a bigger culprit in all this than he would you.'

The truth of the statement calmed Christine down; her mother was right, he would blame her before he would blame his wife. That's what Phillip did, he cast the blame where it suited him. Her mother always looked after number one, so she wouldn't say a word to a soul for fear of reprisals. Really frightening reprisals. Phillip's Catholicism was like a mania at times. She had known him to go to Mass twice a day; he said he felt calm in church, it helped him think. She knew her husband believed he was chosen somehow, that God watched over him personally at the expense of everyone else.

Had she been married to anyone else Christine would never even consider terminating a child's life. But desperate times meant desperate measures. She couldn't do it, couldn't tie herself to her husband even tighter than she already was. She couldn't, wouldn't bring another Murphy into the world. But she believed abortion was a sin nonetheless. For all she knew this child could grow up and discover the cure for cancer, or it might bring world peace. She knew all the Catholic arguments off by heart. Now though, she was frightened this child might grow up like its father, and one of him was more than enough for the world. Still, she couldn't help saying, 'It's a mortal sin, Mum.'

Eileen laughed nastily. 'Yeah, well, it's a bit late for all that, love. You sold your soul to the devil the day you walked up the aisle with him.'

Christine refilled their glasses quickly, but her mother pushed hers away.

'Anyway, the amount you drink, that poor child is probably pickled by now, so it wouldn't be right in the head anyway. Best flushing it away, girl, and forgetting about it.'

Christine didn't answer her mother's harsh words. Her emotions were in turmoil and when she started to cry a few seconds later, she wondered if she would ever stop.

Wondered if any of it would ever stop.

Chapter Ninety-Eight

Philly was lying in the big bed next to Tiffany White. Her mum had babysat the night before so there was no rush to get up. In fact, he was enjoying just luxuriating in the smell of her, the feel of her. As he felt himself getting aroused, he heard her giggle gently. He knew she had been awake all the time. She was a prick tease, as his dad would say. He slipped inside her, groaning at the tightness and the excitement of her body. He had never had sex on tap before, and he was revelling in it. She was like a new world that had opened up, just for him.

Tiffany, for her part, saw him for what he was, a good-looking, well-heeled young bloke, whose father was a serious Face. All her dreams and all her wants had his legs wrapped around her slim waist, and she was going to milk it for all it was worth.

As he rolled away from her a few minutes later, she sighed happily. 'That was good, Philly.'

He loved hearing that from her; she was, after all, far more experienced than he was, which bothered him at times. But he was like his father, a realist, and he knew everyone had to learn somewhere. He felt for her though, he cared for her genuinely, and he appreciated that she would always be special to him. But he also wasn't as enamoured as he had been. He'd learned that he was more interested in the sexual aspect of Tiffany White than her intellect. In fact, her idea of a conversation was to wonder at something she had read, heard or watched about a celebrity. Thick as shit, and twice as dense as his dad would say.

But he could put up with a lot for the pleasure she brought him on a daily basis. He glanced at his watch, a very expensive Breitling, and, seeing the time, he sighed inwardly. His granddad would have his nuts. He was late for work again, though he had to give the old boy his due, he understood his situation with Tiffany much better than he would have given him credit for.

In fact, his old granddad found the whole thing hilarious, which riled Philly at times, although, on the whole, he was now closer to his granddad. They had something to talk about and he appreciated the old boy's quiet ways. In fact, he saw him in a whole new light. He knew his liaison wasn't going to be gossiped about to his granny, and then his mum. His granddad seemed to understand perfectly, and had kept it all more or less hush-hush.

'Philly love?'

'What, Tiff?' He hugged her to him tightly; her body fitted into his perfectly.

'I'm pregnant.' She was holding her breath, not sure that he would take the news as well as she hoped. But she *was* pregnant, and there was nothing he could do now, except stand by her or pay up for the rest of his days. The former was a pretty good option, but the latter wasn't to be sneezed at either. She had the trump card, and she knew it.

Philly, for his part, was reeling from the news. Getting her pregnant wasn't something he'd worried about after she said she was on the pill. She said they were all right. He had been fool enough to believe her. He realised now that he was what was commonly known as a prize prat. He had taken her word for it and assumed she was above this kind of skulduggery.

He now assumed she was nothing but a lying cunt.

Suddenly Tiffany looked grubby to him, used, the place smelled of a trap, not of sex. As she smiled up into his eyes, he saw the triumph in them, the knowledge that he was well and truly fucked. It occurred to him her legs had been open longer than Sainsbury's. Fuck only knew who else she had entertained there. When he thought of some of the things he had done with her! He felt the urge to vomit and escape in equal measures. He also felt the need to rip her head off and drop-kick it off the balcony. Instead he slipped out of the bed and started to get dressed.

Tiffany felt the coldness and the fear coming off him in waves, but she had been prepared for this. Once the shock wore off, he would have to sort it. The baby wasn't to blame, was it? That was her next step in the emotional blackmail. *His* child was snuggled inside her, and he or she would be her ticket to untold riches. Tiffany would play the long game; it wasn't the first time she had pulled this stunt, and she had a feeling it wouldn't be the last.

'Aren't you going to say anything, Phil?' She had the hurt voice down to a fine art.

Philly paused in the act of pulling on his jeans and, after looking at her for long moments, said icily, 'Are you sure you're pregnant?'

She nodded, she had expected that question sooner if she was honest.

'Are you sure it's mine?'

She had not expected *that* one at all. She was up and out of the bed in seconds and, screaming at him at the top of her voice, she said nastily, 'How dare you ask me that! Who the fuck do you think you are?'

He grinned then, a tight, sarcastic grin. 'I'm Philly Murphy, love, and you had better remember that. We had a great time, but it's over now. That baby is *not* going to drag me down all me life, because if you have it and a DNA test says I am the father, then I'll have it off you, darling. No child of mine will be brought into all this.'

He looked around him in disgust, his instincts telling him to frighten her into getting rid of it. He had to make her see that having this child just wasn't an option. And it wasn't just because he was too young and too immature to have a child. It was mainly because his dad was going to go fucking ballistic. As he walked out of the bedroom he said seriously, 'I'll give you a grand to get it done privately, and then there'll be another grand afterwards. But remember this, Tiff, no matter what, I wouldn't touch you with the bloke next door's now. You're scum. If you think you can trap me, you'd better think again.'

Tiffany watched Philly walk out the door, along with all her plans and all her dreams. She was fuming at his words. She had not expected anything like that. She wished she had the nerve to pick up the kitchen knife and run it through his heart. She was filled with rage at his obvious disgust for her and her way of life. She had fucked him raw and what did she have to show for that time and effort? Sweet fuck-all, that's what. She was so angry she could easily cry. His reaction had hurt more than she would ever admit. His complete dismissal of her, and anything to do with her, had really rankled. Who the hell did he think he was? But then she knew exactly who he was, and that was why she had pulled this stunt in the first place. It was over, and she knew it. There was no going back now.

As she made herself a cup of coffee, her sensible head kicked in and she accepted that two grand was better than fuck-all. Because he wasn't coming back. She had overplayed her hand, so it was now about limiting the damage.

Sighing, she lit a cigarette and pulled on it deeply. Life was shit and then you died; she wished she could remember who had said that. Because whoever it was certainly knew what they were talking about.

Chapter Ninety-Nine

Jamsie walked into the arcade and was amazed at the change in people's attitude towards him. He was saluted and hailed from all sides, treated like a conquering hero, and he loved it. For the first time in years he knew what it was to be liked, respected and, more importantly, welcome.

As Breda walked towards him she saw that he was full of his new-found confidence and, smiling widely, she said, 'Hello, little brother, what brings you here so early?'

Breda looked good, and she knew it. As usual, her son Porrick was lurking in the background. He was his mother's permanent minder, and it suited them both. They were close, and they understood each other perfectly which, in their game, was a definite must. A minder and a mindee needed to be in perfect sync. Needed to be able to pre-empt each other to avoid danger and work together to get out of any situations that might arise. In a cash business a good minder was worth their weight in gold. Breda dealt with huge amounts of money, and she moved it around constantly, that was the great thing about cash businesses. You only declared what you wanted to. Consequently, there was a lot of cash to be stashed, as Breda always laughingly said. But she also appreciated how much she needed her boy to keep his eye on her, and everything she did.

'I came in to see you actually, have you got a few minutes for me?'

Breda took him through to the offices, assuming it was

something else about the upcoming wedding. Now it was confirmed, the arrangements were going faster than a five-quid stash. Her mother was seeing to that. Breda was thrilled, it kept the woman off her back. She loved her mum, but she was what was known as an interferer, she thought it was her right as a mother to dictate people's lives.

As she poured them both coffee, Jamsie said hesitantly, 'Would you mind, Porrick, if I spoke to your mum on the quiet?'

Porrick shrugged and at his mother's almost imperceptible nod he left the room, closing the door quietly behind him.

'Why the cloak and dagger, Jams?'

He shrugged and she noticed that he had filled out in the last few months; the skinny, haunted man was long gone. He had always been much better looking than he realised, and she was glad to see him looking so well. He was flourishing. Like her mother she had always had Jamsie on her conscience. And, like her brother Phillip, she had once contemplated killing him. It was a complex situation, and one she was glad was never openly discussed. The arrogance of youth, that was how she referred to it in her own mind, but she knew, just as Jamsie did, that nothing could ever justify the events of all those years ago. She didn't drink like that any more or take drugs; the only good thing to come out of it all was it had made her take a good look at herself and her life. She had prospered ever since.

'I have a bit of a worry on me. I could be wrong, Breda, but I don't think I am. Jonnie Piper is a nice bloke and all that, but lately there's been a geezer hanging round the firm called Dan Smith. Well, I had someone ask about, and it turns out he works for Billy Bantry. What's Bantry got to do with the motors? I mean I might not be fucking Stephen Hawking, but I can smell a rat before it's stinking.'

'Is this Smith there much?'

'All the fucking time, even questions me about orders and

that. It's like he's the boss, the real boss, you know?'

Breda was listening intently, all the time her heart slowly sinking into her stomach. This was trouble – serious, unadulterated trouble. Phillip had left Bantry behind years ago; he had used him as a stepping stone, but they were still tight. Anyone would understand Billy Bantry feeling that maybe he was owed, but they would also understand that now he would not want to push that fact too much. Especially not with Phillip Murphy.

But this was different, this was a sneaky, underhand and definitely dodgy enterprise. Breda knew that Declan and Phillip had their reservations about Piper, but she put that down to Phillip's usual contrariness. He took on a partner, then decided he didn't want them any more. It went from sweetness and light to dark days and thunderstorms overnight. She saw that she had just had some very explosive information dropped into her lap. It also made her realise that she was completely out of the loop about anything to do with the car business, and that annoyed her; a small part of her felt the urge to sort this out herself just to show she could. But the reminder sitting in front of her made her recall with perfect clarity the last time she had thought she could sort things out for herself and she immediately stifled the urge. She was miffed nevertheless. She knew now without a doubt that she was gently but surely being rowed out of the main businesses. The games were as far as she was going to go and, in fairness, that was pretty high in most people's estimation. But it bored her – she could do this job with her eyes closed. This was about Phillip and Declan playing their game of 'Big Boys Only' lately. As much as she enjoyed running the games, she missed being part of the main crew.

She wondered suddenly if it was her age; she was pushing forty, and still on her own, the younger men were getting harder to keep, and she was lonely for someone she could talk to. Not just about her day, but about her life, her work. Even Porrick had a girlfriend – a nice little thing, with a big shy smile, who hung on his every word (and that was no mean feat, because her Porrick, as much as she loved him, wasn't exactly known for his sparkling conversation). But the girl loved him, and he loved her, whatever they saw in one another it worked for them. Now Jamsie had made her see her life for what it was – all work – and, even then, she wasn't really treated as she wanted to be treated, *needed* to be treated. She had been out of the motors since the off.

She saw Jamsie looking at her sadly and he said gently and honestly, 'Look, Breda, I ain't asking you to get involved. I just want you to tell me if I should talk to Phil or Declan. I don't want to cause an international incident if I've got it all wrong.'

She realised then what poor Jamsie needed to do. This information would probably be old news to Phillip and Declan, but Jamsie sussing it would give him the kudos he craved with his brothers, and so she said to him sadly, 'Take it to Phillip, but make sure that Declan's there. They probably know anyway, but they will appreciate you putting them wise. Show them you've got your eyes open to what's really going on.'

Jamsie nodded, relieved at her words. He was nervous about looking like a ponce and he still felt an outsider in some respects, but then Phillip could do that to a body on a whim. 'I'm going round Phillip's tonight to see them about the new orders, I'll mention it then.'

Breda smiled at him, although she was under no illusions that she and Jamsie would ever really be a true part of Phillip and Declan's world. When he went she sat for a long time, trying to figure out what the fuck was really wrong with her, and why she felt so disaffected with her life. It wasn't that her life was bad in any way, it was that she felt it had nothing left to offer her. She had money, prestige, she had respect. So why did she suddenly feel as if everything she had achieved was nothing? Sighing, she went back out to the noise and bustle of the arcade floor. It was all flashing lights and the noise of money being spent, laughter was everywhere. It was undeniably a good business to be in and she told herself how lucky she was. All the same, she wondered who exactly she was trying to convince. Maybe it was the wedding, seeing Jamsie so happy, so settled, maybe she needed something permanent in her life now, before it was too late.

Chapter One Hundred

Philly was nervous, but he knew exactly what he had to do. He had no other choice, and God knew he had tried to find another way out. But where was he going to get a grand from? Two, in fact? He would have to worry about the rest of the money when he had supplied her with the first lot – that was his priority. He would sell something, but he knew his father would notice if anything went missing. He was funny like that – he might ignore his kids, but he didn't ignore their possessions. If Philly could just get the money for Tiffany he would worry about paying it back later. The sooner she got rid, the sooner he would be able to breathe in peace again. He could hear the talk from the kitchen, and knew that his father and Timmy were set for the night. It was strange really, because for all the money, and the huge house, his father still felt most comfortable in the kitchen. It was a real joke that he fought hammer and tong to make something of himself, yet deep down he still felt more at home in what was essentially a woman's domain.

Philly felt his father's haphazard neglect deeply, even though it had happened periodically throughout his life. He was either all over them like a rash, or it was like they were strangers to him. His mother had always tried to tell them that it was only because he was very busy, but he knew that was shite. His father was a nutter, and that was the long and the short of it. He thought he saw more than Timmy did. Timmy was all rugby and lashings of ginger beer. He could step outside it, go to his posh mates and hibernate from the family for a while, whereas Philly wanted, *needed* to be near the man who blanked him on a regular basis. He hoped every day it would change and he would be treated like the golden boy, the first-born. He had always craved his father's attention, and when he didn't get it he felt it acutely. Just thinking about it made him angry. He sat in his bedroom, biting his nails, waiting for his chance to go downstairs and do what he needed to do. He looked around him at the beautiful room he slept in when it suited him. Knew that all his mates were envious of his lifestyle. Yet he would give anything to have their lives at that moment.

He was terrified about this bloody kid, and he could kick himself for not taking proper precautions; he had ridden her bareback, and the thought of what he could have caught was driving him mad. He had to unload her and the kid soon as, then he would get himself looked at properly, buy a gross of condoms, and get himself out and about again. But first things first, he had to assemble a grand because Tiffany would want the money tout suite. She was a thieving, lying slag. And she could be a mouthy mare into the bargain. The way he felt now, he would cheerfully kick the fucking thing out of her if he had to. Anything rather than admit he had been caught out by a fucking female scoundrel with big tits and a brain like a steel trap.

He stood up. He was nervous and he was stoned. Slipping out the door he made his way along the landing. He could hear his mother in her bedroom; as always the TV was on, and he knew she would be sitting in bed drinking and watching crap.

'Is that you, Philly?'

He could hear the need in her voice and, opening her bedroom door, he popped his head round. The last thing he needed tonight was her following him all over the place, and when pissed she was capable of doing just that.

'You all right, Mum?'

Christine was sitting in bed; as always she looked like a picture, even her hair was perfect, how she did it he didn't know. But even pissed out of her brains she could still tidy up behind herself. It was surreal really. She nodded, pleased at his attention and for a split second he felt guilty – for all her faults she loved him and Timmy. Loved them *too* much really, had suffocated them since he could remember. One of his earliest memories was of her picking him up and kissing him, and him fighting to get away from her. Even then he had sensed the naked need in her for human contact, and he knew she wouldn't get that from his father.

'You all right, son? You seem preoccupied somehow.'

He grinned at her, his even white teeth were perfect and, winking at her, he said jauntily, 'Just tired, Mum. Granddad has me hard at it in the shops.'

She smiled, and he saw that she was still a good-looking woman. He knew a few of his mates had harboured salacious thoughts about her when they were younger. 'He's only doing the best for you, Philly. He cares about you, son.'

Suddenly, she was nearly in tears, and he knew it was time to go. She was so emotional lately, worse than usual. Like everyone else, he assumed it was her medication. Everyone referred to her pill-popping as her medication, it made it seem respectable somehow. But he knew that his joint tonight couldn't do half as much damage as the pills she ate like sweets on a daily basis.

'I love it there, Mum. Me and Granddad have a laugh together. He tells me all about when you were a little girl!' He was trying to please her, but he knew immediately he had said the wrong thing. She was shaking her head as if in denial at something, though what that was he didn't know and she wasn't saying.

'I wish you'd known me then, before . . .' She shrugged gently, her slim shoulders making her look frailer than ever. She got on his nerves when she was like this and, walking into the room, he went to her and kissed her on the top of her head. She smelled of Chanel perfume, cigarettes and stale vodka breath. It was a smell from his childhood and he hated it.

''Night, Mum, I have to be up in the morning now, don't I?'

She nodded vaguely. She was already miles away.

He shut the door quietly behind him and, breathing a sigh of relief, he slipped down the huge staircase his father had insisted on having built, and made his way through to the small office at the back of the house. This was his father's domain, and he knew how to get into the safe that was tucked away behind a large framed photograph of Southend Seafront. The photo showed the arcades at night, with his father, his auntie Breda and his uncle Declan standing in the foreground smiling. Breda looked like she had conquered the world. His father looked like he always did whether it was a photo or real life, he just stared at the camera with that fake smile of his. Declan looked younger and happier than he had in years. Taking the photo off the wall, Philly placed it carefully and quietly against the chair beside the desk. Then, as he went to open the safe the door opened, all hell broke loose.

'What the fuck are you doing?' His father was standing in the doorway staring at him as if he was an intruder, a stranger, not his own son. 'Are you trying to blag *my* safe? Nick *my* fucking poke?' He was shouting now, and Declan and Jamsie were already behind him, assuming he had caught someone trying to break in. Philly could see that neither of them expected the culprit to be him.

As he was dragged physically from the room, and thrown into the kitchen he felt the terror envelop him. He was bleeding, he could feel it dripping from his eyebrow, and he knew he had hit the corner of the large, scrubbed pine table. He could hear Declan's voice through the roaring in his ears.

'Stop it, Phillip! Calm down and ask the lad what he was doing.'

Phillip Murphy was like a lunatic now. He hated thieves with a vengeance. He had discovered a weakness in this son of his and it bothered him.

'I know what he was doing, Declan, he was on the fucking rob! He was on his way into my safe! *Mine*. That safe is *mine*. He's a fucking thief, a creeper, no better than a fucking gas-meter bandit. They rob their own and all, you skanking little cunt!'

It took both Jamsie and Declan all their combined strength to hold him back, and it was only seeing his wife's appalled white face at the kitchen door that eventually calmed Phillip down enough to talk with any real lucidity.

'Leave him alone, Phillip. Look at his eye, it's bleeding everywhere!' Christine was kneeling beside her son now; the noise and the blood had sobered her up, and she was trying to stem the bleeding with her dressing gown. Young Philly was letting her do whatever she wanted – he knew inside that his father wouldn't attack him again with her beside him and he was grateful to her at this moment.

'You animal, your own flesh and blood!' Christine was heartbroken, and her voice was loud and angry.

Phillip tried to justify his violent outburst. 'He was trying to rob his own flesh and blood, Chris. Can't any of you see how fucking disgusting that is?' He was looking around him as if he was surrounded by complete idiots.

'What were you doing, Philly? Tell your father the truth.' Christine knew it was the only way out for her son. Phillip held great store by the truth, the hypocritical bastard that he was. Hold your hands up, that's what he had always told the boys. Hold your hands up and take the flak. She hated him more now than ever before.

'Well! Let's hear it!'

Philly looked at his mother before saying brokenly, 'I got a bird pregnant. I needed money for an abortion for her. I would have replaced it, Dad, I swear. But I didn't want you or Mum to know.' He had said all the right things, and he knew it. Phillip was staring down at his son, his eyes screwed up in consternation.

'Not that White bird, Tight Fanny or whatever she calls herself?'

Philly nodded and, pushing his mother's hands away, he saw his father bending down, trying to help her up. Phillip was all gentleness now. His huge hands were underneath her oxters, and she was letting him lift her. It was as if she knew the danger was over. Phillip sat his wife in one of the Carver chairs and, his whole demeanour changing once more, he said softly, 'You all right, Christine?'

She nodded, all the fight gone now that the danger to her son had passed.

Lighting a cigarette, Phillip looked at his brothers and said loudly, 'Fucking imagine impregnating a White. They are like the missing link that lot, her old man still drags his knuckles on the pavement when he walks!'

Jamsie and Declan laughed, but it was laughter tinged with relief. There was blood all over the kitchen floor, Philly looked like he had gone ten rounds with Mike Tyson, and Christine was also covered in claret. It was surreal, because Phillip was acting like nothing had happened. Nothing of importance anyway. He was even chaffing his boy, making a joke about it all.

'You dozy little sod, if you're gonna dip your wick, son, make sure you're wearing something. How much do you need?'

Philly swallowed heavily; he felt sick, and he knew he was probably concussed. He had seen more than a few stars as he had hit the corner of the table. But he answered his father, voice thick with pretend bravado. 'I told her a grand up front and a grand after. That way I could be sure she'd get shot. Money talks, Dad, as you're always telling me.'

Phillip digested what he had been told. 'I'll give you the money, son. It's worth it to get rid of scum like that. But the moral of this story is, tell me when things go pear-shaped and I'll help you, mate. Lie, cheat and steal and I won't.'

Watching on, Declan felt sorry for the lad, but it was Christine that really worried him, she looked awful. Well, worse than usual anyway. Much worse, in fact. She looked like she had been drained of blood completely, her skin was a pasty white and she looked seriously ill, like she had a disease or something.

'Are you sure you're OK, Christine?'

She shook her head and started to heave, loud, dry heaves, and the men instinctively moved a step away from her in case she vomited over them. All except Phillip that is. He knelt in front of her and held her comfortingly until she relaxed then, smiling, he said gently, 'When were you going to tell me, babe?'

She looked into his eyes and she knew then, without a doubt, that he realised she was pregnant. His eyes were soft, yet she could see he was mocking her. He had been waiting to see what she was going to do. As always, he was one step ahead of her, and the knowledge made her finally accept that she would never win. Could never win. Not where he was concerned anyway.

He looked at the cupboard they kept the bin in and winked at her. So he had found the pregnancy tests. If she had not been so frightened and so pissed she would have had the sense to get rid of them properly. It suddenly occurred to her that he probably checked through the rubbish, because he had always somehow controlled her life.

Every last second of it.

The others saw that something was occurring between Phillip and Christine, but none were aware of exactly what it was. Standing back up, Phillip said gaily, 'She's in the club, aren't you, Chris? What a momentous night, a new Murphy.' He looked at his son as he said it. Jamsie was frightened; he couldn't handle Phillip like this, he knew as well as Declan that there was an underlying snide going on, and it felt wrong and it felt dirty.

Declan wondered at a man who could welcome a child with a woman who so obviously needed help with not only her drinking, but her drug-taking and her mental health, yet would offer to play a part in the demise of what was essentially his grandchild. For all Phillip's Catholic beliefs he was quick enough to destroy a child when it suited him. As for poor Christine, she couldn't have another child; she was far too fragile, mentally and physically. He stepped away from the little tableau almost by instinct. There was something wrong here, very wrong, and he was as trapped as the poor mare sitting on the chair.

Philly was in a daze, all he could focus on was the blood. It seemed to be everywhere now. He felt his eyebrow, it was sore, but it wasn't bleeding any more. It was a second or two before he realised it was coming from his mother.

'Mum . . . Mum! What's wrong?'

The terror in his voice communicated itself to the others in the room and, as Christine groaned in pain and doubled over holding her belly, Phillip said loudly, 'Oh, for fuck's sake! Call an ambulance.' Then kneeling back down he enveloped his wife in his arms, as if protecting her from the world. He was playing the worried husband now and, motioning to Jamsie, he shouted, 'Get Philly cleaned up and out of here before the ambulance arrives.'

Jamsie had been watching it all as if it was a film. Philly was battered and bloodied and in obvious need of stitches, Declan was, for the first time in years, speechless and unable to do anything constructive, and Phillip was acting like the most concerned husband in the world. Jamsie wondered if being brought back into this family was something to be considered lucky after all. In fact, he was beginning to wish he was still the fucking outcast. At least then he would be spared all this shit. But he did as he was asked; where Phillip was concerned you didn't really have much choice in the matter.

Chapter One Hundred and One

'Come here, son.'

Declan heard Veronica's voice, and it broke him out of his reverie. He was still stunned at what had happened in Phillip's kitchen. Seeing all that, and knowing that it was just a normal evening for Phillip had reinforced his worries about his brother and his mental state.

He had come straight to his mother's from the hospital; he was sure that would speak volumes to a shrink. But it was the only place he could think to go, because he needed help – they had to do something about Phillip. If he wouldn't listen to him, then Veronica was his only other hope. Phillip needed her to think he was the perfect son, the perfect provider. And she believed it, to his brother's face anyway; but really, she knew better than any of them just how off the wall Phillip really was. Declan loved him, he loved him dearly, but this time Phillip had crossed a line. It wasn't the businesses. Their business was about danger and death. They knew what they were doing there; it wasn't something Phillip would fuck up. What he *was* fucking up though was everyone around him, and that included Phillip himself. He had never been this bad before, and if he wasn't careful he would take his wife, his kids and his family down with him.

'Are you listening to me, Declan?'

He walked to his mother and hugged her and, as she instinctively hugged him back, he wondered how he was going to say what he wanted to say to her. She thought the sun shone out of Phillip, and that was half the trouble. She made him think he was normal.

'Sit down, Mum, I need to talk to you. Can I get you a drink?'

She smiled nervously. 'Do I need one?'

He didn't answer and, as she settled herself down at the kitchen table, he poured them both large Irish whiskies. Placing them on the table he sat beside her, and as Veronica looked at him he wondered how she had managed over the years. She had fed them, clothed them and, in her own way, loved them. Though most of her love had been for her first-born, her Phillip.

She had married a waster, a man who without her would have faded away into the background of life. She had made him work, made him get up and get out there, and she had taken each penny and stretched it into a pound. His father was basically lazy, and they all knew it, he was a born taker and, in a way, that's where Phillip had got it from. His old granddad used to say Irishmen were either drunks or workers, and occasionally a mixture of the two. The workers worked till they made it, the drunks complained about missed chances. Phillip worked, but he begrudged anyone else having an earn; like their dad, he thought everyone else had that bit more than him. But whereas his father would bemoan his fate and lived for the pub, Phillip went out and earned – no one could take that away from him. Like the old man though, Phillip thought the world began and ended with him, and his wants and his needs.

'Come on, Declan, talk to me.' She grabbed his hand and squeezed it tightly.

And so slowly Declan started to tell her about what had happened that night. He told her calmly, and without drama, but he told her everything. When he had finished she had already let go of his hand, and she had physically moved away from him.

Her face was drawn, but he could see the anger in her eyes. Taking a huge gulp of the whisky she finally said quietly, 'Why are you telling me all this, Declan?'

He sighed resignedly. She was already trying to work out how to make Phillip look like the hero of the hour. Oh, he knew her so well. Now this he had to hear, because he had not left out a thing. From the child being lost, to her grandson being battered. He had told her about the hate and the fear that her son had provoked in everyone in that room.

'Because, Mum, Phillip is out of control—'

She interrupted him and, leaning forward in the chair, she said nastily, 'Of course he was out of control! His son had disgraced us all, getting that little whore in the club, and then trying to rob him. His wife had lost a little child in front of his eyes. Only *you* would see that as abnormal. But then that's you all over, isn't it? Neither chick nor fucking child yourself, how would *you* ever understand the mental cruelty of losing your own flesh and blood? Poor Christine, I need to get down there.'

Veronica went to stand up and Declan held her in the seat by grabbing at her arm, practically forcing her to sit back down. He could see the confusion on her face. He knew she was not going to help him, but he needed to tell her whether she wanted to know or not.

'Mum, for fuck's sake, didn't you hear a word I said? You ain't a stupid woman, you know better than anyone that Christine's terrified of him. You also know better than anyone that she should not have another child. She's a drunk, a junkie, and she's been mortally afraid of her husband since the night *you* asked her to stop him from killing his own fucking sister. He did that to her, sent her off her head, and so did *you*, you helped – by colluding with her husband and pretending that everything was all right. She never recovered, Mum, she didn't know what he was like, and once she saw the *real* Phillip, he knew he couldn't hide it from her any more. His big game was up, his wife knew the truth.'

Veronica looked at her son, and it occurred to her that he was right and that, in reality, he was probably the best of the bunch. But she wouldn't have him tell her anything about her family. Who the hell did he think he was? Once you started to talk like this about someone, it was over for them. No one discussed Phillip or his foibles in this family, she had made sure of that over the years and she wasn't about to change now.

'You two-faced little fucker, you'd talk about your own flesh and blood like that? As for Christine, she was always fucking unstable. She should have done what we all do – kept her head down and her arse up. Got on with it. It's called real life, son. Something you and her know fuck-all about. Both of you have been cushioned by him, he gave you everything you wanted, and this is how you repay him? By running him down to *me*, his own *mother*.'

Declan laughed; the irony was not lost on either of them as he said loudly, 'You're *my* mother and all, remember? And Breda's and Jamsie's too. You've got *four* kids, Mum, not one. You sacrificed Jamsie for Phillip, as well as Christine . . .'

She pulled her arm from his grasp. She couldn't deny the truth of what he was saying, but she pushed the thoughts from her mind. As always, she would defend her eldest child, as she had since he was old enough to walk and talk. She would not believe that he was all bad. She couldn't, if she started along those lines Christ Himself knew where it would end.

'Fuck off, Declan, and don't you dare come back here again until you can think straight. As for Phillip, without him where the hell would we be, eh? Think on that.'

Declan sighed and, standing up, he said sadly, 'I'll tell you where his poor wife would be, in a semi-detached somewhere, living a normal life, and her kids would love her. Jamsie wouldn't have been turned into a nervous wreck who had to leave the room every time that cunt showed his face – how many years did he have to live like that, eh, Mum?'

Veronica laughed bitterly. 'I didn't hear you complaining until now. Why didn't you say something if it bothered you so much?'

He pulled on his leather jacket and, picking up his car keys, he said quietly, 'I don't know, Mum. I was frightened to, I suppose. But I ain't frightened of him now. I thought you would listen to me, and get your boy to calm himself down a bit. That was all I wanted, but as usual you were straight in there like a Rottweiler on a fucking poodle. Well, I tried. That's all I could do.'

As he slipped out into the hallway he saw his father had come back from the pub and he was now sitting on the stairs quietly. As he passed him, he heard him say in a whisper, 'She won't forgive this, son. Believe me, I know.'

Declan didn't even bother answering him. He left the house and wondered at a family that had so much, and yet had so little.

Chapter One Hundred and Two

Christine opened her eyes and saw her two sons sitting by the hospital bed. She could tell that they were both really worried about her, and she tried to smile at them.

'You all right, Mum?' Philly asked.

She nodded automatically, all the time looking at her poor boy's face. Philly's eye was already stitched and nearly closed, he looked like he'd been in a car crash. The events of the night flashed into her head, and she felt the usual terror envelop her.

Timmy stroked her arm gently, and said in a choked voice, 'Can I get you anything, Mum, a cup of tea?'

She shook her head, all she wanted was a drink and a few sleepers, in that order. Whatever they had injected her with was wearing off. She knew they had taken her down to the operation room to make sure all the baby had gone, and that suited her, she wanted none of it inside her. Not a fucking iota of Murphy would ever get that far inside her again.

'Where's your dad?'

'He's been with the doctor, Mum, for ages, he's really worried about you.'

She nodded. 'Get yourselves home. Go on. I'm fine, really. I just need to sleep.'

They were gone within five minutes. Once she was sure it was safe, she opened the bedside drawer. She pulled out her handbag, which she had made sure came with her in the ambulance, and, unzipping the side pocket, she put her hand inside quickly.

'Looking for this, Chris?'

She jumped in fright at her husband's voice and, turning, she saw him standing in front of the closed door, a small antique silver hip flask in his hand. He was holding it up in front of his face like a prize he had just been given.

'Fucking hell, Chris, you must need a drink badly, love. Do you think you might have a problem, darling?'

He was mocking her, and she knew that whatever game he was playing now, he'd already won. She started to cry, a deep, raw crying that once started wouldn't stop. She could feel her whole body shaking with the pain inside her. She had snot running down her nose, hanging in loose tendrils and, as she attempted to wipe it away, she felt Phillip's arms go around her, and he was holding her tightly to him. Pushing his face into her hair, and she realised suddenly that he was crying too. Phillip was crying his eyes out, and the sound of it was terrifying to her.

'Our baby's gone, Christine, but we'll get past this. I've booked you into rehab. The doctors here think it's the best thing for you, and so do I, love. You'll come out as good as new. No drink in you, no tranquillisers, and definitely no fucking Ketamine.'

He knew, and the knowledge made her aware of his power once more. He really was like God, he knew everything.

She couldn't wait to go to rehab, and get away from him for a while at least.

Chapter One Hundred and Three

'I miss Mum, don't you, Philly?'

Philly shrugged. He did and he didn't, he just hoped the rehab worked this time. 'I suppose so.'

'What's Granddad like to work for?'

Philly shrugged and, smiling, he said, 'All right really, you'll be fine.' He nearly warned him about good-looking birds with big tits, and the want of a wage coming in, but he didn't. His brother wasn't like him.

Timmy wasn't so sure. He didn't really want to be in the family businesses. He wanted to get a proper job, but his father had suddenly decided that he needed his boys by his side, working their way up through the ranks, learning the ropes, as he called it. Now Philly was working in the arcades, a proper position as well, with a good wage. Philly liked it all, but Timmy didn't. He didn't want to work in the shops, he wanted to be an accountant or something. He liked numbers, and the prospect of a nice office and a good wage was appealing.

As if reading his mind, Philly said gently, 'You'll get used to it, mate and, like the old man says, this is all going to be ours one day, so we best find out how to run it.'

Timmy agreed but, unlike his brother, he didn't care whether he inherited all this or not. He couldn't wait to get away from here if he was honest. It had destroyed his mother, and he wouldn't be surprised if one day it destroyed the rest of them.

It was a façade – the big farm, the easy living, the money, cars and the knowledge that it all came from the rob. It didn't matter how much his father talked the talk, he was still a violent thug, and all the posh houses and expensive cars couldn't hide that fact.

Chapter One Hundred and Four

Phillip was dressed in a dark suit and a pristine white shirt. He looked good and he knew it; he had been collecting admiring glances from women all day, and he had been enjoying them.

As he turned into the driveway of Billy Bantry's house, he was smiling and happy. He was relieved that Christine was away; after the news from the doctors that she'd taken Ketamine and losing the baby, he knew it was in their best interests to put some distance between them. But, as he told himself, she was a piss-head, and piss-heads weren't rational human beings. They were idiots who allowed a substance to rule their lives. So he had to find it in his heart to forgive her for fucking up his baby. His little child, a girl he reckoned. He would have liked a daughter, all men should have a daughter. The child was already dead inside her, didn't have a chance at life.

As he pulled up outside Billy's house he wondered why he still lived so modestly, but that was Billy for you, always frightened to spend a pound. The old joke about Billy was that the fucking Queen herself came to the opening of his wallet. He was one mean ponce.

He waited until Billy came out of the house and jumped into the passenger seat beside him.

'All right, Phillip?'

Phillip nodded and grinned. ''Course I am, I'm always good.'

It was a statement, and he wholeheartedly believed it. Billy

Bantry was used to Phillip talking this kind of shite, it went over his head like a giraffe's fart.

'Where we off to?'

Phillip grinned, it never ceased to amaze him that people were so trusting, he would lay money this fucking ice cream wasn't even tooled up. He was dealing with retards, had been for years, so no wonder he had tucked them up so easily. 'I thought we'd go to mine, Bill. It's quiet there.'

Billy nodded agreeably; he loved Phillip's farm, and always left with a bag of good meat and veg. Phillip Murphy was a lot of things, but mean wasn't one of them. 'Where's Declan today, then?'

Phillip shrugged. 'Busy. You know him – like Breda, if they ain't got a problem they think they're hard done by.'

Billy laughed out loud at the truth of the statement, but he had heard a whisper that all wasn't well these days in the Murphy camp. Of course, Phillip's wife had been carted off again, so that had to hurt. She was mad as a fucking hatter, and who wouldn't be, married to this bloke? That was some of the gossip from the women in their lives; women saw more than men, it was a natural thing inherited from their mothers. Personally, he thought it was so they could all grow up to be perfect mother-in-laws, ferreting out information. His old woman knew far more than he did about the home lives of men he had known all his life. Women talked, that's why a wise man never told his old woman anything of importance. They couldn't keep it to themselves, it was a genetic compulsion with them. You only had to look at a woman's phone bill, and that told you all you needed to know.

'So what do you think about the new moves on Piper's part, Phillip?'

Phillip didn't answer him, instead he changed the subject quickly, saying, 'What are you doing on Saturday night? I was thinking about getting the boys together for a drink up at one of the clubs. It's been ages since we all had a boys' night out, and I want to introduce my lads round, you know.'

Billy nodded enthusiastically, he loved a good piss-up. 'Sounds good. Where and when?'

Phillip laughed at Billy's obvious pleasure; he was all the happier because as always Phillip would make sure no one spent a penny. As they turned into the farm Phillip felt a thrill as he surveyed what he owned; the vastness of his land, and the beauty of his surroundings. No one could touch him, no one. As everyone was going to find out very soon.

Chapter One Hundred and Five

Breda felt sad, but she knew she had to try and cheer herself up for her sister-in-law's sake. Her mother, as always, looked uncomfortable – mental hospitals did that to her. But this place was lovely, cost a fortune by all accounts. She hadn't seen Christine for two weeks and she was a bit nervous.

As she and Veronica sat outside in the beautiful landscaped gardens smoking cigarettes and drinking expensive coffee, they were both shocked when Christine finally walked out of the doorway. She looked like an anorexic and, with her lovely hair scraped back and her face devoid of make-up, older than usual. She resembled someone recovering from a serious illness which, in a way, Breda supposed she was.

'Hello, darling, how are you?' Breda's voice sounded forced even to her own ears.

Veronica didn't say a word she was so shocked at her daughter-in-law's appearance. She looked like the walking dead.

Christine didn't answer at first. She sat at the ornamental metal table and, lighting a cigarette, pulled on it deeply. As she blew out the smoke she said forcefully, in a loud jovial voice that seemed incongruous coming from her slight frame, 'Well, this is nice, isn't it?'

Chapter One Hundred and Six

'You're doing well, young Timmy.'

Ted was thrilled with his new assistant and only too glad to be rid of Philly. He had the call of the clout, as they referred to young men chasing sex on this estate. Timmy wasn't there yet, but Ted was sure it would come. He watched the boy as he lifted the heavy packs of beans and peas. He had to admit it was nice having all the manual work done for him. When young Timmy had earned what his father deemed his apprenticeship he was going to get himself a lad in full-time; it certainly made life easier, and he had to admit he wasn't getting any younger.

'You going to see me mum, Granddad? She's looking much better.'

Ted Booth shook his head and said quietly, 'I'll go in a few weeks. Your nana goes a couple of times a week but, to be honest, it upsets me too much. Seeing her in there . . .' He wondered if he had said too much, but this young lad had the knack of getting you to talk without thinking. He was so truthful and open, it encouraged you to be the same. He was a nice boy.

Timmy picked up on his granddad's fears and said in agreement, 'I know what you mean, but it's quite a nice place, and she seems better, but still very sad. It's funny, you know, Granddad, but I realise now she was always sad. I think that's why she drank and that. But she's sober now, and they are getting her off the meds as well. So that's something, I suppose.'

The shop's electric doors opened and Tiffany White's two brothers came into the small supermarket. The elder of the two, Joey, had just come out from doing a five. He was a big lad, well, man now, and he had the look of a newly released prisoner. He still had the pallor peculiar to them – a combination of cheap processed food and lack of sunlight. As he walked in, Ted knew then and there that it wasn't for a pack of Samson tobacco.

'What can I get you, boys?' Ted was determined not to show his fear; he knew that on this estate it was the most foolish thing you could do. Like animals, boys like these fed off fear, nervousness and intimidation. It seemed that this lad had come out of the stir like many before him, believing he was now what was termed a Face. Oh, the stupidity of youth and incarceration. Phillip Murphy would swat him like an annoying insect. But Ted understood the boy felt he had to restore family honour, though what honour the Whites had he wasn't sure.

'You can get me fuck-all, old man. I want to know where Phillip Murphy the younger is now residing, because he ain't fucking working here no more, is he?'

Timmy watched it all in fascination. He was a big lad, and he knew he could handle himself, but these two had the advantage of being incredibly angry. It was emanating off them in waves, so strong you could almost feel the force of it.

'I don't know where he is and, if you want my advice, I'd drop this now, Joey. Philly and your sister had a fling. It happens so get over it, son. I'm sure she has.'

Joey stepped towards Ted and, as he did, straightened his arm, and a long steel rod that he had hidden up his sleeve slipped down into his hand. The younger brother, Duane, walked to the doors as if standing guard, which of course he was. They must have already warned people off. It had been very quiet all morning, so this was a well-planned operation, which told Ted it would not be resolved with words. He wondered if the cosh was for him or the premises.

'Don't do something you'll regret, Joey. Take Duane and go, and I won't say a word to my son-in-law about any of it.'

The mention of Phillip Murphy did give Joey cause for a moment's hesitation, but he was there on a mission, and he wasn't going to back down now. Especially as he had already told his friends and family what he was going to do. In effect he had painted himself into a very tight corner. His sister was in bits, she had thought she'd got herself fucked and financed, instead she had nothing of value left. He didn't know about the money, of course, all he knew was she had been used and dumped. Now that was something he couldn't ignore, irrespective of what Phillip Murphy might be capable of. This was a family matter now, about family honour and pride. For all she was, Tiffany was still his little sister and she needed his protection. He decided to take the old boy out, and his fucking shop and all. These people had been earning off everyone for far too long, and a lot of the people round the area were sick of it.

As he raised the cosh and walked towards Ted, young Timmy took him out with a tin of beans. He crashed the tin into the back of Joey's head twice, felling him where he stood. Then, as Duane rushed over, he took his fist back, and knocked him out with one well-placed punch. As Duane hit the ground, Timmy started to kick them both, using all the force he could muster, shouting as loud as he could, 'You fucking scum, threaten an old man, my granddad! You're fucking dead . . . I'll kill you!'

As Ted watched in amazement and shock it occurred to him that Timmy was more his father's son than any of them had thought.

Chapter One Hundred and Seven

The farm was empty of people and, as they walked around it, Billy was, as always, impressed despite himself. It was some place. Phillip walked around in his designer wellies and his walking stick like an old-time lord of the manor. It was funny though, somehow it suited him. Phillip did not look as ridiculous as he should have. And, in fairness, he had a lot to be proud of. This place was like a poster for how a farm should be run, it was cleaner than most people's front rooms. The piggery was state-of-the-art, and the pigs were like, well, pigs in shit, Billy supposed. You could see the affection they had for Phillip, and you could also see it was reciprocated. In fact, Phillip got on better with dumb animals than he did with people. As they walked to the top field Billy was feeling just how out of condition he was, and when they finally went into the large barn for shelter, he was secretly relieved at the prospect of a breather.

'See that tractor there? It's a John Deere, best on the market that is,' Phillip couldn't resist bragging.

Billy admired it, as any man admired something you could drive. It was a lovely piece of machinery, and it still looked showroom new. 'It looks it and all, Phillip. This place is fantastic, you're like a regular Farmer Giles!'

Phillip laughed with him and, sitting on a bale of hay, he took out a small hip flask. It was his wife's and, taking a long pull, he passed it to Billy, who did the same. Then Billy took out his cigarettes but, snatching them from him, Phillip said angrily,

'You can't fucking smoke in here! Look around you. This place would go up in a minute.'

Billy shook his head at his obvious stupidity. 'Sorry, mate. That's why you're the farmer and I ain't.'

Phillip put the cigarettes into the pocket of his coat, not trusting Billy Bantry to remember the warning.

'So, come on then, what did you bring me all the way here for? I'm assuming it's something important to do with the businesses.'

Phillip chuckled. 'No flies on you, eh, Bill?'

Then, leaning back on the bale of hay, Phillip picked up a large sabre which he had bought at a house auction. It had apparently been used in the Boer War. Seeing it, Billy's eyes widened in alarm. Shaking his head, he said incredulously, 'You've got to be joking, Phillip?'

Phillip was standing over Billy now and, smiling chillingly, he said, 'I would never joke about something this serious.'

'But why, Phillip, why are you doing this?' It was a serious question, and Billy was genuinely interested in the answer.

'Because you and Piper took me for a cunt. But mainly, Billy, if I'm really honest about it, because I *can*.'

Chapter One Hundred and Eight

'Here he comes, the hero of the hour!'

Timmy walked into the nightclub with a sheepish grin on his face. He was aware that what had happened was the main topic of conversation for everyone around him.

'Come here, son! Is this a chip off the old block or what, eh?'

As Phillip put his huge arms around him, Timmy realised they were pretty much of a size now. Another year or two and he would probably outweigh his father. He saw his brother beaming at everyone; full of pride and pleasure at his little brother's actions. Though 'little brother' wasn't the case any more, he was at least two inches taller than Philly now, and he was much broader. Since the debacle in the shop Timmy had become aware of himself in a way he had never been before. He was what would be termed by the men in this club as a lump. A big, strong lad, he was being treated with respect now. Since taking out the Whites he was like a local hero. People came into his granddad's shop and almost bowed to him if he acknowledged their presence. It was all heady stuff and, he had to admit, he was relishing it. Even the Filth had not bothered – just asked him if he was all right, and put it down as an attempted robbery gone wrong.

His actions had actually surprised him. Seeing his granddad being threatened like that had flicked a switch in his head. His granddad was like his mum, he didn't really know how to cope in the world he had found himself in. Timmy understood that on a very basic level, because he had thought he was the same. But he *wasn't*, he was like his name, he was a Murphy through and through. Accepting it felt like a great weight had been lifted from his shoulders. He knew who he was, and what he was now.

Phillip Murphy watched his two sons with pure pride and the conviction that he had done a marvellous job with them. Poor Christine might be away, but she was on the mend, and his boys were showing the world they were worthy successors to their father. He was so proud he could burst, and taking out that ponce Bantry was just the icing on the cake. Laughing and joking with everyone, he caught sight of Piper surreptitiously watching the door for his little mate Bantry to arrive. He was tempted to tell him that he wasn't coming, that he was burning away at this very moment, his ash soon to be spread on the fields as potash. But he didn't – there was plenty of time for chatting when the time was right. Let them start worrying and wondering, he wasn't going to tell anyone anything until he was good and ready.

Declan had arrived back from his break in Marbella earlier in the day; he was lightly tanned and impressed with what he had found out about the euro situation. A business that would now be wholly theirs, given the untimely demise of their business partners. All in all he was a happy man; once he had tied up a few loose ends, he would be back to his usual self.

Life was looking up, and he decided to make the most of it.

Chapter One Hundred and Nine

Breda was happy enough today and, as she sat in her mother's house drinking tea and eating a big slice of home-made cake, she broached the subject of Christine again.

'Do you think she's getting better really, Mum?'

Veronica was doing the washing-up with her back to her daughter. Rolling her eyes in annoyance, she kept her voice calm as she said, 'I think so, yeah. Sure, she's drink and drug free for the first time in years, so she has to be getting better, child.'

Breda could hear the tinge of irritation in her mother's voice and knew she saw the question as some kind of criticism of Phillip. This was nothing new; Veronica always felt her daughter-in-law's failings were seen *unfairly* as her son's fault.

'I think she looks terrible.'

'Well, you're entitled to your opinion, Breda, as we all are.'

The sarcasm wasn't lost on her daughter and Breda snapped, 'Oh, come on, Mum! Even *you* can't deny the girl looks fucking awful. She's terrified, and we both know what of, don't we?'

Turning from the sink, Veronica faced her daughter; she had to stop herself from taking her hand back and boxing the bitch's ears like she had when she was a child.

'What are you trying to insinuate, Breda? Why don't we cut to the fecking chase, eh? Say what you've got to say and then get yourself home. But I warn you now, girl, you start a fight in this house tonight and I'll fecking mangle you where you sit.'

Breda wasn't surprised at her mother's reaction; it was always

354

the same, the merest whisper of criticism directed towards Phillip was seen as a personal affront.

'Why do you bite like this, Mum? We're talking about Christine here, and I'm sorry, but a five-year-old child can see there's something bothering her . . .'

'Oh, Breda, piss off, would you? As I told Declan, she's just lost a child, it can affect a woman like that. I would have thought you, as a woman, would have understood! But then I should have known you wouldn't get it – you're more like a man these days with your suits and your fecking briefcase. Talking of men, haven't you got a young black man to service somewhere? Get you off my back for a few hours?'

Breda stood up and felt the urge to shake this woman until her teeth rattled. The realisation that Declan had obviously been there before her was a shock as well. But then, he had been present when it happened, so he probably had a tale to tell. This explained why he'd gone off to Marbella so quickly; he was distancing himself from his brother and from whatever had happened.

'Why do you always assume I am going to blame Phillip for his wife's nerves or whatever you call them these days? Why do you always snap the second she's mentioned?'

Veronica didn't bother to answer. She was *not* about to get into a discussion about her son, not with Declan and certainly not with this daughter of hers, whose own life wouldn't bear too much scrutiny. Instead she said angrily, 'Do you know what makes me laugh with you lot? Without Phillip you'd all be nothing, scratching a living as best you could. You're ungrateful and you're disloyal, and I won't have it. When you produced young Porrick years ago, and was whoring yourself from one end of this estate to the other, I wouldn't let anyone say a word against you, so you remember that next time you want to start this up again. I stood by you when you nearly killed my Jamsie. I've stood by you all, you stupid, stupid girl.'

Breda didn't reply. She felt the familiar guilt grip her like a vice – her mother was good at that, making you feel guilty and upset.

Flapping her hand at her daughter, Veronica said dismissively, 'Go, Breda, you've outstayed your welcome as usual. Just go home.'

Chapter One Hundred and Ten

Phillip sat in his house; the boys had just gone up, and he was happy, at least as happy as he could be anyway. Old Sammy was clearly still awake because the lights were on in his cottage and that made Phillip smile. The dirty old fucker watched the late-night porn channels – he should know, they billed him for it. Good luck to him, he thought he was marvellous still having a J. Arthur Rank at his age.

He sipped his Scotch and glanced around the kitchen; it looked beautiful, but it was missing Christine. The Aga was turned low, no one was using it for the moment.

He couldn't deny that she had disappointed him, deeply disappointed him. He worshipped her, he had always seen her as a bit of class; from the first time he had laid eyes on her he had felt the attraction between them, and so had she. When he was driving her pain in the arse of a mother mad at the thought of them together, she couldn't get enough of him, but he lost his temper once, and she acted like *he* was the one with a problem. He felt tears sting his eyes, and relished them. At times like this he was capable of really intense emotions. Christine was the only woman who could make him feel so sad, so unhappy. In his heart, he was still ashamed of Christine seeing him out of control all those years ago; she had never known or even suspected the real him before then. He had loved being the person she thought he was. It was the same with everyone in his life, he showed them all a different side of him. But he had liked the person

357

Christine made him be, he had tried to be a decent bloke, and it had bled into his other lives as well, because he had to take care that she never heard anything untoward about him. Now though, he was like a rudderless boat, drifting aimlessly towards God knows what.

He felt the tears once more. He knew that he would never let her go and, more to the point, so did she. But he still hated to see her so unhappy. When she was sorted, and they aimed her out of rehab, he was going to send her off to Spain for a few months – a bit of sun and a nice relax and she would be right as rain again. He would send her mother with her; Eileen would love it and she'd make sure her daughter stayed off the drink and drugs. It was funny really, Christine taking to the drink and the old Persian rugs when she was such a straight girl in many ways. But, as the doctor said, these days there were more people on prescription drugs than ever took cocaine or the like. It was the middle-class panacea, and she had taken to it like the proverbial duck to water. A small part of Phillip knew he should let her go, that away from him she would blossom, would find some level of peace in that chaotic brain of hers. But, unfortunately, that just wasn't an option; he had married her, and they would stay married until death did them part.

The thought made him smile, and he was still smiling when the boys came down from their bedrooms and said goodnight. He was pleased to see them, and he thought about the men they'd grown into. Philly needed careful handling, he was too much like him for his own good, and Timmy, well, he was still waters all right – who'd have thought he would have took on that scum White and won! He was a handful was that Joey White, and he had seven or eight years on Timmy. He suspected it was all that rugby playing – he was built like a brick shithouse.

'Come and have a drink with me, boys. Pour yourselves a Scotch.'

He pushed the bottle of Paddy towards them and, when he saw how thrilled they were by the offer, he was glad he had made it. When they were settled with a drink he said proudly, 'To my lads – I'm fucking chuffed with the pair of you.'

They were both so exhilarated by his praise, and so grateful for his time, he felt the urge to cry again. He had neglected them shamefully, not just them, but his wife as well, and he swore there and then that once he had sorted Piper, he would concentrate on the family proper. He would become the man Christine had loved again, and prove to her that he could be trusted. He would rein in his anger, and he would romance her back to how she used to be. It never occurred to him that his wife might not want anything from him except peace of mind. Now he had decided what he was going to do, it was like the gospel to him – written in stone – and there was nothing anyone could do about it. He also decided he would blood the boys early; they were ready for it, and the younger you got them, the easier it was. He would let them in on Piper, and they could be invested into the firm easily and with the minimum of fuss. Philly wouldn't be hard to train, he was a natural, and now that Timmy had a taste of the glamour, he would be wanting more. It was the way of the world. Their world anyway.

Phillip raised his glass. 'To your mother, may she be home soon.'

The boys toasted her, but their minds weren't on Christine. They were still basking in their father's attention and, like an animal who sensed weakness, Phillip Murphy played it for all it was worth.

Chapter One Hundred and Eleven

'What are you trying to say to me? How the fuck would I know where Billy Bantry is?' Phillip's voice was loud and incredulous.

Jonnie Piper was not a happy man. He knew, in fact, *everyone* knew, that Phillip had to have had something to do with Billy's disappearance, but as usual no one could prove anything. All the same, he had come down to the office at the arcade to find out.

Phillip's denials, however, were strident and convincing. 'You're out of fucking order, mate, coming in here accusing me of all sorts . . . Even the Filth need something called evidence, even if they have to fabricate it, they can't touch you without it.'

Declan watched in fascination as Phillip played the wronged party; he was good, he was very good. Declan himself almost believed him and he knew *exactly* what had happened to Billy Bantry; after all, he had helped dispose of the body.

Philly watched and learned, he knew better than to offer an opinion of any sort. He knew he had to be silent, but alert, that was what his father always said. He was loving it, being a part of something so dangerous. It suited his temperament perfectly. Timmy was naturally quiet, so he just listened anyway, but he was taking it in all the same. Absorbing it like a sponge, and the more he got involved the more he found he wanted to. But they were both impressed with their father's tremendous power. It was as if he was not human somehow – when he spoke people listened, and they didn't argue with him too much. Even this bloke Piper seemed to be backing off now that Phillip had finally snapped at him.

'I asked you a question, Jonnie. Are you accusing me of doing something to Billy Bantry, to my old mate, the man who gave me a chance in life? Because if you are . . .' Phillip trailed off, as if waiting for the man to answer him, then he took a step towards him, and said angrily, 'Don't go all shy on me now, Jonnie Boy. You had enough fucking bunny a few minutes ago.' He was roaring so loud that he could be heard above the noise of the fruit machines and the computer games outside the room.

Jonnie Piper had never experienced anything like it in his life, and the worst thing was, he knew he was out of order – he had no proof at all. He realised too that he should have kept his fucking opinion to himself; he forgot at times who he was dealing with. Now, he felt like a right snide, as if he was trying to cause aggro where there wasn't any. But Billy Bantry had literally dropped off the face of the earth. Surely that warranted a mention? But that's what Phillip Murphy was best at – making people completely disappear. He had heard more than one rumour that one of his most lucrative businesses was disposing of remains. Nothing would surprise Jonnie, even though he knew, in their line of work, stories got stretched in the telling.

Phillip continued, 'For all you fucking know he has gone on the trot with *our* money because, let's face it, that bastard seems to be capable of anything. Plus he whacks *us* out, he pays *us*, not vice versa. So how much was he actually pulling in? As you and him are so close, like, maybe you can clear up that little fucking mystery and all?'

That was bollocks, but Jonnie wasn't going to voice that to Phillip Murphy. Once Phillip said that to a few people it would become a truth. Oh, Piper knew how their world worked – he was basically fucked. Phillip would set rumours going everywhere, and that was the best way to stop people stating the obvious. Give them a better story, and people would grab at it like a two-bob tart on a charabanc outing.

Phillip was deeply offended now at the aspersions, and he was showing it. 'Oh, why the Helen Keller act all of a sudden, hmm? I mean, he talked to you more than me lately; after all, you and him were already partners when I came into the firm, weren't you?' It was an accusation and Piper knew it. Oh, Phillip was clever. 'Did you have a falling out with him? I mean, you ain't exactly a person to cross either, are you? Like me, you have a temper, and you have a job where, every now and then, you have to put people in their place. Seriously in their place, especially when they start making you look like a cunt, do you know what I mean?'

It was a clear threat. Phillip was showing his hand, and there was nothing Jonnie Piper could do to stop him. He had walked straight into this, and he could kick himself to death because of it.

'I'd hardly be looking for him now, would I, if I had anything to do with his demise?' Jonnie Piper couldn't believe he was now having to defend himself.

'But that's just it, Jonnie. I mean, think about it, you *would* be looking for him, to take the suspicion off, like. I just assumed he'd gone on holiday or something, it never occurred to me that some sort of skulduggery might be afoot. *You're* the one who brought all that to my door.'

Phillip turned to Declan and asked quietly, 'Did *you* see the said Bantry out in Marbella? In fact, did you see anyone even resembling him while you were there?'

Declan had to laugh. Phillip was acting like Miss Marple – raised eyebrows, pursed lips, the lot. He could really take the piss when it suited him, and he was taking the piss now, of that there was no doubt. Everyone in the room was embarrassed for Piper; even the boys were finding it hard not to smile, and they were only kids. This was a story that would be told, and told frequently by Phillip for laughs.

Declan played the game, as he knew was expected of him. 'Not hide nor hair, Phillip. But then his own wife ain't seen him, so he could be off with a bit of strange. Billy always liked the young ones.'

Jonnie Piper saw he was beaten. He'd just about had enough of this man. Admittedly he had been having him over with Bantry since the off, but it still rankled. And now there was the added worry of exactly how much Phillip knew about the situation. If he *had* outed Bantry, and of that there was no doubt in Jonnie's mind, he must know the real score. Declan out in Marbella could mean only one thing – the euro scam. Jonnie needed to regroup, rethink, and decide on his course of action. Which basically meant he had to kill Phillip Murphy before Murphy killed him.

So he changed tack and smiled widely. 'I expect you're right, Phillip. Billy's a fucker though, just going off like that.'

Phillip opened his arms wide, the big, benevolent friend now. 'He went off once for a wedding in Newcastle, and didn't come home for over three weeks. Turned out he had fucked off to Thailand with a local rugby team he'd met on the stag night. You'll get used to these strange southern ways, Jonnie, *I'll* make sure of that.'

Everyone laughed, but no one thought it was funny.

Chapter One Hundred and Twelve

'Mrs Murphy – Christine – I know something is bothering you. I really think that if you would just share it with someone, you would feel a lot better.'

Christine looked at this kindly woman and stifled the urge to laugh out loud. Florence Cartwright was her therapist in rehab and she meant well. Christine just wished she could say that the main thing that was bothering her was the fact that the woman wouldn't wear a bra, or deodorant. She hummed, as the boys would say.

Christine quite liked this rehab, it was nice. She felt safe here, safe and calm. Lovely rooms, quiet time, making your own bed. She liked the people here too, all friendly, all from good homes and backgrounds. People who, like her, had secret problems that drink and drugs assuaged. But *unlike* her, those people could explore them, whereas she couldn't. Daren't. She could just see this stupid woman's face if she did decide to *share*, if she leaned forward in her chair and said confidentially, 'Well, you're right, Florence. It's my husband, see? He is a murdering bastard, nearly murdered his own sister once, but I stopped him. Because, you see, for some reason, he likes me. Loves me in fact. Well, you already know that – you keep telling me how lucky I am to have his support. He arranged for the abortion of his grandchild, while celebrating the news of another child for himself. A child I was determined would never get a glimpse of him or his hate. He is a terror to his sons.

Either ignores them shamefully or suffocates them with his attention. His whole life revolves around criminal activity which, as you can imagine, he doesn't like me talking about. He would call it *grassing*, see, not *talking*, or self-expression, just plain old grassing, so stop writing everything down if you don't want to disappear – for disappear you will. Into the big ovens he had installed on our humungous farm. Unless he wants to make an example of you, of course, to the other therapists here, then your body *will* be found. Stabbing is one of his favourite modes of murder – more personal, like – and then your poor family will have to live with what had happened to you for ever. Believe me, I know. He even killed his mate once, his really good mate. My Phillip is an equal-opportunities killer – he doesn't care who it is – woman, man, friends, family, strangers. He also has most of the police, or Filth as he calls them, in his employ, so they aren't much use either. I am trapped in a marriage that I hate, and I can't leave, you see, because no one leaves my Phillip. He would take that as a personal insult and it would really annoy him, and believe me, *Florence*, you don't want to annoy him. So what do you suggest I do, *Florence*? What's *your* take on the situation?'

But of course she wouldn't say a word, she wouldn't ever say a word to anyone. Christine was a lot of things, but stupid wasn't one of them. It was strange, but since she had been here, and been off the drink and the drugs, she felt better in herself, but she was also able to think more clearly. Maybe it was the environment, knowing she wasn't going home yet, maybe that made her feel safe enough to think properly. Or it might just be that she was straight for the first time in God knew how long. She had at least a few more weeks of not having to deal with the house, and her family, and that included the boys. They were his now, she could see that more and more on each visit they made. It was Dad this, and Dad that. They were even working for him. Even her baby, her Timmy had changed from a nice, likeable lad, to a thug who even her own father thought was some kind of hero. What chance did she have against all that? What chance did any of them have?

Christine turned her attention back to her therapist. 'I wish you'd stop saying all this to me. I just like a drink, that's all. I got used to the tranqs, liked the feeling they gave me, so I took more than was good for me. I had three private doctors at one time prescribing me everything I wanted. You know, Florence, everything doesn't have to be profound, or deep. Some people, like me, are just weak, love. Weak.'

Florence Cartwright looked at this lovely woman and sighed inwardly. Christine Murphy was being eaten up inside and, whatever it was, until she dealt with it, she would never be cured. She had seen this time and time again – women who were unable to cope with their lives so they disappeared inside a bottle. But there was something deeply disturbing about the way this woman kept everything inside herself. She would blow one day and, when she did, the blast would be heard from Land's End to John O'Groats. It had to be something like childhood abuse, probably from someone she trusted. Florence had ruled the father out, there was genuine affection there, nothing untoward at all. Whatever this was, it was consuming this woman like a cancer; you could see the terror in the back of her eyes. Feel the fear that emanated from her at any mention of what might be the root cause of her self-abuse. One thing Florence knew though, she would keep trying to help her. She would talk to the husband again; he was such a nice man, and his obvious love for this broken woman was almost painful to observe.

Christine lit a cigarette, and sat back in the chair. She liked Florence, but God knew, for all her so-called education she was as thick as shit where the real world was concerned. Phillip had given her the usual old flannel he reserved for what he termed posh birds. He made sure he hung on her every word, and agreed with her wholeheartedly, whatever she said. Florence, of course, had loved it. Phillip had charmed her, as he charmed everyone. As he had once charmed Christine herself.

Chapter One Hundred and Thirteen

'Do you think Mum's getting better, Dad?'

Phillip nodded but he was distracted. He was making sure the industrial furnaces he'd installed in the big barn were running at the peak of their capabilities. He loved it in this place, it was a real buzz just to walk in here and know what had happened there and relive it. He could almost assuage his need for violence by coming here. Many a night he strolled up to the barn, with a glass of Scotch and a nice cigar, and he would sit quietly and reminisce alone about the people he had fed into the flames. 'She's on the mend, mate. You know your mum, always liked the drink, I'm afraid.'

Philly looked at his father sadly. 'Do you think losing the baby is what done her head in this time?'

Phillip nodded again and, turning to face his sons, he said gently, 'She lost the baby because of the drinking and the drugs and if she had carried it full-term it would have been seriously damaged. So in a way, it was a godsend. But obviously, we keep that to ourselves, boys. Never let people know the truth about your real life, right? You give people what you want them to know, and you edit your stories so they only hear what you want them to hear. Your mum's situation is something I have lived with for years, and I protect her from herself *and* from gossip, and you two have to do the same, OK?'

The boys looked taken aback at his candour and that pleased him. Phillip believed that if Christine had her way, he would be portrayed as the bad bastard as usual, so he was just getting his side of the story in.

'I knew about the baby for a while, and I was waiting for her to tell me. That's probably why I went for you like I did, Philly. You know, it's hard dealing with someone like your mum. As much as I love her, she is a liability in many ways. She has to be looked after, looked out for constantly, so I get a bit bad-tempered at times. It's frustrating, because I only want to help her, you know? It breaks my heart to see her like she is.'

The boys agreed with him, and he knew they understood it from his point of view now. The baby business had made them both feel very protective of her, and he preferred it when they were nice to her. Still, they hated that she had 'problems', and he used that. Phillip smiled and said in a mock Irish accent, 'If she couldn't cook, I'd have aimed her out the door years ago.'

The boys laughed, pleased that their father was making light of it all; they knew it had to be hard for him. But in fairness, he looked after her in every way he could, he genuinely loved her. She was the one who was always fucking everything up, not him. As he always said, he had to work, and his work was what gave them the life they had. Even Philly had changed his opinion on that, big time. He saw his father as a hero for putting up with her; he wasn't sure he would be so patient if she was his wife. Timmy, for his part, had more sympathy for his mother but felt she should try harder; after all, they could love her to bits, but unless she helped herself, there was nothing anyone could do.

When Phillip thought they had had long enough to digest what he had told them, he changed the subject quickly and, in a businesslike tone, he said, 'Now, boys, look at this gauge. When it's getting full use, it needs to be at its hottest. So that it will incinerate anything – even bone. Right?'

They both nodded; suddenly the gauge on the furnace was the most interesting thing in the world to them.

'Is that just for the animal carcasses?'

Phillip nodded at Timmy, and said jokily, 'Oh yeah, many is the carcass of an animal I've put in this fucker, mate.'

''Course, Dad, it is a farm.' This from Philly who, like his brother, knew exactly what their father meant.

'A very *big* farm, now the neighbours have all gone!'

The boys knew they were learning the craft from the master. Phillip intended to make them legends in their own little lifetimes, and the family would grow bigger and stronger as a result. The next step was grandkids, decent ones, from decent stock, and these boys had the education, the money and, when necessary, the finesse to pass themselves in any company.

Phillip was energised with his plans, now, and his sons were a big part of it. 'Oh and, boys, one last thing.'

They looked at him expectantly.

'Jonnie Piper thinks he is going to kill me, and that means we have to get to him first. Can I count on your support?'

He saw their eyes widen, wondering if he was joking, and finally he saw the acceptance and the desire to help him out, their father. That he was asking for their help he knew would make them feel needed, valued. They nodded in unison and he smiled at them and winked. 'I knew I could rely on you two, you're good boys – the best.'

As they basked in his praise, he was well pleased with his day's work. Piper would never smell a rat if it was shoved up his arse by a nun! Thick, Scally ponce he was. But Phillip understood him better than he realised – if it was just him and his two lads, Piper would feel safe, feel he had the advantage. He would also have to take the boys out at the same time he took him, that was a given. And Phillip saw that as a personal affront. What had his boys ever done to that cunt he would like to know? Phillip was going to get in first, as always. And he would blood his boys at the same time – once they did the first dirty, and got it over with, it would get easier for them. They were willing lads, and he was proud of them.

As for the Liverpool connection, Phillip still had mates up there, and he would see to it that they heard his version of events. Never knew when you might need someone somewhere, or something, so it was best to make sure you always kept a degree of friendliness with certain people. Anyway, once Piper was gone, it would leave a space that someone would feel the urge to fill, and whoever it was would owe him big time for his trouble.

Phillip lit his cigar as they walked back to the house. Oh, what exciting webs we weave, when first we practise to deceive.

Chapter One Hundred and Fourteen

'You're joking, Declan.'

Declan shook his head in annoyance. 'Why would I fucking joke about something like that, Breda?'

'When did he decide this?'

Declan shrugged. 'Who knows when he decides anything? But I talked to him and he's determined.'

Breda sat down at her desk, she felt as if someone had actually deflated her. She couldn't believe what she was hearing, she was so shocked she couldn't really take it all in. 'But they are only lads still. He can't expect them to go through with it, surely?'

Declan shrugged again; he was angrier than he had been in years, angry and disgusted at what Phillip wanted to do, not just to his boys, but to himself. Why would anyone want that for their kids?

'He's calling it "blooding" them. I've already pointed out it ain't like they will be on their first pheasant shoot. They will be killing a person, a real human being.'

Breda didn't answer him. Her mind was working overtime. If Phillip was bringing the boys into this side of it all, then he expected them to become major players, and if that was the case, where did that leave her and poor old Declan? Admittedly there had been a cooling off between them on Declan's part recently – not that Phillip had noticed anything. But she had, and she knew what had caused it. Declan must feel what she was feeling now, he had to see that Phillip, with his usual disregard for anyone else around him, was taking the boys on as if his brother and sister didn't exist. Well, she would make sure it didn't happen to her, she would prove herself to be indispensable. But it still didn't change the fact that, because of the lads, she was now worried about even having control of the arcades. A few weeks ago she had felt as if this was all she had in life. Now, if she wasn't careful, she wouldn't even have that. There was no way she could work for the boys, not until they were old enough to understand what they were doing anyway.

And what about her Porrick? He was *older* than the boys, and he was sidelined as a fucking strong arm. Even though she knew he wasn't capable of much else, it still rankled. It seemed as though Phillip was gradually easing her and now Declan out, and she guessed, rightly, that Declan was having the same thoughts, though he would not voice them until he had considered how to explain his actions.

'Supposing they fuck up? He'll go ballistic.'

Declan didn't even bother answering that. That was exactly what was worrying him. The trouble with Phillip was he assumed everyone was as willing to kill and maim as he was. Declan knew it was part of their world, but he was sensible enough not to court trouble. Phillip, on the other hand, could find trouble within an order of silent monks if the fancy took him. He could be one awkward ponce. And when he decided he wanted change, he made sure those changes were implemented. It was sad really, because Phillip was an excellent businessman – none better. But it was this side of him that was the problem, and it was coming to the fore more and more lately.

It always seemed to coincide with Christine's going off her trolley, Declan had noticed. When she wasn't around, or playing up, as Phillip so nicely put it, it seemed to make him more paranoid, more determined to prove himself. When she was away it was as if he knew he had a free rein and acted accordingly – he wiped people out on a whim. Christine seemed to keep him on an even keel, if not inside the household, at least outside it. Christine's opinion of her husband was very important to him, more important than it should be really. That boat had sailed when he had shown her his true self. Because that was the start of all their problems, especially Christine's – she had never been the same since.

Now it appeared that Phillip was determined to get the boys fully involved and, in some ways, that would be seen as natural to most people. But those boys hadn't been brought up on the estate like his generation of Murphys had. They didn't understand death, not really. The closest they had ever come to it was playing fucking *Grand Theft Auto*, and that wasn't the same thing at all – no matter what people thought. Killing people up close and personal took a lot of bottle, and Declan's big worry, if he was really honest, was that the boys would take to it, and that would be the finish of them.

He lit a cigarette, and coughed harshly; he really should start on the cigars like Phillip, they were better for you.

'Come on, Breda, let's go and get drunk.'

She laughed as she said sarcastically, 'As Phillip always says, when in doubt, do a Christine!'

It was the nearest they had ever got to running Phillip down, and it showed them both just how the times were changing.

Chapter One Hundred and Fifteen

Jonnie Piper was with two of his best men, Colin Banks and Jerome O'Grady. They had worked for him for years and, though not real players in his main games, they were both more than capable for what he needed from them this night. Plus they were dispensable – always a handy trait in this kind of scenario.

'You've got to get to the farm and we'll walk the land, which Phillip will insist on because even *he* wouldn't kill me in his kitchen – no matter how much he pays Lily Law, no Filth will swallow a blatant piss-take like that. When we get to his barn, the big barn, I'll take him out, and then you take out his boys. We can leave them where they lie – let that old fucker who works for him discover them. I know Declan won't be there, he's meeting with Jimmy Mac at the arcades. Even Phillip wouldn't want his boys to be in on a kill, so he must want information from me about the euros. Either way, you make sure you're there for me, right? If there is a welcome committee, then we sort that as and when.'

Both men nodded. They had already done their homework, and they knew exactly how they would enter the premises and leave it. It was all sorted, except for the actual kill, and that would take seconds. It was fifty large each, up front, and that was not a bad wage. Though both knew that considering it was Phillip Murphy it should be a lot higher, which was why they were secretly a bit miffed about it.

'I want them shot in the head and then the face. This is a

fucking warning now to every cunt who thinks they can fucking have me over.' This was personal, and Jonnie was angry. He laughed suddenly. 'I bet his old woman will be over the moon. According to my wife, all ain't as fucking rosy as he would have people believe.'

Jerome O'Grady said seriously, 'I don't think she'll be too thrilled about her sons though, especially shot in the face.'

Jonnie waved his hand at the man in a gesture of irritation, he was a fucking moron to state the obvious so he ignored him. 'Murphy needs removing, and so does his fucking progeny. Fuck them, fuck them to hell and back. But I will have the fucking last laugh.'

'What about Declan and the sister? Won't they be looking for revenge?'

Colin always thought things through and, nodding in his direction, Piper said nonchalantly, 'First, I have a feeling they might not be as fucking angry as they make out. Anyway, once Phillip's gone, so has their strength. Phillip is the one people respect, without him they are fuck-all.'

'What about his mates, have you thought about them?'

Colin was getting on his nerves now, and with thinly disguised annoyance Jonnie said quietly, 'People like Phillip Murphy don't have real mates. What is this, Colin, fucking twenty questions?'

Colin wasn't fazed at the man's words. 'I like to get things straight in my mind, that's all. Look at every eventuality, that way you don't fuck up.'

Jonnie calmed down at that; the man was only covering all the bases, which is exactly what he was paying him to do. 'Yeah, well there's that to it, I suppose, but I am going to enjoy telling people that I think Bantry took him out. See how Declan and that coon-shagging sister of his react to that little gem of information, shall we?'

As Colin's mother was white and his father a Jamaican, he wasn't thrilled at Jonnie's offensive words, but he didn't say anything, not yet anyway. There was plenty of time to react when the dirty deed was over.

O'Grady was watching the clock; they had a lot of preparation to do before the night's work, and he said as much. 'Look, Jonnie, we need to go and get ourselves in position, but don't worry, we've got your back, no matter who he might have with him, OK?'

It was exactly what Jonnie needed to hear. He wanted all this over with so he could get back to Liverpool. Fucking southerners! All they had going for them was a milder climate – other than that the place was a shithole, full of blockheads and fucking thieves. But he felt better now it was all in place, he was even toying with just taking Murphy's knees out at first and letting him watch his boys die. Like Phillip, Jonnie Piper could be really nasty when the fancy took him, especially when he felt he was being had over. And as he was being had over, royally, it was going to stop tonight.

Chapter One Hundred and Sixteen

'Are you frightened, Philly?'

Philly thought about what his brother had asked, before answering him truthfully and with passion. 'I'm shitting it. Aren't you?'

Timmy nodded, but the truth was, he wasn't scared at all – he was excited, exhilarated even. But not in the least bit scared. He remembered as a kid he had dreamed of being like his father, of being without fear, and it had suddenly come to him that on the day he had taken out Joey White he had discovered his true self. He wasn't even twenty yet, and he was already on the cusp of serious crime, and serious crime meant serious respect. He felt like he was living in a Martin Scorsese film. It was every young boy's dream. He knew inside himself that he was born for this. Even more so than Philly. It was his destiny, and as cheesy as he knew that sounded, he honestly believed it. Timmy was champing at the bit to get this over with. He wanted to be blooded, he wanted to know what it was like to have the power of life and death. He wanted, if he was really honest, to *be* his father.

Chapter One Hundred and Seventeen

Phillip was visiting his wife and, as he looked at her strained face, he felt the usual rush of what he thought of as love.

There was, even now, something about Christine. From the moment he had laid eyes on her, he had wanted her, and he would never *not* want her. Of that much he was sure. He could cheerfully take her out at times, fucking strangle her, but he knew he wouldn't, because she represented everything he had ever cared about. Even like this, in rehab, her life in tatters around her, he still felt that pull. She was like something you know you can never have, but you long for it anyway. Even when he had got her, he had never really believed it. He could remember when she had felt the same, when she had run to him as soon as he walked through the door. When they had lain together after making love, and laughed and joked. He had felt like a real person then, the way he knew people were supposed to feel. Because until her, he had never really cared for another human being, not really. He had always seen the people around him as no more than acolytes, even his brothers and sister. They were safe only as long as they were useful to him.

He knew perfectly well he wasn't normal in some respects, but he used that as a strength – it was why he was so successful. Christine had, for a time, given him the belief that he could be like other men, feel as other people felt. Now, he was determined to make her see that he had changed, that he was the man she needed and wanted. He would *make* her believe it, he would get her back onside.

'Do you want another cup of tea, Christine?' His voice was gentle and full of care.

She shook her head, and tried to smile at him, she knew that pleased him. 'If I drink any more tea I'll wake up one morning and find I've turned into a teabag!'

He grinned, and she saw how good-looking he still was. 'Is it hard for you, babe, not drinking?'

It was the first time he had ever directly referred to why she was there, and it threw her for a few seconds. She wondered if he was setting her up, but looking into his eyes she felt instinctively he wasn't. She shrugged. 'Not any more, Phillip. It was at first.'

He nodded, and she saw the tears that were glistening in his eyes, and she felt almost sorry for him. 'I'm sorry for what I did to you, babe. I can't excuse it all, I was a bully, and I was a fucking fool. But you hurt me at times so badly, I had no choice but to lash out. I'm not making excuses, Christine, I just want you to know how I feel about you . . .'

She closed her eyes and swallowed audibly before saying quickly, 'I *know*, Phillip, I *know* how you feel about me. That's the one thing I am sure of, don't you worry.'

It was the nearest she would ever get to sarcasm and they both knew it. Phillip didn't react, he knew he had to keep his temper if he was going to salvage anything from their marriage. He smiled tenderly instead. 'Well, I can't help how I feel, babe. There will only ever be one woman for me, but I won't go on about it. Did I tell you the boys are cooking for me tonight at the house?'

She was amazed at his words, and he saw her face light up. 'You're joking?'

He grinned and, after stroking her face for a second, he sat back from her, as if giving her some space. 'Truth, as true as I'm sitting here. Cooking, *your* handsome sons.'

'What are they cooking for you?'

He laughed then, as if bewildered. 'Fuck knows, probably beans on toast!'

Christine had relaxed a bit, and her laugh in response was genuine. Phillip was lying through his teeth, of course, but she didn't know that. The charm offensive had begun, and he was going to make her love him again. He wanted it so badly, how could it not happen? She would be in here for ages, and that would give him the time he needed to bring her round to his way of thinking. With the help of the boys, he would get her back on track. He would once again be the man she loved and, this time, he would make sure he didn't fuck that up.

Chapter One Hundred and Eighteen

'All right, Breda? Where's Declan?'

She shrugged her answer. 'I dunno, mate. He should be round somewhere, might be in one of the clubs, he's sorting out the stock today.'

Phillip nodded. 'You're looking well, Breda. How's things here? How's the boys doing, that Timmy especially.'

She sat opposite him; when Phillip came in he always took her seat behind the desk. It wasn't that he was making a point or anything, it was just where he felt he should be sitting.

'Both are good kids, emphasis on the kids, of course. But no, Phillip, they are really intelligent boys. Bit young for all this really . . .'

Phillip stopped himself from biting; Breda kept hammering on about their ages, and yet she had been laid down more times than a fucking medieval tankard by the time she was fifteen. So the constant reference to their youth was getting wearing. But he decided to take it as her being a good aunt, rather than because she feared they would be getting her job though he suspected that was the real reason. He could write the fucking script for the lot of them, and it annoyed him that they all thought he couldn't suss them out. There was a reason why they worked for *him*, and not vice fucking versa.

But, in fairness, Breda was good at her job, and that counted for a lot with Phillip Murphy. She was family and, as such, she should understand that his sons were family as well. If they had been cranially challenged like poor Porrick they wouldn't get a chance at anything decent. Phillip wasn't a fucking fool. He wouldn't shoot himself in the foot because they were his kids. If they couldn't earn they would be out. But they had nous, he had to admit that. Now what they needed was experience, and he would provide them with that as well. It's what any father would do for their kids – see they knew how to get themselves an earn.

Breda understood that she had pushed it far enough, so she said, 'Timmy will surprise us, I think. He's deep, Phillip. Still waters and all that.'

He nodded in agreement, satisfied that she had spotted the same potential in his boy that he'd seen. Timmy was going to be the driving force there, he would lay money on it. He felt magnanimous suddenly. His sister was a fucking grafter, and she would kill for him, he knew that for a fact. Smiling, he said seriously, 'Don't worry, Breda, you will always be close to me in the businesses. I have a few things to sort out, as you know, and then I'll want you beside me, you and Declan, because we'll have a lot more work to do. My boys can cut their teeth on this lot, all right?'

Breda almost cried with relief, and he was glad he had put her mind at rest. He had been going to leave her here, but she was a good girl, and she was honest, and she was family. He knew he could trust her with his life. Plus the boys adored her, and they thought the world of Porrick. Personally he thought Porrick was a shitbag, and he would love to know who the culprit was who'd fathered him. But that was a mystery to be solved on another day.

'I want you and Declan at the farm by eleven tonight, OK?'

He saw her eyes widen almost imperceptibly, and he stopped himself from smiling at her obvious surprise.

'Come on, Breda, you didn't think I'd leave you out of something this big, do you? This is a family celebration, darling.'

As an afterthought he said grandly, 'Bring Jamsie and all. Fuck it – let's have a family party!'

Breda was thrilled at the invitation and, going around the desk, she hugged him tightly. 'Thanks, Phillip.'

He grinned happily. 'Why are you thanking me? We're *family*, Breda, we look out for each other, girl.'

'Talking of family, Phillip, how's Christine?'

He laughed then, and so did she when he said cheerfully, 'Mad as a box of frogs, but she's getting there, mate. It's the best I've seen her in years, to be honest.'

'I'm glad, Phillip, I think the world of her, you know that.'

He did know it; it was the truth, and truth meant a lot to him. It occurred to him that he could use Breda's relationship with Christine to help get his wife back on track. If Breda said that he had changed, mellowed, then Christine would believe her, especially if Breda actually believed it herself.

He would play the long game; it wouldn't be the first time, and he was sure that it wouldn't be the last.

Chapter One Hundred and Nineteen

Philly watched Jonnie Piper like a hawk – he was fascinated by him. That he wanted his father dead, and yet was strutting about their kitchen acting like everyone's best friend, was just outrageous.

Philly knew he had to act like he didn't know what was going on, and he felt he was doing a pretty good job of it. Piper would be feeling secure in himself, because he'd assume that Phillip Murphy wouldn't want his sons involved in a murder. But, as his father had explained to them earlier in the evening, that was the genius of the whole plan. It didn't occur to Philly for a moment that no decent man would be dragging his boys into something so serious and so dangerous. Most hardened criminals wanted their kids to be anything but a villain. It was why you earned, to give your kids better opportunities than you had had. Any decent man who had sat in a prison cell for any length of time wouldn't want that for their kids. They would rather see them out and free, not banged up. That was the hardest thing for any parent. But Philly and Timmy took every word out of their father's mouth as gospel; they didn't yet understand that it was really only ever going to be about him and what he wanted, never about anyone else. That was Phillip Murphy – it was how he was made.

Philly felt he was on the cusp of greatness, and he was looking forward to the night's events. He was a bit frightened that he would let his father down in some way, but he was mostly excited about doing something so outrageous, and dangerous. He still couldn't believe his father trusted them both enough to be involved. If he needed any more proof in his father's belief in them, this was it.

'Come on then, lads, who wants to walk the land with me?'

It was just what Jonnie Piper had been waiting for and, picking up his large Scotch, he said jovially, 'Fuck me, Phillip, I thought you'd never ask.'

They laughed as they walked out the back doors, and changed into Wellington boots. Phillip always kept spare sets for anyone who might be visiting, he knew better than anyone the damage dirt could do to a decent pair of shoes.

As they began the quarter of a mile walk they were joking around, and Jonnie Piper was sorry about the boys, because they were nice lads. But needs must and all that – he couldn't leave them as witnesses and, once the dirty deed was done, he would put it out of his mind as always. This was kill or be killed, like war, and these lads were what would be known in wartime as collateral damage.

It was a bright night, and the moon was full, and their voices were loud as they ambled slowly towards what was misleadingly called the 'big barn' but was, in reality, a huge chimney stack with ornamental brickwork, and solid hardwood doors. It looked more like a chapel than a furnace room. Phillip had given the local planning officer a serious drink to get the fucker built in the first place, but it had been worth every penny. After all, Phillip never skimped on quality, that was part of his charm.

Chapter One Hundred and Twenty

Colin Banks and Jerome O'Grady were in the barn, ready. They were calm, and waiting patiently for the night's events to unfold. Both were used to this. Colin had committed his first murder when he was seventeen – he had glassed another lad in a pub in Liverpool's Knowsley district. He had done eight years of a life sentence, and came out far more knowledgeable about murder than when he had gone in. Jerome O'Grady, on the other hand, had learned his trade as a drug dealer's apprentice and he had learned early that if you tucked up a drug dealer, you were dead. It was a real cut-throat business, and that was no pun. He had got fed up with it because it was too obvious, and the likelihood of getting banged up too risky. He now worked for people like Jonnie, clearing up their shit for them, and he and Colin made a good earn. Far more than if they were in a normal legal line of work.

Funny thing was though, people still looked down on them – he assumed it was because they were like the grim reaper. Jerome's wife thought he was a courier; she was far happier thinking he was bringing in diamonds and gold, or even cocaine, than knowing what he really did. Now that *would* freak her out. Colin's wife thought he was a debt collector, and the way she spent she must think he was collecting for Asil Nadir. But it worked for them and, once tonight was over, they would have a drink, get their pay and fuck off home. One good thing about it, as Colin was always saying, the hours were great, and you could piss off from the wife in peace because you could say you had to go to work and she wouldn't question it.

They both heard muted laughter and, even though the only light was from the moon coming through the skylights, they had a pretty good view of the door. They settled themselves in position. They had chosen American handguns for the job; both were untraceable and had been supplied by Jonnie. The Colt 45 was a big gun, powerful and intimidating. Not something most people would pick in this day and age, but it was the gun of choice for the old die-hards.

As the door opened, they were both ready, holding out the guns as if they were playing a part in a film. The two boys were amazed to see them there, and Jerome saw the fear cross their faces as they took in what was happening.

He felt almost sorry for them.

Chapter One Hundred
and Twenty-One

'Let it go, Veronica, will you? I'm sick of hearing about it.'

Phil Senior was annoyed; he wanted to watch the telly, not have another post-mortem on his son's life. As far as he was concerned his Phillip was a fucking lunatic, but a well-heeled, functioning lunatic. The boys had to learn a craft at some point, so why not now?

Veronica was not pleased at her husband's reaction to her worries. She expected him to agree with her, that was how it had always been. Plus she was genuinely worried. In contrast to her Phillip she wasn't sure that her grandsons were capable of making a living on the rob. They were too well brought up after all the money her son had weighed out for their educations. 'Don't you ever think about anything else except drink, sport and telly?'

She watched as her husband shrugged in the chair. 'What else is there to think about in this house? Unlike *you*, Veronica, I ain't obsessed with my eldest son, am I?'

She stood up, and he saw the anger burning out of her bones. He knew he had gone too far. But he wished she would for once stop talking about Phillip; she was like a fucking stuck record, saying the same things over and over again. Who gave a flying fuck? Not him that was for sure.

'You bastard! You ain't interested in any of your children,

that's the trouble – you never were. You ain't interested in fuck-all unless it's the pub.'

He got up and, going out to the hallway, he pulled on his coat.

'Where are you going at this time of night?' Veronica said, following him out.

'I'm going to the pub, there will be afters there, as per usual, and I can sit in peace and have a drink without you giving me GBH of the earhole.'

When he had slammed the front door she walked back into the front room and started to tidy up furiously, removing her husband's glass, the plate he had used for his sandwich, and fluffing up the cushions on the chairs. She hated him at this moment in time, really hated him. She was half tempted to phone Phillip and tell him what his father had said. But she wouldn't. Phillip would kill him, and she knew that as well as she knew her own name. But she was so worried about those boys; they were far too young for the firm, far too young and far too naïve. She had a bad feeling on her about it, and she couldn't shake it off. She just didn't want anything bad to happen to them. It was a filthy, dangerous game Phillip was in and, even though her whole family were involved somehow, she didn't want it for Christine's sons. Because Christine would never be able to cope with them being a part of their father's world and, if she was really honest about it, neither would she.

Chapter One Hundred
and Twenty-Two

Phillip saw his sons' faces, and stifled the urge to laugh. They were both white-faced with shock and horror at what they had walked into. They were diamonds the pair of them, twenty-four carat gold. He looked at Jonnie Piper, who was smiling triumphantly. Jonnie was standing there like he owned the fucking gaff, short-arsed and full of bravado. Phillip acted shocked, worried, but he wasn't – the man hadn't been born yet who could scare him.

'What's going on, Jonnie? What the fuck are you doing?'

Jonnie Piper laughed, the relief now it was actually happening was almost overwhelming; once he had outed this ponce he was home and dry.

'What's it look like?' He was all loose limbed and, thanks to the expensive whisky his host had kindly provided for them, he was almost in a party mood.

Suddenly Timmy took a run at Jonnie and, using his sheer size, knocked him off his feet. Then Philly was on him as well. Phillip watched, proud of his sons' bravery and, pulling them off the man, he said loudly, 'All right, you lads, *relax*. These two are with us.'

Jonnie Piper lay on the floor, felt the cold of the concrete even through his good suit. He glanced at the two men he believed he could trust and felt the sick sweat of dread as it drenched his body.

Jerome laughed before saying, 'You know your trouble, don't you, Jonnie? You're a fucking cheapskate.'

Jonnie knew when he was beaten. He had cut his face on his whisky glass when Timmy had taken him down. He was bleeding heavily, but he knew that was the least of his problems. Philly and Timmy now realised that it had all been set up by their father, and they were relieved as well as vexed.

Phillip hugged his boys to him. 'You were fucking great, but lesson number one, my sons, never believe what you're told, no matter who is doing the telling, right?' They nodded in unison like little boys in front of a teacher. 'You never walk into any situation like this without a weapon, or back-up, such as these two nice gentlemen here. But for all that, you've got heart, and that's ninety per cent of our game. I'm fucking proud of you, at least you would have gone down fighting.' He looked at Jonnie Piper and said, 'They did good, Jonnie, don't you think?'

Jonnie nodded his agreement, but he didn't really give a fuck – all he could think about was what Phillip had in store for him. He wouldn't put anything past Phillip Murphy. After all, he wouldn't be too happy about anyone trying to take out his lads, no one would.

'Can we get this over with, Phillip?' Jonnie's voice was low, and Phillip had to admire the fact he wasn't begging like many other men would be.

'Do it.'

Colin and Jerome each shot Jonnie Piper three times, and the two young lads watched, fascinated, as he bled out on the concrete floor. Afterwards, Colin lit a cigarette while Phillip poured them drinks from the bar he'd had put in for events such as this. All the time he kept a close eye on his sons' reactions.

Philly had already shrugged it off, it was over and done with, but Timmy, he could see, wasn't in the least bit calm yet. He was breathing heavily as Phillip saw him walk over to Jonnie's body. Lifting his foot, he crashed it into the man's face with every bit of his considerable strength. Even Jerome and Colin winced at the sound of crunching bone and sinew.

'Fucking piece of shit! Thought he was gonna fucking take us out.'

Philly pulled his little brother away and, putting his arm protectively around his shoulder, he said quietly, 'Calm down, will you? Dad wouldn't let anything happen to us.'

Phillip Murphy knew then, that out of the two, Timmy would eventually be the brains of the outfit. Unlike Philly, who was a good kid, Timmy would never trust anyone again. Not after this. He would use it as his yardstick for the future. It had been a good learning curve for them both. It was really only Breda's outrage at him wanting them to be blooded that had made him change his plans to have the boys kill Jonnie. Now he was glad he had because it had given him a valuable insight into his sons, and the differences between them. Philly was weaker – not physically, but mentally. Timmy took onboard everything, and he would use the knowledge to his advantage. Philly would be a good leader, but Timmy had the potential to be a great one.

'Come on, boys, drink up and let's get this ponce into the furnace. Then you two can scrub and bleach the floor. Remember, industrial bleach removes everything a forensic will be looking for. So pour a whole drum down the drains, all right?'

They both nodded.

'Right then, young Colin and young Jerome, your poke is waiting for you in that cupboard over there. Separate bags, and used notes as requested.'

Phillip waited until they had removed their money, checked it, and put their weapons inside the bags he had provided, before he opened another cupboard and brought out a large pump-action shotgun. He shot the two men one after the other, the sound deafening, even over the roar of the furnace. Then, looking at his sons' stunned faces, he said jovially, 'Lesson number two, never leave a fucking witness, it only causes you worry. People talk and, with the best will in the world, you never know *when*, *where* or *to whom* they'll do that talking. Now the only people who know what really happened in here are us. And we're family, so that don't count.' He waited till they had digested that bit of information before clapping his hands and saying loudly, 'Come on then, chop chop, this lot won't get up and jump into the incinerator themselves!'

He left them clearing up and walked back towards his house slowly, well satisfied with the night's events. He heard cars pulling up, and knew that the rest of the family had arrived. He was in the mood for a party now. He had everything he wanted and, more importantly, he had everything Jonnie Piper had wanted. His boys were both going places, and he would work hard at winning back his wife's affection; he would be successful, he was sure of it. He would get his family back proper, because at the end of the day, family was all you really had, all you could really rely on. And he had a family to be proud of, a family that most men could only dream of having.

Phillip Murphy was a very happy man.

Book Four

My strength is made perfect in weakness

II Corinthians, 12:9

Train up a child in the way he should go:
and when he is old, he will not depart from it

Proverbs, 22:6

Chapter One Hundred
and Twenty-Three

2009

'Are you sure, Timmy?'

Timmy nodded sagely. 'Fucking telling you, Dad, he's on a real love job.'

Phillip grinned. As always, he was amazed at how his younger son had developed. In the last five years both the boys had come on leaps and bounds, but this fellow here was already becoming a legend. His temper was extraordinary, even Phillip was shocked at his son's actions at times, and that took some doing. He could well imagine how outsiders must feel. Timmy was fair and honest – just so long as you didn't upset him.

Philly was doing well too; he had a good rep, but he wasn't a hard taskmaster like his younger sibling. He was no mug though – he was still worth ten men on the ground.

'What's she like?'

Timmy laughed. 'What do you think? All tits, teeth and designer handbags. Looks like a WAG.'

Phillip knew exactly what he meant. Philly's taste in women was appalling – they were all brainless nowts. But then, as Philly always said, he wasn't exactly after riveting conversation.

'You'll meet her tonight anyway, Dad, she's coming to the club.'

'I think I had better be there then, don't you?'

At that moment Christine walked into the kitchen and, smiling at her, Phillip said, 'Fancy coming to the club with us tonight? Philly's bringing his bird. According to Timmy, he's on a love job.'

Christine laughed in delight, and both her husband and son noticed how young and pretty she looked. 'Oh yeah, count me in!'

Phillip was thrilled, he loved it when she was upbeat like this. She didn't drink too much these days, except for the occasional bender, and they were fucking outrageous. She still depended on her prescription meds though. But she was happier, and that was the main thing. She reminded Phillip at times of himself, she *pretended* she was happy, she played a role and, like him, she had found it made life easier not just for her, but for everyone around her. He pulled her on to his lap and kissed her thick, luscious hair. She smelled good these days – the stale breath was gone, though the vacant stare still lingered at times. But it was all a matter of how you perceived things, and he always looked for the best where this woman was concerned. He loved her, and it seemed that these days, she actually loved him back.

'Fancy our Philly on a love job!' He was laughing with his wife, and that in itself was still a minor miracle. 'What's her name?'

'Finoula McCormack.'

Phillip was astounded. 'No relation to Mad Jack McCormack, I hope?'

Timmy laughed excitedly. 'Yep, his youngest daughter, and she is a stunner. I can't take that away from her.'

'Fucking hell, he can pick them can our Philly. I remember seeing Jack fight – always worth a bet, him, he was the nuts in his day. Him and Roy Shaw were the best. Fucking unbelievable strength those old boys had. You throw Jack or Roy in their heydays into a cage now and this new breed of fighters would run a fucking mile.'

Timmy nodded his agreement; he had met a lot of the bare-knuckle fighters with his dad. It was an exciting sport, but if he was honest he was a cage-fighting boy at heart. It was all to do with age, he supposed. Not that he would point that out to his father – he was far too polite.

'Finoula's a good Irish name, that'll please your mother anyway. She'll be a good Catholic girl!' Christine joined in.

'Fucking hell, never thought of that! They don't come more Irish than Mad Jack. Like the old man's family, Cork men. Hard bastards and all.'

Timmy was laughing again, a deep, friendly chuckle that belied the dangerous man he was becoming. 'I don't know about good. She's been around the track more times than a fucking lurcher.'

Christine sat up straight and said primly, 'That's enough of that kind of talk, thank you very much. After all, if a man has a few girls he's just called a lad. There's such a thing as equal rights, you know.'

Phillip was irritated by that. 'Not where women are concerned there ain't. A bird who puts it about is still classed as a rogue, and should be treated with the utmost suspicion, especially if she wants to get into *my* family.'

Christine didn't even bother answering, sometimes his double standards were so outrageous she could scream. So, as always when faced with this kind of conversation, she tactfully changed the subject. It made life easier for everyone. 'How about you, Timmy, you bringing anyone tonight?'

He shrugged. 'I might, Mum, but don't marry *me* off just yet, I'm only twenty-two.'

She smiled at this handsome son of hers. 'Well, if we're all going out on the town, I'd better get me hair done.'

She jumped up and bustled from the room. When she was out of his sight, Phillip felt a familiar moment's panic. He couldn't imagine a world without her in it, she made his life what it was. Perfect.

Chapter One Hundred
and Twenty-Four

Finoula McCormack was beautiful and, boy, did she know it.

She had long, naturally blond hair and deeply blue eyes, her bone structure was like a young Marilyn Monroe's, and she had the high-breasted slim figure that was peculiar to the women of Cork. Cork women were either amazons, or tiny little birds of women – there was never a happy medium. She had her mother's looks, and her mother's height. She also had her father's feisty disposition. It was a wonderful combination. She was funny, enigmatic, and not as thick as she looked; in fact, she had a quick, agile mind and she was after a decent bloke with a decent earn who could give her a bit more than the average Joe. She was determined not to end up in a bought council house fighting to raise her kids; she was going to make something of her life, and her future kids' lives. She knew her worth; her looks wouldn't last for ever, so she was determined to get what she wanted sooner rather than later. She also wanted someone she loved, not just for what they could give her.

Philly Murphy was all these things rolled into one man, and she cared about him deeply; she wanted his wedding ring and his kids, in that order. She wanted the big church wedding, and the house with the electric gates and a swimming pool. They shared the same dreams, and that was one of the reasons they got on so well. He was even letting her finally meet his family. She already knew *of* them of course, everyone did, and her mum and his nan were great mates, she saw her sometimes at church. But she came from pretty good stock in that way herself. Mad Jack wasn't exactly a mug, and she knew he was very well thought of by Philly's dad; he had come enough times to see her father fight over the years. They were mates, so she had the appropriate in should she need it.

She was excited about tonight, it was the first time Philly had taken her to one of their clubs. They normally went out to other places, neutral places in Romford or up town to the West End. She wanted to look her best, and show Philly that she was someone he could be proud of and, more importantly, that she was someone who could fit in with his family.

Chapter One Hundred
and Twenty-Five

'You sure you're all right, Mum?'

Veronica nodded, but she wasn't, she felt terrible.

'Listen, let me get the quack out.' Breda wasn't buying her mother's lies.

Veronica was already holding her hand palm up. 'No! Now stop keeping on about it. I'm under the weather that's all.' But she knew it was more than that, she just wasn't interested in what it might be. Veronica never went to the doctor, ever. They never told you anything you wanted to hear, it was all doom and gloom. Christ knew she was happy enough in ignorance.

'He'll find out what's wrong with you, and once he knows that he can treat you accordingly,' Breda persisted.

Veronica could hear the worry in her daughter's voice, and smiling now, secretly pleased at her daughter's concern, she said, 'Would you feck off, and leave me be. I'm not a spring chicken any more. Jesus, I won't be seeing sixty again, I'm just getting older, slowing down. You'll be the same one day and I hope that Porrick isn't scalding the heart out of you with constant questions.'

Breda sighed heavily. It was worrying seeing Veronica so thin and weak looking. She still cooked for them all, but it wiped her out these days. Breda had arranged for a cleaner to come in three times a week now the heavy work was getting too much for Veronica. There had been absolute murders when she had first arrived, but now her mother was thrilled with her. She was a lovely Polish girl, very willing, and very polite; she was also a good Catholic and she attended the same church as them, so that was really the deciding factor. But she also kept the place immaculate and, where her mother was concerned, that was the second most important thing. Breda knew her father was glad to get out of the house these days, it was as if the weaker Veronica got, the more frightened he became. He refused to discuss his wife's condition, and Breda knew the next step was to get Phillip involved. Once *he* arranged a doctor's appointment there would be no further arguments, she would have to go, there would be no getting out of it. Breda decided she'd talk to Phillip tonight at the club, then she could relax and stop worrying. It was weird really – Breda gravitated from wanting to punch her mother's lights out, to wanting to hug her on a daily, almost hourly, basis. Deep down, Breda loved her mother even though she accepted that her affections were wholly reserved for Phillip.

'Here, apparently Philly's bringing his bird tonight – we're going to meet her. She's Jack McCormack's youngest daughter and it's a love job by all accounts.'

Veronica was pleased, it was about time those boys settled down. 'What, Mad Jack's girl Finoula?'

Breda nodded. She didn't realise her mother had met her, but then her mother knew everyone who had some kind of Irish heritage.

'Oh, Jasus, she's a lovely girl – beautiful. I've met her a few times with her mother at seven o'clock Mass. She goes every morning with Mary Mac. Done very well at school, I believe. She did a business something or other – I can't remember what, but she runs her father's bookies, and runs them well, I'm told.'

Breda was amazed. She had found out more about Finoula in

two minutes with her mother than she would from young Philly
if she interrogated him for six months. 'I forgot you and Mary
Mac were mates, how is she?'

'Very well, God bless her and keep her. The old breathing is
bad, like, but she loved a fag that one. Always had one sticking
out the side of her gob! Even when she was cooking!' Veronica
laughed in delight at the old memory. She was glad Philly was
seeing someone like *them*, someone who understood their
world. Timmy's tastes were for the more refined, but sexually
accessible females. In short, he never kept them longer than a
few weeks, if that. 'Posh totty' was how Phillip described his
younger son's girlfriends, and she knew it was a derogatory
term, though she didn't really know what it meant. But like
young Philly and his father, one day he would meet 'the one',
and then he'd change his tune like they all did.

Except her Declan, of course – in his forties now and still
without a partner, as they insisted on calling them these days.
Mind you, the same could be said for Breda, but sure, Breda
was more man than the men she came across in her work.
Though her conquests weren't so young these days – well, not
as young as they used to be anyway. Veronica chuckled to herself.
Her daughter had the sexual appetite of a Titan, she got that
from her – not that she would ever tell her that, of course, but
back in the day!

Jamsie had four stepchildren, and now two of his own, so
he'd ended up with six. She was pleased for him though – he
had a good girl there, a damn fine girl. And Porrick, him and his
little thing were married now, and she knew a child wouldn't be
long in the offing with them two. Porrick never said a shagging
word, yet him and his girl were always whispering and smiling.
Sometimes it got on her nerves, but she kept that to herself.
Porrick was her grandson and she loved him, but he was a
fecking eejit to try to talk to for any length of time. Would
aggravate a saint as her mother used to say.

Veronica had been thinking about her life a lot lately since this illness had assailed her. She was sure it was serious and all she wanted was to spend what time she had left with her family, however long or short that might be. Especially her Phillip, her boy, her heart.

As Breda left the house, she pulled her mother into her arms, and she could feel the frailty of her body. Kissing her hard on the cheek, she said quietly, 'We need you, Mum, all of us, so *please* go to the fucking doctors, will you?'

Veronica realised she must look much worse than she thought if Breda was so worried. The knowledge depressed her. She wanted another few years, see them all settled properly, and she would go happily to her maker. After all, that was what happened to everyone, wasn't it?

'Get yourself away, child, and tell me about Finoula and Philly tomorrow. I'll be beside meself until I know what happened.'

Breda left her mother, but she was anxious, and she knew that she had to tell Phillip to get her sorted out. Christine would make sure the doctor was good, and she would go with her to see him. Christine was great like that, she was dependable when it was something important. She did the jobs no one else really wanted to do, and for that Breda would be eternally grateful. The last thing she wanted was to be dragging her mother to the doctor against her will; as her father always said, her mother could make the top of the morning sound like a declaration of war. No, it would be much better if Christine took her.

Chapter One Hundred
and Twenty-Six

Declan was tired. He had just reached Southend Seafront, and now he was sitting like a lemon in the traffic – he should have left his place earlier. With the top down on his BMW convertible he could smell the salt, and the even heavier smell of the doughnut stands which was making him hungry. He had to stop eating – he was getting like a fucking elephant – but it was living alone, he didn't eat properly, but knowing that still didn't make him stop.

As he sat there in the sunshine, watching the girls go by in their skimpy summer clothes, he wondered how the night would be in the club. There had been a lot of trouble in the main nightclub. They had revamped it a year earlier, renamed it Legends and, for some reason, the last few months there had been nothing but fucking trouble in there. Not just fighting – that he could cope with. It was a nightclub in Essex after all and that was part of the Essex experience – a great night out involved a good drink and a good fight, it was almost mandatory really. No, it was the drugs, and the atmosphere they brought with them. There were new dealers coming in all the time. People they didn't know, had never heard of. Like most sensible club owners they used their own people. The franchise would be given to someone who would then deal discreetly and lucratively and they would also take the flak should the Filth decide to raid them. Not a problem in their clubs admittedly due to Phillip's connections, but every now and then there was a fake raid to make things look good. People paid a fair wedge to deal in peace, and so someone muscling in was bound to cause trouble. Which it had. The only thing was they were from out of the county, and all of them were apparently working for a ghost. The man they said had approached them was long dead. A *very* long time dead. He should know, his brother had killed him. It was Billy Bantry.

There was definitely serious skulduggery afoot, Declan would lay money on it. But until they could pin down who had actually given out the franchises, they were no better off. Every description was different, so that meant there was more than one person at work here. It was vexing, because they really didn't need any aggro at the moment; things were going so well, it would be a shame to have to go to war. But a war it would be. Phillip was livid, and taking it all as a personal insult. It would never occur to him that a lot of people thought that the Murphys had a bit too much for their own good and that a bit more of their largesse should be spread about locally. Well, Phillip wouldn't swallow that and, if Declan was honest, neither would he. They were businessmen, not fucking probation officers; there was no law that said they had to make sure strangers were doing all right. It was laughable really. At the end of the day, what did people expect from them? Fucking charity by the sounds of it.

Oh, Declan was annoyed and he was asking round anyone and everyone he could. Trouble was, no one seemed to be off-kilter to them and everyone had a viable excuse for their behaviour. Which left only one thing for definite. Some fucker somewhere actually thought that they could get away with something this fucking outrageous. It was insulting more than anything, and Phillip was losing patience by the hour, hence their constant presence in the nightclub.

Whoever this was would trip up sooner or later, and when they did, he and Phillip would be ready for them.

Chapter One Hundred
and Twenty-Seven

'This place looks fantastic, Philly, really upmarket.'

Finoula was impressed and Philly was revelling in her adoration. He knew this was a decent venue, and something to be proud of. Philly saw himself as a bit of a catch, and he was glad he had won this girl beside him. She was a blinder in every way. A good laugh, fabulous body, a good brain in her head, and a fantastic fuck – what more could a man want from life? He was going to marry her, and he was not going to wait about either. Like her, he wanted kids, and he wanted stability. What he didn't want was someone like his mother, but there was little chance of that: Finoula didn't drink, had never even tried cocaine, and she didn't feel she had lost out because of it. She could sip water all night and still have a blinding time. She was the girl for him all right.

'Come through to the VIP bar, babe.'

He walked her carefully through the crowded club and, seeing the way he was treated by the punters and the staff alike, she felt so proud to be with him as his girl. This was the life for her, this was what she wanted: the respect and the kudos having the name Murphy would bring her. She was already a McCormack and that had given her a small taste of what a name could do for you in life.

As Philly grabbed her hand and walked her into the VIP bar,

she felt the excitement welling up inside her. She could see the envious glances from the other girls there, could almost feel their jealousy, and their surprise at Philly Murphy acting like a love-sick teenager, because that was just how he acted around her. It was part of his charm for her, as though he was lucky to have her. He had told her he loved her, and she knew it was true. Life was just getting better and better.

Chapter One Hundred
and Twenty-Eight

Phillip watched the room through the two-way mirror behind the bar area. All the bars had them; it was the only way to stop thieving and people giving the drinks away for free. Though, in fairness, their staff were loyal and honest enough. It was the agency fuckers you had to watch out for. They were only there for one night and they went all out to make sure it was a good earner for them. That is until they were caught, of course – then they realised they had skanked off the wrong person. He was watching the VIP bar, eager to see this little bird of Philly's and, when they walked in, he had to admit she was a looker. She could have stepped out of the pages of a magazine, but then that wasn't too hard in Essex. All the girls were lookers. It was almost a genetic thing – they knew what was in fashion, what wasn't and where to get whatever they wanted. Even through the mirrors, Phillip could see she was special though, and watching his son's beaming face as he escorted her to the bar, it was clear that she was going to be a part of their lives from now on. She was from good stock, and it seemed like she could handle herself; if she ran the bookies as well as he had heard, she would be an asset to them. She had a business degree by all accounts, so she wasn't the usual tits and teeth – she had a bit of nous as well. His Philly had done well by the looks of it.

Christine watched as her husband spied on his son and his

new girlfriend, because that was exactly what he was doing, spying on them, and it annoyed her.

'Come on, Phillip, let's get out there and say hello. She looks like a nice girl.'

'I just wanted a sneak preview. If she was a Hammer Horror I was going to fuck off home to avoid them!'

Christine laughed despite herself, Phillip could be amusing when the fancy took him. Through the mirror she saw Breda walking towards Philly and his girl all smiles and camaraderie, and she felt a rush of affection for her sister-in-law. She might get on Breda's nerves at times, but she knew Breda felt a lot of guilt over what had happened all those years ago, and genuinely cared about Christine. Breda just wanted everyone to be happy, everyone in her family anyway. As Christine watched her with her elder son it occurred to her that Breda was probably closer to him these days than she was, and she was amazed to find that the realisation didn't bother her as it would have once. She had learned to live with a lot of things over the years, and she had also accepted that it wasn't what happened to you, it was how you *dealt* with it. And she dealt with things as and when they happened now, she didn't let herself get in a state over things she had no control over. It wasn't an ideal life, but it was the best it had been in years, and all because she made a point of not letting herself think too much. That had always been her trouble.

'She's very pretty, Phillip,' she commented to her husband.

He nodded, but she knew that the girl's looks wouldn't affect him – if she was seventy-five, he would still want her rather than anyone else in the world. She told herself that it was a compliment, most fathers would have been drooling over this little girl and her tight young body. She decided the girl had a lovely smile, and that she liked the way she looked at her son, as if she had been given a lovely present, and was thankful for it.

The gunshot, when it came, was deafening, even though they

were inside the offices away from the club itself. As her son sank to the floor, and young Finoula started screaming, Christine realised that it was her Philly who had been the target, her baby had been shot, and blood was seeping through his lovely suit and on to the carpet she had chosen so carefully.

She could hear someone screaming, screaming louder than everyone else, and it was a few seconds before she realised that the terrible noise was coming from her.

Chapter One Hundred
and Twenty-Nine

'He's still in the operating theatre. This is fucking madness.' Phillip's voice was loud in the small room, loud and aggressive sounding. 'Who would dare? Who would fucking dare!' He kicked the wall in outrage, and the thud was audible to them all.

Declan didn't answer him; he was thinking exactly the same thing, so it was pointless repeating it. If the lad died, he knew there would literally be murders, though the way Phillip was acting now, he wouldn't put it past him to take out the poor surgeon if he didn't tell him what he wanted to hear.

'Will you calm down, Dad! For fuck's sake, this ain't helping anyone, is it?' Only Timmy could have got away with that, and even Breda was impressed that the boy was saying what they all wanted to but daren't. Even more astounding was the way Phillip swallowed it – anyone else would have been dismantled in seconds. 'Whoever is behind this is a fucking dead man, Dad, that's a given. Let's just concentrate on getting him better first. How's me mum? Has anyone been down to see her?'

'She's all right, Timmy, I sat with her until the sedative worked,' Breda said from her place beside Finoula, who looked bedraggled and covered in blood. Finoula had held Philly in her arms until the ambulance had arrived, and travelled with him all the way to the hospital. She had been outstanding, and they

413

knew she would be accepted by every one of them for this night's performance. If Philly survived he would be a lucky man to get this girl full-time, and they would tell him that as well. Phillip, especially, was impressed with her; he knew she had been terrified, yet she had lain over Philly, as if protecting him from further harm. The girl loved his son, of that there would never be any doubt.

The door opened and they looked expectantly towards it. When Mad Jack walked in, Finoula ran to him and, bursting into tears, she sobbed brokenly, 'Someone shot Philly, Dad! Some bastard shot my Philly.'

As he held his daughter to him, Mad Jack looked at Phillip and shook his head sadly. It said a lot for him that he didn't question what had occurred, or make a scene about his daughter's condition and the danger she had been in. Like everyone in the room, he saw this as an occupational hazard. And, like them, he would move heaven and earth to find the culprit. This was personal now – whoever had done the dirty deed had risked his daughter's life in the process.

'Fucking terrible business, Phillip. Any idea who it was?'

Phillip shook his head. 'Nah, but there's a hundred grand reward for any information, so I don't think it'll be too long before we have a fucking name.'

Mad Jack inclined his head in agreement. 'Fucking filth they are. We'll find them, Phillip, don't you worry about that.'

Phillip nodded, and felt the anger spiralling through him once more. 'How dare they! How dare they shoot *my* boy! I'll fucking torture and maim the cunts responsible, I'll take a fucking oath on that.'

Mad Jack didn't even react to the venom in his words, none of them did. At the end of the day, Phillip was only saying out loud what they were all thinking. Whoever was behind this night's work would pay, and pay dearly.

Chapter One Hundred and Thirty

Veronica was heartbroken, and she knew that if her grandson died she would not be long following him. She still couldn't believe it had happened, that her lovely boy Philly had been shot. Shot in a crowded nightclub, and no one had apparently seen a thing. The shooter had been in and out in no time. In the pandemonium a gunshot always causes, he had dropped the gun on the floor and just disappeared amongst the people fighting to leave the building. There was nothing, not even a decent CCTV picture. It was unbelievable. Who the hell would *dare* to do something like that to *her* family? That was what she wanted to find out, and she was placated only by the knowledge that her Phillip was doing everything possible to find out who the culprit might be. Between him and Timmy, Declan and Breda, they had to find out sooner rather than later. Of that, she was convinced.

As she looked at Finoula, still bloodied and bedraggled and sitting a vigil at Philly's bed, she felt the tears once more sting her eyes. The girl had been there beside him for two days, and she hadn't even gone home to change her clothes or have a bath. Her mother had brought her in a pair of jeans and a shirt, but she hadn't opened the bag containing them. She had been there since he had come up from theatre and been placed in the ICU. Her hair was like a rat's nest and her make-up was smeared all over her face. As Phillip remarked, no one could accuse her of being vain – she looked dog rough. But then her Phillip was always brutally honest about most things. Still, Veronica knew he thought the girl was a diamond. She understood that Finoula was frightened that if she left Philly, even for an hour, he would die. This little girl wouldn't go anywhere until she knew that he was going to be OK. They were all very impressed with her. She was loyal and decent and, most importantly, she hadn't been fazed by the events like a civilian would have been. Her father had been shot before, as had one of her uncles. She knew the pitfalls that came with being part of a family like theirs.

She saw the worried eyes of Ted and Eileen Booth and, for once, she didn't have the guts to return their stares. They had gravitated between their daughter, still flat out in a side room, unable to cope with her son's injuries, and their grandson, who was not out of danger yet, not by a long chalk.

She felt the pain inside her belly again; whatever was wrong with her was getting worse. But all she could do was ignore it, and do what she did best: support her family. When this was over she would worry about her own troubles and, until then, she would do what she always did when in doubt, she said the rosary over and over like a mantra. Though even she had to admit, the hypocrisy of her life wasn't lost on her these days.

Chapter One Hundred
and Thirty-One

'Has he fallen out with anyone that you know about?' Phillip was questioning his younger son.

Timmy shook his head.

'An argument with someone? I mean, you know Philly – he can be an awkward cunt. Maybe he mouthed someone off, and they took umbrage?'

Timmy was still shaking his head, he was getting frustrated now with the barrage of questions. 'Look, Dad, do you think I'm fucking stupid or something? I've even asked about in case it's an ex of Finoula's, but there's nothing, Dad, nothing at all.'

His tone was insolent and Phillip looked at this son of his and imagined the boy's reaction if he battered the fuck out of him. Because he might just do that before long.

Declan watched the two men, and he knew that one day there was going to be a battle for supremacy and, if he was honest, he wouldn't write either of them off as the loser. They were both too aggressive for their own good. Whereas Phillip was not averse to letting his feelings known to all and sundry, Timmy was usually good at keeping them under control. But his brother's shooting had shocked them all. It was outrageous.

'I think this has something to do with the clubs and the drug boys, Phillip. We keep hearing Bantry's name and, let's face it, either someone's got a fucking strange sense of humour, or they are trying to send us a message of sorts.'

Phillip nodded, he had been thinking along similar lines himself. But as he had taken out everyone who had anything to do with Bantry, he couldn't see what could be gained from all this. He knew there were still people who believed he had done away with Billy, and that included the Old Bill, but they could think what they wanted. It was proving it that would be the hard part. He had been accused of all sorts over the years, and he had laughed it off. Some things he was responsible for, and others he wasn't. He never said a word either way; he knew there was mileage in letting people think he was the culprit. It gave him a status, and that was what they relied on in their line of work.

But this was scandalous and, standing up, he said quickly, 'Right, round up Breda, all the doormen, and every hard fuck we own. We're going on a manhunt. We're going to visit every cunt in the vicinity, and see what they have to say.'

Timmy smiled at his father's words.

Declan felt uneasy. 'We don't want to be falling out with people just yet, Phillip, we might need them down the line.' He was, as always, the voice of reason, but he knew neither Phillip nor Timmy would listen to him.

'Just get everyone assembled at the farm, and tell Breda to get those black boys on the case. They must have supplied the gun to someone, the Filth have already shown it to me. I'll get Benning to remove it from his evidence locker and we'll see what the fuck they have to say about it.'

Declan sighed inwardly. There was something not right here, because a hundred grand large should have brought every fucking grass out of the woodwork, but they had not even had a nibble, let alone a bite. This felt wrong, it felt very wrong. There was no one big enough to take them on, *no one*. As Timmy pointed out, there were a lot of new little Faces coming up.

They all thought they were fucking cowboys, but even *they* would have to be fucking stupid to have a go. There was one family you kept away from – the Murphys.

Chapter One Hundred
and Thirty-Two

Breda was in the big barn with Jamal McBride, a huge Rasta with Scottish-Jamaican ancestry. She had dealt with him a lot over the last few years, and found him astute, despite being stoned most of the time, and intrinsically honest. He never promised what he couldn't deliver, and he had never let them down.

Most guns came out of South London, then were dispersed all over the Smoke, so it was strange that Jamal professed to know nothing about the one used on Philly. Still, once he saw the weapon in question, it might jog his memory. She could only hope, because Phillip and Timmy were both getting angrier and more vindictive by the hour.

'I assume these are the legendary ovens that I hear about whenever the name Murphy comes into a conversation?'

Breda laughed at his tone. She knew that if a dog went missing the joke was that Phillip Murphy had incinerated it. The farm was often referred to as Auschwitz by some of the braver, often drunken, locals, though if Phillip knew that there *would* be fucking murders. He hated the Germans almost as much as he did the French, the Welsh and the Italians. It was an open secret, the big barn, but there was nothing here that could ever incriminate them. The ovens were cleaned almost daily, and any debris was well hidden from the public gaze. Phillip had a crime-scene bloke on the payroll who was quite happy to ensure there was nothing left that could be used against anyone. It was about keeping up with current procedures – if you did that you were safe. Phillip had an analytical mind, he never left anything to chance. This place was probably too clean, in fact, but that was how things were, and how they would always be.

Phillip and Timmy came through the doors and Breda was reminded just how powerful they were together. Timmy was smiling, he always seemed to be smiling at the beginning of any meet. It was his way of disarming the person they were talking to. He looked like any handsome man; the real Timmy was hidden away, waiting to pounce.

'All right, Jamal?'

Jamal shook hands with them, and waited patiently for the real conversation to begin. He wasn't happy about Benning being with them; he always felt uncomfortable around the Filth. But this one was tame, so he would swallow. If he was honest, he would rather this meet had been on his own turf, but Phillip Murphy wasn't the kind of person you forced your opinion on. If he wanted to meet on the moon, you found a way to get there.

'So, what can I do for you gentlemen?' Jamal was a naturally polite man, which worked for him, and he rarely fell out with people through arrogance or rudeness. His mother had drummed into him from an early age that being nice got you further in life than being mean. Especially if you happened to be black. She was a very intelligent woman, and he had listened to her closely.

Phillip waved a hand towards Benning. 'Show him.'

They were given latex gloves and, once they were on, the gun was taken out of the plastic evidence sack and placed in Jamal's hands. Jamal looked the gun over like the professional he was. It wasn't a particularly good gun, but it had a high calibre and it would easily kill someone at close range. It wasn't a make he dealt with – in fact he hadn't seen a Russian gun like this in years, it should be in a fucking museum.

He said as much. 'Russian, as I'm sure you know. Not a gun you see often these days, it's more of a collector's piece. Whoever provided this must have had it hanging around somewhere. It's been well looked after, but it's practically an antique. There's no way I would shift this, no one would want the fucker, plus there's no profit in it. Now if it was a grenade launcher, I could sell it like Tesco sells bread rolls. Sorry, Phillip, but this ain't from a regular supplier. Even the fifteen year olds want a decent firearm these days.'

'That was basically what Benning said, but it never hurts to get a second opinion,' Phillip replied.

Jamal sighed. 'For what it's worth, Phillip, I ain't heard a *whisper* about who might be behind this, not even a speck of gossip, and that ain't natural. Gangsta's talk, we are all guilty of it, you know what I'm saying? You sure this ain't from over the water? Spain, wherever? Because I don't think this is anything to do with the Smoke. No one could keep something like this secret for so long.'

Phillip considered Jamal's words. That was exactly what had crossed his mind, but he knew there was no one in Spain who would dare to do something so outrageously stupid. His reputation was too entrenched in the minds of everyone who knew of him for anyone without influence to even dream about taking him on.

'I know where you're coming from, Jamal, but I can't see it.'

Phillip was already investigating it though, as he was sure Jamal had guessed. He was also going to visit every fucking ponce who thought they were a villain and give them a taste of the old Murphy charm. He would find out who was behind this if it killed him, though he had a feeling it would not be *him* who would be getting killed. He looked at Benning, and decided to cut his fucking money down. He was as much use as a fucking chocolate teapot, you'd think a Filth might have heard a fucking whisper. That was their job for fuck's sake.

'Any new firm on the scene with dreams of the big time?' Timmy's voice was flat, but it had to be asked.

Jamal shrugged. 'They all think they're big time till they come across the real Faces, but no, no one this fucking daring. A few have possibilities, like – there's a little crew in Brixton, none over twenty-two, and they are well organised. But what the fuck would anyone there want with the south coast? They might *visit* the place, but they ain't gonna be living there, know what I mean?'

Phillip understood him perfectly and, his business head coming to the fore, he said with interest, 'Would these kids be any use to me? Are they up for the earn?'

Jamal nodded, and smiling now he said, 'They're good kids, Phillip. Just need a firm hand, that's all. I'll give you their numbers, you can arrange a meet. They'll be thrilled, I can tell you.'

Phillip smiled. He bet they'd be thrilled; his talking to them was the criminal equivalent of being summoned by a king.

'Well, I'm off now, and listen, your Philly is a strong little fucker, he'll be home before you know it. I got shot in the gut ten year ago, and look at me now, still eating me curry goat and rice. It's lucky it didn't hit the heart.'

They all hoped Jamal was telling the truth. Philly was too strong to die. It was what everyone was relying on.

Chapter One Hundred
and Thirty-Three

'Once he regains consciousness I'll be a lot happier, Mrs Murphy, but he is definitely on the mend. Now, how are you?'

Christine didn't answer the doctor she looked out of the window at the lovely sunshine instead, and felt the urge to sleep again. People would be taking advantage of the weather, normal people anyway, going to the beach for the day with their kids and making her husband more money, because you couldn't go to the seaside without going in the amusements, could you? Other people would be arranging to visit their families, or have a picnic, normal people who didn't live in the shadow of violence like her family did. Now it had her son's life in the balance, her Philly's. She could still see him the moment he was shot, saw the surprise on his face, the blood as it oozed from him, but she also saw the man who had done it. She had noticed him a few seconds earlier, recognised him from somewhere, but she couldn't place him. And that was what was worrying her so much.

She yawned. She was so tired, but she knew it was because of the injections they were giving her. It was nice to slip into unconsciousness, leave all her troubles behind. Now she had an even bigger worry.

'Are you listening to me, Mrs Murphy?'

The doctor's voice was irritating her, but she answered him

nicely. ' 'Course I am, Doctor. Can I go and see my son now?'

He nodded. Christine Murphy was a strange woman, and he didn't like dealing with her, or that husband of hers. They thought they *owned* the hospital, even going so far as to take over all the family rooms – no one else got a look in. So the sooner that boy could be moved to a private facility the better, as far as he was concerned. Everyone in the hospital treated them like celebrities and, though he wouldn't say any of this out loud, thugs like these were not people he particularly wanted to have to placate on a daily basis. They behaved as though he was their own personal physician, calling him at all hours, walking into his consulting rooms as if he was a plumber or something, not a highly skilled surgeon. They had even arranged for professional cleaners to come in. MRSA was constantly on their lips, and these were people he would have assumed had trouble saying the most basic of sentences. His wife said he was a snob, but if she had to deal with people like the Murphys every day she might understand his feelings a bit more.

There were other ill people in the ICU, people who didn't live in a world where getting shot was treated as a normal occurrence. People who were ill through no fault of their own. And he would rather spend his time and energy on them than on this shower, who seemed to think that the world turned specifically for them and their cohorts.

Chapter One Hundred and Thirty-Four

Finoula was tired out, but she wouldn't sleep. She was still sitting by Philly's bed, holding his hand tightly. He looked so vulnerable lying there with all the tubes and the machines around him. He couldn't die, she wouldn't let him, and thankfully the doctors seemed to think he was over the worst. As she looked around her at the bareness of the walls, and smelled the disinfectant and the underlying scent of death that these places always seemed to have, she felt the urge to cry once more.

'Hey, Philly, I've just thought, maybe me and you could go on holiday when you're recovered. A bit of sun and sangria maybe? Nowhere too far, just a few hours away.' She was always talking to him when they were alone; it made her feel better. She had read once that the hearing was the last to go, and if he was going to go, then she wanted him to go hearing her voice. 'I love you, Philly, please wake up, please talk to me.'

Why was he still unconscious? No one seemed to know the reason for it. The doctor said it happened occasionally and it was because of the anaesthetic. But his stomach was sewn up, and he should eventually be all right if only he would come out of his coma. She laid her head on their joined hands and started to talk again.

'Timmy and that will be here soon. They always come around

this time, and they bring me something to eat – not that I have any appetite, of course. But it's nice they think of me, eh? Your nan's gone home, and your mum's been in. She looks awful, bless her, but then I would be the same if it was my son.'

She wiped her eyes with her free hand, and sniffed loudly. She knew she needed to have a good blow, but she was loath to let go of his hand, and her tissues were in her handbag on the floor by the doorway.

'Stop crying, Finoula.'

She looked up then, into Philly's eyes, and saw he was looking at her.

'Oh my God! You're awake!' She was almost screaming in her excitement. Throwing her arms around him, she kissed his face and cried uncontrollably. He was awake, he was talking, and he was the love of her life. God, she knew, really was good.

Chapter One Hundred
and Thirty-Five

'Now this is much more like it!'

Philly laughed at his brother's words. The private hospital was like an expensive hotel, and he thought it was great. Sky Sports, the lot. 'I bet it's costing a pretty wedge?'

Timmy grinned. 'You always have to price everything, don't you? Who cares, we can afford it.'

'Oh, don't worry, bruv, I ain't complaining.'

Finoula had left them to talk, she was good like that, and Timmy said as much. 'That Finoula was nearly out of her mind with worry, Philly, she's a fucking diamond bird.'

It was strange hearing Timmy talk at times; he spoke Mockney, like Guy Ritchie and other posh boys who thought they were Cockneys. He had always had a lovely speaking voice, and he could speak like the Queen when the fancy took him. But then Philly supposed he was the same in many respects. But he took umbrage, for some reason, at his brother referring to Finoula as a 'bird'.

'I'm marrying her, if she'll have me.'

Timmy grinned widely, he had been expecting this, they all had. 'You should, Philly, she never wavered, bless her, not once. Most girls would have been on the trot at the first whiff of cordite.'

Philly laughed, because it was true. 'Anything yet?'

Timmy shook his head in bafflement. 'Not a fucking word, it's just not possible, is it?'

Philly didn't answer his brother. That was what was bothering him so much. It was as if he had been shot by a fucking phantom and, as they all knew, that was not something that was easily accomplished. Especially not when it involved people like them. No one would be willing to do the dirty deed, it was too risky. It was like all this shit about Bantry calling people in to work the drugs in the clubs. Bantry, if he had still been alive, of course, wouldn't have touched something that high profile in a million years. That was a young man's game. Dealing was never part of their businesses. They controlled it, yeah, but they wouldn't get involved in the day-to-day, so none of it made any sense. It was the old bullshit baffles brains scenario, but he would suss it out eventually. He was missing something, they all were, it was just a matter of finding out what.

'Is Dad still dragging people out of bed at three in the morning and interrogating them?'

Timmy laughed as he said, 'No, thank fuck. He nearly found Bin Laden a couple of times in East London! He fucking went after everyone – Asian, Greek, fucking Slovakian . . . You name any country, and I bet he has threatened at least one of its citizens.'

Philly was roaring now; they often laughed at their father's actions, though never to his face. But Philly was pleased to know that his father was determined to get to the bottom of all of this. It was a diabolical liberty, and it was personal. Phillip Murphy would never let this one go, and neither would his elder son. It was funny, but getting shot had done Philly a lot of good, made him realise that life was for living. More than that, it had given him a personal insight into the damage a gun could do. It would definitely be his weapon of choice for the future and, like his father before him, he now believed wholeheartedly in the old adage: shoot first and ask questions later. Wipe the fuckers out, off the face of the earth, never leave anyone in a position to come back at you. Somewhere along the line, someone had been nursing a grudge, and that was why he had been singled out. He believed that his brush with death was not because of something *he* had done, it was payback for something his father had done in the past. Someone had waited, and they had planned, and they had eventually felt confident enough to act on their feelings.

These were thoughts he would keep to himself for a while; he would keep a close eye on exactly what came out in the next few months, and only then would he give voice to his inner thoughts. It seemed he was more like his father and brother than he had been given credit for.

Chapter One Hundred and Thirty-Six

'Are you sure, Finoula? I mean, love, he's just been shot. Remember that – you could have been burying him, and been left with a couple of kids all on your own. Not that I'm saying a word against him, mind, he's a lovely lad. But I want you to be sure about what you're taking on.'

Finoula loved her dad, but he was a worry-guts at times. 'I understand what you're saying, Dad, but I love him, and I want to marry him. This has just made us both realise how much we want to be together.'

Jack McCormack nodded, it was what he had expected. But, as her father, he needed to say what he had said. One thing was for sure – if the boy had died and left her a widow, she would never have wanted for anything, and that counted for a lot in his world.

'Then you've got my blessing. Congratulations, Finny. He's a good one, even with a belly like a tea strainer.'

Mary Mac was pleased too; she had always liked Veronica Murphy, and the two women would enjoy sharing a marriage like this.

'So when is the happy day?'

Finoula shrugged. 'Soon, Dad. Philly wants you and Mum to come in the hospital and talk it all over with his mum and dad.'

Mad Jack grinned. 'Come here, and give your old dad a kiss.'

431

Chapter One Hundred and Thirty-Seven

'I think she's a wonderful girl, Philly, and you'll both be very happy, I know it.'

'Thanks, Mum.' He knew she meant every word she said. It was funny but her and Finoula got on like a house on fire, which was strange in a way because a lot of people didn't really get his mum. She could come across as a bit odd. But Finoula seemed to understand her, and she treated her with the utmost respect.

'How are you feeling, son, really?'

Christine asked the same thing ten times a visit, and he answered with the same words. 'I'm fine, Mum, truly. Now stop dwelling on it.'

She didn't answer him, she knew he wouldn't tell her anything of import, none of them ever did. She was like a child as far as they were concerned, not to be worried with trivialities. But *she* knew who did it, and the knowledge frightened her. It wasn't so much *what* she had seen that was bothering her now, it was what it *meant* for all of them.

'Do you think you'll ever find the culprit, son?'

Philly shrugged. 'I hope so. It's something I would like to know because I think shooting someone is a pretty serious action, don't you? I want to find the person who wanted me dead, Mum.'

She nodded. 'If you did find them though, you or your father or one of you lot would kill them, wouldn't you?'

He remained silent. It was the first time she had ever referred to his life in the business, and he wasn't about to get into any discussions with *her* about serious matters that had fuck-all to do with anyone except the people concerned. He could just imagine her face if he decided to tell her the truth about the lives they led, especially as it had already sent her into the madhouse on more than one occasion. She was a strange cove, this mother of his. The weirdest thing was that, for once, she seemed genuinely interested in what was going on; he supposed that was because she had nearly lost him. He looked at her then, sorry she had been given all this worry, and appreciative of how much it must have affected her.

'Come on, Mum, let's drop this now, eh?'

Christine smiled sadly, and he saw that she was genuinely vexed. Hugging her to him, he said loudly, 'Let's get this wedding arranged, shall we? You and Finoula will make sure it's a blinder.'

But Christine couldn't hold back her tears. She was crying now, sobbing, and he held her gently to him, wishing she wouldn't do this to him when he still felt so weak and so tired. But he understood the fright she must have experienced, and he knew it was his job, as a son, to put her mind at rest as best he could.

Chapter One Hundred and Thirty-Eight

Declan was annoyed, but he knew it was a futile emotion. They had turned over every stone in the fucking Smoke, Spain and even fucking Portugal, and still there was nothing to go on. Not even a murmur.

It had been three months since the shooting, and they were no nearer to finding out any more than they had been at the beginning. Initially they had believed that they would be inundated with fucking accusations, theories, the lot. They had expected the usual nutters trying to get an old score settled by saying their mortal enemy had done it. But no. Nothing. Had he really thought they were in with a chance of naming the fucker concerned? How naïve were they, thinking it would all be over in a few days? It seemed now that whoever was responsible had the nous *and* the clout to make people forgo a hundred grand reward. That took a serious amount of fear; most people they dealt with would grass up their own fucking grannies for a tenth of that. Even Phillip was beginning to think they would never solve this fucking mystery, and if he was getting disheartened then things *were* bad. But no one seemed to know anything, and that in itself was suspicious. Someone, somewhere, *had* to be in the know.

Breda knew what they were all thinking, so she said what was on her mind. 'Look, Phillip, your Philly is a bit of a hothead at the best of times, are you sure he ain't had a tear-up with someone and conveniently forgot about it?'

Phillip shook his head. 'Crossed my mind, don't worry, Breda, but he says no, and so do his associates. Anyway we would have heard a whisper about something like that. People talk. Stands to reason.'

She nodded. That made sense, someone would have mentioned something so obvious. 'This is fucking mental, it's like they shot the wrong person or something!'

Phillip was in absolute agreement. 'Don't think that hasn't occurred to me and all, Breda.'

Declan sighed, and wished he was anywhere else on the planet but in this office, on Southend Seafront. He said slowly and deliberately, 'Well, we're out of fucking options, Phillip. Even though it grieves me to say that, but you know the old saying, it all comes out in the wash. This *will* come out eventually, it's just waiting till that happens.'

Breda's mobile rang and she answered it quickly. After a brief conversation she called off and, looking at Phillip, she said tersely, 'That was Timmy. Christine's on a bender, he had a call from the Moonraker pub. They want her out by the sounds of it, in case *you* find out she's been served, Phillip. They've got a new barmaid by all accounts, didn't realise the score.'

Most of the pubs in Southend knew better than to serve Christine Murphy, Phillip had seen to that years ago. But she still slipped past the safety precautions occasionally. Plus, there were a lot of pubs these days that changed hands frequently thanks to the ridiculous no-smoking laws. People were going out of business hand over fist. So it was getting harder and harder to police her.

Phillip rolled his eyes to the ceiling in frustration. 'Oh for fuck's sake! This is all we fucking need. Her on a fucking tear-up around Southend Seafront.'

Breda sighed. She felt sorry for Christine a lot of the time, she thought she had been doing well, and she said as much. 'Well, be fair, Phillip, she has been good until now. I don't know if I could have coped so well had my Porrick been shot.'

Phillip was furious now and he said snidely, 'Your Porrick wouldn't even notice if he got shot. He's a fucking moron – no brain, no fucking pain, him. I hope that baby his bird's having ain't as thick as him.'

Declan saw Breda's face drain of any colour at the vitriol in her brother's voice. Standing up she said quietly, and with tears choking her voice, 'Thanks a fucking lot, Phillip! That's my boy you're talking about. Whatever he might be, he's still my son, and I love him. Just because he ain't a fucking intellectual you look down your nose at him, but he earns his wage and you know it. Still, it's always good to know where we stand with each other, ain't it?' Then she left them.

Declan looked at his brother and, standing up, he shouted in abject disbelief, 'Feel better now, Phillip? You've just hurt your sister, and not just hurt her, but embarrassed her and insulted her. Well, do you know what, mate, *fuck you*. Because Breda is a fucking grafter, and you should remember that before you put your fucking mouth in gear. You're a bully sometimes, because you know she can't fight you back. You know there aren't many people who *can* fight back where you're concerned. I thought you hated bullies, Phillip. That's what you've always said, ain't it? Now I am going to see that she's all right. You can do what you fucking like.'

When the shock of his brother's words had worn off, Phillip remembered his son years ago, when he had attacked old Donny, and he had accused him of being a bully. Yet Phillip was the bully now; he had just destroyed poor Breda for no other reason than because he felt like it. He was annoyed, so he had taken it out on her. Where was the man he had prided himself on being all those years ago? Who was known for his good manners and his care for the people around him. He had understood, at a young age, that when you did the kind of work he did, goodwill was mandatory. If the people you grew up with wished you well, and the people you employed thought you were a good person, you were on the way to untold riches. He liked that people thought he was a good person; it was all the more important to him because if *they* believed it, then it must be true.

Phillip ran from the office suddenly and, tearing through the packed arcade, he burst out of the front entrance into the late September sunshine. Seeing Breda and Declan standing together on the pavement by her car, he went over to them. He had to make this right, he knew that much. She was crying, and he realised for the first time ever, that Breda was not just his sister, or his colleague, she was an intrinsic part of his life, and she was one of the main reasons it ran so smoothly. She took a lot of the shit from him, and she sorted it out without complaining. He also knew that without Declan he would never survive, Declan's loyalty meant a lot to him. He was one of the only people he actually respected.

'I'm sorry, Breda, I am so fucking sorry, darling.' And he meant it, because whatever he might think inside, he knew that he was lucky to have his family around him. They were grafters, and they relied on him to an extent. But he knew that without them he couldn't run any of the businesses as well as he did now. You couldn't trust anyone like you could your own flesh and blood. So for that alone, he would make sure Breda didn't think she was unappreciated.

'I'm so fucking eaten up with my Philly, and now Christine out on another fucking bender. I daren't walk round to the pub to get her, I'll fucking lay her out the mood I'm in.'

Phillip was looking at his sister with what she saw was genuine remorse. Breda was so amazed at the turn of events, she couldn't even speak a word.

Declan saw that Phillip had understood his warning very well.

Breda – all of them, actually – needed a little bit of respect and a little bit of encouragement sometimes.

'I love your Porrick really, you know that, Breda, and he's already asked me to be godfather to the baby, so I can only say I'm sorry, love.'

She was nodding, but even *she* thought Phillip was stronging it now. He hardly said two words to the boy. She appreciated the sentiment anyway. At least this would clear the air if nothing else.

If Declan knew one thing, it was that they would have to draw a line under this soon, because it was causing them to start infighting, and that could be fatal. Something like this made onlookers think, look for a chink in the family's armour, and it was a time when they needed to be seen as tighter and stronger than ever. If they weren't careful, this would become bigger than them. And there was nothing bigger, or more important than the family.

Phillip knew that, which is why he was outside the arcade trying to placate his sister. Normal service *had* to be resumed as soon as possible. Not that this would all be forgotten, of course, that was a given, but it had to stop being the only thing they focused on.

Chapter One Hundred
and Thirty-Nine

Christine was happier than she had been for ages. Vodka could do that, she found. It was ages since she had been on a real drink-up, and today she had decided, quite suddenly, that it had been long enough between bouts. Starting early, she had bought a half bottle of Smirnoff from the local off-licence in Leigh-on-Sea, because they didn't know her there, and she had polished that off in no time in her car. She realised with a jolt that she had left the car somewhere, but she couldn't remember where. The police would find it, they always did, and they would have it delivered to the farm. It was handy being Mrs Phillip Murphy at times. She had gone to the Wheatsheaf next, a lovely old pub, and she had downed a lot more vodka there before walking to the Three Crowns, where she sat outside looking at the sea, drinking herself even further into oblivion. She vaguely remembered getting in a cab, or being put into a cab if she was being totally honest, and ending up at the Moonraker, which was where she was now.

She was looking at her son, and wondering why she was so anxious to get home. Phillip would be annoyed; he hated it when she tried one on like this, he said he was worried about what could happen to her. But she didn't believe him, she thought it was because he couldn't control her when she was drunk. The thought made her laugh.

'What's so funny, Mum?'

'Nothing. Why, who are you, the laughing police?'

Even Timmy smiled at that.

'I want to see my Philly, take me to see my Philly!'

'Philly is at home, Mum, remember? Finoula's there with him.' He was talking to her as if she was a child, and a stupid child at that. She hated feeling like this, maudlin and depressed. She wondered if she had any pills stashed at home. She didn't think she did, but you never knew; she was always the optimist.

As they drove along, she watched her son's profile, it was dark now but, in the light of the car, he looked like his father with his pursed lips and his obvious annoyance at her condition. She knew the boys hated her drinking, but they were grown men now. Philly was getting married soon. She was a grown-up as well – if she wanted to get pissed then that was her right, surely? It was probably in the Magna Carta or something. After all, she was an adult; not that they treated her like one, of course.

She tried to justify her drunkenness. 'My son was shot like an animal in front of me, and I *needed* a drink today, not every day like before, but just today.'

She thought the words were very profound, and she opened her bag to get her cigarettes. Timmy didn't even bother to answer her and, as she lit her cigarette, he said quietly, 'I don't like smoking in my car, Mum, if you don't mind.'

It was the way he delivered the words that set her off. Off-hand, irritated, as if she was some kind of moron he was being forced to babysit. She turned on him then. 'Don't you talk to me like that! Who the hell do you think you are? This ain't *your* car, it's your *father's* car. Like you live in *his* house, and you eat *his* food. So don't you dare talk to me like that again, boy. I've had you and your attitude up to here.' She made a chopping motion across her own throat to emphasise her point. 'All that money for private school and you haven't even got any manners.'

Timmy sighed in annoyance; she was a fucking pain when she

was like this. He knew one thing – he would never marry a drinker. Finoula didn't drink, and he wondered if Philly knew how lucky he was because of that. When he thought back to this woman's antics over the years . . .

'You're pissed, Mum. Just put a fucking sock in it, will you?'

It wasn't just the words, it was the complete dismissal in them, as if she was nothing, a no one. But she supposed, to her sons, that is exactly what she was. After all, she had never really been there for them, always too caught up in her own problems, in her nightmare that passed as a life. But this one here, her Timmy, her baby, for him to speak to her so disrespectfully somehow made it seem so much worse. But deep inside, she knew she had no one to blame for this but herself, herself and her weakness. If only she could have taken them as far from Phillip's orbit as possible, but he would never have allowed her to do that. She should have left them there, with him, and saved her own life, because they were like him, so very like him. In every way. Phillip had made sure of that. Especially this younger son of hers.

She knew she was crying, she could hear herself, and she wished she could stop.

Chapter One Hundred and Forty

'I've never seen your mum pissed, is she really terrible then?'

Finoula was genuinely interested. Philly had told her about his mother's 'problems' – he'd had to since she spent so much time at the house – but, in fairness, his mum had been pretty good recently, considering.

'Not terrible, more sad. She's always suffered from a deep depression. I think it started after Timmy was born, at least that's the impression I get from me nan.'

'Postnatal depression they call it, Philly.'

He shrugged in bewilderment. 'Whatever. Anyway, she goes on benders, but not that often these days. When we were kids she was out of her nut twenty-four-seven, on pills and booze. To be honest, I don't know how me dad's stuck it. In and out of rehab, it was like living with an old Amy Winehouse.' He was trying to make light of it, but Finoula could see that it hurt him.

'I like her, I think she's lonely, Philly. She always seems as if she's not really a part of anything, do you know what I mean?'

He knew exactly what she meant, and he loved her for it. She had sussed it all out, and he knew he was lucky to have someone like her, someone so understanding, and so kind.

'She don't mean any harm, Finny, but sometimes when we were kids, she was so embarrassing, pissed out of her nut, talking shite.' He started to laugh then. 'She came up the school once in odd shoes. Honest, me and Timmy nearly died, they were different colours and everything – she was *so* drunk the school wouldn't let her drive home again, so me dad came and got us. But she was doing her crust, effing and blinding.'

'What, your mum?' Finoula's voice was incredulous, she couldn't imagine Christine Murphy being like that, she was such a nice woman.

Philly nodded at her and said seriously, 'The drink and the pills change her, she's like a different person – it's mental to see her. She talks like a drunken road builder.'

'I hope she's all right tonight. We'll look after her, yeah?'

He nodded, hoping that his mother wasn't on one of her rants against his father. 'Everyone always talks about her when she was young, how pretty she was, how clever. To me and Timmy it's like they're talking about someone who died, because we don't remember her like that at all. See, me and Timmy, we only remember her drunk or stoned, or both. Trying to kiss and cuddle us, and all we could smell was stale breath, and vomit. That was how bad it was at times.'

Chapter One Hundred and Forty-One

Timmy watched his mother as she listened at the doorway to Philly and Finoula chatting unawares. She had her hand at her throat, and her eyes screwed shut. He wondered if she realised just how much she had neglected him and Philly over the years so she could drink.

She had wandered inside while he had parked the car and called his father to see where he was. Seeing the devastation on his mother's face at what she had heard made him feel bad now, because no one should hear that about themselves, not even her.

Phillip came in just as she was opening a bottle of white wine in the kitchen and, as he opened his mouth to protest, she put the bottle down on the side and, running to him, she threw herself into his arms. As he held her close, she kept repeating over and over again, 'What have I done?'

Chapter One Hundred
and Forty-Two

'You have what is called a gastric ulcer, Mrs Murphy, and once we get you on the medication the pain should subside greatly. You just have to take better care of yourself. Other than that, you are as well as a woman of your advanced years could expect.'

Veronica didn't like this doctor, he was an arsehole of the first water, talking to her as if she was a newspaper or something. She didn't care how much he charged, he needed to be taken down a peg. 'Is that so, Doctor? Well, let me enlighten you now. My son has paid a fecking fortune for your opinion, and my advice to you is next time you have a woman of *my advanced years* in your office, remember to talk to her as if she was a grown-up and not a shagging errant teenager. Because, for all your grand education, you could do with a few lessons in good manners and social interaction.'

The last bit was something Finoula had said about Gordon Brown, and Veronica felt it was a good put-down; she only hoped she had used it in the correct context.

Christine and Breda didn't laugh until they were out of the consulting room, then the two of them started to roar.

'Fucking hell, Mum, what brought that on?'

Veronica was still annoyed, but she could see the humour of the situation. 'Who the shag do these people think they are?

445

Talking to me as if I'm a fool. And with that eejit Phillip paying him good money. I might not be in the first flush of youth, but I'm not in me fecking dotage yet.'

Christine took Veronica's arm. 'Come on, let's get to mine. I've put a casserole in the simmering oven and it'll be ready when we get there.'

Secretly Veronica was over the moon. She had thought as they all had that it was going to be bad news, but it wasn't. God had seen fit to give her a few more years, as she had requested, and she felt as though a great weight had been lifted from her. The anxiety had been keeping her up at night. An ulcer of all things! Who would have thought it? A little voice inside was telling her it wasn't even caused by worry – it was guilt. But she ignored it, just as she had been ignoring that voice for years as well.

Chapter One Hundred and Forty-Three

'This is beautiful, Christine. Would you teach me to cook?'

Christine smiled at the wonderful girl her son had somehow managed to bag. She was lovely, really lovely, and not just in looks. She was a kind girl and so thoughtful.

''Course I will, Finny! Anything you particularly want to know how to cook? If you start with things you like it's easier. Then as time passes you go on to more complicated things.'

'Like life?'

They both laughed.

'Yeah, I suppose that's a good comparison. But you and Philly seem so happy, love, I don't think you have anything to worry about there.'

Finoula grinned, her perfect, overly white teeth looked incongruous in the early morning light that flooded the kitchen. She was like a photograph, not a real person, but Christine knew that was how girls were now. They were fighting off ageing before their twenty-fifth birthdays, and everything was about how they looked, not how they felt inside. Maybe they had the right idea. It was the whole Cheryl Cole concept and look how successful she had been! If girls nowadays had an original thought it would die in their heads of loneliness – all they cared about was being pretty. Christine knew she was being harsh, because this girl here had more than a good brain, she had the street smarts to go with it.

'I do love Philly, Christine, he's my world.'

Christine knew Finoula spoke the truth and, having been in the same position once, she couldn't help but be frightened for her. Grabbing her hand tightly, she said seriously, 'That's a good thing, my little love, but remember what I am telling you now. He'll always have his life and his job, but you'll end up at home with the kids, and that can be the most rewarding job on the planet, but also the loneliest. Always keep something for yourself – get a good nanny, au pair, whatever, and make a life for *yourself* outside your front door, outside your marriage. Don't be dependent on any man – eventually they resent you for it. Keep your friends, even the ones he doesn't like, and make sure you see them regularly. Don't become just a wife – it's never enough for most men.'

Finoula was a bit shocked at what her future mother-in-law had just said, but she understood she was trying to help her, and she was also perceptive enough to see that she was telling her the truth. Finoula grinned at her conspiratorially. 'Don't worry, Christine, I've already decided to keep my hand in with the bookies. I think if I was at home all day I would go off me nut!'

She realised what she had said, and just stopped herself from apologising. Christine, however, laughed at her choice of words. 'Well, take it from someone who's experienced exactly that – it's no fun, I can tell you!'

They laughed together companionably and, once more, Christine wished she had heard her sons talk about her years ago. If anything could have stopped her drinking and pill-popping, it would have been the words she had heard from her elder son the other night. Listening to her Philly telling this girl what he had really thought and how he had felt over the years had been the jolt she needed to finally clean up her act.

The real surprise had been how pleased she had felt to see

Phillip standing there. She had seen the sad look on his face, because he knew how much it would have hurt her; Timmy had obviously filled him in on the night's events. She was amazed at how eagerly she had run into his arms. He had seemed like her lifesaver at that moment, she had felt such relief at seeing him in the kitchen. She had to admit, no matter what had happened over the years between them, he would *always* be there for her, and she was aware that she had always relied on him for that. No matter how much she had hated him, she had still needed him.

Her life was set now and she would never get away – not unless one or the other of them died. But there was still hope for Finoula, and she wanted her to have her eyes wide open to the life she would be taking on when she married a Murphy. The lying, the deceit, the knowledge that her husband could be taken from her at any time; either with a gun, as had been proved already, or by a court giving him twenty years. She wanted this girl to know that the security around her would be suffocating at times – armed men patrolling the grounds because of a deal that had upset someone enough to want them all dead. She would have to learn about keeping her thoughts private, because a careless word could bring terror to her doorstep. And stashing every receipt because you might have to prove purchase one day for the most mundane of things; the tax were shit-hot, and the one set of people you couldn't buy. There was still so much this girl had to learn. She might have the benefit of being Mad Jack's daughter but, in comparison to her family, Mad Jack was an amateur in the criminal stakes.

Finoula hugged the woman who would soon be her mother-in-law. She really liked her, and she sensed that she was very unhappy. 'I can't wait to start learning to cook properly. Philly always talks about what a good cook you are. Your food's legendary.'

She was being kind. Christine knew her son loved her food,

but she had a feeling he would much rather she had served it to him sober.

'Even the doctor thinks he's putting on weight properly, and you cooking him such wholesome food has been a real help.'

She smiled, but she didn't answer the girl; instead she walked to the kitchen door and motioned for Finoula to follow her. As they walked up to the big barn, Christine observed the girl's pleasure in her surroundings.

'It's a huge place, isn't it?'

Finoula nodded.

'When we bought the house there were only a couple of acres, but we own everything now. Do you see that farmhouse over there in the distance?'

Finoula nodded; it was a nice property, really big and it had wonderful brick chimneys.

'Phillip's giving it to you and Philly as a wedding present.'

Finoula looked at Christine to see if she was joking with her; she clearly wasn't, because she looked very serious and contemplative.

'The people who owned that house had farmed there for over two hundred years. Phillip offered a fair price for it and they refused. Eventually, after their water supply had been poisoned, and their barn burnt to the ground, he got the place for a song. They live in the village now, their children spread all around the country. They were nice people, they even brought us over some lovely cuttings when we first moved in . . .'

Finoula was nonplussed. She didn't know what Christine wanted her to say, didn't know how she was supposed to react to these revelations.

'I don't want to hurt you, Finny, all I am trying to say is that things in this family aren't always like they seem. Not with Philly – he's a diamond – but we always get *everything* we want. Remember though, it's often at someone else's expense.'

Finoula nodded. She understood and she knew this woman

was only trying to help her. Even though she had a strange way of showing it.

'Enjoy that house – it's crying out for a family – but never forget how you came to acquire it.' She waited for the girl to digest her words before she added, 'And see that building there, with the huge chimneys?'

Finoula nodded.

'*Never* go in there, and *never* ask about what happens there.'

'Why? What happens there that's so mysterious?'

Christine smiled, an enigmatic little smile. 'I don't know. What I *do* know is there's an unspoken rule in this family, and it's that the big barn is off-limits. You'd do well to remember that, Finoula, and never question *anyone* inside or outside the family about it.'

Finoula was uneasy now; there was more going on here than met the eye. But she consoled herself with the fact that this woman was off her tree most of the time, and this was probably one of those days. The pleasure she was getting from her surroundings was gone, however, and the huge open spaces were suddenly not beautiful and picturesque, but isolated and frightening.

'Come on, let's go back and make a pot of coffee, shall we?'

Finoula agreed in relief, but although they chatted about normal things for the rest of the day, Christine's words stayed with her.

Chapter One Hundred
and Forty-Four

'Well, the dirty deed has been done!'

Phillip, relaxing back into the living-room sofa, sounded happy. The wedding had been a success on every level. The bride had looked spectacular in a Vera Wang creation – whatever the fuck that was! – and the groom had looked suitably terrified and happy at the same time. The guest list had read like a who's who of the criminal underworld; everyone who was anyone had accepted their invitation, and Phillip had put on a show of spectacular proportions. People who had flown in from abroad were picked up in chauffeur-driven limos, and provided with top-class accommodation. It would be talked about for years, from the wedding itself to the spectacular entertainment provided.

Poor old Mad Jack! Phillip had seen the relief on his boat-race when he had found out that all he had to pay for was the booze – and that was a pretty penny. Even then, Phillip had slipped some stuff in himself on the quiet. The gift of the farmhouse had been very well received, although Finoula had looked a little frightened by it; he expected that was because she wasn't used to such largesse. Money, serious money, frightened people. Like those cunts who won the lottery and still went to work in shit jobs. He could understand the shock might make them nervous, but the whole idea of the lottery was to change your boring life. He shook his head at the stupidity of the average person – then they bemoaned the fact they lived like fucking serfs. It was the welfare state, that's what it was – made people frightened of success.

As he sipped on his brandy, and looked at his happy but tired-out wife and around his wonderful home, Phillip finally felt like he had made it. The day's events had set him back the national debt, but it had given him the opportunity to show the world just how fucking well he had done. He had seen the looks from the guests, seen the envy mixed with utter admiration for him, his family and his way of life.

Philly had been determined to marry from the farm and he wanted his reception there, whereas Phillip had wanted a top class hotel in the West End, somewhere discreet but classy. But now he was glad it had been on the farm. Because once the marquees had been erected, carpeted and hung with chandeliers, he had been able to indulge in a different kind of showing off. He had the best chefs, and they had cooked only what he grew, from the meat to the veg. That had really impressed so many people; they had thought he played at farming, he realised that now, they didn't see it for the lucrative business it actually was. No, that had been a coup really, people had not comprehended just how successful he was outside of Southend Seafront. He had shown the world that they had the one thing money could never buy: class.

And his Christine, she had looked fantastic. Really gorgeous, and everyone had remarked on it. She had stayed on water all day too, only sipping at the champagne for the toasts.

Oh, he was like a dog with six lamp posts, he was so happy. It had been a triumph for him, and now he was savouring the feeling that came with it.

'Come on, Christine, one glass of brandy won't kill you! Join me in a toast to our son and his lovely bride.'

She moved closer to him on the sofa, and nodding she said happily, 'OK. It was a lovely day, wasn't it?'

'It was a perfect day, and did you see the way everyone was looking around? We fucking showed them all right, they know the real score now.'

Christine felt a moment's sorrow for this big, ignorant lout she was married to. When he talked like this she saw the child inside him, always trying to prove that he was someone, that his family were someones. She closed her eyes and savoured the Courvoisier; he still had cheap taste in brandy, for all his expensive bottles, he still felt the Big C, as he called it, was the only brandy to drink. It wouldn't surprise her if he didn't even *like* it, it was just another part of his persona. He should have been an actor, because he could act the part of anything with conviction. At the moment he was the proud father, who had just seen his elder son married. But he wouldn't have thought about the happy couple once, though the speech he gave didn't reflect that – it had been amazing. All he was really interested in was what other people thought of the day, how it would have shown him in a good light. It was *always* about him in the end. He hugged her to him, and she could almost feel his satisfaction.

'Lot of old faces here today, Christine.'

'Yeah, Phillip, four hundred of our closest friends!'

Even he laughed at her droll delivery. 'All right, Christine, but you know me, I like people to see how well we're all doing.'

She nodded. She wasn't about to start a fight, she couldn't be bothered any more if truth be told. It was easier being nice to him, pretending everything was fine. And occasionally, like now, (and she hated admitting this, even to herself) Phillip, when he was happy and content, could be very good company. At moments like this, she could almost pretend they were young again, before she had found out the truth about her husband.

'People were impressed all right. Fucking hell, *I* was impressed, Phillip, and I helped arrange it!'

He laughed in delight; it was just what he needed to hear, and his Christine like this was the cherry on the cake for him.

'Did you see Mad Jack with those *amuse-bouche* things! Fucking hell, Christine, he looked at me and his face was so bewildered I just burst out laughing. I told him later though that you had to explain them to me the first time! He's a great man. Philly did well with that girl, she's got a bit of savvy. Reminds me of you, back in the day.'

She smiled, but she didn't answer him, she wasn't getting into any conversations that might open up old wounds. 'Your mum enjoyed herself too. She loves a show-off – she's worse than you!'

He made a wry face and she laughed.

'Probably where I get it from, eh? Timmy seemed a bit subdued. I thought he would enjoy the party more. I mean, he didn't really mix that much, or was it me imagining things?'

Christine thought about it for a few seconds before she said slowly, 'Now you come to think of it, he *was* very quiet. Mind you, Phillip, they are close those two. Seeing his big brother married off probably made him realise things would change between them now. Especially as Finny wants a baby soon as they can manage it.'

'You're right. I saw him up by the big barn with that horrible little fucker Philly used to knock about with, I couldn't stand him. Graham Planter – snide of the first water, him. All the Planters are the same. His father's a fucking grass, everyone knows that; you can't deal drugs like they do in full view of the Filth and not get a fucking serious talking to. He's never been nabbed once, and that tells me one thing – he's offering the Filth an alternative income. Scum. I kept me temper though, but Timmy could see I wasn't impressed. I told him last year that I didn't want Planter in the arcades. Timmy was all right about it then. He should never have found his way to the wedding reception.'

'Did you say Graham Planter?'

Phillip nodded; the memory had marred his perfect day now, and that rankled. 'Our Timmy can be a right awkward ponce at times, don't you think, Chris?'

She was nodding but thinking of nothing except the fact Graham Planter had been up by the barn. He had not been at the reception, she would have noticed him because his face was stamped on her memory. Graham Planter had shot her Philly. When everyone else had been looking at Philly's wounded body that awful night in the club she had noticed him. He was older, and he had one of those stupid flat caps pulled over his eyes like the DJs wore, but she had recognised his face. He had been Philly's childhood friend not Timmy's. So why would he have been with Timmy at the big barn? She felt sick at the thoughts that were suddenly going through her head.

'Where is Timmy anyway? Did he go back to his flat or stay here?'

Phillip frowned. 'He was drunk, so I assume he's upstairs in his old room. Why?'

She shrugged as if she wasn't that bothered. 'I just wondered, that's all.'

But the shine had gone from the day, and her nerves were once more jangling inside her body. She threw back the brandy in one gulp and then, holding her glass out for more, she said with forced joviality, 'Fuck it, Phillip, let's have a party, shall we?'

He laughed delightedly. 'Anything you want, darling, you've got it. We made history today, you and me. It was perfect, babe. Everything was just perfect.'

Chapter One Hundred and Forty-Five

Finoula and Phillip were at the Hilton Heathrow. They were flying to LA the next day for their honeymoon and they were both happy, tired and randy.

'Fucking Los Angeles, I still can't believe it! I bet that was your idea?'

Finoula nodded and laughed. 'Your mum asked me where we would really like to go, and I said I wanted to shop on Rodeo Drive, eat at The Grove, and see the Hollywood sign. Plus, I thought you might like a few days in Vegas!'

He popped the champagne with a flourish. 'I'd go to a caravan in fucking Norfolk if you were there in the nude! But I can cope with LA and Vegas. At least there will be a bit of currant bun anyway.'

She took the champagne flute and said dreamily, 'What a day, Philly! It was so wonderful, I've never been so happy.'

He could hear the tears in her voice, and he felt a rush of pure love wash over him. 'Come on, Finny, don't start crying now. I want me leg over!'

She couldn't help laughing at him, and his choice of words; he was funny was her Philly. She knew how lucky she was. 'There'll be none of that, mate, not now I'm a respectable married woman!'

It was an old East End joke; both had heard it a hundred times before but they still laughed together.

'What about the farmhouse and all! My dad did us proud today. He thinks the world of you, Finny. I think your dad's a bit of a hero to him, you know. They get on so well, don't they?'

She nodded. Her father had been taken aback by the scale of the day's activities, but he was pleased for her, she knew that. Jack had known he couldn't compete with Phillip Murphy, and he had stepped back and let the man have his way, well, let Finoula have her way really. Her and Christine's. Christine had such exquisite taste – you only had to look at her own home to see that, and between them they had arranged everything exactly how they wanted it. The only blight on the day was remembering what Christine had warned her about. She shivered, as if a goose had walked over her grave as the old dears would have described it.

Philly noticed and said in a concerned voice, 'You all right, Finny? You better not be coming down with anything.'

She smiled, but the ghost of fear was still on her shoulder. 'I'm fine, Philly, just tired out with the excitement of the day.'

But a cloud had passed over her happiness, and she felt an inexplicable urge to pick up the suitcases and run away, away from everything, not just for a few weeks, but for ever. It wasn't an option though, and she consoled herself with the fact they had so much to look forward to – a new home, a new life, and a baby at some point in the future.

Philly grabbed her none too gently, and pulled her into his arms on the king-size bed, spilling the champagne everywhere.

'Come here, you silly mare! Let's consummate this marriage, it's all I've been thinking about all day. I hope now it's legal it will still be full of the usual excitements!'

As she lay with him, she forced the worries from her mind,

telling herself it was just wedding-night nerves. After all, it was a big step they had taken, and in a Catholic church as well. This was for life, and that was a very big commitment. For both of them.

Chapter One Hundred
and Forty-Six

Christine waited until her husband was asleep, then slipped from the bed and crept down to the kitchen. She was worried, really worried, and her first thought was to get herself a drink. So she opened a bottle of vodka and, sitting at the kitchen table, poured herself a large glass, added a couple of ice cubes, and tossed it back in two gulps. Then she poured another immediately, waiting for the trembling to stop. Lighting a cigarette, she pulled on it deeply, blowing the smoke out noisily. Then getting up she raced through to the downstairs bathroom. Standing on the toilet seat, she placed her hand behind the cistern and, frowning, she realised there was no little plastic pack of pills hidden there. Phillip had probably had the place swept by the drugs squad.

Back in the kitchen, she took another deep draught of the vodka. But it was no good, she still felt unable to think about the problem in hand. It was all too outrageous, but she knew in her heart it was the truth.

Timmy, her younger son, and the person Philly had chosen as his best man, was behind his shooting. He had wanted his brother dead, of that she was sure.

She felt the sickness assail her once more. What the fuck had she bred? Was it Phillip's fucked-up DNA, or was it because she had been drunk most of their lives and they had been left to drag themselves up? Was it because Timmy felt, as the younger son, he wasn't getting what he felt he was entitled to? Or was it because, and this was her real belief, he really was his father's son? Like Phillip, he removed any obstacle that might be in his way. Looking back he had been that way as a kid, but she hadn't realised it till now. Quiet little Timmy, who you overlooked because, unlike Philly, he didn't demand, or shout about his feelings. He just waited, and waited, and then took what he wanted at the appropriate time. He was the good boy, the good son. Philly had been seen as the little bastard, but he'd just been like other boys his age. Foolish, selfish, but not really bad. Jesus Christ, how had her life come to this? She felt the useless tears of futility and anger, and wondered what she was to do with this knowledge now she had it. She thought of Philly, on his honeymoon and unaware that the person he thought was his best friend, as well as his brother, was behind his attempted murder.

Who could she tell? That was the thing. Phillip was questionable, she knew that. He would probably just weigh up the pros and cons and decide which boy he was going to keep! Declan? He might be worth approaching. Once it would have been Breda, but she would not tell her any of this. Something had happened between her and Phillip, and he treated her like some kind of Mafia don these days. Asking for her opinion on everything, and giving her the most lucrative Legends to run for him. She was overseeing the boys and they answered directly to her. So Breda wouldn't want to rock any boats – even her Porrick was now on the proper payroll, running a new business Breda had set up putting fruit machines in pubs and cafes. No, Breda was too close to Phillip at the moment, it would have to be Declan. But she knew Declan wouldn't be able to keep something like this to himself. He would see it as something Phillip needed to know.

She felt a wave of nausea once again, the worry inside her

gnawing at her, making her feel like she had years ago when her nerves had started. It was the same hollowness in her stomach, the terror of each day and what it might bring down on them all. But even that was nothing compared to this latest trouble. Her own son, her baby, wanted to take out his own brother. She was too frightened to ever say any of this out loud.

Suppose she was wrong? Suppose she had got the wrong end of the stick? Maybe it was like what Phillip said when he ranted about the judicial system, he was always going on about circumstantial evidence. How people might *look* guilty, but that didn't mean they *were*. He could go on for hours about the subject, and frequently did. She was pretty sure that wasn't the case here, but she still grabbed on to the thought. So, with Declan and Breda out of the running there was no one else she could trust enough to tell. Even her Philly would think she was just off her chump again – she knew how crazy it would sound.

It was weird, her intuition was eating her up. Phillip mentioning Planter's name was fate, and she believed in all that – she believed things were meant to happen. Like Philly surviving the gunshot wound – he had survived because he had just stepped forward to kiss Finoula, and that had stopped the blast from hitting its mark. It had to be a death sentence Timmy ordered for Philly – there was no reason whatsoever for him to just get his brother shot, that had no value to him or anyone else. She had not been married to Phillip Murphy all this time without picking up some bloody tips on how their world worked.

Philly was away for ten days, but he had to be back to sort out the clubs for the spring openings. Phillip always had them professionally cleaned and any necessary repairs made; it was important that the places looked new and smart, as befitted the clientele. Philly and Timmy would be working flat out on that, as well as everything else that made up their job descriptions. So she had ten days to talk to Timmy, and carefully gather as much information as she could. She only hoped she had the guts to go through with her plan. When Timmy discovered she had sussed him out would she be next on his list? There was so much to think about, and so much to worry about, not least the fact that her child was capable of killing his brother. A brother who was just starting out on his married life, and who had no idea what had really happened to him. The worst thing was, she knew that if Timmy had tried to kill her husband, his father, she wouldn't have lifted a finger to stop him. But then, she assumed Phillip would be next on Timmy's list.

She was in a quandary all right; she had to decide which of her sons would live. Because even *she* knew that Timmy couldn't be allowed to ever get a chance like that again. Philly didn't deserve any of this, and that was what was so bad. She would have to choose between her sons, but she knew, deep inside, that she already had. It seemed that the hypocrisy that Phillip had instilled in them all, so many years ago, was still alive and rampant inside her as well these days.

If someone had said she would one day be faced with a dilemma like this she would have laughed in derision, yet, thinking back, it was a wonder something like this had never happened before now.

Chapter One Hundred and Forty-Seven

'You all right, Mum?'

Timmy was watching Christine from across the room. She looked spaced as usual, but he knew she wasn't on anything, she was just like Dilly Daydream, staring into space.

'I'm fine. Why aren't you at the airport with the others?'

He grinned. 'What, meeting up with the conquering hero? He's been on honeymoon, Mum, not a fucking tour of Iraq.'

He was good, she couldn't deny that. His words sounded like a joke, but she heard the underlying meaning. She watched him warily again, he was fascinating to her these days. She loved him – he was still her son, and for that she would always have some feeling for him – but it was not like before. It could never be the same again.

She glanced away from him, and saw him looking her up and down carefully in the huge antique mirror over the fireplace. Before she could stop herself she said innocently, 'Seen anything of Graham Planter lately?'

As she spoke she turned in the chair and looked him directly in the face. His pupils widened and for a few seconds his eyes were almost black. She knew that she had frightened him and she grew braver with the sensation.

'What makes you ask that?' He had recovered his composure now, but she knew he was rattled.

'I just wondered. It's funny, son, but he was never your friend. Then your dad said he saw you and him at the wedding, up by the big barn. That's where your father keeps those guns, ain't it? That Jamal delivers them. Contrary to popular belief, I see a lot more than any of you have ever given me credit for. Oh, and tell Graham I liked his hat that night at the club – nearly didn't recognise him in it.'

They were looking deep into each other's eyes now, and she could see a small tic pulsing at the side of Timmy's right eye. That she had rattled him, she had no doubt; she couldn't have made it any plainer. He knew she knew all right, he was just deciding what to do about it. It was like watching Phillip at work, it was almost uncanny. Her son had inherited his father's complete disregard for human life.

'Are you trying to tell me something, Mum?'

She shrugged as nonchalantly as possible. 'Such as? What are you on about?'

'Well, that's what I'm asking you, ain't it?'

She sighed heavily, as if all this was well over her head, and she had no idea what he might mean. 'You are a bit odd today, Timmy. Been missing your brother I expect.' She smiled as easily as she could manage with the trembling that was now threatening to take over her whole body. But she was nearly there, and she knew she had to act as if she wasn't scared of her child in the least. 'He's home tonight. Oh, and they're staying here, by the way, not at the flat. Me and Finoula are going to look over the house tomorrow.'

He nodded as if in agreement with her, but he knew she was warning him that she would be watching him. Watching out for Philly.

'I've cooked them a lovely coq au vin, used a real cockerel. There's enough for you, if you've still got some appetite after my little bombshell.'

Christine had to make him think she wasn't afraid of him.

But it was hard, so hard. Still he didn't say a word, and as she looked at him she recalled what he was like as a kid; he could go quiet for days, and they had all laughed, and said he was deep. Deep, yeah, but also dangerous. If only we could have a glimpse of the future when our kids were small how much easier life would be.

She took a deep breath before asking quietly, 'Can I say something to you, just between us, like, Timmy?'

He nodded, she could see he was more than eager to hear exactly what she had to say for herself. 'Fire away, Mum. I've always got time for you.' The sarcasm was there, along with the pun, and the smile that went with it said it was meant as a threat. He was trying to intimidate her, and the knowledge didn't frighten her, it just made her more determined to tell him what she wanted to tell him. She stood up and poured herself a large brandy and, after knocking it back swiftly, she poured herself another one.

'Don't I get one, Mum? Or are you drinking alone as usual? Good at that, aren't you? But then you've done enough of it, I suppose.'

She didn't answer him. She just carried on with what she was doing, gathering her courage as best she could before it failed her altogether. Then, walking to where he was standing, just inside the huge picture windows, she stopped right in front of him. Looking into his face she said seriously, 'If anything happens to my Philly, I will hold *you* personally responsible. If he breaks a nail climbing out of his car, I will assume it had something to do with you. If he fucking so much as catches the flu, I will blame you, and if he *ever* gets shot at again, I will blow your fucking world so far into orbit, you'll be thumbing a lift from the Hubble Telescope to get back down to earth. Do you understand what I am telling you, Timmy?'

He didn't even flinch at her words, but she could tell he was worried, and wondering how to get out of this without anyone else finding out the score.

Timmy scoffed at her, 'Like anyone would listen to *you*! You're a drunk, Mum.'

She could feel the heat enveloping her body, and she knew he could smell her fear.

'You're a joke to everyone in this family, Mum, especially *your* Philly. No one would give your story a second's credence.'

'I'll be watching you, boy.'

He grinned then and, pushing his face close to hers, said quietly, 'And I'll be watching *you*, Mum. Keep that in mind, won't you?'

Before she could answer him, the door crashed open and Philly's voice was booming out. 'Hello, Mum, the wanderers have returned!'

Timmy pushed her gently out of his path, sidelining her and, holding out his arms, he said to his brother, all smiles and familial affection, 'Fuck me, look at you, bruv, brown as a berry! And where's the lovely Mrs Murphy? Don't tell me she's fucking left you already.'

As Finoula came into the room, Christine said her hellos and then, using the excuse of needing to check the dinner, she almost ran to the kitchen. What had she started? Oh dear God in heaven, what the hell had she started? She was so afraid of her younger son, she was beyond relieved to have her husband in the house with her.

That alone told her just how bad things really were.

Chapter One Hundred and Forty-Eight

'Please, Phillip, I've never asked you anything about your work before, but please tell me what's going down. I can sense that something is different.'

Phillip Murphy looked at his wife, clearly weighing up how much to reveal. It annoyed her more than she believed possible. Her new-found interest in everything pertaining to the businesses and the boys was getting a bit wearing as far as her husband was concerned, but she didn't care. She had to know.

He shrugged suddenly, as if he had decided something very serious, and said, 'Someone is coming to pick up the guns. Now, can we drop it, Christine, please? You know I don't like to discuss things like this, especially with you. What's come over you lately, mate? You're either stoned on the pills the doctor gave you, or you're following me around like a fucking puppy. Is something bothering you, Christine? Because if it is, you only have to tell me and I'll sort it for you.'

She felt the urge to laugh out loud; he was starting to sound like Florence, her therapist of old. And, like Florence, she could just see his face if she told him what was actually on her mind. Phillip didn't even come into the equation any more – in fact, she could cope with him, and since the shooting he had been really good. It was the boys that were sending her off her head.

Her Philly didn't even guess there was anything untoward going on with his brother, and that was the most frightening thing.

'I've got a funny feeling on me that's all, Phil, it's since Philly, you know . . .' she trailed off.

Christine only had to mention the shooting and Phillip was immediately all husbandly concern. He understood how deeply she had been affected by it, and Phillip had always admired how much she cared. Christine knew he was fascinated by other people's emotions, and how they affected them and their everyday lives. On a basic level, he needed to observe them, so he could attempt to imitate them. It was how he had survived so long without being sussed out. So the briefest mention of Philly being shot, and he was all over her, worried it would make her ill again, make her have to go away from him again.

Christine also knew he was still puzzling over who the culprit could be, and she had nearly told him so many times in the last few weeks. But she couldn't. She was frightened – if she *did* tell him, she couldn't predict what he would do. Being Phillip Murphy, he would decide whether that was a sign of strength in his son, or a weakness that meant he had to obliterate him. Even though she felt he would choose Philly, with this man you could never be sure. Like King Herod, who had killed three of his own kids, Phillip had the capacity not just for great brutality, but also great kindness. He would also assume, as she had, that he was next in line for the chop. And she didn't want anything to happen to Timmy either – not because of her anyway. It was such a quandary, and it was her fault, all because of her, and a determination many years ago to best her mother. The more her mother had been against her marrying Phillip Murphy, the more determined she was to have him.

All she had wanted was to be a part of a big, happy family; well, she had got her wish – to be part of a big family anyway – for all the good that it had done her. She had married a murderer, and she had given birth to two sons, one of whom was capable of literally anything, and another one who she felt might just have a chance at a normal life because he had married Finoula. She was a sensible girl, a decent girl. Philly respected her, and the way she had acted after he had been shot had shown them that she had the staying power needed to be married to a Murphy. Christine had a terrible feeling on her that, many years ago, Veronica Murphy had thought the exact same about *her* where Phillip was concerned. Had seen her as his saving grace, because if he loved her so much he had to have some good in him. Philly was ruthless, yes, too caught up in his father's world, true, but he was basically a good person, a good man and, at the moment, Christine was holding on to that fact like a lifeline. She had to believe that some good had come out of her marriage or she would never rest easy again.

After all, they had to have some of her in them, didn't they? They were carried inside her, she had given them half their DNA. Had the only thing she had given them been her weakness? Her Timmy had indeed turned out to be like the spit out of his father's mouth – someone had said that to her just after he had been born, and it came back to her now. Philly, on the other hand, looked like his father, but didn't have the same mannerisms like Timmy did. Philly did have his father's utter disregard for what other people wanted or needed though; it was all business to him.

She was worrying herself now with her thoughts. So she did what she always did, she just pushed the troubling thoughts from her head. Philly *wasn't* like his father, it was *Timmy* who had turned out like him, in more ways than one. She couldn't eat, she couldn't sleep. She couldn't think straight. But because of her history no one thought she was acting that strange, so it was giving her a bit of an insight into how bloody weird she must have seemed to them all, especially the boys. In some ways, for years she had never felt so normal as she did now. It was as if this had kicked her into touch, made her see her life and her sons' lives for what they actually were. This had to stop, this all had to stop.

The question was, how?

As Phillip left the house to go to the big barn, and get ready for the visitors, she watched Timmy and Philly from the doorway laughing together on the drive. Her heart was in her mouth as she saw Timmy look behind him, and straight at her; he waved in a friendly manner, and then Philly did the same thing. Timmy was acting as if nothing untoward had taken place between them, but she knew, deep inside herself, he was just waiting for the opportunity to finish all this off once and for all.

As she watched Philly walking towards Old Sammy, Timmy turned so he had his back to his brother and, making a pretend gun with his hand like a child playing at cowboys and Indians, he pretended to shoot her. He was laughing as he did it, and she knew then that it had gone far enough.

She walked slowly up to her bedroom and, locking the door, she took a deep breath. Then, her heart hammering in her ears, she picked up the phone and began to dial.

Chapter One Hundred and Forty-Nine

'Hello, Breda. Oh, look at him, young Porrick Junior.'

Phillip made a big fuss of his nephew's baby, and even though Breda knew that, in actuality, he had no real interest in it she played the game. With Phillip that was often the best way. She smiled at him and walked through to the kitchen to see Christine.

'All right, Chris?'

Her sister-in-law smiled, but Breda could see she was not right, she was a bundle of nerves again, and she sighed inwardly. This was a serious bit of business tonight, and she was relying on Christine to watch the baby for her while she was out at the big barn. Trust fucking Porrick to choose tonight to take his bird for a meal and the pictures. Still, she could have refused to babysit, they wouldn't have minded, they were pretty good like that. But she had loved this child with a passion since she had first seen his little scrunched-up red face. She looked after the child as much as possible, and her son and his bird were quite happy for her to do just that.

'You seem a bit preoccupied, are you sure you're all right, mate?'

'Fucking hell, Breda, what's this – act like the Old Bill night? I'm fine, just a bit tired that's all. Give me a fucking break, will you?'

Breda was taken aback. 'All right, *relax*, I was only asking,

Christine. You're fine. Fuck me, I get the picture.'

She stormed from the kitchen, and Christine felt a twinge of guilt. But it didn't last, she had too much on her mind, and she hoped to God that she had done the right thing. She felt sick with apprehension and fear at what was going to happen soon. She saw Timmy looking at her, and she turned away from him.

'Have you two had a fucking row or something?' Phillip was standing in the doorway, his eyes flicking from one to the other.

Timmy shrugged as if he didn't know what his father was talking about, and Christine just shook her head. But she was pleased to see that Timmy, for all his pretence at non-chalance, was actually nervous. The knowledge gave her a thrill, and she was ashamed of herself for it. But God, it felt good to know she was affecting him; it proved he knew she might be capable of taking him down.

'Don't be silly, Phillip! What would we argue about? Don't be so fucking stupid.'

Phillip laughed at her but said seriously, 'You haven't stopped effing and blinding all day, Chris.' Turning to Timmy he said, 'And as for *you* . . .' He smiled half-heartedly before pointing his finger at him. '*You* are acting like something is on your mind too. So why not cut the fucking bullshit, and tell me what's occurred? Not another fracas like last night, I hope.'

Timmy pushed past his father, but he was careful not to be too aggressive. 'I don't know what you're on about, but about Mum's swearing, I think you're spot on. She ain't stopped since this morning.'

Christine went to the huge larder and opened it. Inside it was neatly stacked with jams and chutneys, bottled fruits and veg. To her, all it represented now was the hours she had spent trying to act like a *real* wife, a *real* mother. Feed the kids, make the jams, and pretend your life was fine.

But they had needed more than sustenance – they had needed a mother who had the guts to take them away from the hurt and the anger they had been born into. In her heart of hearts though, she knew now that for Timmy it would still have been the same. He had his father's personality for, like Phillip, he only understood his own needs, and his own wants. They would always be the most important things to him.

The larder also held the household cigarette quota and, opening a carton of Marlboro Lights, she ignored her husband's questions and said instead, as normally as possible, 'What time's Declan and Jamsie getting here? Will they want feeding?'

Phillip walked into the larder with her and, shutting the door behind him, he said quietly, 'Look, Christine, I don't know what's going on here, but it all feels a bit odd. Now tell me, has Timmy upset you? Because if he has, I'll fucking knock him out. He's getting too lairy by half lately. Do you know what he did yesterday?'

She shook her head and whispered, ''Course I don't, what happened?'

'He only went and hammered one of my best fucking customers. Slapped him all round the fucking arcade. In full view of the other punters.' He shook his head in disbelief at his son's idiocy. 'I've told him time and time again, *never* lose your rag in public, and *never ever* let anyone see you raise your hand to anybody. That's what God created dark alleyways and fucking empty houses for. Privacy means no witnesses. Honestly, it's like he's fucking simple or something lately. You talk to him, and he's fucking miles away and, to be frank, Christine, he's getting on my wick.'

It pleased Christine that she was getting to him, that Timmy was anxious about her and what she knew. He was worried all right. Worried she would be believed. Well, if it went to plan, she would show him once and for all who was fucking stupid. She knew he had thought she was too weak, too frightened, to tell anyone what she knew. But now he wasn't so sure.

'Phillip, will you promise me something?'

He nodded. 'Of course, anything.'

'Will you keep near me and Philly tonight?'

He laughed tiredly and said in disbelief, 'You and Philly?'

She nodded. 'Yes, Phillip, *me* and *Philly*. Just promise me.'

He rolled his eyes in mock annoyance, and she was reminded yet again just how good-looking this man she had married was. Phillip could see she was desperate for him to tell her what she wanted to hear, so sighing heavily, he said in his best placating voice, 'If it will make you happy, darling, then I promise.' He laughed, all joking and full of mischief. 'Cross me heart and hope to die!'

She smiled back at him, playing along as she had for so many years, and realising, not for the first time, just how fucking wearing it could all be. 'Good.'

She felt better now and, going back into the kitchen, she called her elder son in and made them both a stiff drink. Sitting at the big scrubbed pine table she chatted to her son about his new home, his new wife, his new life. And so began her vigil. Phillip was as good as his word and came in and out often, giving her a conspirator's wink every time to cheer her up. She was aware that Breda was annoyed about her monopolising the men. Especially as she had to empty the holdalls containing the handguns and the sawn-off shotguns herself. Eventually though, Philly got up and excused himself from the kitchen. As Christine wandered into the large sitting room, to catch sight of Timmy sitting there calmly with Philly, she nearly walked into the coffee table. Steadying herself, she went over to the window and stood with her back to the room, looking out.

Breda looked at her strangely and said, 'Are you feeling all the ticket, Christine? You seem nervous.'

She turned on her then angrily. 'I'm fine, Breda. What's the matter with you? Are you trying to pick a fight with me? Because the mood I'm in girl, you are liable to get one.' Christine's words caused a hush in the room. She saw her husband and sons stare at her as if they had never seen her before.

Chapter One Hundred and Fifty

This waiting was killing her. Christine was sick of this, so sick of it. Breda had been walking around with a child in one arm and a shotgun in the other, her sons were both acting as if this was normal behaviour. Her husband was obviously thinking she was out of it again, when she was saner than she had ever been in her life before, even with the pills her doctor had prescribed. She felt like she was in a play. Acting out a part. Yet this was her life.

As she saw Timmy get up and go to pull his jacket on she said loudly, 'Where do you think *you're* going?'

Timmy laughed as if she had made a really funny joke. 'Why, what's it got to do with you?'

Breda was watching them as if they had both gone mad.

'He's going to pick up some stuff from his flat. What's wrong with you, Mum?' Philly was genuinely perplexed; he was looking at Breda now, and they were both shaking their heads at one another, as if she was the nutter on the bus.

'He ain't going nowhere.'

Timmy had put his jacket on now, and he said tiredly, 'Why don't you go to bed, Mum, and let me get on with what I'm doing.'

But Christine knew in her heart that if she let him leave this house, he would disappear from their lives, and none of them would be safe ever again. This son of hers would never rest until he had got his own back, not only on her, but on all of them.

477

She had inadvertently stumbled across his real agenda, and he knew she was ready to let the secret out. He was leaving all right – leaving the family for good. But she wouldn't allow that, she was determined to make sure that he never got the chance to repeat his attempt on Philly's life. Whatever had made him like this, she would probably never know for sure, but she would protect Philly if it was the last thing she ever did.

'You can't let him leave, Philly. Where's your father?' She wanted Phillip here, wanted him nearby.

Timmy was pushing past her when Phillip walked into the room and announced, 'Declan is already at the barn, and he wants me to meet him up there. Apparently him and Jamal came in through the fields. Why the fuck would they do that? Has this whole fucking family gone funny tonight? He sounds as fucking nervous as you, Timmy.'

Philly and Breda glanced at one another again, and Christine saw that they both guessed something was going down. But looking at Breda with her grandchild in her arms, and at her Philly, who didn't know his days were numbered, she knew she had to take control of this situation now. Timmy wasn't going to go anywhere without a fight, and Breda and that poor child didn't need to be caught up in the middle of this. She had made this happen, the least she could do was see it through to the bitter end.

'You stay here with the baby, Breda, I need to talk to Declan about something. Philly, do me a favour, will you?' They were all looking at her again as if she had just grown an extra tit and was feeding a lion cub with it. 'Stay here and ring Finoula for me, me and her have a surprise for you.'

She was talking utter shite, but she was desperate to keep them there so Timmy couldn't get away. Then she saw the lights from a car coming down the drive, and she felt the tension seeping out of her. He had done it. She had trusted him and he had done it for her. So when she burst into tears of relief, Baby

Porrick joined in, only louder, and with much more energy.

Phillip Murphy, shaking his head in bewilderment, went to his wife and said sadly, 'What the hell is wrong with you, Christine?'

At that moment Jamsie Murphy came in the back door and, grabbing Timmy by the throat, said angrily, 'Wait till you see what I've got in my boot, you treacherous little cunt.'

As Phillip and Philly stepped towards Jamsie menacingly, their only thought to protect Timmy who was now trying desperately to break free of Jamsie's chokehold, Christine cried brokenly, 'Leave Jamsie alone! Just listen to what he's got to say.'

She was nearly hysterical with grief now, realising the enormity of what was going to happen, and knowing it was because of her. Timmy was looking at her with such hatred even Phillip was stopped in his tracks at the sight of it. It was so deep it was almost tangible.

'You fucking drunk! You're scum, Mother. Fucking filth . . .'

Phillip Murphy dragged his son away from his brother, all his anger at Jamsie forgotten now he was faced with his son's disrespect for the woman who had borne him. Forcing him to the ground he said angrily, 'You *never*, *ever* speak to her like that, do you hear me?' Then he hit him, and before she knew it Christine was watching her son being battered. She was nodding her head as if egging her husband on. For the first time ever, she was taking an active role in the family's penchant for violent retribution but, as yet, no one in that room except Jamsie knew why.

Jamsie went to her and, taking her gently by the arm, he pulled her to one side. 'It's all right, Christine, you did the right thing, love.'

She was nodding again; tears were still running down her face, but they were silent tears now. 'I know, Jamsie, I know. But it's still hard.'

Phillip had stopped punching Timmy and, standing up, he

looked from his wife, to his brother, to his son. Timmy was just lying there, looking at them all, no emotion showing on his face, nothing. Then he turned to his father and said laughingly, 'I was this far –' he held his finger and thumb about an inch apart – 'this far from taking you and him out. But I tell you now, *Mum*, I don't regret a second of it. I just wish I'd taken you out years ago. Because you're nothing, you're just a drunken fucking no one, who let *him* rule all our fucking lives.'

Phillip was amazed at the diatribe, and even he was loath to ask what it was about, but he couldn't help himself. 'Right, I've just about had fucking enough of this shit. What the fuck is going on here, people?'

Philly and Breda were watching it all like a nightmare they had accidentally stumbled into, even Baby Porrick had quietened down as if interested in finding out what the hell was actually going on.

Christine exploded angrily, and with utter credibility, 'For crying out loud, Breda, will you take that child from the room? He doesn't need to see any of this!'

Breda, for the first time ever, did as she was asked without an argument. She had a feeling that whatever this was about, she didn't want to know, and she certainly didn't want to get involved.

Christine looked at her husband and, nodding her head towards her brother-in-law, she said with conviction, and searing clarity, 'Now then, Phillip. You better listen to what Jamsie has to say, and you, Philly, had better get Graham Planter out of the boot of Jamsie's car.'

For once, to her amazement, they did exactly as she asked.

Chapter One Hundred
and Fifty-One

Christine was sitting on the sofa in the semi-darkness, a drink in one hand and a cigarette in the other, when she finally heard the back door open, and footsteps walking across the kitchen flags. She looked at the doorway, and saw the figure of her husband standing there. Even in the half light she could see the devastation on his handsome face.

'Is it over?'

He knew exactly what she meant, and he nodded.

'In the furnace, is he?'

He nodded again, almost imperceptibly.

They were both quiet for long moments, and she knew there had been a subtle shifting in their positions in the last few hours. Phillip had not imagined anything like this could ever happen, it was beyond his comprehension really. She knew he would not see it all for what it was, that Timmy had turned out just like him, and had acted just as *he* would have acted had he been in his position. Timmy had learned subterfuge and treachery at the knee of the master, but Phillip would see this as someone else's fault, mainly Timmy's.

'Are you all right?'

She nodded in the darkness, then, leaning over, she turned on the lamp nearest her. Its light was as unexpected as it was brilliant. She saw her beautiful room, the antiques, the expensive carpets and curtains. Saw the beauty of her surroundings, as if for the first time, knowing she had made it all so lovely to cover up the muck and the filth that it represented.

'Do you want another drink?'

She sighed. As bad as it was, she also felt as if she had finally shrugged off some of the fear that she had lived with for so long. 'Yeah, why not.'

He poured them both drinks and, as he handed her the glass, she saw the bruises on his hands and the blood that he had not bothered to rinse off properly. She knew then that her son had not died an easy death, and yet at this moment she didn't care. She felt nothing, but this feeling of numbness would eventually pass, and then it would hit her like a ton of shit.

'I still can't believe it, Christine.' And he couldn't, she knew that.

'I am leaving you, Phillip. I should have left years ago. I can't live like this any longer. You got what you wanted, you finally made me a part of all this whether I wanted it or not.' She gestured around the room to emphasise her point. 'I had to choose between my sons, and I did what I thought was right. I know I was right, I *know* I was. Even though this will all haunt me for the rest of my days. But I *am* leaving you, Phillip, and if that means I end up in the furnace, then so be it.'

It was a good few minutes before Phillip answered her. She was holding her breath in anticipation of his words, and they surprised her when they finally came.

'Where do you want to go?'

She knew what it had cost him to say that and, as much as she hated him at times, she felt a small spark of sorrow for him, because she knew more than anyone what it had taken for him to utter them.

She shrugged. 'I don't care, Phillip. Anywhere. Spain maybe.'

He nodded. 'Do you want the farm? You can have it, Christine, you deserve it.'

She shook her head, and sipped deeply at her drink. It was seventy-year-old Scotch, and she wondered at how she could gulp it down and still feel as sober as a judge. But she supposed murder could do that to a person. She was probably still in shock.

'You keep it all, Phillip. I never want to see this place again, to be perfectly honest.'

'You can have whatever you want, Christine. I'll be generous. I suppose I owe you. I certainly owe you my life, and that's a big debt.'

'You owe me Philly's life and all. God love him, I bet he's devastated.'

'Well, put it this way, he ain't exactly celebrating, if you know what I mean.' Phillip tried to laugh it off, but even he was having trouble accepting what had happened.

Christine placed her drink on the table and, getting up, she straightened her clothes. She could feel her husband's eyes watching her every move. 'I'm off then. I've packed a bag, I'm going to me mum's.'

He nodded, and she knew he would let her go now. He had no power over her any longer. She was leaving.

'I love you, Christine, remember that.'

She looked down at him then and, smiling gently, she said frankly, 'No, you don't, Phillip, you never did. You don't know what love means and neither did our Timmy. But Philly does, so you can do me one last thing – promise me you won't take that away from him.'

Epilogue

I do not wish them [women] to have power
over men; but over themselves

Mary Wollstonecraft (1759–97)
A Vindication of the Rights of Women (1792)

The unexamined life is not worth living

Socrates (469 BC–399 BC)

Chapter One Hundred and Fifty-Two

'Hello, Finoula, how are you feeling, love?'

Christine was visiting from Spain. She finally had the life she had dreamed of, and now she had a new grandson to celebrate.

Finoula looked tired but outrageously happy. And that was how it should be – she had only given birth a few hours before, and she needed a good night's sleep and her husband to herself.

Philly was so proud of his newborn son, he looked fit to burst. He placed him in his mother's arms carefully, and Christine looked down at the child with love already in her heart. He was dark-haired and blue-eyed. He was Phillip Murphy all over again, and she was surprised that it didn't bother her as much as she had thought it would.

'He's beautiful, really beautiful.'

'We like him!'

Christine laughed at her son's unashamed pride in his new baby. 'I better warn you both that me mum's on her way.'

They laughed with her.

Then Phillip walked into the room and, looking into his wife's eyes, he said quietly, 'Hello, Christine, you look well, mate.'

She took the compliment well, and she gave it straight back. This was their new way of communicating. It was all very civilised, and she knew she was very lucky. Phillip had let her go, and she knew how hard that had been for him. She wouldn't strong it in any way. There could never be another man, not that she wanted one. She would always have to see him from time to time, because of Philly, and now this little fellow. They shared a deep secret, and it was only because of that they could continue with their lives. 'So do you, Phillip. Isn't he gorgeous?'

Phillip looked at the red-faced child and said seriously, 'Good genes, that's what it is, love.'

She didn't answer him, the words provoked so many emotions in her. She saw the baby grab her husband's finger tightly and, pulling on it to show the child's strength, Phillip said loudly, 'He's a Murphy, all right! Another Phillip Murphy – we'll end up a dynasty if we ain't careful.'

They all grinned happily, except Christine. She felt the urge to run from the room, run away from them, but she wouldn't. She was only over from Spain for a few days, then she would go back and resume her new life. They came out to see her often, Finoula and Philly, and they respected her decision to live so far away. What more could she ask for?

Eileen and Ted burst into the room then. Both were over-excited at the birth of their first great-grandchild, and Christine stepped back, watching them all together.

Chapter One Hundred and Fifty-Three

'It looks lovely, Veronica.'

Christine was admiring the new sofa and TV that Phillip had supplied. Veronica nodded, not interested in her home for once, and Christine followed her out to the kitchen where she was making one of her endless pots of tea.

'Isn't he gorgeous, Christine? A great-granny again! Now that makes you feel your age, I can tell you!'

Christine smiled the requisite smile, and waited for the real conversation to begin. It was only a matter of time, and, actually, she had thought it would have been sooner than this.

They were halfway through their tea when Veronica finally said sadly, 'Any news about Timmy?'

Christine shook her head. 'Not a word. He's just disappeared.'

Veronica nodded as if in agreement, but she wasn't a fool and they both knew it. 'Can I ask you something, and will you promise me you'll never repeat it to a soul?'

Christine nodded, knowing what this woman was going to say to her. 'Of course, anything.'

'Is Timmy's . . . *disappearance* . . . anything to do with my Phillip?'

It spoke volumes that this woman had guessed her son had murdered his own child. But Christine made sure she looked suitably shocked – she was getting very good at it. 'What on earth makes you think that?' She sounded incredulous even to her own ears.

Veronica was looking at her now through slitted eyes and she said slowly, 'All right, have it your own way. I'll not ask again, but I'll remind you of this much – it seems funny to me you two splitting up like that, and poor Timmy on the missing list. There's a story here, and one day I'll get to the bottom of it.'

It was almost a threat, and Christine had had enough of threats and veiled accusations and all the other shite that went on in this so-called *family*. She leant forward in her chair and, looking into the older woman's eyes, she said quietly, but with conviction, 'Do you know something, Veronica? There's some things in life you're really better off *not* knowing, and this is one of them. You've spent your life protecting Phillip, but believe me when I say this, you didn't do *him*, or *anyone* around him any favours, and that includes me. If I had known all those years ago what you had bred, what you *knew* you had bred, what your son really was, I would have run a fucking mile and maybe saved my own son's life. Now I am going soon, and I doubt I'll be back for a long while, but I know this much: if I *never* see you again it will be too soon.'

Chapter One Hundred and Fifty-Four

'Are you sure you're all right, Christine?'

'Oh, for fuck's sake, Mum, give it a rest, will you?'

Eileen didn't argue with her daughter, she just pursed her lips and waited for Christine to apologise.

'Look, Mum, I'm sorry, but I've told you over and over. I'm all right, I'm not really happy yet, but I'm getting there.'

Eileen nodded sadly. 'If they found his body . . . If we could bury him . . .'

Christine rolled her eyes to the ceiling. But her mother was mourning the loss of her grandson, and she had to remember that. Remember that not everyone knew him for what he was or, more to the point, knew what had happened to him, and why. Her mother still missed him, loved him. So why didn't she? Christine hated him more with every day that passed, yet she didn't hate his father any more. In fact she felt nothing for Phillip, nothing at all.

Ted Booth looked at his daughter and shook his head sadly. Christine knew he had guessed a lot, and that she should have listened to him all those years ago. But, as everyone finally found out, hindsight really was a wonderful thing.

Chapter One Hundred and Fifty-Five

'I appreciate this, Breda, you've always been good to me.'

'It's great to see you looking so well, to be honest. You off the drink and all?'

Christine laughed. 'Not really, but I don't drink like before. It's strange, but what happened with Timmy, it sort of straightened me out somehow. Made me see my life for what it was. I should have sorted meself out years ago.'

Breda sighed heavily. She always drove her sister-in-law to the airport. They enjoyed their private time together when they could both talk without fear, and they did just that. They talked about everything and anything.

'I know what you mean, I feel the same really. I've taken a huge step back from the businesses. I'm getting too old for it, I think. Timmy left a bad taste with us all, Christine. Not just me, but Declan and Jamsie. It's as if we knew it had gone too far. Phillip, on the other hand, he feels he should have guessed something – he's bothered about the fact he hadn't sussed it out. But then, that's Phillip, obsessed with himself as usual.' It spoke volumes that Breda could now say things like this. 'Do you know what? All I want to do is spend time with little Porrick. He more or less lives with me now. I just want to hold him close, and keep him safe from harm.'

Christine understood that, much more than even Breda realised.

'Aren't you lonely, over there on your own?' Breda asked suddenly.

Christine smiled sadly. 'I was much lonelier when I was married, Breda.' She could say that to her sister-in-law now.

Breda sighed and then said, 'I never thought of it like that, Chris, but I can see what you mean. It must have been hard over the years.'

Christine didn't answer her, she wasn't getting into any conversation like that ever again.

'Are you sure you want to do this, don't want to go straight to the airport?'

Christine shook her head. She knew exactly what she had to do.

Chapter One Hundred and Fifty-Six

Phillip was watching Christine from the kitchen doorway. She had refused to even go into the house, and it was cold and raining as she walked up to the big barn. Inside, she stood and looked around her. Nothing had changed, but then she had not expected it to.

The furnace was humming as usual, that low sound it had, and she felt the sting of tears suddenly. It was hot in there, as always, and the heat made her think of her son's last moments on this earth. Inside her head, she could hear the sounds of the boys when they were young. Their voices, childishly high, calling for their mum. She saw Timmy on his first day of school, his eyes so wide and not a scrap of fear in them. Saw him standing by the Christmas tree in his pyjamas, all excitement and curiosity at what might be wrapped up for him. And she wondered, for the thousandth time, what had changed inside him, when it had changed, or if it had always been there. This was the nearest she would have to a gravestone and, as she knew she would never come here again, she felt she had to do this one last time.

'Goodbye, son.'

Her words echoed in the silence around her and, turning slowly, she walked away. Outside, she stopped. She looked at the farm one last time and, as she went back towards the house, she heard the familiar sounds of rural life.

She was going back to the sunshine, to her art classes, and to her bookclub. She was going back to her new life, without the violence and the feeling of dread that accompanied her old one. She knew suddenly, without a moment's doubt, that she would never come back to England again – not even her grandchild would be enough to bring her back to this place, and the memories it held.

She got to the car and, seeing Phillip watching her, she raised her hand in what they both understood was a final gesture of farewell. Then, getting into the passenger seat, she sat quietly as Breda drove her away from her old life, and towards her new one. As the gates of the farm closed behind them, she felt a huge sense of relief overwhelm her. The sun was coming through the clouds, and the rain had finally stopped.

She would never be happy, not like other people were happy. Too much had happened, and it would always be there in the back of her mind. She still woke up in a cold sweat remembering her life, and what it had finally become. But she knew that she was slowly but surely finding a measure of peace inside herself and, after living like she had for so many years, on her nerves, and with a bottle or a pill, that was a start.

She had wanted a family, to be a part of a family, so badly, she had sold her soul for the privilege. Well, now her family was decimated, and she was the reason for it. But for the first time since Timmy's demise, she felt a faint glimmer of hope for the future and, as they drove through the rolling countryside, she felt her heart becoming lighter. Felt the dread seeping from her bones. It was ironic really, and the thought brought her up with a jolt. She knew she had to leave her family – what was left of it anyway – behind her, even her brand-new grandson, if she was to finally have some kind of stab at a real life.

She closed her eyes. She would be home in a few hours, the

sun would be shining and the villa would be waiting for her. There would be no Phillip, no violence, and no fear.

And all of this, she knew, would finally seem a long way away.